Over the Devil's Back

An evil act that could shatter a family...
A cherished friendship...
A young boy's burden of silence

A Novel By

MELVA HAGGAR DYE

ISBN 978-1-956001-41-9 (paperback)
ISBN 978-1-956001-42-6 (eBook)

Printed in the United States of America

Dedicated to the memory of my aunt,
Martha Morgan Scruggs

and to all those who have been blessed with
One. True. Friend.

Acknowledgements

Special Recognition and Sincere Thanks

To my Editor, Krista Hill, L. Talbott Editorial
Her professional edit, constructive input and encouragement
were invaluable to me throughout the development of this novel.

To my husband, Charles Lewis Dye,
for the amazing life that we share.

Introduction

"…And what're you doin' hanging 'round the house this fine sunshiny mornin', anyways? You ought to be out playing with friends! 'Les, of course, you'd rather sit here and shell peas all day long," Mosell cackled.

Her gnarled fingers stopped their work and lay still on her apron-covered lap. The rhythmic creaking of her rocking chair stopped as she looked directly into her grandson's eyes and continued the one-sided conversation. "What's the matter, boy? You ain't said half a dozen words all week long. You got somethin' you wanna talk about?"

The young boy took a deep breath before he answered her with a question of his own. "Moam, what did you mean when you talked about the devil's back?"

"Huh? Oh, you mean las' night when your daddy and me was talking. What I said was: 'what goes over the devil's back, is gonna come crawling under his belly.' It's what my pap always said. Now, what that means is that whatever you done, be it good or bad, it's gonna come right back around to you for sure.

"You see, child, if you walk hand in hand with the Lord, then good things be coming your way. But if you play leap-frog with that ole devil," she paused and lowered her voice to a whisper, as her eyes locked on those of the boy, "well, then, the bad you done gonna keep coming back to haunt you."

Mosell shook her head sadly and wiped a tear off her cheek with the back of her hand. "And whoever done harm to that child—the devil gonna be coming back around to him for the rest of his days!"

Prologue

Creating illusions: that's what people like us do best. At least, that's what YOU do best. You delude the senses and you set the mind awhirl. You project an image different than it actually is. No, no, that's not right; that is not what you do. You project an image as it SHOULD be.

Why, just look at yourself—the quintessential southern gentleman, which is exactly what you are. You've never looked better than you do tonight with your perfectly-knotted tie, perfectly-pressed pleated shirt; the diamond stickpin's a nice touch.

Just how many men in the ballroom are clad in a custom-tailored tuxedo? Nothing rented or off-the-rack for you, no sir; you noticed. Hell, anybody who'd ever set foot outside of this rag-tag county noticed. The ones who hadn't didn't matter, anyway.

And self-control? You were perfect. Not a trace of second thoughts. Yeah, you really wowed 'em with that speech tonight, didn't you? Of course, that was essentially accomplished years ago when you made your mark with the hayseeds around these parts. No social graces, none of 'em!

Anybody ought to know that you don't talk business at a shindig like this. But how're you supposed to answer the likes of: 'What's your stock pick this week?' 'I wonder if you'd mind taking a look at my portfolio.' Or, 'What do you reckon the Fed's going do at their next meeting?' Like they'd understand your answers anyway.

What you'd like to explain to the Bubbas of this town is that off-shore banking does not imply stuffing cash in a Thermos jug and anchoring it out in the Peedee River.

You don't say that, though. Instead, you smile, look him in the eye, pat him on the back, compliment him on marrying the prettiest woman in the county and make him beg—yes, **beg**—you to let him deposit his money in your banks. Yeah, that's what you do, and you do it so well. Calls to mind that old saying: 'He who rules the gold, rules.'

You had 'em eating out of your hand tonight for sure. The old-fart has-beens that barely remembered what it felt like to be on top all the way down to the wet-behind-the-ears wanna-be's were hanging on every fucking syllable that came rolling off your silver tongue.

And the women? Man, you still got your pick. You had 'em all twitching, even the old cronies, twittering and fanning their selves over every little smile you flashed in their direction. And just how many perfumed notes got tucked discreetly into your jacket pocket over the course of the evening by young, smooth, silvery-nailed hands? Of course, you're not going to take any of them up on their offers; but still, those high tight asses wriggling themselves up onto that polished Louis XVI desk of yours—a man can dream.

Stop yawning. You're not tired, you're just trapped. Oh, but you've got the sure-fire keys to freedom. Just a pinch of this fine white ambrosia—there, now, just a thin line from the crystal vial balanced on your knife blade—voila! Your world changes back into the exciting, magical kingdom it should be with you in your rightful place as ruler.

Who would've thought it—goddamn sharecropper's son!

Easy, now, chill; focus on what really matters. It's show time. Check the mirror, touch up the Cartier cologne, a little breath freshener, and it's back downstairs to give 'em more of what they want.

Yeah, baby, you da man!

C'mon, now, move; you need to get back to the party, back to your court, to your admirers. So, why's it so hard to do it? Move your ass, you cowardly prick. All you gotta do is push the down button, step in the elevator, push 'M', get off on the mezzanine, and she'll be right there waiting for you.

Or maybe she's on her way up here to see what's taking you so long. You wouldn't want that, now would you? No, no, she can't come up and see you standing here frozen in front of this goddamn mirror, sweating like a pig, crying like a freakin' baby!

Shouldn't have done that second line. One was just perfect; two's bad, bad, bad! Big mistake hitting the hard stuff. And at your age, too. Folks saying that *things get better with age is just a load of horse shit. What you'd give to go back to when you were young and do it all over again. And some things you'd never do at all. Speaking of that, what are you going to do about this letter? What possessed you to write such a thing in the first place? Ought to tear it up right now.*

Whew! Man, you gotta get a grip, gotta get your golden ass back downstairs and mix and mingle. What is it you always say: act like you know what you're doing, and you'll get away with it?

That's right.

Maybe a breath of fresh air is all you need before you head back down there to walk the walk, talk the talk. Yeah, just a minute out here on the rooftop.

Man, what a beautiful night, just look at the stars. You never notice the stars anymore. You used to look at them all the time—back in the day.

Brrr, it's getting a mite chilly out here. You better get back downstairs; they'll be looking for you. You can do it; you can go right back down there this minute.

See, it's not that far down there, only four floors. Funny thing, this old building used to seem like the tallest building in the world. Just look down there; why, you can almost hear what the doormen are saying to each other, almost hear who they're talking about.

Whoa, steady now; don't get too close to the edge!

Close your eyes and breathe deep; that's it. You can take just a minute longer out here in the dark, just a minute to silence the whispers. Goddamn those whispers! Why won't they ever stop?

Shhh, relax, calm down and get your bearings. So, what if the whispers have gotten louder over the years, no one besides you ever hears them. And if anyone else did hear, who in their right mind would ever repeat such vile words—liar, rapist, murderer? Who would dare to even think pedophile?

"SHUT-UP!"

Sicko-loser words, dregs-of-humanity words, words never to be associated with you. Why? 'Cause you're the best of the best, man!

Just look at 'em down there, scurrying around like a bunch of pissants. They don't know how good they've got it, always having someone looking out for them, looking after their interests, telling them what to do. Hey, all you little people, look up here at who's taking care of you, why don't you? Look up here at your hero, your ruler, your god!

No one understands just how hard it is to be at the top, keeping it all together, never slipping, never giving in… well, almost never.

"I said SHUT-UP!"

Hush, now. It's past time to go, and just look at you—you're a mess.

Take another deep breath, now; steady yourself. You can pull this off, can't you? Of course, you can. Hell, man, you can do anything.

You're the Illusionist.

* * * * *

Deshaun Freeman sat behind his desk, drumming his fingers on the scarred surface. How he would conduct this morning's interview was foremost in his mind.

He looked around his office at the clutter. He probably should have asked Keisha to file the stacks of case records that currently sat in precarious columns on the floor. And it would have been a good idea if the cleaning crew had done a little extra touch up yesterday.

Wait a minute—are you trying to make an impression instead of doing your job?

He decided that his office was just fine. It was a functional workspace, albeit jerry-rigged, comprising four glass walls extending from the floor all the way up to the twelve-foot ceiling. The heating and air-conditioning vents were already ensconced in the creaking, oiled-board floor. The glaring, outdated fluorescent lamp and decrepit ceiling fan hung where they always had; so, no complicated wiring had been needed.

Deshaun was proud of the simple design that he had come up with during his first week on the job. Simple indeed—his very own sixteen-by-sixteen-foot glass box, complete with the ancient walnut desk that dominated the center of the room, used by more predecessors than he could name. That desk served to remind him of the only design flaw in his first architectural undertaking: the door was too small to facilitate its removal.

He was not a man of expensive tastes. His chief of detectives, Omar Landry, must have recognized that fact when the young deputy, Keisha Jackson, had attempted to replace the split, cracked and squeaky desk chair with a slick new La-Z-Boy from Bowman's Furniture. Wisely, Omar had complimented Keisha on her good taste and suggested that she keep the new chair for herself.

At the time, Deshaun had wondered what all the fuss was about. Why, the only thing that old chair of his had needed was a few more strips of duct tape to cover the new splits and it was good as new. So as not to cause hurt feelings, though, Keisha had been given a small allowance to cover the purchase of two chairs and a side table to make visitors comfortable. And the plants and throw rugs did add some color.

Deshaun never envisioned his workspace as a place of comfort, quite the contrary. He, himself, didn't stay put long enough to warrant it; and the *guests* he entertained were as a rule not deserving of creature comforts and were usually whisked away in a timely manner to other locations within the hulking three-story City Hall building.

The *Fish Tank*, as the square glass enclosure had been dubbed, served a two-fold purpose. It gave him a heads-up on anyone entering the department, but more importantly, it conveyed an image of accessibility to his staff and to the townsfolk in general. That was the idealistic premise behind his actions. He was more than just a flash in the pan, and he needed the people he served to know that. He needed them to know there was more to Deshaun Freeman than merely being the first African-American Police Chief of Antioch, South Carolina.

Keisha poked her head in his office. "You know what time it is?"

Deshaun couldn't help but smile at her rare display of enthusiasm. He answered, "Yes ma'am, Ms. Jackson, I got me a good view of that Coca-Cola clock on the wall yonder. That's how come I made these walls glass. Why, I'll even be able to see him when he comes through the front door." Deshaun mocked her good-naturedly; he knew what sparked her animation this morning. "He's not due 'til 10:30."

"Oh, m'God! Oh, m'God, he's here!" Sally Ann May's shrill voice carried from the main room, proclaiming the arrival of the man who had occupied Deshaun's thoughts for the past seventy-two hours.

"Do y'all know what he's driving? A Mercedes SL, that's what!" Sally Ann emphasized each word. "Hear me, people, an SL!"

Keisha had already made her way to the window to join her blond, boisterous counterpart. "Shucks, Sally Ann, he's walking to the coffee shop across the street."

"Yeah," Sally Ann responded dreamily; "and would you just look at that walk."

The two women giggled and whispered like teenagers, prompting some friendly chiding from Desk Sergeant Roy Kennedy. "Now, Sally Ann, don't you think you might ought to leave Mr. Washington to Keisha? After all, ain't he just a bit too young for you—not to mention a little too dark?"

Sally Ann rose to the bait, turning saucily and wiggling her plump backside. "A man too young or too dark? Why, Roy, honey, there ain't no such animal."

The guffaws and hand-clapping made Deshaun grin. He recognized every day how fortunate he had been to have assembled—through inheritance as well as good hiring practices—a team such as this. No acrimony lived here. No rivalries arose. His people could joke with each other about race, family skeletons, politics, sexual preferences, whatever, and still perform together to do their job of protecting the citizens of this small town.

He also knew the importance of allowing his staff a moment of lightheartedness after what they'd dealt with during the past days. Roy Kennedy especially had been shaken. After all, tragedy such as the one that occurred on Saturday night shouldn't happen in Antioch.

Deshaun waited for the moment of merriment to subside before directing his crew back to the business at hand. "Let's get back to work, ladies and gents. Mr. Washington's got twenty more minutes before his appointment. I don't 'spect he'll be late."

"Right, Chief. Believe I'll turn the A/C on; it's getting awful warm in here." Sally Ann said, as she made her way to the far side of the office, fanning herself and relishing in the snickers of her fellow workers.

Deshaun turned his attention to Omar, whose meaty right hand had just descended into the Krispy Kreme box for another treat.

"Them things gonna kill you, man. Clog up your arteries, cause diabetes and all kinds of bad things." Deshaun tried to act nonchalant, but he worried about the older man. Omar had no family to look out for him.

"Hmm, can't see no arteries," Omar replied. "And I don't worry 'bout nothing I can't see. I already got diabetes, so that takes care of that."

He met Deshaun's gaze levelly and continued speaking. "Now, I appreciate your concern, Chief; but the way I figure it is if them two bullets I took las' year during that meth raid didn't do me in, then I reckon it's up to these here donuts, the fat-back in my beans and the fried catfish on Friday nights to take me out, 'cause I ain't giving up none of 'em."

Deshaun held up his hands and said, "Sorry, man; promise I'll quit nagging."

"Uh-huh, till next week when Sally Ann brings in the donuts."

"Okay, till next week, then;" Deshaun said as he filled his coffee cup and headed back towards the tank.

"You think Washington can shed any light on this mess, Chief?" Omar asked.

"Can he? Or better yet, will he? I don't know, Omar. Only thing I know is what I've got, and that's a dead man and what faintly resembles a suicide letter written personally to Leander Washington. I sure hope that he can shed some light on it."

"He ain't been 'round these parts for quite a spell, now. I remember him as a boy, though." Omar wiped his hands on a paper towel and limped back to his desk, his feet obviously hurting him.

"I remember him 'cause he was the smartest little kid I ever did see. Had manners, too; Carl Lee made sure of that. Yes, sir, all three of them Washington kids was real nice; but that Leander—smartest I ever *did* see," he repeated.

Deshaun closed his office door. Oh, he remembered, alright; but some of his memories ran deep and were tough to wade through. Like Omar, he remembered Leander Washington as being smart. Actually, *smart* wasn't a suitable adjective to describe the person who, by all rights, should have been named valedictorian of his high school graduating class. Deshaun chewed on that particular memory, finding it most difficult to swallow, even after twelve years.

Most of Deshaun's freshman year had been spent practicing football plays, playing football or thinking about practicing and playing football. His talent as a running back was recognized early on and provided the perfect excuse for the miniscule amount of time he'd spent on academic endeavors. Less than passing grades on exams, missed classes and 'lost' assignments were forgiven by his teachers at Antioch High in eager anticipation of another 2-A state championship.

But even Deshaun's intense passion for football did not overshadow the travesty carried off against that year's senior class. It was bad enough to have the entire student body subjected to regular poetry readings by Principal Hadley's insipid daughter, Amelia, at the weekly school assemblies; but to hear the announcement that she and Leander Washington were tied for class valedictorian was ludicrous.

The image had stayed in Deshaun's memory over the years: old man Hadley, flanked by two members of the school board, standing in front of the student assembly, his nasal twang intoning short, contrived sentences like he was explaining some abstract theory to a bunch of morons.

"The selection of this year's valedictorian is difficult. That is because the number of points earned is exactly the same for two students. These two students are Amelia Hadley *(doting smile)* and Leander Washington *(polite hand-clapping)*. Now, the only fair thing to do is to administer a test, and the student with the highest score will be named valedictorian. This test will be held at 11 o'clock on Saturday morning. Good luck to both of you fine young people."

Leander had not been able to take that test at the appointed time, as it conflicted with the funeral service for Mosell Washington. *Moam*, as she was known to her family had passed quietly, without realizing her dream of seeing her only grandson graduate from high school and go on to college. She doted on Leander and never missed an opportunity to brag on him.

"You jus' watch," she would say to anyone who would listen. "That boy's gonna shed his rags one day."

The contrived fiasco played out to Hadley's liking. "We hate it for you, son, but I can't see changing the test date. Teachers have made plans, and it's hard to set something like this up and then start making changes. You understand, don't you?"

Of course, Leander had understood. Everyone had. That's the way things were done back then. Change had come grudgingly to Antioch. Understanding had not made it any easier to swallow, though, especially since Hadley and his cohorts were unable to hide their pleasure. The swaggering walks, the elbowing, back-slapping, and teary-eyed snickers barely suppressed behind pink, ham-like fists had set the tone for the final days of that school year.

The old guard had their way. Amelia's name was announced the following Monday at assembly, to a modicum of applause, while the announcement of Leander as salutatorian received a standing ovation from the student body.

Things sure have a way of coming back around, though, Deshaun mused. Old man Hadley died a couple of years after that from liver disease, and the last he'd heard about Amelia was that she'd gotten knocked-up, dropped out of college and lived in a trailer park over near Greenville. Leander Washington, on the other hand, was a full partner in Remington Banking & Investments, LLC.

Deshaun's thoughts immediately returned to the business at hand. He was a little unsure how he would go about questioning Leander this morning. They had both grown up in Antioch and had attended the same small schools, but three years' difference in age seemed infinite when you were in your teens. Their friends and interests had been practically polar opposites. While sports enticed one, the other was rarely seen outside of the school library.

Added to the mix, too, was Leander's closeness with Gabrielle Westin's family, and that in itself cast the two boys in vastly different social venues.

He stood as Keisha approached the glass door, followed by a tall man with the same noble bearing and pleasant face that Deshaun remembered from years past.

"Chief, uh," Keisha stammered, her posture ramrod straight, her dark eyes huge, "Chief, Mr. Washington's here, sir." She ducked her head and sidled back to her desk before Deshaun could respond.

"Come in, please." Deshaun himself was six feet tall, but he had to look up to meet Leander's gaze. The two men joined in a firm handshake. "Please have a seat," Deshaun gestured.

"Thank you, Chief." Leander said, but made no further attempt to converse. He removed his suit coat and casually draped it over one chair while settling into the other chair with cat-like grace. He waited.

Deshaun was impressed. Had the other man practiced the toss of his jacket so as to reveal the *Armani* label, or was it just a fluke? *Mercedes automobile, Armani suits? I guess we finally overcame, but nobody told me!*

"You probably don't remember me, but we went to high school together—for one year, anyway. I was a freshman when you were a senior." Deshaun opened the conversation.

Leander surprised him with his response. "As I recall, you were quite a football star at Antioch High. All-State Running Back, correct? Scholarship to Clemson, I believe.

"I'm flattered," Deshaun said. "My career got cut short, though; blew out my left knee my sophomore year. After that, I actually studied some and managed to graduate with a degree in Criminal Law.

"After college I came back here, married Nikki Logan, and the rest is history. How 'bout you? I believe you go by Lee now, right? No point in us being so formal since we're both hometown boys. Call me Deshaun." He hoped he could put both of them at ease. "Can I get you some coffee, a donut, maybe?"

Leander studied the other man for a long moment before answering. "No, thank you, Chief Freeman. How can I be of help to you?"

So, that's the way it's gonna be. Deshaun tried once again to establish some rapport. He said, "I run into Gabrielle ever once in a while; she tells me you spend most of your time in the Cayman Islands. Must be nice."

"The partners have offices there," Leander responded. He crossed his legs and remained aloof.

Deshaun took a deep breath before he spoke. "Mr. Washington, I believe that you know why you've been asked to come here. First, though, allow me to express my deepest condolences. Please convey my sympathy to Gabrielle and the entire Remington-Westin family. I'm sure most everyone is still in shock."

"Thank you."

Deshaun realized that there was to be no rapport between the two of them. He fumbled with some papers on his desk and pressed on awkwardly.

"His blood alcohol level was 0.13 and," he paused for emphasis, "he had cocaine in his system as well as on his person. Do you have any idea what prompted him to commit suicide?"

Leander's eyebrows shot up. "Pardon me, Chief, but you seem to be contradicting yourself. First, you call attention to the fact that he was drunk and under the influence of drugs, not to mention the fact that he was wandering around on the rooftop of a building with *no* guard rail. This was obviously a horrible accident. Wherever did you get the idea it was a suicide?"

Well, now—just maybe I can get a rise out of him yet. Deshaun kept his voice flat. "Oh, maybe the suicide angle came to me from this."

He reached into one of the file folders that lay atop his desk and removed a sheet of white paper sealed in plastic. The crumpled page looked as if it had been folded and unfolded many times before it had been smoothed out. Although the dark red stains partially blotted out some of the lettering, the message remained legible.

Deshaun studied Leander as he slid the plastic-encased sheet deliberately across his desk. He said, "The family members appeared sincerely shocked when I shared parts of this letter with them. How 'bout you?"

At first, Leander seemed to be afraid to touch the letter. After a moment, he picked it up. He looked at it for a long time—far longer than it should have taken to read the four short paragraphs.

Deshaun watched closely for some sign of emotion to cross the other man's face. Surely, he'd catch a fleeting glimpse of shock, fear, sadness, or dread—*nothing.* "Well, Mr. Washington?"

Leander held his hands palms up and shook his head slightly as he responded. "Well, what, Chief Freeman? Look, I've been told about the letter, and it contains some troubling thoughts, to be sure; but suicide—hardly. More like alcohol and cocaine working together to fuel grief, conscience, whatever. Can we possibly go into the, uh, the past details another time? It wasn't suicide, Chief, I am certain." He said as if the matter had been resolved.

He checked the Rolex on his left wrist and prepared to stand. "If that's all, I need to get going. As you can imagine, I have a ton of phone calls to make as well funeral arrangements to finalize."

Deshaun was furious with himself. In the span of that few seconds, he had almost succumbed to the easy way out. He was so close to knuckling under to The Man.

It didn't matter that they were both members of the same race and that both men had shared similar upbringing, they were worlds apart. *Yes, sir, Mr. Harvard-educated rich man, 'course you're right. No bad publicity for the partners, no sir. An unfortunate accident is just what it was.*

Bull shit!

"Sit down, sir," Deshaun spoke quietly but with authority. "The time to discuss the 'past', as you put it, is *now*. This letter alludes to an incident that occurred some twenty years ago." He picked up the plastic-encased letter, all the while keeping his eyes locked on Leander's. "And this incident, whatever it was, supposedly led to *another* death.

"Now, since this letter was written to you *personally*, Mr. Washington, I must assume that you know something of that incident. What about it?"

Leander's facial expression remained unchanged. "We invite trouble when we begin to assume, Chief," he said.

Deshaun bit his tongue. "All right then, let's *not* assume anything. Why don't you tell me what you know about the twenty-year-old crime mentioned in this letter?"

"Drugs and alcohol played an unfortunate part in his life. And as far as my name appearing at the top of the letter, I believe there's an explanation for that." Leander paused briefly.

"It's common knowledge that he and I had our differences. I wanted Remington Investments to be more customer-friendly, I suppose you could say. I thought that we should invite input from all our investors, not just the top tier. He, on the other hand, had serious doubts as to the sharing of information and so on. We butted heads frequently, but that's to be expected in any business environment."

Leander stopped speaking momentarily, and Deshaun recognized his hesitation as a bit of mild embarrassment. He seemed to collect his thoughts, then continued.

"Chief, you probably also know that the banquet last Saturday night was held in my honor. I imagine that envy or jealousy—whatever, led him to direct his ramblings to me. I don't see how I can be of any further help to you."

"For starters," Deshaun said, "why don't you and I stop circling each other like a couple of junk-yard dogs. This is a police investigation, in case you haven't noticed, and *I* am the police. So please stop wasting my time and start at the beginning."

Leander's expression turned to one of mild amusement. "The beginning? That's quite a long time ago, wouldn't you say so, Chief Freeman?"

Deshaun would not be mocked. His fist came down hard on the desktop—too hard. File folders stacked high slid in disarray, and Keisha's vase of fresh-cut flowers wobbled unsteadily.

He was vaguely aware of the six people in the outer office jumping up from their chairs, only to freeze in anticipation of his next move. He held his hand up, signaling that all was well, and then riveted his gaze on the man before him. His voice was no longer amicable. He spoke forcefully and with barely contained disdain.

"You, sir, may answer to your entourage of multi-millionaire investors, but I answer to the people of this town. That's my job, and I take it very seriously. I don't have much to go on in this death, but let's look at what I *do* have." He paused.

"I've got one of the leading citizens of Antioch—hell, of the entire state of South Carolina—who, it appears, took a header off your bank building and ended up splattered all over the town square, right in front of the Confederate Soldier's monument!"

Deshaun had begun to rise slowly from his chair. As he spoke, each word grew louder and more forceful, reverberating off the glass walls and turning the fish tank into an echo chamber. He placed his hands flat against the desk and stared daggers into the other man's eyes.

"Now, that dead man that I've been talking about just happened to have in his pocket what *looks* like a suicide letter written to *you*. In that letter, he took to rambling on and on about another death. That's the beginning I'm interested in, Mr. Washington, not the 'In-the-beginning-God-created-beginning', but *that* beginning!"

PART I

The Beginning
May 1999

1

"Eenie-meenie-minie-mo, catch a nigger by the toe. If he hollers—"

Whump!

The group of children froze in shocked silence as the chubby red-haired boy's hands flew to his face. They watched his Adams's apple bob up and down as he fought unsuccessfully against his tears. "Gabrielle Westin, you done broke my nose!"

"Oh, no I didn't!" the young girl said. She took an intimidating step towards her wounded classmate and appeared to enjoy a moment of victory as he inched backward and away from her. "But, Eddie Crabtree, if you *ever* use that ugly, hateful word again, I just might break your nose. Anyways, I'll whup you good you ever say it again!"

The boy had managed to swallow his sobs. He wiggled his red nose gingerly with his fingers as he looked around at the circle of eight other children who were gathered on the dusty playground of Antioch Elementary School. A couple of the girls giggled nervously, but the boys appeared to be as embarrassed as the injured one. Not Gabrielle, though; she stood defiantly before him with her hands on her hips, staring him down.

Eddie rubbed his nose again. "I didn't mean nuthin' by it, Gaby. It's just a word, that's all. Besides, everybody says it."

"No, it is *not* just a word, and we don't say it in my house!" She paused a moment and then continued with her lecture.

"It's not just a word to Leander, it's hurtful to him. He's my best friend, so don't let me hear you say it again." A strand of honey gold hair had fallen across her face. She tucked it behind her ear and turned away from Eddie. "And," she concluded, tossing one final insult at the boy, "only my friends call me Gaby; *you* will call me Gabrielle!"

She wasted no time in marshalling her classmates into a circle once more. "*I'll* count off," she announced. "Eenie-meenie-minie-mo, catch a piggy by the toe. If he hollers, let him go; eenie-meenie-minie-mo. I choose y-o-u, you old dirty dish-rag, YOU! Okay, Leander, you're 'it.' Now remember, count to one hundred by fives; and no peeking. Ready, set, GO!"

Leander had remained quiet during his classmates' confrontation. He was, in fact, self-conscious at being the catalyst for Gaby's anger. But now that their game was on again, a more rational thought occurred to him: he was almost always *it*.

He had figured the odds of that happening, and it did not seem possible that he could be chosen as frequently as he was. Of course, he realized that the chance of him being chosen was greater when fewer children gathered to play hide-and-seek. But even on days like today, when the usual group of nine was all present, Leander was *it* three out of five times.

He had tried to discuss it with Mr. Woods, his third-grade teacher, after their math lesson one day. He had shown the man his calculations, as well. The teacher, however, just stared at him and walked off, mumbling that some kids were entirely too smart.

Oh well. Leander didn't mind being the one hardly ever allowed to hide. In fact, he looked forward to being included in the daily games of this group of children, so much so that he would probably have agreed to be 'it' every time.

The boy had no misconception, though, that all the children liked him and wanted him to play with them. The fact that he was the only black child included in their games was, he knew, due to his friend's intercession.

Gabrielle was spunky and a natural-born leader. She could also be bossy at times, which made her disliked by some of the girls in their class. Leander thought her unpopularity was probably due to jealousy on their parts.

Her dark blond hair hung in a smooth, straight cascade past her shoulders. In the summer, her skin would tan without a hint of freckles, to match the glossy gold of her hair. But it was her eyes, although slightly crossed, that garnered attention. They were amber in color and reminded

Leander of the picture of the lion that hung in the school library. He had overheard some of the grown-ups in town remark that Gabrielle's eyes kept her from being pretty. He disagreed.

He saw her as an angel, surrounded by a shiny, golden halo. She was his angel, anyway, and his dearest friend. He would die for her.

Gabrielle was also someone to be reckoned with. Leander snickered to himself as he thought about fat Eddie Crabtree and his bruised nose. Today was the last day of the school year, and he was sure going to miss these games.

"One hundred!" he called out loudly. "Ready or not, here I come!"

* * * * *

"That was fun," Gabrielle proclaimed thirty minutes later as the children made their way from the dusty playground and back into the brick schoolhouse. "You found everybody 'cept me. Now, only two more hours, and we're outta this place for the whole summer."

"I'm going to miss it," Leander said. "I love school."

"That's 'cause there ain't nobody else as smart as you, not even the teachers," Gabrielle said, praising her friend.

Leander stopped dead in his tracks, looking sternly at his friend. "There *ain't nobody else*? Come on, Gaby! You know that's terrible grammar. You should have said, 'There *isn't* anyone else' or, no one else is as smart—"

"Yes, Professor," she interrupted him, using the moniker his grandmother had bestowed on him a couple of years earlier when everyone began to notice the degree of his intelligence. "I don't see what difference it makes. You understand what I'm saying even if it ain't— *isn't*— correct."

"It makes a difference whether you get good grades or not. It will certainly make a difference when you want to go to college someday."

Gabrielle shrugged. "Who cares about going to college? When I grow up all I want is to get married to somebody like my daddy who's gonna take care of me and let me have babies. Besides," she fell silent, and Leander thought she looked a little sad. "College is for smart people, like you."

"You're smart, too, Gaby, you just have to try harder. And, you should have a back-up plan," he said as he winked at her and grinned. "You might not find anybody who even *wants* to marry you."

Gabrielle punched his shoulder playfully as the two friends entered their classroom. "You better watch it, Leander Washington; I'll whup you just like I done fat Eddie."

"You mean, 'just like I…'." He stopped speaking, closed his eyes, and shook his head. "Never mind."

Gabrielle giggled and skipped across the classroom to take her seat. Their teacher had discovered what his predecessors had: that the two children were practically inseparable and had to be parted to avoid whispering and note-passing in class. She turned suddenly and hurried back to Leander's side of the classroom.

"Are we gonna do it this afternoon?" she asked.

"If you're still sure that you want to," Leander answered.

She took a deep breath. "I'm sure."

2

"Free at last!" Gabrielle shouted as she turned a cartwheel off the schoolhouse's front steps. She landed gracefully on her feet, brushed her hair back from her face and grinned at Leander. "Let's race to the creek. Bet I can beat you," she said as she got a head start on the boy.

"Of course, you can beat me! I've got all the books to carry!" Leander called out after her, referring to the six books he had borrowed from the school library for the summer months. The stern-faced librarian had smiled and congratulated him on wanting to read during his vacation.

"What in the world are you gonna do with them books, anyways?" Gabrielle asked him as he caught up with her.

"*Those* books," he corrected her. "What do think I'm gonna do with them? I just might read them."

"Whatever," she said, shaking her head.

Leander recognized her expression as one of bewilderment where academia was concerned. The two of them had talked of little else for the past week except Dalton's Creek's deep swimming hole, rainbow trout to be caught and trees to be climbed.

She slowed her skipping pace to walk beside her friend. "So, did you bring the knife?" she asked him.

"I did," he answered. "You're still sure you want to do this?"

"I said I was sure, didn't I?"

Leander could tell that she wasn't sure, but she must know that he'd never allow her to be harmed.

The two children waved good-bye to friends as they left the school grounds and began walking down the two-lane gravel road toward their homes. The mile-long road was flanked by hundred-year-old live-oak trees, interspersed with huge camellia and azalea bushes, and dotted with perfectly tended beds of rose bushes and seasonal plants, coming to a picturesque end in the circular driveway of the Westin house.

In truth, it was never referred to as the "Westin" house, but rather the "Remington" house. Gabrielle's grandfather, William Llewellyn Remington, had built the mansion forty years earlier and still resided there as the family's powerful patriarch.

Leander's family lived less than a mile from the big house in one of the estate's modest frame rental houses. His father managed the farming and livestock breeding activities, which allowed Mr. Will to devote the necessary time to mold Remington Banking and Investments into a multi-million-dollar company.

In other words, Carl Lee Washington was a sharecropper: a modern-day overseer who looked after the interests of the master of the plantation. Of course, no one thought of Carl Lee's position with the leading family in the county in such demeaning terms—no one except perhaps Mr. Will.

Taking the familiar path that took them away from the gravel road and through the bullrushes, the two friends soon arrived at their destination. "Here we are!" Gabrielle exclaimed as she dropped to the mossy ground and began pulling off her tennis shoes and socks. "I can't wait to stick my feet in that cold water. You ever knowed a hotter day in May, Leander?"

"No, Gaby, I've never *known* a hotter day for this time of the year," Leander answered on a mildly sarcastic note.

"Me, neither." She grinned devilishly as she kicked water from the stream towards him. "Come on! Let's wade over to that big rock yonder. We can do it there," she said, boldly splashing farther out into the middle of the stream.

"This is serious business, Gaby;" Leander said a few minutes later when they were both seated on the large flat bolder.

He took the knife from his pocket and carefully pried the blade open. "When this is done, you and I will be blood brother and sister for all our lives." He turned the knife over and over in his hand.

"I know. I'm ready," Gabrielle responded as she wiped the palm of her left hand on the bottom of her tee shirt and held it gingerly toward Leander.

The small white hand lying in Leander's equally small black one trembled slightly as the shiny blade traced a thin line along the curved contour of her palm.

A heartbeat later, he made an identical cut on his own palm. He laid the knife down on the rock and looked into her eyes.

"Okay, now, we have to press our hands together just right so that our blood mixes," he instructed. "Like this." They clasped their left hands together tightly.

"It stings," Gabrielle whispered, "but not too bad, huh?"

"It's okay. We're supposed to say something, you know," Leander prompted.

"I'm not good with words like you are. You say it."

Leander nodded his head and spoke. "This makes us more than friends; we're blood brother and sister now. We'll look out for each other all our lives, and we'll never have any secrets between us. If you ever need me for anything, you just call. No matter how far away I am, I'll be there for you, Gaby. I won't ever let you down. I so swear."

"I so swear," she whispered reverently.

Slowly, they pulled their hands apart. Leander bent forward to wash the smeared blood from his hand. Gabrielle followed his lead.

"So," she began, looking at him quizzically, "our blood mixed together, right?"

"That's right," he answered as he pressed his hand on his shorts and checked to make sure no red remained.

"Does that mean that I might turn black?"

Leander turn to stare at her in disbelief.

"Of course not. What a ridiculous question!" Her giggling made him grin.

"I'm not *that* dumb," she said. "Come on, you silly boy. Let's wade back over to the bank. I got some cookies and Kool-Aid in my lunch box. We can have a picnic."

The shady creek bank welcomed the two youngsters as they munched Oreos and took turns sipping lime Kool-Aid from Gabrielle's Thermos cup.

"What'cha want to do tomorrow? I know," she babbled on before he could respond. "Let's come back down here and bring our fishing poles and some bait. I bet we could catch our supper."

"I thought Remy was coming home today. Don't you want to spend time with him tomorrow?"

"Yeah, he's driving in this evening. But if I know him, he'll stop by the Olsen's house first and smooch with M'Lyn. Then he'll probably sleep 'til noon tomorrow, him and Mason both. Mason's spending the summer with us. I told you that, didn't I?"

"Yes, you did. I guess he'll be working with Remy down at the bank, huh?" Leander remarked idly. He liked Gaby's big brother, but his best friend, Mason Carlisle, gave him the creeps.

"Probably. Anyhow, you want to go fishing tomorrow, or not?" Gabrielle asked as she sat upright and wiped perspiration from her forehead. "Damn, it's hot!"

"Yes, I want to go fishing," Leander answered firmly, "and do *not* cuss."

"Sorry," she said. "Hey, let's jump in the deep part of the creek now. Come on."

"We'll get our clothes wet," Leander objected.

"Not if we take our shorts and tee shirts off, we won't. I got my undershirt on, so you can't see my titties." Gabrielle scrambled to her feet and began tugging off the navy-blue shorts and navy and white striped shirt that was their school's warm weather uniform.

Leander looked up at her in amazement. "Girl," he said, "you ain't *got* no titties!"

In the blink of an eye, he knew the grave mistake he had made, as his friend whirled around, her face aglow with surprise and glee.

"What did I just hear?" she shrieked. "Did I just hear Leander-smartest-boy-in-the-whole-school-Washington say '*ain't*'?

"Better yet," she kept on teasing him as she skipped in circles delightedly, "did I just hear Leander-never-says-anything-wrong-Washington say '*ain't got no*'?"

Her antics were contagious, and soon they were laughing uncontrollably. They collapsed on the mossy earth, holding their sides and losing their breath in merriment.

Weak from laughter, they began to roll down the sloping bank towards the swimming hole. Their lithe young bodies picked up bits of moss and leaves along the way, only to end up being washed clean in the cool, crystal waters of Dalton's Creek.

And so it was that after a blissful afternoon spent with his dearest friend, nine-year-old Leander Washington would become caught in a web of chilling horror.

3

Gabe Westin strolled along Antioch's Main Street. It was barely after nine in the morning, and only a few of the shops were open. Although several parking spaces stood empty in front of his destination, Gabe had chosen instead to park in the public lot at the far end of the street. He'd hoped the long walk would calm his nerves a bit. He nodded to several folks he recognized along the way and thought how nice it was to see life coming back to downtown.

He soon reached his destination and paused, still unsure of just what he would say to someone he hadn't seen in close to twenty-five years—someone who had rarely been out of his thoughts in all that time.

The shop was one of several new businesses that had recently opened up in the block of long-vacant and disheveled brick buildings that lined Antioch's town square.

Gabe turned the knob and opened the glass door of *Tess' Fine Lingerie* to the merry sound of tinkling bells. He had to duck his head slightly as he entered. *Folks sure must have been a lot shorter when these old doors were set nearly a hundred years ago*, he thought.

He immediately took notice of the interior's pointed contrast to the vintage façade of the building. The fresh wallpaper's muted shades of pink and mauve served as a backdrop for the many racks of colorful gowns, robes, and kimonos.

Sleek, glass-topped tables stood on the polished oak floor and held neat stacks of all things frilly. The merchandise was illuminated by a dazzling crystal chandelier hanging from the recently painted, twelve-foot domed ceiling. The old brass wall sconces had been shined and put to good use with candles emitting a pleasant vanilla aroma,

Gabe heard sounds coming from beyond the curtain just the other side of the perfume counter. He cleared his throat to announce his presence.

A woman immediately entered through the curtain, smiling as she spoke: "I'm so sorry. I didn't know anyone was here this early. I was in the storeroom and didn't hear the bell. Welcome to—"

"Hello, Tess. Welcome home," Gabe said, his voice shaking. "You must've been living somewhere in a time warp. You still look fifteen years old." He could feel his eyes misting as he swallowed hard.

She took her time responding. Briefly, she closed her eyes, and when she opened them, it seemed to Gabe that the fleeting shadow of sadness he had just seen was gone. She smiled and shook her head as she spoke. "And you, Gabe Westin, are just as silver-tongued as you ever were. Come here and give me a hug."

The two embraced awkwardly.

"I saw your cousin, Betsey Ledford, at the Stop 'N Go last month, and she told me you were moving back to Antioch and opening a store," Gabe began the conversation in earnest, his voice steady again. "It's hard to believe that you decided to move back here, Tess. I heard that your designs went over real big in Atlanta."

"So, you've kept up with me, huh?" she said, grinning as she playfully poked a finger at his chest. "Actually, the decision to come back to Antioch was made *for* me. Maw-Maw Bradley is sick; she's got lung cancer. Never smoked a cigarette in her life. Go figure. I'm all she's got, and since she wouldn't hear of coming to stay with me in Atlanta, here I am. Maw-Maw was always there for me." She paused and shook her head thoughtfully. "What is it they say about the child one day becoming the parent?"

"Whatever happened to D'Andre? Can't he help with your grandmother?"

Tess raised her eyebrows. "That no-good uncle of mine? He's probably in jail somewhere. I haven't even bothered to look for him. He wouldn't be any help to us, anyway. He and my mother were just alike; all either one of them ever did was take money from Maw-Maw, break her heart, and then leave us." She spat the words angrily, reminding Gabe of the *other* Tess.

The telephone rang, startling them both. Tess excused herself and walked back to the counter to answer it, giving Gabe a brief respite from the gaggle of emotions that being with her again evoked. He watched her and listened as she spoke professionally into the receiver.

"Yes, ma'am. We specialize in bridal showers, and we have a registry at the shop here as well as at the one in Atlanta. It's worked so well for our clients. The bride can enter her wish list items. That way, everyone knows her tastes and there won't be any duplication."

She certainly knows her business, Gabe mused. He had never doubted for one minute that Tess Bradley would be a success at whatever she undertook. The uncertainty came from her. She never believed she was good enough or smart enough. She always fretted over what folks thought of her.

It was during those times of insecurity that the *other* Tess would come out—the one ruled by depression. She would close herself off for days, not even responding to Maw-Maw. And when she emerged from whatever dark place that had held her captive, the thin razor cuts along her arms would tell the horrible story of just how far into self-loathing she had sunk. Gabe hadn't known how to help her back then; he'd been too young to know.

He succeeded in shaking off those bad memories as he watched her write down information from the telephone call. He hadn't lied earlier: she *did* look as young as she had back in high school, and just as pretty, too. She had kept her dark hair short, accentuating the fine bone structure of her face and her long neck. He remembered the feel of her skin, like caramel-colored velvet beneath his trembling hands.

Stop it!

Tess ended her telephone call and turned to Gabe. "Well," she announced triumphantly, "I've just booked my first bridal event of the Antioch social season. Elise Pettigrew is giving her daughter, Shelby, a lingerie shower next month."

She seemed pleased, and that pleased Gabe. He said, "Back to what we were talking about before the phone rang—I'm so sorry to hear about your grandmother, Tess. Be sure and give her my regards. Let me know if I can do anything for her."

Tess looked up at him thoughtfully. "Maw-Maw always liked you, Gabe. She used to refer to you as 'that nice, polite white boy.'" Tess chuckled and then went on. "What she did *not* like one bit was you and me keeping company."

Gabe joined in the liveliness of the moment. "I remember the very first evening I stopped by your house to ask if you'd go walking with me. When we were going down your porch steps—"

"Maw-Maw said, 'Humph! Some folks don't know where they supposed to stay!' I didn't know if she meant me or you."

Their laughter melted into an uncomfortable silence. Gabe finally spoke. "I saw your ad in *Cosmopolitan*. You made it, Tess. I'm so happy for you." He walked over to a rack of gowns and began to examine them. "These sure are pretty."

"Well, I never made it to New York like I swore I would. But Atlanta wasn't bad, I guess." She fell silent for a moment or two. "I didn't do it all on my own, Gabe. I had a…I had help."

"You had talent. Don't you ever sell yourself short," he said emphatically.

She studied him, frowning. "Why are you here, Gabe?" Not allowing him time to answer, she continued speaking. "Now, don't misunderstand me. I appreciate your welcome and your compliments. But if you're here for a stroll down Memory Lane, you'd best know that road's been closed a long, long time."

Gabe waited, knowing that she had more to say. She walked behind the perfume counter and perched on a stool before she spoke again.

"When I said that I didn't succeed all on my own, I was speaking of a man I met soon after I ran off to Atlanta. He was an older, very wealthy white man. A *married* man," she added.

"Tess, you don't have to explain."

She held up her hand, silencing him. "You're right, I don't have to explain anything!" The *other* Tess spat the words angrily.

"I don't *have* to do a damn thing, Gabe. You know why? I'll tell you why. 'Cause that old, rich, white, married man picked up a raggedy-assed, scared-to-death, dirt-poor little colored gal from the boondocks of South

Carolina at the Greyhound bus station in Atlanta! And do you know what that man did?"

Her voice trembled, but her eyes remained dry. She spread her arms wide and tried to smile, but it came across as a sneer. "That man took a sow's ear and gave the fashion world a silk purse."

Gabe knew that her self-effacing sermon was over. He also knew it was best if he didn't comment. He pretended that the row of gowns on the rack in front of him had captured his attention. When she broke the silence, her voice was calm again.

"His name was Colonel Samuel Alexander, retired Army. He'd just dropped his aunt off at the bus station. Oh, I remember how alone I felt that night, standing out on the sidewalk, trying to figure out which way to start walking.

"I guess he could tell I didn't have the vaguest idea of where to go or what to do when I got there. So, he says, 'Young lady, may I offer you a ride downtown?' I told him that I could walk downtown just fine on my own. Then he told me that it was gonna be a mighty long walk, 'cause I was headed in the wrong direction."

Tess chuckled before continuing. "He took me to a motel, paid for the room, and told me he'd pick me up the next morning for breakfast. I didn't know what to make of him, but I was ready the next morning. Breakfast lasted through lunch and dinner. When that day was over, I knew there would be many more.

"That man was something else! He was easy to talk to, and when I told him I wanted to be a fashion designer, he never stopped pushing me to do it. He made me read every fashion magazine that was ever printed. He even sent me to design school. When Sam died five years ago, my shop in Atlanta and my condo were paid for, and I had five hundred thousand dollars in the bank.

"And that's the story of my success." She was done talking about herself. "What about you, Gabe? Tell me about the last twenty-some years in the Remington dynasty."

Her question brought him back to reality. She always did have a way of doing that—reminding him of the reality of his life, instead of the way he had wanted it to be.

"Vivian and I married right out of high school. After I graduated from Wharton, I went to work at the bank. Remington Investments has done well over the years. The partners own several banks and an insurance company as well. I'm the bank's president, but don't let that fool you—Will still calls the shots."

"And family?"

"My son, Remy, is just finishing up his freshman year in Columbia. We had a dry spell, and then Gabrielle came along. She's nine now."

Tess walked around the counter and came close to him again. Their eyes met for a long time before she repeated her earlier question.

"Why are you here, Gabe?"

"Like I said before, to welcome you back to Antioch. And, I came to buy a birthday gift."

"Oh, it's Vivian's birthday?"

"No, it's Remy's birthday. He'll be home sometime this evening for the summer. Tomorrow's his nineteenth birthday." Gabe tried to act nonchalant and hide his amusement at her confused expression.

"And you're shopping for him in *my* store?"

Gabe laughed heartily. "If you could see the look on your face!"

"Well, kindly explain to me just what you're talking about," she demanded.

"It's like this: I've always bought Vivian a gift on Remy's and Gabrielle's birthdays," he said. His voice was soft, almost apologetic. "It's my way of thanking her for giving me the children."

Tess didn't comment. After a while, she straightened her shoulders and walked briskly to the opposite side of the shop and opened a mirrored armoire door.

"These are my newest designs. I believe this occasion calls for…" she stopped speaking for a moment and flipped through the armoire's contents. "This one."

Gabe let out a whistle under his breath as he reached out and tentatively touched the silk gown that she held out to him.

"That's beautiful, Tess. You designed this? I don't believe I ever saw anything so pretty. What color do you call it?"

"This is periwinkle blue," she answered. "That's Liz Taylor's color."

"Uh-huh. Well, you're right. That's the one. I'll take it."

"I remember Vivian's strawberry-blonde hair and blue eyes," Tess said as she began to box the gown. "This should look lovely on her."

Gabe handed her his credit card and picked up the package while he waited for his receipt.

"You're going to do splendidly here, Tess. Antioch's womenfolk have never had a special shop like this one. Please don't forget to give your Maw-Maw my regards."

"Thank you, Gabe. And I sure do hope you plan on getting your *son* a birthday gift, too."

"Not to worry. His granddaddy will take care of that. Will Remington lives for that boy," he told her.

"Well, I'd better get going. I've got lots to do before Remy's party tomorrow night. I-I've really enjoyed our visit, Tess. And I meant what I said earlier: you look wonderful."

"Thank you. Now you watch yourself in this weather," she said. "I remember how the heat always bothered you, and we're in for a record-breaker today."

"I will. Bye, now." Gabe had grown uncomfortable and was relieved when he reached the front door.

His hand was on the doorknob when her voice stopped him. It wasn't her pleasant, lilting voice of just a moment ago, nor was it the *other* Tess's voice. It was a voice caught somewhere in between.

"Do you ever think about *our* boy, Gabe?"

Her words sliced into him like a knife. He turned slowly to face her once more. She was staring beyond him and gently rubbing her arms. She wore long sleeves on this hot day, and his heart broke at what he knew they covered up.

"For God's sake, Tess," he pleaded in a whisper, "please, don't!"

"I visited him the first day I was back here," she said, speaking in a monotone as if she had not heard him. "I took flowers. He's right there behind the King David A.M.E. Zion Church, second row back. I had a marker put up when I started making money in Atlanta. Before that, we just had a little wooden cross. Maw-Maw never had the money." She stopped speaking and closed her eyes. When she opened them, they were clear and focused again.

"What do you want me to say, Tess? What *can* I say to you that I didn't say twenty-five years ago? That, that we'd go away together somewhere? That everything would be okay? How 'bout that two fifteen-year-old kids could somehow…" His throat felt like it was on fire as his words dissolved.

"Old Doc Stamey said that me being so young and my body not ready for pregnancy was why he was so small. Oh, Gabe, he was so tiny. He could almost fit in one of my hands. He never cried, and babies are supposed to cry, you know.

"But for one magic moment, he opened his eyes and looked right at me, like he knew who I was. It's true, what they say, babies do have blue eyes. 'Course with those brown eyes of yours, and me being dark, his eyes would've turned brown. But they were blue then. And then he closed them."

She remained quiet for several minutes, and when she spoke again, Gabe knew she was close to being finished. Her voice was the sensible, matter of fact one that she had used before.

"They told me that I had to give him a name. I couldn't think of any except for the one I gave him: *Angel Bradley*. That's what's on his little marker."

There was nothing left to be said by either of them. He turned the doorknob slowly and stepped out of the shop and into the oppressive heat of mid-morning.

The door must have upended the little bell, for it didn't jingle cheerfully as it had an hour ago. Now, it sounded dull, out of tune, and lifeless.

4

M'Lyn Olsen had perfected the pout. Practicing in front of her vanity mirror for hours on end, she had mastered all the facial expressions that a southern beauty needed to gain attention—and anything else her heart desired.

She studied her image in the mirror critically, posing first one way then another. Her smile was perfect, worth the years of corrective braces that she'd endured. Her complexion was without blemish—*thank goodness, no zits this month*. She decided that she liked her hair in the French twist that Roberta had done for her earlier; it made her look sophisticated.

M'Lyn's frequent analysis of her reflection had led her to select the left profile as her best pose. That was the one she had chosen for the senior yearbook picture. She glanced over at the framed 8x10 that she intended to give to Remy for his birthday the following day.

She leaned closer to the mirror and continued to practice her facial expressions. Her mother had been right: a lady could speak volumes without ever using words. And she was prepared to use those expressions—plus a few other little tricks she had *not* discussed with her mother—to get what she wanted most of all: a diamond engagement ring from Remy Westin.

She practiced a while longer. *Let's see now, disappointment, boredom, mild embarrassment growing into outright shock, happiness*—all of them perfected, she decided. Why, she could even think about her little dog that got run over last summer, and her blue-diamond eyes would fill with tears.

M'Lyn stood up from her dressing table, yawned, and stretched. She ambled over to the wall of closets across her large bedroom and began to flip through her vast assortment of clothing. The next hour was spent trying on one outfit after another, until she finally decided on the white mini shirt and blue tank top.

After her shower, she donned a new white push-up bra, matching lacy thong, and her chosen outfit. She pirouetted in front of the full-length mirror, noticing the way her nipples appeared visibly erect through the thin tank top and the mini skirt barely covering her butt. She snickered as she prepared to leave her bedroom and go downstairs to wait for Remy.

The way she looked, coupled with *the pout*, and that poor boy didn't have a chance. That diamond ring would be hers before summer's end!

She stepped around the pile of clothes that she had tried on earlier and opened her bedroom door. "Roberta," she called out loudly, "come hang up these clothes, please."

* * * * *

"Hell, man, you'd better slow this mo-chine down! You gonna total it before you put a thousand miles on it." Remy hung onto the armrest of the '99 Mazda RX-7 as he cautioned his friend. "I still can't believe your old man sprung for it. Shit, what I'd give for a ride like this."

"Not to worry, good buddy," Mason Carlisle replied. "This baby was built for speed. Besides, if I *did* wreck it, dear ole dad would just arrange for a new one the next day."

He slowed the car in preparation for the turn into the Olsen's driveway, and then went on talking. "It's their way, you know, Dad's and Step-Mommy's, for not having to include me in their trip to Italy. Not that I wanted to go with them, anyway. I'd much rather spend my summer vacation right here in bum-fuck-Carolina with you, buddy boy." He brought the car to a stop under the portico at the side entrance of the Olsen home.

Remy knew his best friend was just putting up a front. He had obviously been hurt when his father had informed him rather contritely last week that 'things just hadn't worked out' for him to accompany them to Italy for the summer months.

"Maybe next year," Layton Carlisle had said as he patted Mason on the back and handed him the keys to the Mazda. "Enjoy the car, son. You've earned it."

Layton had then wasted no time in wedging his short, square frame into his Jag convertible, adjusting the steering wheel to just barely miss his belly, and affecting his exit from the Columbia campus with Mrs. Trophy Number Four nestled in the seat beside him.

"Come on in with me," Remy invited as he opened the passenger's door and prepared to exit the car. "Mr. and Mrs. Olsen are probably still at the mill, but Roberta can make us some sandwiches and cold drinks."

Mason cocked his head at his friend in disbelief. "You ain't seen M'Lyn since Easter, and you're asking me to come in? Looks like I'm gonna have to have a *long* talk with you one of these days."

Remy laughed. "Yeah, well, just my luck that she's determined to wait 'til she's married before she gives it up," he responded to his friend's teasing. "Today will end like all our other times together with her letting me go only so far then getting all weepy on me and saying I just want her for sex, and me apologizing and leaving with a hard-on the size of Kansas."

"Well, my good man, just leave it to Dr. Carlisle," Mason continued to goad his friend good naturedly. "How 'bout I give you an hour with the luscious Miss Olsen, and then I'll come back by and pick you up. I guarantee that where I'll take you, you won't leave with nothing but a smile on your face."

Remy shook his head. "Uh-huh, a smile and a dose of the clap."

"Never fear," Mason countered as he patted his shirt pocket. The two friends laughed at the rustle of cellophane. "A boy scout is always prepared."

Remy reached behind the seat and retrieved his backpack, then studied his friend for a brief moment. Mason had inherited the Layton short, stocky frame, but that in no way made him less attractive to the opposite sex. His curly black hair and cobalt-blue eyes, coupled with his self-assured demeanor, attracted the coeds like bees to honey.

Remy alighted from the car, then bent down to the open window and spoke. "I can't understand it, man. You could have your pick of girls like M'Lyn. How come you like to troll in the slums?"

Mason started the engine and revved it a couple of times before he answered. "Simple. I like 'em young, willing, and uncomplicated. See you in a couple of hours, pal."

Remy jogged up the brick steps and rang the doorbell. He was about to decide that Mason had the right idea—just a good time with complete satisfaction and no strings attached. But then, the leaded-glass door opened, and he was met with that saucy little grin. Wordlessly, M'Lyn took his hand and pulled him decisively into the room and closed the door behind him.

She stood on her tiptoes, wrapped her arms around his neck, and began to brush her lips across his. His hands traveled down her back to lift the mini skirt and cup her bare buttocks. As he sucked gently on her swollen lower lip his breathing grew labored, and when her tongue slid easily into his mouth, all thoughts of Mason and his uncomplicated way of life vanished.

5

At just past noon, the day was already stifling with the air so heavy you could drink it. Mason lowered the Mazda's windows anyway. He adjusted the A/C controls all the way down, cranked up the soft rock music on the radio, and drove leisurely through the slightly blighted neighborhood.

It wasn't exactly the slums, but it was close. A few modest houses were still standing, but the area known simply as The Project consisted mainly of a cluster of cheaply-built, three-story buildings. These buildings housed a segment of the town's population who relied on government-subsidized rent to inhabit their apartments.

Mason dodged a pot-hole on Westside Avenue and stopped at the first of two traffic lights on the narrow street. His butt was numb from the long drive and he was hungry. Maybe he should have taken Remy up on his offer of lunch at M'Lyn's.

He moved the driver's seat back one position and stretched his legs as much as he could. Out of the corner of his eye, he saw her approach the passenger's side and lean down to the open window.

"Hi, handsome," she purred. "You lonely?"

He studied her briefly before nodding his head slightly. She opened the door and slid gracefully into the leather bucket seat. She was young, dark-skinned, and pretty—or, she would have been pretty had she not been wearing too much makeup and that ridiculous platinum wig.

"How old are you? And don't lie to me," Mason instructed before she could answer his question.

She straightened her shoulders slightly and said: "Okay, I'm sixteen. So, what'cha want?"

"How much?"

"Depends," she answered, shrugging and trying to act like she wasn't new to this. "Right here, right now, twenty bucks."

This was just what he needed to start his summer off right. "Tell you what, dahlin', you get the job done before I get to that next traffic light, and I'll make it thirty." He grinned at her and unzipped his shorts.

She grinned back, showing perfect white teeth, and he thought again how pretty she'd be if she wasn't all painted up.

The light turned green, and he inched the Mazda forward.

"Thirty bucks, please," she said, holding out her hand and straightening up a minute later as he brought the car to a stop at the second traffic light.

She stuck the bills in her purse, opened the door, and stepped out. She leaned back down and her halter top fell open, giving him a full view of small, perky breasts with dark brown nipples.

"I'm here most every day now that school's out for the summer. You come on back anytime, you hear?"

Mason winked at her and pulled away without a word. *That certainly took the edge off.* He was sweating, thirsty, and ravenous.

He stopped the car at a one-pump gas station at the end of the street advertising a hot lunch counter. After rolling up the car's windows, he alighted. He made sure he locked the doors and then went inside.

The interior of Curley's Gas 'N Go was even more dingy than it had appeared from the street. The air was thick with stale cigarette smoke and the smell of fried pork rinds.

Thinking that maybe he wasn't that hungry after all, Mason headed for the cold drink case against the far wall. He selected bottled water and a can of soda from the meager contents. He was about to pay the bald-headed man behind the counter with the name tag that read *Curley*, when the voice behind him broke the silence.

"You better have one of these here pulled pork sandwiches, Mister, to go with that Dr. Pepper. They's the best sandwiches in town."

Mason turned around to the grinning face of the young girl behind the lunch counter. She looked to be in her early teens and was as pretty as a picture.

"Well, now, my first day back in Antioch and I done met the future Miss America," he said.

She giggled. "You want a sandwich, or what?"

"What," he answered, winking and flashing his smile in her direction.

"What else for you, sir?" Curley asked him rather brusquely.

"I do believe I'm gonna have one of those pulled pork sandwiches that this lovely young lady offered," Mason answered.

"You hear that? Fix this gentleman a sandwich," Curley instructed. "You want that to go, sir?"

Mason was about to say that he'd have his lunch at the only table in the establishment, when the battered screen door burst open to the sound of a boom box and the loud voices of four local youths.

They were all talking at once and jostling each other. One of the young men knocked over a potato chip rack, and they all laughed riotously as it clattered to the floor.

"Cut that goddamn noise off!" Curley's voice boomed. "And pick that rack up! Now, whatever you come in for, get it, line up here and pay for it one at a time, then take your leave. You all understand me?"

Mason guessed that Curley must have a reputation that preceded him. The young man sporting the boom box on his shoulder immediately turned the volume down.

"Sorry, suh," came the sullen reply from the group's apparent leader, a light-skinned black man who had trouble keeping his pants pulled up. "Tru, pick up that rack," he ordered.

"Didn't knock it down," the smallest of the men responded sullenly.

"Don't matter. I said to pick it up!" the leader repeated threateningly.

When he had been obeyed, he turned to Curley and said: "Sorry. You got any cracklins today?"

"Fresh made this morning. How much you want?"

"Let me have a pound. And four of them pork sandwiches, too."

Mason had stepped away from the action. He watched as the group selected several more items and moved politely to the counter.

"How much for everything?" Baggy Pants asked.

"Eleven-fifty-five, all together," Curley answered.

When the four had left, Mason stepped back to the counter. "You certainly put the fear in them," he said.

Curley met his gaze as he responded. "It's not exactly me they's scared of; they done heard 'bout this." He reached under the counter and brought out a sawed-off shotgun. "I had a run-in with a couple of their buddies some time back. They got good memories."

He changed the subject. "You got this gentleman's sandwich, honey?"

The young girl walked from behind the lunch counter and handed Mason a paper bag. "Yes, sir, Gramps. Here it is."

Mason could see that she was even younger than he had originally thought. Although her facial features belied her age, her mannerisms were those of a child. She swayed back and forth on the balls of her feet and looked down at the floor as she addressed him.

"I sure like your car, Mister."

"Well, thank you, dahlin'. When you grow up, I just might take you for a ride," Mason teased. He grinned at Curley, whose countenance remained guarded as he handed over change from the twenty-dollar bill.

"Thank you, sir. Good day to you," Curley said.

Mason caught the inflection in the older man's voice and knew he was being respectfully dismissed. As he gathered up his purchases and prepared to leave, he saw Curley direct his granddaughter back to the lunch counter with a firm jerk of his head.

She's gonna give you some kind of trouble, Pop, Mason mused as he headed out the door. "You folks have a nice afternoon," he said.

Mason hopped in the Mazda and drove a short distance beyond Curley's store to where the narrow street petered out and the black-top melted into a large, overgrown lot. He remembered this as being the old wagon road that was used by settlers over a hundred years ago. It had at one time led to a row of slave cabins located on the back side of what was once a thriving cotton plantation.

Now, that narrow trail wound through untended land covered by kudzu vines, across a rickety old wooden bridge that spanned the town's unauthorized trash dump and came to an end on the back side of the Remington property.

Mason turned the Mazda around to face the street he had just traversed and prepared to eat his lunch.

He liked this part of town, even if it was considered the slums. His youth included fond memories of his and Remy's carefree summers spent in and around the worthless patch of ground, taking pot shots at rats and snakes with B-B guns from the safety of the old wooden bridge and hiding from the watchful eyes of parents.

Those were good times, broken up by his father's bonanza in the stock market and his insistence that they move from Antioch to Charleston where, Mason knew, they would not be looked upon as having *new* money. He still resented his dad for uprooting him from Antioch. He couldn't remember his mother, and the only family life he'd ever experienced was in the home of his best friend, Remy.

They had kept in touch throughout high school, though, and were now reunited as college roommates. Remy's dad, Gabe, had always been rather distant to Mason, but he could tell that Mr. Will liked him. After college, Mason felt certain he'd have a position with the old man's bank.

He finished what was, in fact, the best pulled pork sandwich he'd ever had, wadded up the paper wrapping and tossed it out the car window in the general direction of the rusted-out, overflowing trash receptacle beside the road. It fell on the ground, right in front of the "Antioch is too beautiful to litter" sign.

Mason needed to pee. He exited the car, walked behind a clump of weeds, and relieved himself. After stretching his legs, he got back in the Mazda and started the engine.

Up ahead he saw the screen door of Curley's Gas 'N Go open and the young girl step out. She looked down the street in Mason's direction, stood still for a full minute, then turned around and began a slow and deliberate sashay up the street towards the town square.

"Oh, yeah, Pop," he whispered. "That one's gonna be trouble!"

He slipped the car in drive and resumed his slow cruise.

6

"I sure missed you, baby," M'Lyn whispered in Remy's ear. "I just think about you all the time."

She flicked her tongue along the outer edge of his ear and down his neck to his collarbone where she knew he liked her to nibble. He groaned, and the thought occurred to her that she'd better stop him soon, or neither one of them would be able to resist the inevitable.

M'Lyn had allowed his hand to stroke her thigh, and she'd even parted her legs slightly to his more intimate caress. The temptation was exquisite, but she would not give in.

"Stop, Remy," she ordered breathlessly, as she gently pushed him away and sat up on the settee in the den. She began to smooth her hair and pulled her mini-skirt down as far as it would go. "Let's go in the kitchen and get some lunch." Her voice was shaky.

Remy couldn't speak at all. He was on the verge of throwing her back down on the settee and ripping that ridiculous strip of lace off her and giving her what they both wanted. Damn her for dressing like that! He closed his eyes and stretched back against the back of the settee and tried to wish away the ache in his groin. It didn't work.

When he opened his eyes, she had already left the room, and he could hear her moving around in the kitchen.

"What's for lunch?" Remy asked a few minutes later as he entered the kitchen and perched on a bar stool.

"Roberta made chicken salad. I'm fixing you a sandwich, now," M'Lyn answered. "She made strawberry shortcake, too. How does that sound?"

Remy watched her flit around the room. "Strawberry shortcake's not exactly the dessert I was hoping for," he said, making one last plea.

She turned around slowly and presented him with dewy eyes and the much-practiced pout. "Now, Remy," she began sweetly, "I've told you that I am not going to have sex until I'm married. I meant it, too. When I walk down that aisle at the First Baptist Church, I'm going to be wearing Mama's white lace wedding gown that she wore when she and Daddy got married, and I'm going to *deserve* to be wearing it."

"I know, sugar. So…" he drew a deep breath then fell silent.

"So, what?" M'Lyn prompted.

He reached across the island counter and took her hand in his. "So, let's get married. This summer."

M'Lyn's eyebrows shot up and her expression brightened briefly. "Oh, Remy," she squealed and bounded around the counter and into his arms. Before he could respond, she went on talking.

"But it takes a year to properly plan a wedding, with all the parties, showers, the invitations, reception—everything."

"We don't need all that," he said. "You can wear your mama's dress, and we can just have our families and close friends at the church."

M'Lyn had to think and think fast. This was what she wanted alright, just not *how* she wanted it. She walked to the refrigerator and poured herself a glass of iced tea before she spoke again. When she did it was with much emotion.

"Remy, I just can't do that to Mama. Why, it just about destroyed her when Suzanne eloped with Ritchie. She and Daddy had saved and planned for her wedding just like they have mine, and they were just crushed. 'Course, with my big sister being knocked-up, it was best that she did elope. But I'm not going to cheat them out of a big wedding. You do understand, don't you?" She finished her speech and watched him expectantly.

"Yeah, I guess. My folks would be disappointed, too. We'll get engaged, and you and your mother can plan the wedding for next summer."

This time, she practically knocked him off the bar stool when she jumped in his arms. "Yes, yes, yes! Oh, Remy, I love you, and I'm going to make you so happy." She backed off and gave him her most glowing smile.

"I want a diamond, okay? A big one, bigger than Pamela Sue Murray's. She prissed around school all year long, showing off her diamond and telling everybody that it was a carat and a half. We couldn't even have cheerleading practice without her shoving that ring in our faces. Can we get a big one, baby?"

"Sure thing. I'll talk to Granddaddy," Remy agreed. He pulled her close once again and began to run his hands down to her buttocks. She kissed him hungrily just as the telephoned on the counter jangled noisily.

"I better answer that. It's probably Mama. Hello?" M'Lyn spoke into the receiver as she turned and blew a kiss in Remy's direction. "Why, hello, Mason. How are you? I'm hurt you didn't come it to say hi to me," she purred.

After a moment of silence, she asked: "Nothing's wrong, is it? Yes, he's right here. Just a minute. *Car trouble*," she whispered as she handed the receiver to Remy.

"Hey, man, what's up?" Remy asked. .... "So, what am I supposed to do? It's ten miles from here to the house. I'm not walking that far on any day, much less in this god-awful heat. ...Whatever!" He finished the conversation on a note of disgust and hung the phone up decisively.

"He said his car was giving him trouble. I thought it was brand new," M'Lyn commented.

"I'm sure he's got trouble," Remy grumbled. "I'm just betting it's not with his car."

M'Lyn finished making sandwiches and set the plates on the counter. "It's about time for Mama and Daddy to get home from the mill, anyway. One of them can drive you home. Shall we tell everybody at your birthday party tomorrow night?"

"Tell them what?"

She looked at him in amazement. "That we're engaged! What else have we been talking about?"

Remy swallowed half of his sandwich and chased it with a swig of iced tea. "Don't you want your ring first?" he asked, managing to avoid the storm he saw brewing on her face.

She took a deep breath and then nodded her head thoughtfully. "You're right, baby. When do you reckon that might be?"

"I'll talk to Granddaddy over the weekend. How 'bout some of Roberta's strawberry shortcake?"

M'Lyn set about serving the dessert just as the kitchen door opened.

"Remy, how nice to see you," Lynn Olsen said as she entered and moved to embrace him. "I'll bet you're glad to be home for the summer."

"Yes, ma'am, Miz Lynn, I sure am," Remy answered. He smiled and turned to shake hands with her husband, who had entered behind her.

"Good to see you, Mr. Tom. How's things down at the mill?"

"Doin' fine, son, just fine," Tom answered. "That cake looks good, baby girl. Cut your daddy a piece of it."

"Now, Tom, remember what the doctor said about your blood sugar," Lynn cautioned.

"To hell with that doctor," Tom said, ending the subject. He perched his heavy frame on the bar stool beside Remy and began to attack the cake heartily.

"How's your granddaddy, son? I been meaning to call him and get him down to the mill to talk about setting up some 401k's for our employees. I'll get with him tomorrow night at the barbeque," Tom said, as he wiped whipped cream off his mouth with the back of his hand. He slid his empty plate across the counter and motioned to M'Lyn for a refill.

"Remy needs a ride home, Daddy. Mason Carlisle dropped him off, but his car's broke down or something."

"Sure thing. Let me finish this cake and we'll get going," Tom responded between bites.

7

Mason slammed the receiver back on the telephone so hard it made a ringing sound. He hadn't meant to do that.

"I'm sorry," he said apologetically. "Please excuse me. I'm sure you can understand why I'm so upset."

The heavy-set lady behind the bar of Denny's Dream Lounge looked at him with hooded eyes. "Uh-huh," she responded dully. She inclined her head in the general direction of the open front door. "There's yo' wrecker." She turned away from him and began to slowly wipe the cracked marble countertop.

Mason slapped a ten spot on the bar and walked outside without another word.

Two skinny boys, neither of whom looked old enough to drive and both with cigarettes hanging out of the sides of their mouths, had already hooked the Mazda up to the tow truck. They stood side by side, grinning and waiting on instructions.

"Where to, Mister?" the taller boy asked.

"The closest service station, I suppose," Mason answered. "Any suggestion?"

The boy shrugged his shoulders. "The Shell station on Raven Street is where I'd take it," he said, the cigarette bobbing up and down as he spoke.

"They fix tires, but I don't think they's gonna be able to fix these. I think you're gonna need two brand new ones."

"It looks that way," Mason agreed. "Okay, the Shell station it is. Can I hitch a ride with you?"

"Sure thing. Hop on in," the boy said as he and his friend climbed into the truck's cab.

Mason had reached the truck when a voice behind him made him pause and turn around.

"You know why this here happened, don't you?" The lady from the lounge had followed him out to the street and stood propped against the door frame.

Mason motioned for the tow truck driver to wait a minute and walked over to the woman. "No, ma'am," he said, "I can't imagine why this happened. Why would someone slash two of my tires to shreds for no reason whatsoever?" His tone was sharp; Mason felt like crying.

"You got no place here, that's why," she answered flatly.

"What's that supposed to mean? I came in here for a couple of cold beers on a hot day. I sure as hell didn't deserve this," Mason retorted. He shook his head and prepared to return to the truck.

"No to both," she said, still showing no emotion.

Mason turned back to her. "What do you mean by 'no to both'?"

The woman studied him for several seconds before she answered. When she did respond, Mason thought he detected a bit of genuine concern in her voice.

"Well, first off, no you did not deserve to have your tires ruined like that. And second, you did *not* come in here for cold beer."

She crossed her arms and continued with her lecture. "You came in here looking for black gals to have some fun with. *That's* what you come in here for, and *that's* why you got trouble. The customers here don't take kindly to white boys coming around."

He was about to respond when the woman held up her hand to silence him. "Leave now, son," she said, "and be glad that your tires was all that got cut up."

* * * * *

"Jeez-Louise! Somebody sure did a number on your tires, young feller," the grizzled old mechanic at the Shell station exclaimed.

He spat a stream of tobacco juice on the ground and shook his head. "I ain't never seen tires cut up that bad. You got trouble with somebody, son?"

Mason ignored the man's question. "How long will it take to get two new ones put on?"

"Won't take no more'n an hour to put 'em on," the old man answered.

"Good. Go ahead and get started. I'll wait inside, if that's okay."

Mason stepped toward the station door as another brown stream whizzed by him.

"I said it'd take an hour to put your tires on," the old man said. "It's gonna take probably three days to get 'em here."

"Three days? Why so long?" Before the questions were out of his mouth, Mason remembered that he was not in Charleston or Columbia.

"These here tires," the old man began to explain patiently, "are special order; we don't stock 'em. They got to come out of Greenville. Tomorrow's Saturday, and we don't get no deliveries. Probably get 'em in Monday late, Tuesday morning, I'm guessing. You want me to order them?"

Mason sighed heavily and realized he didn't have a choice. "Yes, sir. Go ahead and order them. How about my car? Can I leave it here?"

The old man flashed him a brown, nearly toothless grin. "Son, your car ain't going nowhere on its own, that's for sure. You need a ride somewhere?"

"No thanks. I'm staying at Mr. Will Remington's home, and I can walk from here."

The old man straightened his shoulders slightly before responding. "You staying at Mr. Will's? Don't you worry; your car will be just fine. I'll put it in that back bay over yonder. Nobody's gonna mess with it, I guarantee."

"I appreciate that, sir. Can you call the house or the bank when it's ready?" Mason inquired, extending his hand to the old man.

"Sure thing, son. Give my regards to Mr. Will. Tell him Jesse said howdy."

"I'll do that, Jesse. Thanks." Mason smiled at the old man and turned to leave.

"You sure you don't want a ride? It's mighty hot today," Jesse called out after him.

"No, thanks," Mason replied. "It's not that far. I believe I'll cool off in the creek, and then cut through The Ramble. I'll be there before long. Thanks again, sir."

"Glad to be of help," Jesse said.

Seems like a real nice young fellow, the old mechanic thought as he turned to re-examine the Mazda and its shredded tires. "Wonder who he pissed off," he muttered under his breath. He gave directions to one of his employees for the car to be put into the empty service bay and went into his office.

As he reached for the telephone to place the order for the two tires, he realized that the young man hadn't even asked how much they were going to cost.

8

"Bye, Remy. I'll see you tomorrow night," M'Lyn called out from the kitchen doorway as she watched him follow her father to his car. When he turned around to acknowledge her, she gave him her most seductive smile and flicked her tongue across her lower lip.

Remy stopped momentarily in his tracks and closed his eyes. "See you tomorrow," he said weakly. He stumbled while getting into the car and was still looking at her when Tom pulled out of the driveway.

M'Lyn grinned as she turned and went inside. She wouldn't say a word to anyone until she got her ring. Then, she and her mother would start planning the wedding.

Oh, she could already see the pale blue, engraved invitations: *Mr. and Mrs. Thomas Olsen request the honor of your presence at the marriage of their daughter, Millicent Lynette, to Mr. William Remington Weston.*

She was going to do everything right. No hasty, shotgun wedding for her, no sir. Every step of her life was going to be orchestrated, with each event taking place just as it should.

M'Lyn yawned and stretched, deciding a nap before dinner was in order. As she slowly ascended the curved stairway to her bedroom, she continued to organize events in her mind. First, the ring; next would come the announcement, the parties, the formal invitations, and finally the biggest wedding of the season.

The house, of course, would come after an extended honeymoon, then children. Well, *maybe* children—M'Lyn wasn't sure she even wanted them. Just look at poor Suzanne and what three of the little beasts had done to her figure. She'd think about that later. After all, eighteen was much too young to be thinking about children.

Yes, her life would continue along its smooth path to perfection. She was glad she had made the decision not to give in to Remy, much as she wanted to. Remaining a virgin until her wedding night was a goal she fully intended to realize.

M'Lyn paused as she neared the top of the stairs, a frown creasing her forehead. Well, there *was* that one time when she was what—thirteen? But that didn't count because it was just adolescent curiosity and not passion.

And what was that boy's name? Tyrone, maybe? Tyrell? Oh, Ty-something. Anyway, it was just that one time, long ago. She remembered warning him that if he told a soul, she'd have him boiled alive in a tub of hog lard for daring to even touch a white girl!

He must have believed her—she didn't think he had said a word about it. When it came time to pick the peaches the following year, his family hadn't shown up.

M'Lyn reached the top of the staircase. "Roberta," she called out, "come take my hair down and brush it, please. I'm getting a headache."

* * * * *

"Mr. Tom, there's no use in you getting your Cadillac all dusty on the driveway," Remy said. "I can walk from here. Truth is I'd like to walk through The Ramble today; I've sure missed being home."

"Well, if you're sure, son. I don't mind driving you all the way to the house at all." Tom Olsen chuckled as he brought the car to a stop where the pavement ended. "I'll be driving up the driveway tomorrow, anyway."

"Yes, sir, but I feel like walking today." Remy hopped out of the car. "See y'all tomorrow," he said. He waved as Tom turned the car around and drove away.

Actually, he did *not* feel like walking. Thanks to M'Lyn, walking was painful. But he needed to be alone and think things through. *Damn, you are going to be a married man in one year.* The notion struck him full force. *Still in college, with a wife!*

Oh, well. His dad and mom had married right out of high school. He should talk to them. But he knew he couldn't: he'd never been able to talk to either of them about anything. He would talk to Granddaddy, though, just as soon as the time was right.

Granddaddy was the only person who could put things into perspective for him. He would keep everything from closing in on him, like it sometimes did. Remy sat down on one of the stone benches beside the road. Out of the blue, he felt miserable. He leaned forward and rested his head in his hands. Why was he suddenly in such a funk?

The day had begun on a high note, with him and Mason heading home in that fabulous new car, each one of them looking forward to his summer job at the bank and the generous paychecks that would come with it. And, of course, for Remy there were those summer nights with M'Lyn.

"But, married?" he lamented.

He got to his feet slowly and turned toward the familiar, pine-scented woodland trail that would lead him home.

9

The Ramble, a crescent-shaped tract of land encompassing close to four densely wooded acres, was once the main entrance to one of the largest antebellum plantations in the upstate. The Mossbank Plantation mansion had survived the Civil War relatively unscathed and was still standing, albeit beyond repair, when Will Remington purchased it in mid-1960s.

Although several Mossbank descendants still resided in Antioch, the old plantation, comprising a hundred-plus acres of rolling meadowlands dotted with overgrown garden plots and boggy lowlands, quickly became known as the Remington Estate.

The dilapidated old house had been demolished and the new, red brick Georgian mansion erected. Will, being a bit ostentatious, had insisted on abandoning the original approach to the house as being too narrow for anything wider than a horse and buggy. Truth be told, the simplicity of the winding driveway nestled between huge live oaks heavily adorned with Spanish moss was simply not grand enough for him.

"We need the entrance to our property to make a statement," young Will had said to Lily, his wife, as he explained his reasoning for bypassing what was to her the most beautiful part of their property.

"But you're making the new driveway straight," Lily had replied. "How can a straight stretch of road make a statement?"

"You'll see," Will's said as he set about doing it his way. And he had made a statement, alright: by investing a fortune with a landscape architect to design the entrance to his liking.

Lily rarely understood her husband, but she never questioned his decisions. She was content to remain in the background, simply being Will's wife. Her pet project of cleaning, grubbing, pruning, planting, and generally caring for The Ramble resulted in Will grudgingly admitting that she had created as beautiful a park as was anywhere in the county.

Of course, it didn't hurt that he had allowed her a blank check to cover the many stone benches, fountains, statuary, and plants and flowers of every kind to fill her paradise. When the weather permitted, Lily had worked tirelessly in The Ramble until she became too advanced in her pregnancy to bend over. Following Vivian's birth, she retreated once again to the solitude of her Eden.

With her infant daughter in the capable care of their housekeeper, Rosie, Lily's daily treks to tend the gardens grew from a hobby to an obsession until the morning when she awoke to blood on her pillow and uncontrollable coughing spasms.

As she lay dying, six months later, she weakly remarked to her nurse that her two regrets in life were that she had not given Will a son, and that her beloved Ramble would never be finished.

Remy had heard the story of his grandmother's devotion to her gardens many times. True, no one had ever worked in The Ramble after her death, but the tons of fertilizer, mulch, and topsoil that had been poured into the area at her direction had taken hold.

The azalea, camellia, and other flowering shrubs had grown to be the size of trees and created dense hide-a-ways for the young lovers who strolled there. Especially popular with the children who came from town to play among the trees were the ancient crape myrtles. Their huge, multi-stalk trunks were smooth and splinter-free and made for superb feats of climbing.

It was easy for someone unfamiliar with the labyrinth of trails that wound through the wooded area to take the wrong path and find themselves lost in flowering confusion. In fact, many of these smaller trails had succumbed years ago to the ivy that now threaded its way to make walking difficult. The main path had remained clear, though, and Remy knew it like the back of his hand.

He smiled as he entered The Ramble, remembering his happy childhood. Stepping into the shady grove was like stepping into the embrace of an old friend. Maybe his growing frustration—both physical and emotional—would abate by the time he reached his home.

* * * * *

Mason sank to the mossy ground beside Dalton's Creek, unzipped the garment bag that he had taken from his car and removed a small, leather pouch. After deftly rolling a joint, he lit it and inhaled deeply. He needed to veg out before he continued to the house.

What a disaster this day has turned into! He lay back on the cool earth and pulled on the joint again as he thought about how great the day had begun. *Oh, well. Could've been worse,* he reasoned. The lady from the bar had been right—he was lucky that tires were all that had gotten cut up.

He couldn't sit still—even the weed couldn't get him mellow. *Only one thing can do that,* he thought ruefully, and he didn't see any sweet, willing babes around here. He finished his smoke, stood up, and shucked off his shorts and tee-shirt.

The cool water immediately refreshed his naked body, and soon his mood began to brighten. Thank God he wasn't like his best friend, Remy. Otherwise, he would stay depressed for days over a couple of tires.

Mason wasn't one to stress himself too much over anything, especially something that money could fix. Remy, on the other hand, would work himself up into an absolute frenzy over something as insignificant as a bad grade on a test, or the thought that his granddaddy would somehow find out that he'd spent his entire month's allowance on booze. "Who freakin' cares?" Mason muttered as he submerged one last time in the cold water then headed back to the creek bank to dry off before he dressed.

With the sweat washed from his body, he felt like a new man—but he wasn't a new man, though he longed to become one. Hopefully, this summer spent with Mr. Will and Mr. Gabe at the bank would ignite a sense of purpose in him. Perhaps time spent in their presence would turn him away from the path he currently walked—one of self-destruction. His father and their tenuous relationship played into the mix as well, and it disturbed him to admit that the only positive role models in his life were someone else's family.

Mason recalled Remy's earlier words, reminding him that he could have his pick of pretty, young coeds from prominent families. Why, he wondered, when so many fine things had already been laid at his feet, did he step over them and reach for that which had no value? What hunger gnawed inside him that could not be satisfied?

Mason continued to mull over his past behavior until he became bored with self-analysis. *Oh well*, he thought, *they say that recognizing the problem is half of the cure.* If one wanted to be cured, that is.

He stood up, stretched, and put on his clothes. A sudden lightheadedness gripped him, and he leaned against a slender crepe myrtle to steady himself. But the shakiness passed as quickly as it had struck.

"What's with that? Too much pot, maybe?" he wondered aloud and then dismissed the thought as just the end result of a shitty afternoon. He checked the time as he adjusted the band of his Rolex—another gilt goodie from dear old Dad. It was almost three o'clock. After a stroll through the Ramble, it would be time for a couple of Mr. Will's Gin Rickeys, followed by some home-cooking. *Sounds like a plan*, just what the doctor ordered to get him started in the right direction.

Actually, except for the destroyed tires, the day hadn't been that bad, Mason reasoned, suddenly recalling the teenage prostitute. A devilish smile crossed his face, and in the blink of an eye his resolve to redirect his ill-fated life vanished. When he got his car back, he just might make another trip down Westside Avenue. But he would steer clear of Denny's Dream Lounge, that was for sure.

10

Gabe returned home from his trip to town in time to, he hoped, have lunch with Vivian. He wanted to make the day special for the two of them. He knew that Remy coming home for the summer would lift her out of her usual melancholy. And she was sure to like the gown that he had bought for her.

Gabe had never stopped trying to shape some measure of closeness between them, even as he witnessed his wife slipping farther and farther away from him with each passing year. It had been good between them when they were first married, although he had been away at college. His trips home had been laced with passion and planning, and the birth of their son. He shook his head, recalling that Vivian was never quite the same after Remy was born.

Their anniversary trip to New York ten years later had resulted in a few precious days spent with the contented and effervescent Vivian who had been a part of his life since they were young children. Her clever banter he had enjoyed throughout their adolescent years had resurfaced as they strolled along Park Avenue. It was on that trip that she had reached for him in the night after so long, confirming what Gabe had known for most of his life—that he and Vivian truly did belong together.

Upon their return home, they learned that she was pregnant with Gabrielle. It was then that Vivian had quietly moved from their bedroom to her own suite at the far end of the mansion.

Gabe believed that his wife still loved him, and he knew that she adored their children. So, what had happened? He had tried on several occasions over the years to talk to Will about Vivian's lack of interest in anything, and to suggest that perhaps she needed to see a professional. Will was not a man who believed in the need of psychiatric help, though.

"Hell, Gabe!" he had shouted at his son-in-law, "my daughter's a woman. Can't nobody figure 'em out!"

Gabe walked from the carport at the end of the house and up the stone steps to the kitchen door. He didn't necessarily want to figure his wife out; he wanted to help her. Perhaps his gift, as well as their son's homecoming, would coax her from that dark place that held her captive.

"Hey, Rosie. Has my wife had her lunch yet?" Gabe asked their housekeeper as he entered the kitchen.

"No, sir, Mr. Gabe. She told me this mornin' after breakfast that she was going to lay back down for a while. I was just about to take a tray up to her."

"I'll take it up," Gabe responded, reaching for the tray. No one knew exactly how old Rosie was, but she had been with the Remington family since Will had been a boy. Gabe guessed she was in her mid-eighties.

"You need to save your energy for tomorrow night."

Rosie seemed relieved. She plopped her large frame onto one of the oak kitchen chairs. "Yes, sir. I sure don't need another trip up them stairs this mornin'. I done made half a dozen already today."

Gabe climbed the back stairway that led from the kitchen to the second floor. He hoped Vivian would be in her sitting room, but she wasn't there. He called out to his wife as he rapped lightly on her bedroom door.

"May I come in, dear?"

"Of course, you may," Vivian said as she opened the door. "I looked for you earlier, but Rosie said you left right after breakfast."

Gabe set the luncheon tray on the writing desk in front of the tall French doors that opened to a balcony spanning the front of the mansion. He knew that this was where his wife spent most of her days now, sitting at her desk and writing in journals that no one was ever allowed to read.

"I had a little errand to run," he said. He walked across the Persian rug, hugged her gently, and kissed the top of her head. Her hair smelled of lilacs, and Gabe thought again of their youth. He handed her the mauve-colored gift bag. "I hope you like it."

Vivian became animated. "Oh, Gabe, you are a treasure. You always give me gifts on the children's birthdays, and I love it," she gushed. "Now, let me see what you've come up with this time."

Gabe settled himself into the cushy velvet chair facing her. He was grinning from ear to ear as he watched his wife eagerly tear into the elaborately wrapped package. Her eyes widened and she sucked in her breath as she lifted the lid and pushed back the tissue that covered the gown.

"Well," he asked tentatively, "do you like it?"

"It's beautiful," she whispered. Her hands touched the silken fabric as if it might break, and when her eyes met his, they were shining with tears. "I've never seen a more beautiful shade of blue."

"It's called periwinkle—that's Liz Taylor's color," Gabe quoted.

"Well, I don't look anything like Liz Taylor."

"No, you don't," Gabe said, his voice conveying emotion. "You're more beautiful than Liz Taylor."

Vivian continued to admire the garment as she lifted it from its nest. She stood up, walked to the full-length mirrors that concealed a wall of closets, and held it up against her.

"It looks like the perfect size. Wherever did you find this, Gabe?"

Gabe remained silent. He was enjoying his wife's pleasure with her gift. Her eyes widened as she looked at the label. "An *original*—Gabe!"

"Just like you, my dear.".

But she didn't seem to hear him. "An original design by Tess," Vivian read aloud, the lilt gone now from her voice. She carefully folded the gown and laid it back into its box. A tiny frown creased her brow as she turned back to him.

"Tess *Bradley*?" she questioned.

Gabe tried to act nonchalant. "Yes, you remember her. She's a designer, now. Moved back to Antioch and has opened a shop in the old Cosgrove Building. It's been renovated. You know, it's that brick building down at the end of Main. Real pretty things there, Viv. You should go take a look." He paused, then added, I think she'll do really well."

Vivian had turned her back to him now and stood looking out the French doors.

"I do remember Tess Bradley," she said with no emotion. "She was in our class at school. I seem to remember she dropped out during our sophomore year." She paused, sniffed, and went on with her monologue.

"They *say* she went out and got herself pregnant!" She enunciated each word in that slow, simpering southern drawl that Gabe detested.

He hoped he could salvage something of their earlier pleasant mood. He remarked cheerily, "Well, if she accomplished that, then she'd be in the record books."

His wife directed a questioning look at him, obviously not understanding his quip.

"You know," he explained, "someone getting *themselves* pregnant?"

"Oh," Vivian dismissed his attempt at humor with a wave of her hand. "You know what I meant." She sat once again at her desk and met his gaze. "I remember something else, too, from back then."

Gabe didn't respond this time. The earlier joy of giving his wife a gift had evaporated, and his patience was wearing thin. He looked at her until she continued speaking.

"I remember how you raised eyebrows in town when you came to the Memorial Day picnic with Tess. My, oh my, you certainly had tongues wagging."

Gabe was livid. It was at times such as this that he was thankful for tolerance. At that moment, he longed to tell her how furious he was with her. But he wanted nothing to spoil Remy's homecoming or the grand party that had been planned for him the following night.

He leaned across the writing desk and patted his wife's hand. He said: "We went to school together, Vivian. We walked to the town picnic together. That was all. I don't know why tongues would wag."

Was it such a bad lie if one told it to spare another's feelings?

"Hmm. Of course, dear," she responded in the tone of voice that let him know she didn't believe him for one minute. She gently extricated her hand from his.

"The gown is lovely, Gabe. Thank you." She turned her chair around to face the window. He was being dismissed.

"You're welcome. Perhaps you could wear it for me tomorrow night after the party. I'd like that."

She kept her back to him. "It will be late when everyone leaves. We'll be tired, I'm sure."

Gabe stood, crossed the room to the door, and left without another word.

"You want your lunch now, Mr. Gabe?" Rosie inquired as he clattered down the stairs and into the kitchen.

He gave her no answer and left through the door he had entered earlier, allowing it to slam behind him.

11

William Llewellyn Remington was cut from a far different cloth than that of his predecessors. His father and older brother had been contented all their lives to sit opposite one another at their old partners' desk in the office of Remington Savings & Loan. The substance of their lives had lain in making certain that the books they pored over daily held no misrepresentation that might lead to a depositor being deprived of a penny's worth of interest.

But Will had wanted more.

He studied the gold pocket watch in his hand and thought of the regimented life of his late father.

Precisely at nine o'clock every weekday morning, his dad would walk through the front door of his downtown bank, pause, and check the time on this very pocket watch against the chimes of the grandfather clock that stood in the bank's lobby. His brother, Steadman, would mimic their father by checking the serviceable Bulova wristwatch he wore.

On days that he had been allowed to accompany the two of them to the bank, young Will always wondered why this repetition seemed so necessary. He guessed it must have something to do with owning the small town's only bank. Their actions would be repeated at one o'clock each day when they returned from lunch and at 5 o'clock each afternoon as they left the building.

The old man and his brother had been gone for many years, now, and Will wondered what had prompted him to think of the two of them this morning. Perhaps it was the pocket watch that had conjured up the memory.

Will had removed it from the display case on his antique desk earlier and had been toying with the idea of giving it to Remy for his birthday the following day. He had always promised Vivian that he would do so, but now he wondered if wasn't too soon.

A nineteen-year-old kid would most probably toss the timepiece into a drawer and not think of it for years. Will wanted the watch to mean something to his grandson, so maybe he would wait a few more years before passing it along.

Besides, the birthday present that he had for Remy would certainly dwarf a pocket watch. Both Gabe and Vivian were going shake their heads and chastise him for being so extravagant with the boy, but what the hell good was money if he couldn't indulge his only grandson?

Thinking of money always got Will's juices flowing—not the money, per se, but what it represented. Yes, sir, he had inherited one antiquated, little old savings and loan establishment from his father and had built it into three branch offices as well as purchased several smaller banks and founded Remington Investments.

Part of Will's success was because he was, if nothing else, a risk taker. He had the touch, alright, and so did his son-in-law. Why, Gabe could easily run the entire corporation by himself, but Will had no intention of letting that happen for quite some time. He enjoyed the financial climate, and as long as he got a rush out of making money for his investors as well as for his family, he fully intended to continue to steer the ship.

Will had decided to stay home today, as he wanted to be there when Remy and Mason arrived. He wasn't going to give Remy his present until tomorrow evening at the barbeque, and he didn't want him snooping around the property and finding it. *That would spoil the surprise,* he thought with a chuckle.

He strolled through the French doors that led from his study out to the front veranda and settled into one of the white wicker rocking chairs that filled the spaces between Vivian's potted ferns. His daughter had certainly inherited her mother's green thumb.

Lily—he could see her smiling face as clear as if she were standing before him now. He steeled himself against the memory of his dead wife, sending her image back to the past where it belonged. He flipped the pocket watch open and checked the time: one o'clock.

"Rosie," he bellowed, "I'll have my lunch out here."

12

"Afternoon, Rosie. Where's the missus today?"

Rosie shook her head. "Now, where you think she is, Miz Claire? Why, she's up in her rooms all by herself, as usual. Mr. Gabe, he went upstairs earlier with a big gift bag in his hand. He come down 'bout ten minutes ago, looked like he'd jus' had the wind knocked outta him. He didn't say a word to me.

"Then, I seen him go walking off down toward The Ramble." Rosie paused to put finishing touches on a luncheon tray she was preparing before resuming her monologue. "Them two has got everything to be happy 'bout, but they ain't."

Claire Washington knew the housekeeper was itching to engage in a little gossip, but she would have none of it. She directed a stern look, punctuated by the raising of one eyebrow, towards the older woman and then gently rebuked her. She said, "I merely asked Miz Vivian's whereabouts. I do not need your opinions, Rosie. She's my best friend. Do you understand?"

"Yes, ma'am. I got to take this tray out to Mr. Will, anyways. I ain't got no time to sit and talk."

Claire watched Rosie waddle through the kitchen door, past the formal dining room, and out the French doors to the veranda. Although her thoughts mimicked those of the older woman, she was not about to take part in idle chit-chat with the help.

She filled the vase of flowers that she had gathered from her garden with water from the kitchen sink and tripped up the back stairs to visit her friend.

Claire, above all others, knew that Vivian's *good days* were far exceeded by the bouts of melancholy that had plagued her for most of her adult life.

51

She firmly believed that Will's poorly disguised disappointment that his daughter had not been born a male child was the origin of that depression. Claire despised him for that very reason—among others.

"Good afternoon, sunshine," she called out cheerfully as she knocked on Vivian's door and opened it simultaneously. "You sure picked a good day to stay indoors; it's hotter'n Hades today."

Vivian stood up from her chaise lounge and smiled brightly. "Hey, Claire. This is a nice surprise. I thought you had to take Miz Mosell to the doctor today."

"Now, you know my stubborn old mother-in-law is not going to do one thing anybody tells her that she needs to do. No, sir, no doctor for her today," Claire responded. "Oh, well, she'll most likely outlive us all, anyway. Here, I brought you something," she added, setting the vase of tulips on the writing desk. "This hot spell will just about finish these off."

"They're beautiful, Claire. Thank you for thinking of me. Just look how they brighten the room!"

Claire folded her arms across her chest and studied her best friend. "These flowers," she said, beginning her lecture, "are much prettier outside in the garden. But, how would you know that?" Her facial expression was stern, as she had intended, and her trademark raised eyebrow left no room for misinterpretation. "How long has it been since you were out of these two rooms, Vivian?"

"I'll have you know that I had dinner with Daddy last night in the dining room. Gabe took Gabrielle to the awards night at school."

"I know. I saw them there. Carl Lee and I both went. Gabrielle got a certificate for perfect attendance. Why weren't you there?"

Vivian looked away. "I told you. Gabe went with her. He told me that Leander got the award for making the highest grades in their class. You must be so proud of him, Claire."

"Of course, I'm proud of him, and his daddy is so puffed up that he's just about to bust." Claire paused and shook her head. "Lord knows where that boy gets his smarts.

"But it's not Leander I was talking about," she continued. "When was the last time you went *out*? We used to go shopping at least once a week.

And lunch—we haven't been to the Magnolia Room for lunch in ages." Her voice lost its sharp edge. She reached out and gently took Vivian's hands in hers. "I'm worried about you."

Vivian studied her in silence. Finally, she smiled wanly and squeezed Claire's hand. "Come on, let's go *outside* and sit on the balcony. Remy and Mason could possibly get here early," she said, checking her watch. "When I see them coming up the drive, then I'll know that my boy is home safe."

The two women settled themselves in rocking chairs on the balcony, and although they sat in silence for some time, Claire could read her best friend's thoughts and knew that she was struggling. She waited for her to speak first.

Vivian drew a deep breath, exhaled, and said, "The reason I do not go out very often, Claire, is that it doesn't matter one iota to the people in this house what I do or what I don't do." She spoke emphatically, and when her companion gave no response, she continued. "I am little more than an afterthought to my family."

Claire waited until the impact of Vivian's words had taken hold. "Then, help me understand," was her simple response.

"Daddy has always dismissed me with a pat on the head and a 'That's fine, sugar. Now run on and let Daddy work.' In my thirty-eight years, Claire, he has never included me in *any* conversation of any importance."

"It's simply because he's old school, and he doesn't believe women have any place in the business world. Mr. Will has spent his whole life making yours as safe and secure as possible. It's obvious that he adores you." *Can't believe I'm defending the old bastard!*

Vivian chuckled. "No, dear. Daddy does not adore me. He adores his grandson. And his position in the community. And his money." Her voice broke and she blinked back tears. When her composure returned, she went on talking.

"You know I'm right, Claire. Surely you remember the minute that Remy was born, how Daddy took him away from me. It was as though my purpose had been served and now, I could slip back into obscurity with another pat on the head. And Will Remington finally had what he'd longed for above all else—a male heir."

Claire stood up and walked into the bedroom. She returned with the glass of now-watery lemonade from the untouched lunch tray.

"Here," she said, "drink some of this, Viv. It'll make you feel better."

Vivian complied and then continued pouring out her heart. "When I found out that I was pregnant the second time, I prayed for a little girl. And when Gabrielle was born, I was ecstatic. I thought that finally I would have someone who would want to be with *me*. Finally, there was someone who would run to *me* with both skinned knees and a broken heart, and I would know how to fix both. But that hasn't happened, and it never will."

She took another sip of lemonade and blinked away more tears. "My daughter runs only to her father or to her big brother."

"Do you ever talk to Gaby? I mean, like you and I talk about things?" Claire asked. "It seems to me that she would respond to you if you reached out to her like a girlfriend."

"Mmm, good advice, sweetie," Vivian answered. "But I wouldn't have the slightest idea of how to begin such a conversation with her." She stopped her struggle against emotion and allowed a lone tear to trail down her cheek.

"How sad it is that I cannot think of what to say to my nine-year-old daughter that I love more than my own life."

"Now don't you start crying," Claire fretted. "We'll work on it together, just like we do about everything. Two heads are better'n one, I always say." She quickly changed the subject. "Let's you and I get our plans all finalized for tomorrow evening. We want Remy's birthday bash to be unforgettable."

"Oh, it's going to be unforgettable alright," Vivian said. She banished the remaining tear from her cheek and continued speaking. "I found out what Daddy bought for his grandson. Gabe has always told Daddy that he was going to ruin Remy. They'll have words over this, for sure."

Claire raised her eyebrow. "That good, huh?"

"You'll see. And you are so right, we need to go downstairs and check our lists. If you don't mind, you can call the band and the caterer while I go over everything with Rosie again. She's getting so forgetful, you know. But aren't we all?"

Vivian stood up and went back into her room with a bit of a spring in her step. "Yes, ma'am," Claire said, "we'll get everything firmed up. And then I've got to get back home and make sure them two girls of mine have got the house cleaned and supper started. Carl Lee went to Greenville this afternoon to pick up a new part for the big lawn mower, and he won't be back 'til late. But Leander ought to be getting home any time now."

"I wouldn't count on that," Vivian said. "I'm sure that he and Gaby are just now getting out of Dalton's Creek. You remember our school days, I know. We couldn't wait to get in that cold creek water on hot days like today."

Claire nodded. "I remember *all* our good times, Viv, and I loved them all. I love you," she said. "That's why I worry so about you sitting up here all by yourself and feeling sad like I know you do." She paused briefly. "I'd fix things for you, if I only could."

Vivian reached for the other woman and hugged her fiercely. "I know you would. And you know you are my very best friend—my *only* friend."

"I don't have to be your only friend, though," Claire tried once more to interject a positive note. "You would be welcomed at the ladies' luncheons at the Country Club. You know that. And you used to love playing tennis— you could start back—"

"And why on earth," Vivian interrupted her, "would I want to be with people who thrive on gossip and delight in the misery of others? Now, you know very well that I'm right about that, don't you? And if I did join the ladies at the Club, do you think for one minute that they would welcome you, too?"

"I would understand," Claire answered simply.

"Well, I wouldn't. Oh," Vivian whirled around to face her, "I almost forgot. I have a present for you. We'll call it an early birthday gift." Her sudden animation was infectious.

"My birthday's not for another month," Claire said as she watched Vivian hurry across the room to one of the mirrored closets and return with a gift bag.

"Like I said, this is *early* birthday. Go ahead," Vivian coaxed as she handed the package over, "open it."

Claire sat the bag on the bed, removed the box from inside, and lifted the lid. As she parted the perfumed layers of tissue, her smile of a moment ago evaporated. She looked at the gown in silence.

"Well?" Vivian prodded. "Do you like it?"

"I can't accept this, Viv. I'm sorry."

"Why on earth not? I told you it's for your birthday, and I promise I won't buy you anything else. Now come on, hold it up and go look at yourself in the mirror," Vivian prattled on. "I won't take no for an answer."

Claire still did not touch the gown. Instead, she turned a stern expression towards the other woman and said, "*You* didn't buy this. Gabe did. I know he always gives you a gift on the kids' birthdays, and he gave you this. Why would you want to give it away?"

"I don't care for the color, that's why," Vivian replied a little too casually as she moved across the room to her dressing table and began to brush her hair.

"That's a load of crap!"

Vivian responded without turning around. "Claire Washington, such talk."

"Why?" Claire repeated her question.

"Everyone wants to dress me in blue, and I simply do not like it. That's the truth. I prefer yellows and greens. Blue makes me—well, *blue*." Vivian's voice had started to quiver. "Oh, why can't you simply say thank you and accept my gift? That's the way I want it!"

Vivian was becoming more agitated: their afternoon was perilously close to ending with another one of her stabbing migraines. Claire rewrapped the gown, placed it back into the gift bag, and turned to face her friend. This time, her smile was back in place.

"Thank you," she said. "It's the most beautiful garment I've ever had. I will treasure it always."

Vivian returned her smile. "That's my girl. The color is called periwinkle," she said, pointing to the bag, "Liz Taylor's color. She has black hair, and so do you. It's perfect for you. Now, let's go downstairs and go over those lists."

"I'm right behind you," Claire said, closing the door to Vivian's suite. She had seen the label on the gown and now shook her head in disgust. *Gabe Westin, how can one man be so dumb?*

13

Will was lost in thought and only dimly aware of Rosie's measured steps as she carried his empty luncheon tray back into the house.

"Thank you, Rosie," he called out absently. He leaned his head back and closed his eyes. He was not a man of leisure and couldn't remember the last time he had taken a day off and done nothing. Admittedly, when he was away from his offices, he floundered like a fish out of water.

Today wasn't half bad, though. The whisper of the ceiling fans was mesmerizing, and he felt himself drifting off to sleep when voices from inside the house roused him. He could hear his daughter's laughter and Claire Washington's mellow response. Will had never understood that friendship.

With Lily's passing, he was left a widower at twenty-two with an infant daughter that he had no idea what to do with. He now saw the mistake he had made by moving Martha Mackey and her fatherless baby, Claire, into the guest house to take over the care of Vivian. The two girls had grown up together and were inseparable.

Will was baffled by his daughter and had never approved of her choice of friends. He recalled one of the few conversations he initiated with her during her adolescent years. His awkward attempt to remind her of the Remington family's position in the town and to point out the importance of mingling with only the *right* people had been met with her accusation—albeit delivered respectfully—that he was a bigot.

Maybe he was, Will reflected, but so what? He had asked Vivian on more than one occasion just what was the sin in being rich, powerful, and white?

Her response had been swift: "Nothing, as long as you reach out to those who aren't."

Will was infuriated. There *were* differences in people, and those in the class of the Remington and Weston families needed to remember that.

And look at Gabrielle—just like her mother! He scowled as the image of his granddaughter running rampant throughout the county with a black boy. "God Almighty," he muttered under his breath; "what's going to happen to this family?"

It was some consolation as he thought of his grandson's choice of friends. He liked Mason Carlisle. Actually, he saw more of himself in that young man than he did in his own flesh and blood. Mason just needed to tone down that bulletproof veneer of his, but that would come with age.

Will stood up from his rocking chair, stretched away his lethargy, and walked briskly down the front steps. He checked his pocket watch again: three o'clock. Remy and Mason would be getting in from Columbia soon. He had sat idle far too long, and his inherent need to take charge surfaced.

He would inspect the backyard to make sure Carl Lee had the tents in place properly for the party the following evening. Will smiled: he'd check on Remy's birthday present, too.

14

Since purchasing the old Mossbank Plantation years ago and constructing the mansion, Will had never posted the property. Anyone who might want to drive along the stately access road, or wander leisurely among the gardens and wooded maze of The Ramble, were made to feel welcome. And many did come to admire the property.

Should a stranger happen upon Will during his afternoon stroll, he would most surely see a dignified man who looked much younger than his sixty years. At six-foot-three, Will did not have an ounce of fat on his large frame and still walked with a spring in his step. His flaming red hair and florid skin tone made it necessary for him to wear a hat and a long-sleeved shirt, even in the heat of summer, to avoid sun damage.

If the stranger were to make his acquaintance, he would be hard pressed to ever forget Will's face. He was not a handsome man, as such. But his wide-set blue eyes conveyed a look of innocence, and his thin lips were naturally tilted at the corners, making it appear that he was always smiling.

Even during times of displeasure, he presented the image of a mild-mannered, friendly statesman. Only those who knew him personally could discern the difference between his truly affable smile and the rigid set of his mouth that seemed to say *Careful, now. Pay-backs are hell.*

And so, after a firm handshake and a few well-chosen words from him, the stranger would take his leave thinking Mr. Will Remington to be a most gracious southern gentleman when, in truth, he would be turning his back upon a cold and calculating man with a mean streak rarely equaled.

Having finished his inspection, Will made a mental note to instruct Carl Lee to move the larger of the two tents closer to the barbeque pit so the presentation of Remy's birthday gift could be made easier.

"Do I have to think for you, too?" he grumbled aloud, reinforcing the notion that he was the only person on the entire estate capable of rational thinking—well, he and Gabe, that is. Certainly, none of the hired help could be trusted to perform even the simplest of tasks without supervision.

His thoughts were interrupted by the sound of the kitchen door closing. He stepped around the corner of the house in time to see Claire come tripping down the stone steps and make her way along the well-worn path between the high hedge rows of bottlebrush that led to the house she shared with her family. His steps quickened and his most pleasant smile was in place when he called out to her.

"Afternoon, Claire. You and my daughter got everything ready for tomorrow evening?"

"Yes, sir, Mr. Will," Claire answered, glancing back over her shoulder as she ran along.

"Wait up a minute!" Will called after her. "I want to thank you for helping out—Carl Lee, too. Why, I don't know what we'd do around here without the two of you," he praised. "The whole place would probably just fall apart."

"Oh, I 'spect you'd get by just fine, Mr. Will." She turned away from him once more and resumed her walk toward home. "We'll see you tomorrow," she called out.

"You coming over here on such a hot day to help Vivian—don't know how I can ever thank you," he said.

Claire stopped walking and turned to meet his gaze. "Friends help each other," she responded stoically. "No thanks are necessary. Bye, now."

Will ignored her parting words. "You look mighty pretty today," he said. "'Course, don't nobody set off a cotton dress quite like you do." He took a step closer to her. An amused expression crossed his face as she retreated.

He continued speaking. "A day as hot as today puts me in mind of that time when I came upon you standing in the middle of Dalton's Creek, soaking wet with that thin little cotton dress sticking to you, and not a stitch on underneath. *Whoee,* now that was a glorious sight for a man to behold!"

Claire's tone was steady as she met his gaze. "I had no idea anyone was around. Like you said, it was a hot day. And, it was a very long time ago."

"But you see, I remember it like it was yesterday," Will said glibly. He smiled as his eyes raked her figure from head to toe.

"Well, it's been nice talking with you, Claire. Have a good evening. By the way, what's in the bag?"

She realized that she had been clutching the gift bag in a near death grip. She relaxed slightly and answered him. "It's a gift from Vivian—an early birthday present, actually."

He moved closer to her and placed his left hand at the small of her back, then trailed casually up her spine to take hold of her hair in a forceful grip. He pulled her head back, making it virtually impossible for her not to look up and into his face.

"Let me go." Her voice trembled, but she met his gaze bravely.

"Ahh, Claire, Claire," Will whispered, bringing his right hand up to trace little circles on her cheek, "I just can't get that image of you in that wet cotton dress out of my mind. So, how 'bout you and me take a stroll down to Dalton's Creek and relive the past."

"I said to let me go!" She pushed hard against his chest, dropping the gift bag and almost falling to the ground in the process. Swiftly, she regained her balance and retrieved the parcel. She whirled around to face him, pointing a shaky finger.

"Don't you ever lay your hands on me again!" She spat the words angrily, not even bothering to hide her tears.

Will held both hands up in mock surrender. The little smile remained in place as he spoke. "And here I thought that you'd enjoyed our time together."

"*Enjoyed?* I was barely thirteen years old, no more than a child! I was terrified! And you were a, a god to me.

Back then, I didn't know what to do. Guess I figured that somehow it was my fault. Anyway, I never told a living soul. But if you ever come near me again, I swear to God I will. I will tell Vivian."

Will narrowed his gaze. "Now you listen here to me, girlie!"

"I was not put here for your pleasure, and I am NOT your girlie! My name is Claire Washington—Mrs. Carl Lee Washington." She then turned and continued walking toward her home.

Will chuckled under his breath. "Well, then, you have a pleasant evening, Mrs. Carl Lee Washington."

Without turning around, Claire shouted, "And you go to hell, Will Remington!"

Will was livid. He could fire her husband. He could throw her entire goddamn family out of *his* house and off *his* property for good. He could make it impossible for any of them to get work anywhere in the county.

But he wouldn't do any of those things, and Claire knew it.

Of all the females around, his daughter had to be best friends with that uppity wench. He gritted his teeth. *Just where did she get off talking to him like that?*

Will realized that he'd been walking fast—almost running, in fact—towards The Ramble. He slowed his pace and took a deep breath. His heart was racing, and he needed to calm down.

As he entered the shady umbrella of crepe myrtles, the stifling heat lessened. He took his handkerchief from his pocket and, after clearing the leaves from the nearby stone fountain, dipped it in the cool water and applied the compress to the back of his neck. He felt a little better.

The memory of his late wife resurfaced, enticing him along the pathway and deeper into the forest. Will cared little for the outdoors and being here was certainly not what he had intended.

Perhaps it was what he needed.

15

The smooth, flat piece of shale rock fit perfectly into the curl of Gabe's index finger. He dropped his left arm down to hip height and flipped the stone forward and across the surface of Dalton's Creek.

"Three, four, five, six, seven," he counted under his breath. "Look at that! I broke the record!"

A sad little smile teased the corners of his mouth and then faded. He watched the circular ripple swell and then disappear, along with the stone, from the water's surface, like they had never existed.

"…six times, Gabe. I bet nobody ever skipped a stone six times. You ever skipped one six times?" She danced around in circles, delighting him.

"No, Tess, I'm sure I haven't. You've set the record."

"…been the best day of my whole life, Gabe!"

"The very best day," Gabe whispered aloud. He eased his tired body down to sit cross-legged on the creek bank. Absently, he picked a nearby daisy and twirled it between his fingers.

Her dark eyes sparkled; her smile was tentative, questioning, as she slowly plucked the petals from the flower she held. "…he loves her, he loves her not; he loves her, he loves her not…"

"He loves her." Gabe's words and the caress of his hand had been her answer.

Gabe shook his head. Twenty-four years of living had raced by without ever overtaking the memory of that one unforgettable day.

"What do you want to do, Tess? I mean, after high school. Do you know?"

"Oh, that's easy. I want to design ladies' fashions. I make all my clothes, you know. Made the dress I wore to the spring dance last Saturday night."

"You looked so pretty. I wanted to ask you to go to the dance with me; I just…"

Just what? Just scared of what Will would have said? Or, had he feared hurting Vivian? *Come on, admit the truth. Weren't you just a touch embarrassed to be seen with her?* After all these years, Gabe still didn't know which scenario had weighed him down the most. But *she* had known. And she had made it easy for him, like always.

"And after high school, you'll go on to college. And then you'll go to work in Mr. Will's bank. And then you'll marry Vivian and have a happy life."

She had prattled on matter-of-factly, forcing young Gabe to face the stark reality that they had no future—not together, anyway.

He stretched out on the cool ground and closed his eyes. "No future," he muttered to himself. "Oh, but we had *that day!*"

There had been many days, in fact, during that steamy summer of their fifteenth year. A summer ushered in by furtive glances across the classroom, a barely acknowledged nod of the head in the school cafeteria, and culminating in the awkwardly orchestrated meeting on the way to the Memorial Day picnic.

Gabe had thought himself to be the personification of cool, only to realize later how obvious to everyone his actions were, especially to Will. The admonishing lecture had been delivered sternly but accompanied by the ever-present smile and a special twinkle in the older man's eye.

"It's understandable for a man to—ahh, sow his wild oats, son. You might even say it's expected for a man to, uh, get experience from someone who he—well, someone who he wouldn't want to be seen escorting to social functions."

Will had gone on to tell him in all sincerity that he loved him like the son he'd never had, and to finally point out that Vivian was crushed that he hadn't yet mentioned the upcoming dance to her.

Fifteen-year-old Gabe could barely remember coming to live in Will's house when he was seven. Orphaned by the fatal car accident that was never properly explained to him, he found himself the heir apparent to the Remington fortune. And, he had learned quickly what was expected of him. That evening after dinner, he had dutifully asked Vivian to go to the dance with him.

Gabe finished plucking all the petals from the daisy and absently tossed the stem towards the creek. A tiny eddy along the water's edge caught it and sucked it under the surface.

"Don't let go of my hand, Gabe. I can't swim a lick, and I just might get caught in a whirlpool or somethin'."

"I won't let go, Tess. Come on, now, step on one rock then another— barefoot's best. I got your sandals…"

There couldn't have been any other ending to that glorious day but to have it melt into a night of passion and promises.

"Stop saying you're sorry, Gabe. The two of us wantin' love ain't nothin' to be so sorry for…"

Gabe blinked his eyes and looked around, momentarily confused. He didn't remember leaving the creek bank and walking into The Ramble. But here he was, standing on the leaf-covered ground, inside that tent of weeping willow, still seeing, feeling, tasting the splendor of *that day*. He wished that he could live it all over again. At the same time, he wished to God that it had never happened.

He took the handkerchief from his pocket, wiped his eyes, and blew his nose. It was time to close the door on the past once and for all before it overtook the present. He began to trudge along the main path, determined to reestablish the benchmark of his character—defining what was real and what was fantasy.

But the two seemed to be hopelessly intertwined. The benchmark had shifted.

16

"This has sure been a good day, huh, Lee?" Gabrielle said, draping her arm across Leander's shoulders. He returned the gesture, and they began slowly walking with their arms entwined towards home.

"The best," Leander responded. "I wish it didn't have to end."

"We'll come back tomorrow. You ain't gonna get yelled at for being late, are you? I bet it's nearly four o'clock."

Leander ignored her. After a few seconds passed, she spoke again.

"You *aren't* going to get yelled at?"

"No. Mama's most likely still over at your house. And Daddy had to go to Greenville this afternoon. He won't get home until late."

Gabrielle disengaged her arm from his and shifted her backpack to the other shoulder.

"Meet me back here tomorrow around noon. We can fish for a couple of hours and still have time to get ready for Remy's party." She began to walk up the gravel driveway.

"Hold on," Leander called to her. "Aren't you going to cut through The Ramble? It's way shorter and cooler than walking in the hot sun on that old dusty road."

"Naw," she answered him, turning around and waving as she skipped backwards. "I don't want to miss seeing Remy and Mason if they was to come driving up."

"If they *were* to come. See you tomorrow."

Gabrielle rolled her eyes heavenward. "Bye, Professor."

"That's *Brother* Professor to you," Leander shot back, not allowing her time to respond as he headed toward the shady respite of The Ramble.

Leander smiled as he entered the well-worn forest path. This was a paradise to him, but far from quiet as one might initially imagine.

His arrival was heralded by a grey squirrel, who barked raucously from its overhead nest in a tall pine tree. A female mockingbird—no doubt with young ones nearby—engineered a half-hearted dive at his head before flying away.

The virtually impenetrable cane break to his right soared more than ten feet straight up, separating the property from the main road. Even with only a hint of a breeze stirring, the bamboo whispered around him like a hundred hushed voices.

A fleeting thought occurred to Leander that, had it been nighttime, he would have been less than brave and would have joined Gabrielle on her chosen route. But in the daylight, any thought of monsters was dispelled. He barely took notice of the sudden rustle of leaves behind him as an innocuous chipmunk scampered out of sight.

A straight, smooth branch lay alongside the path, and Leander picked it up. *A hockey stick!* And the pinecone puck was just ahead.

He wondered if he could do it—keep the puck on the path while toting the heavy book satchel at the same time. He'd have something to brag to Gaby about if he could.

* * * * *

What a frustrating day this has turned into. Be glad when it's over, that's for sure. Tomorrow will be better—hope so, anyway. Has it really been such a bad day? Maybe disappointing is more the word. Right this minute, though, is pleasant.

Been a long time since you were here in The Ramble, sitting on this bench all by yourself, enjoying the beauty. You gotta quit letting things get the best of you, getting you down. Illigitimis non carborundum—don't let the bastards grind you down. Ha-ha.

You just need to look on the bright side. Everybody is going to be together for the summer months and that's good. Things will certainly go your way. You won't lose—you hate to lose.

Whoa, wait a minute. Where did that come from? Why would you even think about losing? And what is there to lose, anyway? Nothing. And everything to gain.

So, stop the pity party. And remember: don't EVER lose your cool.

"Do you hear me? Get a grip!"

"Who you talking to, Mister?"

The young girl materialized from nowhere. She was leaning against a tree, studying him intently.

He jumped straight up, his heart skipping at least one beat.

"Good God Almighty! You scared me half to death, girl. Don't you know better'n to slip up on a man like that?"

"I-I'm sorry," she stammered, the shock of being chastised showing on her face. "I didn't try to scare you; I thought you heard me walking up. I didn't mean no harm." Her eyes darted from side to side and her chin quivered.

"Oh, now don't start sniveling. I'm sorry I yelled at you. But you just about gave me a heart attack, girl."

"Guess we both done scared each other, huh?" she replied, closing the distance between them as curiosity overcame her fright.

"You was talking to yourself," she said matter-of-factly. "I do that sometimes, too. Actually, I do it a lot, 'cause I ain't got nobody much to talk to. You got folks to talk to, sir?"

He eyed her a few moments. "Yes, I have folks to talk to. And look who we've got here. Your parents are probably wondering where you are."

When she didn't move, he continued speaking. "So, you'd better be getting on home now."

"Don't have no parents. My daddy died when I was little, and my mama just up and left 'bout a year ago."

Her lack of emotion in describing her dismal situation registered immediately. "Well, I know you have family. You do have a home to go to, don't you?"

"Uh-huh," she answered. "Me and my grandparents got a nice home, but they're old. I get bored sometimes."

"So, when you get bored you just wander onto other folks' property and strike up a conversation with a stranger?"

"Everybody in town comes to cool off in that creek over yonder and to walk through these woods," she said defensively. "And besides that, you ain't exactly a stranger."

"Mmm, guess not. But I don't know your name, now, do I?"

She didn't respond. He was becoming mildly amused by this girl. He watched as she removed the headband from her long black hair. She deftly combed through the tight ringlets with her fingers and fashioned a ponytail, which she secured with the headband.

She was pretty and her movements were lithe, graceful, and *very* self-conscious.

"Well, if you're not going to tell me your name, at least tell me how old you are."

She didn't answer immediately. "I go to Antioch High," she said, obviously fibbing.

"Uh-huh, and I'm the King of England."

"Huh?" she asked, then she grinned. "I'm in Junior High."

When he didn't comment, she quietly added: "Well, I will be this fall."

"So that makes you about twelve, thirteen, maybe?"

"Maybe. How come you keep holding your head? You got a bad headache? My grandpaw gets bad headaches sometimes. Before my mama left, she used to rub his temples. He said that was the only thing that helped. I rub his head now. Hey, you want for me to rub your head?"

"No, no, that's okay. You'd better go on home, now. Your folks might be worried."

"My grandmaw's real sick. She lies down in the afternoons. And my grandpaw, he's still at his store," she chattered. "They don't worry 'bout me, 'cause I don't give 'em no reason to worry." She finished with an offhand little nod of her head.

Simple philosophy. Why couldn't everyone adopt it?

It was too simple, that's why. Folks don't want simple. They want to complicate everything with a bunch of bullshit rules.

First thing you do is to write the rules. Then, you need people to enforce those rules for the asswipes of the world who won't obey them.

Then, just when everybody learns the rules, somebody says we ought to change the rules, and here we go again.

Oh, God, where is all this coming from—all this crazy shit bouncing around inside your head? If only the dazzling would stop, those dazzling lights that keep things from making any sense!

"Ahhhhh—"

"What is it? You having a stroke or something?"

He jumped at her touch on his forearm.

"What? No, no, nothing like that. I'm not having a stroke. I get headaches with bright lights, stress, that's all."

"Uh-huh, just like Gramps," she stated confidently. "I can help." She moved behind him and placed her fingertips against his temples.

He was beyond objecting. In fact, he felt as though he would fall off the stone bench if the nauseating pain became any worse. He tried to open his eyes, but even the diffused forest light was too much.

You can't just sit here. You've got things to do. Get to the house and take a couple of aspirin; that usually helps. And a drink won't hurt, either. Must be 'bout time for cocktails, anyway. Miserable headache, you can't think straight with this pain.

"That better now?"

He could barely hear her whispered question.

"Umm," was all he could say in reply. After a time, he tentatively opened one eye, then the other. The dazzling lights had all but gone, and he no longer felt as though he was going to vomit.

"I believe so," he finally answered. Carefully he lifted his head up, arched his back, and sat in an upright position. Her hands had migrated from his temples to the base of his skull, still maintaining the same kneading pressure as before.

"Unbelievable. Headache's practically gone," he said. "In what, five minutes? Damn, girl, you ought to be a doctor."

"It was more like twenty minutes. And I thought one time you was gonna pass plumb out," she responded.

"I've already done some doctoring," she added. "I seen a baby get born once. Me and my mama helped. That was right before she took off."

She had stopped massaging his head and had moved around in front of the bench to face him. "Well, alright, then. You need any more help?"

Finally, that quagmire of pain, jumbled memories, and blinding flashes of light are gone. Whew! That was a bad one, for sure, but now you can think clearly again.

Better check the time: close to three-thirty. You've been here way too long—here with this pretty little slip of a girl.

He studied her for a long moment. "How 'bout you and me take a walk down that path over yonder?" he asked offhandedly. "It leads to a secret garden that I bet you've never seen before."

She hesitated. "Maybe I better get on home."

"But you said your folks won't be worried," he coaxed. "Come walk with me a bit. Besides, we can't say goodbye 'til you've told me your name."

17

The pinecone puck skidded along the path in a circular motion, proving to be a bit more challenging than Leander had originally thought. The activity also failed to hold his attention, as did sports in general. He would much rather be mentally challenged by math problems or puzzles any day.

He hitched the heavy book satchel higher up on his shoulder and began his trek homeward in earnest. He had spent entirely too much time *lollygagging*, as his mother would say. And, he'd promised Moam that he would read to her before supper.

His grandmother had never learned to read, and it gave Leander great pleasure to share his time with her. He usually read from the Bible, but tonight he had a surprise for her. One of the books the school librarian had loaned him was about the early days of the railroad in South Carolina. Moam had told him that her daddy had been a railroad man, so it seemed logical to Leander that she would enjoy the book.

He rounded a curve in the trail and immediately froze. Only a few feet from him stood a spindly-legged fawn, looking at him curiously. Oh, it was beautiful, and he wished Gabrielle were here to see it, too.

Stealthily, Leander inched backward and into the bushes alongside the trail. There were probably adult deer nearby, and he might catch a glimpse of them as well.

The fawn all but ignored the boy, turning instead to gaze into the laurel thicket on the opposite side of the trail. There they were—a doe *and* a buck.

Doggone it! if I only had my camera!

In the days to come, Leander would try to reconstruct the events that filled the next hour of his life. His inherent need for structure would propel him to not only try to remember each detail, but to recall them in their proper sequence.

He would fail miserably.

* * * * *

"Hello? Where is everybody?" Gabrielle called out loudly as she entered the kitchen. The house seemed unusually quiet—her brother and Mason must not have arrived yet.

"Hey, my darling," Rosie said as she limped from the pantry into the kitchen. "Did you have a good day today?"

"I sure did. But where is everybody?" Gabrielle repeated. "I thought I'd see Mama and probably Granddaddy sitting on the porch waiting on Remy. I guess Mama's up in her room, though."

"Don't know where Mr. Will got to. But yo' mama went walking a little while ago. And Mr. Gabe, too, down towards The Ramble, as a matter of fact. You come that way?"

Gabrielle shook her head as she hopped up on a kitchen stool and downed the frosty glass of lemonade that Rosie set before her.

"Uh-uh, but Leander did. I walked up the driveway so I wouldn't miss Remy." She motioned for more lemonade and wiped her face with a napkin. "I sure do wish everybody would hurry up and get on home."

Rosie placed her hands on her hips. "Well, now, *I'm* home. Don't I count?"

Gabrielle scrambled off the stool, threw her thin arms around the old woman's waist and hugged her fiercely.

"Of course, you count! You're the best, Rosie."

Rosie patted her head. "And, you, my sweet," she whispered, "are this family's shining light."

"Why you always calling me a 'shining light'?" Gabrielle asked.

"'Cause you got goodness inside of you, Gaby girl—I can see it. Now, you best run on upstairs and get cleaned up for when everybody else gets home. You smell like creek water." Gabrielle giggled as she shooed her towards the kitchen door.

She paused at the threshold and turned towards the housekeeper. "I love you, Rosie," she said.

"I knows it, child. I can see that, too."

18

The first thought that came to Leander's mind was that the big buck crashing through the trees directly in front of him was going to trample him to death. That very well could have been the outcome, had he not executed a split-second dive to his left.

When he scrambled to his knees and looked around, the buck was long gone, and there was no sight of the doe or the fawn, either. It was as though they had never existed.

Leander absently rubbed the side of his forehead where it had met with a fallen log. He felt a little dizzy and wondered what had caused the deer to bolt in the first place. He knew he had not made a sound, but something had startled them.

And then he remembered that, just before the buck jumped, he had seen the animal raise his head and flare his nostrils. *He smelled something that frightened him.*

Leander began to feel a bit uneasy. He had heard some of the older kids in town—his two sisters included—talk about having seen wild cats and even a bear in The Ramble. He didn't believe it, mainly because his dad said it wasn't true. He decided that those kids had tried to scare him out of jealousy, because he could move about the entire wooded area and never get the least bit turned around, much less lost.

But now, as he sat all alone on the mossy earth in the shade-darkened woods, he couldn't help but wonder what the deer had smelled. Well, he could wonder 'til the cows came home, as his grandmother often said. The fact was that he had to get moving. Mama would be upset if she got home and he wasn't there to get started on his chores. Leander got to his feet, dusted himself off, and retrieved his books.

He was just about to step from the dense clump of rhododendron and laurel when he heard it—the muffled sound of someone crying. Warily, he retreated into the bushes, his ears alert. After hearing nothing for several seconds, he decided the sound must have been a bird.

Wait. There it is again.

This time, Leander knew it was not just a bird, nor was it his imagination. It was the unmistakable sound of sobbing. There was something strange about the sound that the boy could not put his finger on. Gingerly, he hunkered down and parted the thick vegetation to get a glimpse of what lay beyond.

He had a clear view of the main path, with its cluster of ivy-choked trails branching off in many directions. The sound had seemed to come from his right—the trail that led to Miz Lily's secret garden. He didn't know why it was called the *secret* garden, since everybody knew where it was. Gabrielle had told him that it was where her grandmother, Mr. Will's wife, had asked that her ashes be spread.

Mr. Will had complied with his late wife's wishes, setting the stage for many stories—sworn on the Bible—from folks having seen Lily herself, on a night of the full moon, wearing a flowing white dress, walking along the forest path and into her secret garden. Leander didn't believe those stories either. Still, at that very moment, he would have given a month's allowance money to be walking on that hot, dusty road alongside Gaby.

When he heard the sound again, it was louder and closer. Leander held his breath and continued to peer through the bushes. At that moment, he realized what had seemed so strange to him about the crying sound—it was coming from a man.

He had never heard a grown man cry before, except at funerals. And certainly not the deep sobs he was hearing now. From his hiding place, he watched intently as the man came into view. He was facing away from Leander as he stumbled backward from the secret garden path. He veered from side to side as he held his head and continued to moan.

The man stopped and bent forward at the waist, whimpering and sobbing.: "No, no, no," he said, over and over. Then, when he stood up and turned around, the boy barely suppressed a gasp. *Why, it's…*

What's wrong with him? What's he doing here? Why is he crying? The questions screamed for answers.

Leander thought that maybe he should offer his help, knowing all the while that he couldn't move, even if his life depended on it. Spellbound, he watched as the man's demeanor abruptly changed. He drew several deep breaths and straightened his shoulders before he sat down on the ground in a cross-legged position and began to talk to himself.

His voice was hoarse and shaky, but understandable. "Y-y-you did not mean for this to happen! It was an accident, and, and it could not be helped. Calm down, calm down now. You just need to figure things out! W-w-what to do!"

Leander's heart was pounding as he watched him rock back and forth, like he was in a trance. After a while, the man stood up and began to walk at a somewhat normal pace along the path that would take him to The Ramble's exit closest to the Remington house.

"This was *not* your fault," he addressed himself as he walked along. He appeared to be less upset but continued to glance back over his shoulder toward the secret garden.

"This was an accident, nothing more," he went on, "and you will tell no one. No one can *ever* know!"

19

✦✦✦✦✦

Leander didn't move for a long time.

Only when his legs went to sleep, and the pins and needles became more than he could bear, did he have the courage to stand up. He tried to stomp his feet quietly, but his movements sounded like an elephant crashing about.

When the circulation returned to his legs, he parted the thick bushes and stepped cautiously from his hiding place and into the clearing. He knew exactly what his next move should be. He should hightail it home right now.

But he wasn't going to do that.

Never had Leander seen a grown man so upset, and he had to know why. Besides, Gaby would want him to find out what was wrong, wouldn't she?

He left the heavy book satchel along the main path and started walking down the narrow trail that led to the secret garden. It hardly resembled a trail at all. Only someone who had explored virtually every foot of The Ramble as Leander had would even know it *was* a trail. Fox grapevines had flourished during the years of neglect and now competed with thick ropes of wild honeysuckle to form a canopy so dense that sunlight could not penetrate.

Leander pressed on as the green tunnel seemed to swallow him. He walked more slowly now, not only due to trepidation, but because the thick, sweet air made breathing a chore. Rivulets of sweat ran from his head down the center of his back, making him itch. He thought of tiny spiders, like the ones he and Gaby had seen earlier, emerging from their egg and flying away on silken threads. He backed up to a sycamore tree and scratched his back on its curly bark.

The spongy earth around him was covered with violets, lady slippers and Jack-in-the-Pulpit. *Just like being in the greenhouse at the Four-Lane Garden Center, only smaller.* On the way back, he would pick a big bouquet for Mama and Moam and one for Gaby, too. They would like that.

Leander froze. The sudden noise made his heart skip a beat. For an instant, he couldn't decipher it. There it was again—the unmistakable sound of footfalls. Someone or *something* was walking just beyond the thick wall of bramble briars to his right. He swallowed hard, recalling the stories of wildcat and bear sightings. *Miz Lily in her flowing white dress?*

"Cut it out," he whispered to himself. He was hearing the deer, that's all. Deer sounded just like a person walking through the forest. Besides, the sound was growing fainter by the second—the deer were walking away from him. He remained dead still and counted in his head until he no longer heard the steps.

Drawing a deep breath, he pressed onward. After a while, the trail took a sharp turn to the left, and Leander found himself in a clearing. He brushed some low-hanging vines out of his face as he ventured a few steps farther and into what remained of Miz Lily's garden.

Two stone benches sat on either side of a large fountain no longer in use. His dad had told him that Mr. Will stopped maintenance on the electrical wiring years ago, and most of it had rotted away.

A thick layer of moss carpeted the benches, one of which had sunk into the ground, rendering it useless. Leander sat hesitantly on the other one, hoping there weren't any snakes lurking underneath it. He had been here only once before, with Gaby. It was even more overgrown now. He studied his surroundings, trying to imagine how it must have looked all those years ago.

There were many big stone pots that probably held flowers at one time. Some of them lay broken now, and the others contained only straggly weeds. What were once hanging baskets had been reduced to misshapen masses of rusty metal that now dangled haphazardly from vine-covered tree limbs.

The area directly in front of him had at one time been cleared of all trees. A few saplings had sprouted from the roots and grew straight up in their search for sunlight. Wildflowers were abundant. Leander frowned. He certainly wouldn't pick any of these, though. They were all broken and smashed down. *Why?*

He rubbed his forehead: it was sore and very swollen. He felt guilty—this was just something else to worry his mama. He would rest a few minutes longer, then pick flowers and get his hynie home. A big glass of ice water would sure be good right about now—better yet, some of Gaby's lime Kool-Aid.

Leander closed his eyes and told himself that there was no mystery here. Whatever it was that had been so upsetting had obviously happened elsewhere and not in The Ramble at all. Rational thinking lost out though, as the young boy's need for answers continued to fret him.

What kind of accident could it have been? And why had he been crying like that?

A vague uneasiness settled over Leander as the forest sounds became more pronounced in the gathering dusk. Two bullfrogs echoed each other from the stagnant green water in the fountain's base, and the crickets began their incessant chirping from tall oak trees.

The sudden rustle of leaves directly behind him caused him to leap from the bench and whirl around: a wild turkey scratched the forest floor for food.

He was all alone.

20

In hindsight, Leander would recall that he should have paid far less attention to the sounds around him and watched more closely where he was stepping. He should not have tried to run. Had he walked in a normal fashion, he wouldn't have tripped over the tree root. And had he not tripped over the tree root, he would not have reached for the laurel bush in an effort to break his fall.

Leander crashed head-long through the spindly laurel and landed with a thud and a moan among the crushed wildflowers.

He lay still, trying to figure out which part of his body hurt the worst. He had tried to break his fall by using his hands, and both stung badly. His knees had hit the ground as well. They would be scraped and might even by bloody. He sat up gingerly—*nope, no blood, nothing broken.* He began to brush bits of leaves and flower petals off his head and face, ignoring the pain in his palms.

From the corner of his eye, he caught sight of an object partially hidden underneath the laurel bush. *Who in the world would leave their shoe in the woods?* In a squatting position, he pushed aside the laurel branches.

He froze in horror.

He did not want to see, but he could not look away. He thought that he would never stop screaming, until he finally realized that his screams were only in his mind. He was unable to utter a sound.

Leander shut his eyes tight and counted to ten, praying all the while that the fall had momentarily addled his brain. He prayed to the Lord Jesus that, when he opened his eyes, the scene before him would have vanished and all he would see would be an abandoned garden with a silly, over-imaginative boy sitting on the ground, all alone.

Instead, he opened his eyes to the sickening realization that the young girl lying just beyond his reach was dead.

Leander couldn't remember seeing a dead person before, except at a few funerals at the church, but that was different. Those folks had been old and sick—and they'd been in caskets. And the preacher had said that death was a part of living.

This was *nothing* like that kind of death!

He swallowed the bitter bile that had risen in his throat and tried to distance himself mentally from the scene as both revulsion and fascination caused him to inch ever closer to the lifeless body. He looked first at her feet. She had on only one tennis shoe, as the other one lay several feet away where he had seen it. Her navy-blue shorts were all twisted, making her tobacco-brown legs appear to be broken.

Trance-like, his eyes traveled up her legs to the scaly stains that had dried on her upper thigh. A horsefly buzzed in and landed there. Leander shooed it away angrily. He wanted to grab that fly and rip its wings off for daring to touch her.

He closed his eyes again and swallowed hard, then continued his inspection. He noticed that her shirt was bunched up, exposing her belly which showed a large, darkened bruise. Her right arm lay at an awkward angle across her chest and was dotted with small scratches, like the ones he got from picking blackberries.

Leander sat very still on the ground, his eyes no longer focusing on anything. After a time, the wind began to blow and a wayward breeze somehow found its way through the thick shelter of trees, stirring the leaves and letting in a small shaft of light. Something glinted, causing him to rise on his haunches and lean a little closer for inspection. He drew in his breath. *Could he possibly get that close to her?*

He moved gingerly and retrieved the shiny object lying just underneath her left arm, taking care not to touch her. He held it in his hand for a long time, studying it, before putting it into the pocket of his shorts.

Now came the hardest part—looking at her face. His gaze lingered briefly on the thin line of dried blood that ran from her left nostril and across her parted lips. But it was her eyes that shook him loose from his stupor. They were open and looking right at him! A sudden chill crawled up his spine, causing him to shudder. Maybe he should reach out and gently close her eyelids, the way he'd seen folks do on the endless reruns of *In The Heat Of The Night*, that show that Moam watched on afternoon TV.

He didn't do that, though. Instead, he stood up on shaky legs and wiped tears from his eyes as he slowly backed away from the ghastly scene before him.

What in the world am I going to do?

It was perfectly clear in his mind exactly what he *should* do. He should run home this very minute and tell his mother, and they should call the police. And when the police came, he should tell them about seeing him crying and what he had said about something being an accident. And then he should lead the police right back here to where she was.

But then the police would go to Gaby's house.

Leander staggered, not only from the weight of the cumbersome book satchel, which felt a hundred times heavier than it had hours earlier, but from the sheer burden of the circumstances. He trudged, zombie-like, along the main forest path until he reached the clearing and the big stone fountain that still functioned, marking his exit from The Ramble.

Through the low-hanging archway of crepe myrtle branches, he looked across the green lawn toward the Remington mansion. Gaby was probably getting ready for supper with her family right about now. She'd been saying all week how great it was going to be, having everyone together.

"...Granddaddy, Daddy, Remy, and Mason, too, since he's part of the family. And Mama, of course...it's gonna be a great summer, Lee, I can't wait!"

Leander sank to his knees under the enormity of what he had seen. Without warning, his stomach lurched. He leaned to his right, braced his shaking sore hands on the ground, and heaved. The soured lime Kool-Aid blistered his throat as hot tears scalded his eyes. But his thoughts were finally clear. He knew what he was going to do.

"...everybody together, Lee, my whole family..."

He slowly got to his feet and walked the few steps to the stone fountain. The water smelled like Moam's old trunk when she opened it in the fall and shook the moth balls free from her wool clothes. He swished some water from his cupped hand and spat it on the ground. It tasted horrible. As an afterthought, he splashed more water on his face and dried off on his shirttail.

This time when he hoisted the book satchel, he didn't even notice its weight. He lifted his head and began the trek to his home in earnest. He would do nothing to destroy Gaby's family. Instead, he would break the solemn oath he had sworn to her earlier.

He would keep a secret from her. He would keep it forever.

21

Carl Lee drew a deep breath, closed his eyes, and leaned his head back against the worn upholstery of his pickup truck's seat back. He slowly exhaled. All this was done in a concerted effort to—as his wife instructed him all too often—calm down.

He had been looking forward to putting this hectic day behind him and spending a relaxing evening with Claire and the kids—until this latest hurdle loomed.

"Always something," he muttered under his breath. He hastily scribbled a note on the back of an old bank deposit receipt: *Jesse, can you fix her one more time? Sounds like the water pump. Call me. Thanks, Carl Lee.*

He exited the truck and dropped his note and keys into the night deposit slot in the Shell Station's door. The parking lot and Raven Street were deserted, but Carl Lee knew it wouldn't be that way for long.

This part of Antioch was halfway respectable during daylight hours and quiet after dark, until around eleven p.m. or so. That's when the dingy alleyways and condemned buildings of West End, as this part of Antioch was known, came alive with the shadowy inhabitants that the gentile folks in town refused to admit existed.

It was a little after seven o'clock and Carl Lee didn't feel threatened—yet. After putting the newly purchased lawn mower parts in a canvas tote bag that he kept in the truck's cab, he locked the doors and began his walk home.

From this end of town, his most direct route would be to cut through The Project and cross the rickety old bridge that spanned Hobo Jungle. From that point, it was only a mile or so to his house.

He left the parking lot, crossed the street, and made his way between the rows of public housing buildings. Streetlights had been installed when this area was first developed, but eventually the bulbs in all but two of them had burned out. Even so, Carl Lee could see clearly since most of the apartment doors stood open, their occupants hoping to catch a bit of cool night air.

Nothing ever seemed to change in The Project, and tonight was no different. Cars lined the narrow streets, their engines running. The deafening *thump-thump* of amps helped to muffle the sounds of babies crying, dogs barking, and the occasional outbreak of swearing as the inhabitants wrestled with the day-to-day reality of their lives.

Carl Lee made his way between the terraced rows of apartment buildings, careful not to trip over bags of garbage, old lawn chairs, and scattered toys that lay in disarray on the rarely cut grass. Some of the residents sat on the small stoops in front of their units, watching the youngsters skateboarding or jumping rope in the street.

He nodded to several folks in passing but no one acknowledged his greeting. He didn't expect them to. He had come to realize long ago that belonging to the same race and living a lifetime in the same geographic area didn't always make for close ties. In this case, it didn't amount to a hill of beans. Carl Lee did not belong here.

As he neared the far end of The Project, the clatter of stereos, car engines, and voices began to ebb but not before one wizened old man made his presence known. He could barely stand on his own but was shaking his walking cane and shouting at a couple of brothers in a car.

"Get away from here! I know what you all is doin'! You is selling drugs to our children!" He was bent and frail, but obviously had no fear. "You sons-o-bitches are killing our babies! Get on outta here now, or I'm calling the cops!"

"Shut-up, old man!"

"Get yo' ass back inside where you belong, Pops!"

"Daddy, come on back inside, goddammit! You gonna get us all killed!"

"Shut up, down there! I'm trying to get my baby to sleep!"

"Fuck you and your baby!"

"No, fuck you, asshole!"

Carl Lee rounded the corner of the last building. Blessedly, the darkness and silence enveloped him. Although he breathed a sigh of relief as he left the chaotic scene behind him, he did so with conflicting emotions.

Why, he wondered for the umpteenth time, did he feel guilty for the relative comfort of his life? True, he toiled daily to provide for his family, even though he knew that he would always be a tenant and not a landowner. He chuckled to himself, thinking that he didn't even own a reliable vehicle.

He retrieved his flashlight from the tote bag and followed its halo down the last terraced slope of The Project's grounds and onto Westside Avenue.

The few rundown businesses that remained on Westside had closed hours ago. His boot heels made an especially loud clatter on the pavement as he made his way past the last building, a boarded-up barber shop, and stepped from the asphalt surface. The silence was immediate.

He stopped walking and mopped the perspiration from his face with his handkerchief before continuing along the overgrown path. A bit further and he would step onto the old wooden bridge that had miraculously not collapsed into the deep ravine below. Carl Lee had no idea when the bridge had been built—it had been there as long as he could remember. And every time he chose this route, which was rare these days, he sent up a silent prayer that he would reach the other side safely.

22

"Well, here's Mr. Perfect now! Mama's been beside herself worrying over you. How come you to stay out after dark, anyway? You know how she frets over all of us, Leander. And, to make matters worse, I'm late for my shift at the mill, 'cause I couldn't leave Mama here without the car in case somebody was to call and say you'd had an accident or something. If I get fired, it's your fault!"

Accident?

"I-I-I'm s-sorry, Carleen. Time just got away from me, that's all," Leander mumbled weakly. "Where's Mama?"

"In the living room on the phone, calling everybody she knows, asking have they seen you." Carleen stopped her lecture, folded her arms, and continued to glare at him. When Leander finally lifted his head and his eyes met hers, she dropped to her knees to envelop him in a fierce hug.

"We were scared that somethin' bad had happened to you, boy! Where've you been, anyway?" She wiped away a tear before holding him at arm's length to study him more closely. "Lee, are you sick? You've been crying and you smell bad." She didn't give him a chance to respond before calling out loudly: "Mama, he's home!"

"Thank you, Lord Jesus," Claire said, practically running from the adjoining room and into the kitchen. "Leander, you *know* that you are to always be home before it gets dark. Why, I've been worried half to death! I just got off the phone with Rosie, and she said Gabrielle got home hours ago. Now, just where've you been?"

Over the course of her speech, his mother's tone of voice had migrated from relief to frustration, ending on a stern note that Leander recognized all too well. He was going to be punished, and he didn't even care.

"I'm sorry I worried you, Mama. Guess I lost track of time." His words were barely audible. "I-I don't feel so good."

"He *is* sick, Mama," Carleen said in her little brother's defense. "He smells like he's been puking."

"That true? Are you sick?" Claire asked, reaching out her hand to feel his forehead. "You don't have a fever."

"I got sick walking home and I rested awhile in The Ramble," he answered. "Can I go lay down now?"

"Not before you take a bath and eat something, you can't," Claire said. "Carleen, you go on to work, now. We'll be fine."

"Okay. Daddy ought to be getting home soon. I'll see y'all in the morning. Goodnight, Moam," Carleen called out. She tweaked Leander's shoulder affectionately and whispered to his mother as she prepared to leave: "Go easy on him."

His mother studied him, examining the bruises on his arms and legs, as well as his filthy clothes.

"Leander, tell me the truth. Did you get in a fight?"

"No, ma'am, I did not," he said. "I tripped and fell in a briar patch. And I got sick."

She heaved a sigh. "Alright, then. Go get in the bathtub. When you get done, I'll fix you some soup. As he turned to leave, she added: "I thought you'd had some kind of an accident, Leander, and I was so scared."

Accident?

He hesitated briefly before responding much louder than he intended: "No accident, Mama. I just want to be left *alone!*"

"Don't you be giving me attitude, boy," his mother's voice cautioned him as he slammed the bathroom door behind him.

With his back braced against the door, Leander closed his eyes and began to slide downward until he lay in an exhausted heap on the cool tile floor. His head hurt and the many cuts and scrapes on his body smarted.

Far worse that physical pain, though, was the emotional turmoil that raged inside him. His thoughts were little more than a mass of baffling pieces to a jigsaw puzzle. His decision of an hour ago had seemed so clear at the time. But now, after being confronted by his mother, all he wanted to do was open the door, run back to her, bury his face against her neck and pour out the details of what he had seen.

Leander scooted across the floor to the bathtub, put the stopper in the drain, and turned on the warm water. He laid his head on the tub's edge and watched the water slowly begin to rise. It made him think of the water in the swimming hole at Dalton's Creek. A sad little smile tugged at the corners of his mouth as he recalled the wonderful day he and Gaby had shared.

"…and we won't ever have any secrets."

He stood up, shucked off his grimy clothing, and climbed into the tub. He lay back until only his nose remained above water. The sounds of his mother's voice on the phone and Moam's television dimmed to white noise. The water was not only cleansing but soothing, and Leander wished he could remain there forever.

Finally, he sat up and mechanically began to scrub his sore body, barely wincing as the soap stung his wounds. As he climbed from the tub and reached for his towel, clarity took hold of him. Right or wrong, the decision he'd made earlier would stand. He would never tell a living soul what he had seen this day.

* * * * *

"Well, I do believe I've let everyone know that Leander's home safe," Claire said as she hung up the phone. "Can I get you anything, Moam?"

"No, dear, I'm fine," her mother-in-law answered. "I know what happened to our boy today. Now, you jus' think about it, Claire. The las' day of school, and what you reckon he had to eat? Cakes, candies, soda pop, that's what. After that, he done swallowed some water outta Dalton's Creek. Hmm, it ain't no wonder he got sick."

Claire smiled. "You're right, as usual, Moam. Don't guess I'll ever quit worrying about my children."

"'Course you won't. That's what mothers do: they worry. And pray," Mosell added.

"I sure did my share of worrying *and* praying today," Claire said. She fell silent.

"And you're still worrying. Am I right?"

"Yes," Claire answered, "I guess I am. Leander seemed…" she paused, at a loss for words.

"Go on," Mosell prompted.

"He seemed *different*," Claire responded. "Almost like he was a different child when he came home tonight than the happy, sweet little boy I sent off to school this morning. Oh, I know you're right about what he ate today making him sick. But he's had an upset stomach before. And taking a tumble in a briar patch is nothing new to him."

The two women sat quietly for several minutes before Claire spoke again. "Tonight is the first time Leander has ever raised his voice to me." She shook her head, pondering her young son's actions.

Mosell leaned forward in her rocking chair to lay a hand on her daughter-in-law's shoulder. "Now, you listen to me, my dear," she said, "you ain't raised no boys before. What you're dealing with is simple: growing pains." She nodded sagely and went on:

"I know you remember when Carleen and Reva was younger. Why, they would bust out crying at the drop of a hat. Drama: that's what girls gives you. But boys? When boys start getting older, they just go into theirselves and won't talk to nobody. Yes, ma'am, a boy will just sull up like an old possum. Growing pains, Claire. That's all you got going on with Leander."

"I know you're right," Claire said. "But he's only nine years old. When did Carl Lee start having *growing pains?*"

Mosell grinned from ear to ear. "From the time he could talk."

23

The old bridge groaned with every footfall, and Carl Lee wondered just how long it would be before the ancient structure collapsed into the ravine below. Even as this thought occurred to him, the beam from his flashlight illuminated a gaping hole just ahead where one of the slats had rotted away.

Carl Lee stepped over the opening and quickened his pace. There would certainly come a time when the old bridge would be no more. He dreaded that inevitable outcome, as he knew it would not be replaced. The realization saddened him, not only because it would eliminate his short-cut from the back of the Remington property into town, but with its demise would go happy memories from years gone by.

The creaking and groaning subsided as he passed the half-way point on the bridge. He stopped walking and, after testing the stability of the railing, leaned against it to rest. The night sky was illuminated and provided the perfect backdrop for the vine-shrouded *creatures* that rose up from the ground below: *a giraffe, an elephant, a castle, and, of course, a whole family of dinosaurs.*

Most folks, especially farmers, landscapers, and those charged with keeping the roadsides mowed, cursed the creeping kudzu vegetation. It seemed that nothing could eradicate its presence. Only the winter's cold brought the vine to its knees. But when spring returned, so did the dreaded kudzu with a vengeance.

Every year the vines grew with lightning speed, smothering other plants under a blanket of leaves, encompassing entire trees and easily scaling utility poles. Carl Lee rather liked the vines despite their encroachment upon other plant life. He knew what else lay in that gully below the old bridge. Hidden now by the creeping vines but fully exposed in the winter months was the evidence of how little some people cared for their surroundings.

Bags of garbage carelessly tossed over the railing, scrap metal, an old washing machine, countless broken toys and bikes, cast-off clothing, piles of old tires, carcasses of dead animals—and maybe even worse—littered the ravine's floor. The encroaching kudzu transformed it all into an extravaganza for the imagination.

Carl Lee remembered not only his own childhood fantasies but bringing his girls here when they were little to see who could spot the most animals. He smiled as he recalled those times. How those little girls of his would squeal with delight as they huddled between him and Claire, pretending to be hiding from *monsters*. Reva especially would squeeze his hand a bit tighter as darkness enveloped them and the images grew more sinister.

Leander, on the other hand, had informed his parents at an early age that pretending to see creatures when there were none was silly. Carl Lee's thoughts turned to his son and, as always, they were accompanied by a sense of wonderment. His son was first and foremost a miracle, since the doctor had said Claire would not be able to conceive again following Reva's birth. But, nine years later, there he was.

Almost from the time he was a toddler, everyone recognized Leander's intellect. *"We got us somethin' special in that boy,"* Moam said on more than one occasion. His mother had been right: Leander *was* special. As his thoughts centered on his son, he recalled a buying trip a year ago or so to Antioch Feed 'N Seed when Leander had gone with him.

"That'll be $89.90 total," the clerk, a skinny boy of about eighteen with dirty blonde hair brushing his collar and a cigarette hanging out of the side of his mouth, said after totaling up the items in the basket. As Carl Lee was reaching for his wallet, he felt a tug on his britches and looked down at his son. Leander simply shook his head.

"Would you mind adding that up again, please?" Carl Lee asked politely.

"You sayin' I'm a liar?" the young man responded loudly, obviously trying to impress the other customers who were standing around.

"No, sir." Carl Lee answered. "I'm simply making sure that I account for Mr. Will Remington's money. That's all." He smiled politely.

"Mr. Will, huh? Well, sure. Uh, yeah, I'll add it up again. This old cash register, it ain't been working real good, so—"

"Thank you," Carl Lee interrupted.

"Uh, yeah, like I said, this cash register ain't working. Let's see, now, with tax that comes to $77.49. Sorry."

"No problem. Here you are. I'll need the receipt," Carl Lee said.

"Sure. You need help toting everything?" Blondie asked with an actual hint of respect in his voice.

Carl Lee shook his head as he lifted the two bags from the counter. "Have a good day," he said as he and Leander left the store.

"How did you know that I was getting charged too much, son?" he asked when the two of them were on the way home.

"I added it up while you were putting stuff in the cart," Leander answered.

"In your head?"

"Yessir."

When Carl Lee related the incident to Claire that night, her reaction had echoed his thoughts exactly. "Scary," she'd said.

Scary, for sure, he mused now, recalling last night's awards program at Leander's school. His son, with the highest grades in the entire class! He couldn't have been prouder. Carl Lee was proud of all three of his children. Carleen had a good job at the mill and was talking about moving out into a place of her own. And Reva—finishing up her junior year in high school and working two part-time jobs. They were good girls, and pretty, too, just like their mama.

Claire's skin tone was lighter than his, and she had passed that along to her two daughters. Leander, on the other hand, was dark like his father. But thank God, all three kids got their mama's good looks, especially her nose. Carl Lee thought that his wife's nose was her best facial feature. It was so small and delicately formed that he could not imagine it ever encountering an unpleasant odor. He had told Claire that when they were dating, and she had remarked that he ought to be a poet. He chuckled at the memory, glad that the bulbous feature that occupied the center of his face had not been passed on to any of his children.

Carl Lee picked up the tote bag, turned on his flashlight again, and started on the last leg of his journey home. The old bridge groaned in relief as he stepped from it onto the dirt path. From the corner of his eye, he glimpsed a fleeting movement in the woods to his left. He ignored what he knew to be harmless.

Hidden from view now by the thick kudzu vines were the makeshift shelters of cardboard and plastic lean-tos that made up Hobo Jungle. But when the trees were stripped bare and the vines withered by frost, the blue tarps and tiny pinpoints of firelight would materialize amid the growing mounds of trash. And when the wind was right, the stench of rotting garbage mixed with the odor of unwashed bodies and human waste would make even Claire's exquisite nose wrinkle in revulsion.

The shadowy inhabitants of this crude village located in the ravine just below the old bridge had haunted Carl Lee for most of his life. Occasionally, he would come face-to-face with one of the wandering homeless with their dull, unmoving eyes that seemed to convey only that they were waiting. *Waiting for what?* he wondered: a handout, a kind word, death? How could society allow these ever-shifting groups of homeless poor to remain adrift, seemingly invisible to those belonging to a realm of wealth and privilege?

Troubling as the sights and smells of this sad place were to him, it was not the tangible that haunted him. Instead, his mind played out the scenes of what might have led a person to lose everything and find themselves banished from society. What tragedy could push someone to the point of giving up on life?

Carl Lee picked up his pace and soon stepped from the dirt path onto the gravel driveway that led to his home. Blessedly, the images of lifeless eyes and the stench of decaying hopes and dreams receded. He managed to shake himself free of his gloomy thoughts and reminded himself that he did not belong to that shabbiness any more than he belonged in the Project.

What made the difference? The answer was clear: *this* made the difference, he realized as he walked up the three steps to the back porch of his house. This home, his wife and children, his job and the mother who had raised him—*that's* what had made the difference in his life.

Silently, he offered up a prayer of thanks before opening the kitchen door to the sound of Moam's TV coming from the living room, the sight of Claire's smiling face as she turned toward him, and the smell of pork chops and apples sizzling on the stove.

24

"Some homecoming party *this* has turned out to be!" Gabrielle's voice cracked noticeably as the tears threatened. To hide her emotional side—one she deemed a weakness only to be attributed to *sissies*—she turned her back to the group assembled in the formal dining room and stomped up the stairs to her room.

"Now see what you've done, Remy! You've gone and broke your little sister's heart." Gabe spoke sharper than he had intended and immediately regretted his tone. "I'm sorry, son. But Gaby's been beside herself all week waiting for you to come home. And then for you to tell her you don't feel like talking is shameful."

"Oh, now, Gabe. She'll get over it. Why, she'll forget all about it come morning," Will said, defending in his blustery fashion anything Remy ever said or did. It was a scenario that Gabe had grown tired of years ago.

"Yes, Will, Gaby will get over it. And in the morning, she'll be her usual sweet, forgiving self because that's what she is: a sweet and forgiving little nine-year-old child." Gabe held his father-in-law's gaze amid the silent group gathered around the dining table. After a few seconds, he went on:

"I know you're tired, Remy, and let's face it, it seems as though we've *all* had a bad day. But that's no reason to hurt your sister's feelings. You should go up and talk to her right after we finish dinner."

"Sure, Daddy. I will," Remy said.

"That's my boy. Takes a big man to apologize," Will spouted as he reached over to slap Remy on the back, giving the impression that *he* was the one bringing harmony back to the dinner table. "It sure is good to have you home, grandson—and you, too, Mason. I'm mighty sorry about your tires.

But, don't you worry. It'll be taken care of. I'll tell Ginny to get a check over to Jesse first thing Monday morning."

"That's not necessary, Mr. Will," Mason said. "I appreciate it, but it's my fault. I never should have stopped in that part of town. It was just so hot, and I needed a cold drink."

"Nonsense. You work for the bank, and we take care of our own," Will said emphatically. "Don't you agree, Gabe?"

"That's fine," Gabe said. He changed the subject. "I hope you don't mind, Vivian, but I'm going to skip dessert tonight and retire early. It's been a full day."

"Of course, I don't mind, dear," his wife said. "But you've barely touched your steak. Are you feeling ill?"

"I'm fine." Gabe rose and planted a kiss on his wife's upturned cheek. "Goodnight, boys. It's good to have you both at home." He rounded the table and patted his father-in-law on the shoulder. "Have a good night, Will."

"You, too, Gabe," Will answered. "I'm going to skip dessert myself. I have an appointment in town, probably won't be back before you boys hit the sack. I'm sure we'll all be in better spirits in the morning." He chuckled. "Leastwise, we'd all better be in a good mood, 'cause there's gonna be one heck of a shindig here tomorrow."

Will rose from his place at the head of the dinner table and made a token trip to the far end to pat Vivian's hand. "Have a good night, daughter," he said.

"Daddy, how in the world did you get such a terrible bruise on your wrist?" Vivian touched his hand, causing him to recoil.

"How the hell should I know? My skin—yours, too—we bruise!" Will snapped, exiting the dining room in a huff.

The grandfather clock in the entry hall chimed eight o'clock, breaking the awkward silence that had fallen. Vivian was accustomed to her father's brusque treatment, but it still embarrassed her even in the company of family. She smiled and began to smooth an imaginary wrinkle in the linen tablecloth.

"Well, it looks like you two handsome college men are stuck with only my company for dessert and after-dinner drinks. But we'll manage, I'm sure. Just let me help Rosie clear these dishes, then I'll bring our dessert into the living room."

Mason rose from his seat and swiftly moved to assist his hostess as she began to rise. "Let me help you, Miz Vivian," he said as he pulled her chair away from the table. "I believe I'm going to skip dessert myself. This has been a mighty long day, and I didn't realize how tired I was 'til just a little while ago. I hope you'll forgive me, but that guest house bed is calling."

"I'm turning in, too, Mama," Remy said. "I'm beat. Like Granddaddy said, we got a big day tomorrow."

Remy started to leave the room behind Mason. Unexpectedly, he turned, walked back to Vivian and wrapped her in his arms. The spontaneity of that embrace—not to mention the warmth it conveyed—caught Vivian off-guard and rendered her momentarily speechless. Her son rarely displayed emotion, and never toward her.

"Thanks for everything, Mama," he whispered against her hair. "Sorry tonight's been such a downer."

She found her voice. "Remy, are you feeling all right? I didn't want to mention it, but you're pale as a ghost tonight. You barely touched your dinner, and you *must* know that Rosie made her famous banana pudding, your favorite. Are you sure you don't want some?"

"I'm sure. I probably got a little dehydrated today walking home. You, too, huh?" he said, playfully punching Mason's arm.

"No doubt. Goodnight, Miz Vivian. Later, man," Mason said, flashing a grin as he took his leave.

"Alright, then. You boys get a good night's rest," Vivian said. "We'll all feel better tomorrow."

"Yes, ma'am."

"Thank Rosie for us, Mama."

Automatically Vivian began to stack the china plates, salad bowls, glasses, and silverware onto the butler's cart to be rolled into the kitchen. She shook her head as she surveyed the remnants of Remy's welcome home dinner. The preferred menu of all the menfolk in the family of rib-eye steaks, baked potatoes, salad, and Rosie's homemade yeast rolls sat cold and barely touched.

"Oh, my goodness!" Rosie exclaimed as she stood up from her rocking chair in the kitchen. "I reckon I must have dozed off. Here, let me tend to those." The old housekeeper stopped and gazed forlornly at the heavy-laden cart.

"Was somethin' bad wrong with the dinner? Why, nobody hardly touched a bite."

"No, Rosie. The dinner was delicious. Everyone said so. It's just been a very tiring day for all of us. And Mason's trouble with his car gave us quite a shock." Vivian hugged the older woman. "I'm just going to empty the plates and stack them. You go on to bed. You need to rest up for tomorrow."

"Yes, ma'am, if you sure. I'm powerful tired, myself," Rosie said, wasting no time in removing her apron and limping toward her bedroom door.

"I'm sure," Vivian replied brightly. "I'm going to enjoy some of this banana pudding along with my brandy, and then I'll be turning in as well."

Vivian's smile was in place until Rosie closed her bedroom door. Then, she chucked the leftovers in the garbage and rinsed and stacked the dishes. After filling her dessert dish with a generous helping of pudding, she walked back into the dining room and poured herself a brandy.

The formal living room was rarely used by the family anymore, but it remained Vivian's favorite room in the mansion. She settled herself comfortably on the overstuffed sofa to enjoy the remainder of her evening. Moonlight and landscape lighting caressed the room and made the chandeliers unnecessary. Massive bay windows at the end of the room overlooked the property to the east, away from the main entrance and towards an unusually high rock face referred to as "The Bluff".

From the time she could walk, Vivian had felt no pull toward The Ramble as her mother had. Instead, her little feet would take her to The Bluff to daringly peer over the edge and send Nanny Martha into fits of panic. As a bribe to keep her away from the overhang, Will had hired a carpenter to construct a playhouse fit for a princess. It was a safe enough distance from the dangerous rock ledge to reassure the adults but close enough to satisfy the young Vivian. It was there that she and Claire played as children, overcame the fears and insecurities of adolescence, and reached womanhood together—she without a mother, Claire without a father.

When Vivian had outgrown the playhouse, it was converted into a gazebo for summer parties. It had remained her special place. *The night of her sweet sixteen birthday party and Gabe's first kiss, his awkward proposal on one knee when they were barely eighteen—so many memories.*

The family seldom used the gazebo for entertaining any more, not since the precocious five-year-old Remy had taken a bad fall after trying to "parachute" off the railing onto the ground with an umbrella. His broken arm had been the catalyst that prompted Will to brand the gazebo unsafe.

Vivian still went there, though, usually alone. A frown creased her brow as she recalled Claire's earlier apprehension that she spent far too much time alone. *Maybe this summer will be different*, she thought, recalling Remy's warm embrace. Was it too late to bond with her son? Perhaps she and Gaby could find some common ground as well.

With dessert now finished, she placed her dish on the coffee table and burrowed into the sofa cushions. She sipped her brandy and continued to mull over the Remington-Westin family dynamics. It was easy for her to lay the blame at Will's feet for her lack of closeness with Remy. And what little girl didn't favor her daddy over her mama?

But she and Gabe—now *that* was complicated.

25

"Whoee, something sure smells good!" Carl Lee exclaimed as he dropped the tote bag on the floor and moved to the kitchen sink to wash his hands. "How'd you know I been thinking 'bout pork chops all day long?"

"You're late," Claire said. "Supper just about cooked too long. I didn't hear you drive up."

"Yeah, well, that's 'cause the truck's sitting at Jesse's."

"Again? What is it this time?" Her voice carried her discontent.

Carl Lee dried his hands, hung the towel back in place, and moved behind his wife to embrace her. He nuzzled her hair: it smelled like jasmine. "Won't know 'til Jesse calls me, but I'm betting it's the water pump." He walked to the kitchen table and sat heavily on one of the wooden chairs.

"Sorry, babe. I know you been wanting us to take a trip up to Asheville. Maybe this fall."

"That's okay," Claire said. "Better time, anyway. When the leaves turn." She put her frustration aside and began filling dinner plates. "Reva!" she called loudly in order to be heard above Moam's television, "your daddy's home! Come to supper!"

Carl Lee looked quizzically into the living room. "Where is everybody?"

"Well, Carleen's working the evening shift, Moam's already had supper, and Leander is lying down. He's sick. So, it's just you, me, and this soon-to-be high school senior here." Claire jostled Reva playfully as she entered the kitchen.

"Hey, Daddy," Reva said as she bent to peck his cheek.

"Wait just a minute," Carl Lee demanded. "What's this about my boy being sick? How come you didn't say so first thing?"

"Because there's nothing to worry about, that's why," Claire answered. "He got sick to his stomach from eating too many sweets today at the school party. Then, he wore hisself out swimming in Dalton's Creek." She fell silent as she settled herself into the kitchen chair and reached out her hands to her husband and daughter in preparation for the blessing. "And to top it off, he took a bad fall in a patch of briars. Now, let's get to our supper."

When Claire finished saying grace, Reva said, "I heard Leander crying in his bedroom when I came in a while ago. I knocked on his door and asked what the matter was, and he told me to go away and leave him alone. What's *that* all about?"

"Most likely he still upset 'cause I fussed at him for coming home so late," Claire said.

Moam's slipper-clad feet shuffled along the hardwood floor as she entered the kitchen. "I told you all what's going on with our boy—ain't nothing but growing pains." She helped herself to a glass of iced tea from the fridge and began her slow progress back to the living room.

Carl Lee was growing more agitated by the second. "First of all, you tell me that Leander's sick, then I hear that he's in his room crying when that boy don't never cry, and now I find out he was late getting home! Anything else you think I might ought to know?"

"Calm down, please," Claire spoke evenly. "Of course, I would have told you. I knew you'd be tired and might want to have supper before you talked to him, that's all."

There was a knock at the front door and Claire looked at her watch.

"Now who in the world could that be? It's after eight thirty."

"I'll get it, Daddy," Reva said, rising from her chair and hurrying into the other room. Moam lowered the volume of her television as Carl Lee heard a low-pitched male voice.

"So sorry to bother you folks, but could I speak with Carl Lee, please?"

"Sure thing, sir. Come on in," Reva said. "Daddy, Mr. Jerome is here to see you."

"Who?" Carl Lee asked as he walked from the kitchen. "Oh, hey there, Curley. How you doin', man?" He reached out to shake hands.

Claire had followed him from the kitchen and welcomed the visitor as well. "Hello, Curley. What brings you out tonight? I do hope Tavish is feeling better," she said.

"Thank you, Miz Claire," Curley said. "Tavish is tolerable these days, that's all. The chemo been mighty hard on her, for sure."

After a brief silence, Carl Lee asked: "Curley, you want to sit down?"

"No, thank you. I didn't come to visit. I'm going around asking everybody I know have they seen my granddaughter any time this afternoon or tonight, 'cause she didn't come home. She always goes right straight home from school or from my store, but she didn't today, and Tavish is beside herself with worry. And I don't mind telling you, I'm worried, too." The words tumbled from his trembling lips.

"Tawney, that's her name, right?" Claire asked.

"Yes, ma'am," Curley answered. "You see, she's a good girl and she knows how her grandmaw worries 'bout her. She wouldn't do nothing to worry her no more. Besides," he paused, nodding his head for emphasis, "Tawney left my store this afternoon and she left this behind." He pulled the item from his pocket and held it out. "This is her inhaler. She don't go nowhere without it 'cause she gets bad asthma attacks and has to have it to breathe."

"I've been in Greenville all day," Carl Lee said. "Got back to town a little before dark but had to leave my truck at Jesse's and walk home. I came through the Project, but I didn't see your granddaughter. Of course, I don't know if I could recognize her. Kids grow up quick these days."

"What grade's she in?" Reva asked.

"She finished sixth grade today," Curley said. After a moment's hesitation, he added: "She'll be going to junior high this fall."

"Let's asked Leander if he saw her at school today," Reva suggested.

"Leander, come on out here, son!" Carl Lee called loudly.

The room was completely dark except for the blue light coming from his aquarium in the far corner. The darkness hugged and comforted him as he lay on his bed, staring into the blackness. He had tried to fall asleep, but each time he closed his eyes, he saw it all again. *Everything.* Would he ever been able to close his eyes again? What would happen to him if he never slept again? Would he die?

The creak of his bedroom door and the shaft of light spilling from the hallway beyond brought him out of his inertia. "I need you to come out to the living room, son," his dad said.

"Okay," Leander croaked as he sat up slowly and swung his feet to the floor. He was dizzy. "I'm coming, Daddy."

He gritted his teeth against the new wave of nausea and took one weak step after the other until he was standing before the circle of adults in the living room. His eyes locked for an instant on those of Mr. Jerome Simpson's before focusing on the floor. "What's the matter, Daddy?" he asked.

"Leander, Mr. Jerome is looking for his granddaughter, Tawney, 'cause she never got home today. Did you see her at the school this afternoon?" Claire asked.

The floor continued to hold his gaze. His tongue felt paralyzed.

Carl Lee placed his hand on the boy's shoulder and said: "You hear your mama, boy? She asked did you see Tawney today."

Leander lifted his head and looked at everyone before responding. "S-s-she's in the grades ahead of mine. Their classes are upstairs, and we're not allowed to go up there." He swallowed hard and waited.

"Okay, I guess you can go on back to bed, now," Carl Lee said. "The boy came home sick today, Curley. You got to excuse him."

"That's alright. Thank you, son," Curley said, and then turned his attention back to Carl Lee. "I'll be going now. I need to check with some of her friends. Maybe she's with them."

"I would definitely check with her close friends," she said. "Does Tawney have a boyfriend?"

"*Boyfriend?*" Curley seemed shocked at the question. "Why, no, ma'am. She ain't but twelve years old."

Leander noticed that Moam, who had sat silent the entire time, turned her head toward Curley and lifted her eyebrows.

"Please do let us know when she comes home, Curley," Claire said. "And tell Tavish I'm thinking about her. If she needs me to run errands or do *anything* for her, she's to call me. You hear?"

"Oh, yes, ma'am. And thank y'all." Preparing to take his leave, Curley turned back to Leander. "You feel better, lil' man," he added.

Leander nodded and managed a weak smile. As he turned back toward his bedroom, Reva placed a comforting arm around his shoulders. The gesture was too much, though, and brought another round of tears perilously close. He pulled away from his sister's touch and hurried to the dark solitude of his room.

Carl Lee returned from walking Curley to his truck. As he closed and locked the front door, he said, "I sure do hope that girl's back home by the time he gets there. That old couple—they live for that granddaughter. Have ever since their boy, Terrance, passed." He moved to his recliner and sat heavily. His day had caught up with him, and he was suddenly exhausted.

"I never did hear why Tawney's mama up and left like she did," Claire said thoughtfully. "Probably couldn't take care of Tavish any longer. But to leave your daughter like that…" Her words evaporated.

"Mmm," Carl Lee grunted wearily. "Curley's got a hard row to hoe, that's for sure."

"That's right. 'Specially if he thinks twelve be too young for a boyfriend," Mosell commented as she shook her head. "Growing pains," she murmured under her breath.

26

✦ ✦ ✦ ✦ ✦ ✦

"Hey, Will. I didn't know you were coming over tonight. I was just about to take Gypsy for her evening walk. You want to come along?" Belle Fontenot asked as she hooked her arm in his.

The frisky terrier sniffed at Will's feet and whined for attention. He stooped to scratch the dog's ears. "No, babe," he answered. "You go on. I'll wait inside. Too goddamn hot for me even after the sun goes down."

She studied him momentarily, her expression quizzical. "Is anything wrong, Will?" she asked.

"No, no, nothing's wrong," he said, turning away from her intuitive gaze. "I just felt like some good company tonight."

"Didn't Remy and his friend get in?"

"They did."

Belle waited. When he offered no further comment, she said: "Well, then, I'll make it a quick walk."

Will climbed the steps of Belle's restored Federalist house to the screened porch. He abandoned his initial destination of air-conditioned luxury for the modicum of relief afforded by the gallery's whirring ceiling fans. He sank into the padded cushions of the glider and watched Belle make her way down the narrow sidewalk toward the small park at the end of the cul-de-sac. His smile widened a bit as he watched her walk. "Still the best-looking ass I ever saw," he muttered under his breath.

Belle was a handsome woman. She was tall, nearly five ten, and big-boned. Her large features were softened somewhat by the thick mane of curly blonde hair, which routinely hung in disarray past her broad shoulders. She was rarely seen in public without her artfully applied makeup and a tasteful selection of expensive jewelry adorning her fingers, ears, and wrists. And never *ever* would she be seen—even on an evening stroll with the dog—without her trademark high-heeled sandals. She wore them all *very* well. *As a matter of fact,* Will thought as he sat, captivated by her undulating progress down the sidewalk, *when Belle entered a room—any room—she owned it.*

Will had made her acquaintance some twenty years prior, during one of his business trips to Charleston. His offer to purchase a small, family-owned bank had been gratefully accepted by the surviving grandson, and the two men had set out to seal their deal with a night on the town.

Belle had made a positive first impression on Will for several reasons, the least of which was her good looks. Beautiful women were everywhere, but damned few of them knew how to wear their beauty without flaunting it. Belle did. Even fewer women had a good business head on their shoulders and knew how to go beyond simply earning a living by rising above all others in their chosen profession. Belle did.

She hailed from New Orleans, she had told him, left there at seventeen and had not been back. After living for short periods of time in Florida and Georgia, she'd settled in Charleston because she loved the history of the city.

During their early talks, Will had told her of his father's relentless tutoring, guaranteeing that he would reign supreme in the banking industry. Belle had laughed sarcastically then and said, "Yeah, unfortunately, my father gave me the same kind of tutoring in *my* profession."

Not many women could have risen above such an upbringing. Belle had.

Her establishment was in the most exclusive part of Charleston and literally took one's breath away upon entering. Her gourmet dinners, accompanied by vast selections of fine wines, were the envy of chefs throughout the city. Her clients were wealthy beyond imagination. Her employees were hand-picked, well-educated, gorgeous, and always accommodating.

And Belle Fontenot herself was at the top of the heap—the most esteemed Madam in the city of Charleston.

Several days after their meeting, Will had asked Belle what was it about him that had enticed her to leave her table on the second-floor balcony that night and come down the stairs to personally greet him. She had answered him without hesitation. "Three things: you didn't gawk, you addressed my hostess as *ma'am*, and you were wearing a hand-tailored suit."

After Belle's welcome to her house, she had asked Will which one of the ladies he might like to share a drink with. "I'm looking at her," he had replied.

That night had been the beginning of only the second *relationship* in Will's life. Many dalliances, meaningless encounters, and scores of forgotten names—both before and, regrettably, after Belle—had served as poor substitutes for affection. It was during his brooding times like tonight, when his closeted regrets rose to the surface to haunt him, that he sought her company. He listened to her footfalls on the steps and thought that their years together seemed to have passed in the blink of an eye.

"You okay?" she asked as she entered the screened porch and proceeded to remove Gypsy's leash.

Will raised his head, moistened his lips, and stated flatly, "I said a while ago that I am fine."

"I just asked because you were sitting there all bent over with you head in your hands. Now what else am I to think, except that something must be bothering you, Will," she said.

Her tempestuous response was something else Will had always admired about her. It appeased him immediately. "Sorry, babe. I didn't mean to snap at you," he said, grinning. "You know what I'd like right now?"

She stood before him with her hand on her hip. Her smile widened and her tongue flicked her lower lip enticingly. "Oh, I got a pretty good idea," she murmured.

Will chuckled and shook his head. "Not that. How 'bout you go and find that high-dollar bottle of brandy that we bought on our last cruise. You know the one I can't pronounce. Bring it and two glasses back out here. That sound good to you?"

"Sure. Just let me freshen up a little. That walk made me break a sweat. I'll be right back, sugar."

"Oh, and put something on the stereo, will you?" he called out. "Not that goddamn noise folks play today. Something I can understand the words to."

It was Belle's turn to laugh. "How 'bout Dean Martin's Greatest?" she asked.

"Perfect."

Will sat comfortably on the glider, his left foot on the floor, gently pushing it back and forth, and his right foot propped on the coffee table. Belle filled the other side with her feet in his lap, and Gypsy lay tightly wedged between them. The bottle of brandy, over half gone now, was every bit as good as touted on the label.

Dean had sung his last a while ago, and now Sinatra's *My Way* made Will grunt pleasurably. "Sure do wish this night could go on forever," he said. He meant it, he realized. He didn't want to leave her and go home, but he had to. He wasn't even looking forward to the party tomorrow, and that thought disturbed him. For weeks now, he'd been eager to give Remy his birthday present and to see the look on the boy's face. Surely, his excitement would return with the morning.

He stretched and patted Belle's thigh. "You coming tomorrow, aren't you?"

"I'm going to try, but it'll be late when I get there," she answered. "I'm scheduled at the Clinic from noon 'til five. It being Saturday, you know how many snotty-nosed little kids are gonna be brought in. Also, Mrs. Blevins three houses down broke her ankle last week, and I told her I'd go to the grocery store for her tomorrow sometime. Oh, and I need to drop off some clothing at the Good Will office. Anyway, if I don't make it tomorrow, you tell Remy to stop by soon. I got a present for him."

Belle had sold her property and relocated here to Antioch shortly after she and Will began keeping company. Her patented answer of "I'm retired from public relations," seemed to have satisfied anyone who asked her about her past. Her constant obsession with various charity efforts were obviously her heartfelt attempts to atone for her past, and at times irked Will. Not tonight, though, and he let her know it.

"You're a good woman, babe. In fact, you're the kindest, most generous person I know."

"Yeah, well, you know what they say about the soft heart of a whore."

He turned toward her, bringing his face close to hers. "Don't do that," he said pleadingly. "Don't run yourself down, Belle. It hurts me when you talk like that."

At that very moment, his belly rumbled loudly, and the sound caused them both to laugh. "Did you have any supper?" she asked.

"Not very much, I guess. Sorry."

"How 'bout some scrambled eggs and toast?" she asked.

Will nodded. "If you don't mind."

"No trouble at all. I'm kind of hungry myself." Belle stood up and stretched as she cleared the brandy and glasses from the table. "Come on in and sit with me while I cook," she said.

He watched her walk across the porch. She was fifty-eight years old and still had a spring in her step. She was special, and just being with her tonight eased his mind. "I should have married you, Belle," he said wistfully.

She paused for a long moment with her hand on the doorknob before responding. "What," she finally said; "and ruin a perfectly good love affair?" As she entered the house, she called back nonchalantly over her shoulder, "Come get your eggs."

27

Carl Lee lay propped up in bed by an array of throw pillows and tried to decipher what his wife was saying from their adjoining bathroom. How did she expect him to understand her when she had a mouth full of toothpaste? "What did you say, Claire?"

"I thed that I wath weally worried 'bout Tawey."

"Uh-uh. It just might be that Mama's right and she got herself a boyfriend," he said.

"I don bewee dat fo one minwet."

"What?" Carl Lee was growing frustrated. "Why don't you finish brushing your teeth and come on out here where we can talk? I can't understand a thing…"

He stopped speaking as Claire stepped into the doorway. Silhouetted by the bathroom light, the blue silk clung to her body as if it had been painted on. Slowly, she moved toward the bed.

"Lord, have mercy!" was all her he could say.

Claire chuckled. "I guess that means you like it," she said.

"I never saw anything so pretty. Where in the world did you get something like that?"

"It was a gift from Vivian. Early birthday present, she *said*. But I'm not buying it," Claire stroked the fabric where it hugged her waist. "It feels like I'm not wearing anything."

Carl Lee grinned at her. "In a minute, you ain't gonna be," he said.

Claire slapped at him playfully, and then settled herself into a cross-legged position on the foot of their bed. "Carl Lee, I'm awful worried 'bout Leander," she said.

"Wait a minute, woman! You been flittin' around like a June bug. First off, you're worrying over Curley's granddaughter—and I'm not saying you shouldn't be. But then, you come in here looking as pretty as when I married you, talkin' 'bout Vivian giving you that gown but you not believing why she did. And now, you jumping to Leander!" Carl Lee finished, his voice growing louder by the second.

"Shhh," Claire cautioned. "You'll wake up the whole house. When I went over to the big house today, Viv was up in her rooms, as usual. Anyway, we had a nice visit and was about to go downstairs and go over everything for tomorrow's party, when she said that she had a present for me. She said that we would call it an 'early birthday'.

"Well, when I opened the box, it just took by breath away. But I *knew* she didn't buy it. Gabe did. He bought it for her, and I told her I knew that and asked her why she wanted to give it away." She paused to catch her breath.

"What did she say to that?" Carl Lee asked.

"She *said* that the color was better for me and that she didn't like to wear blue. But I'd already seen the label and I knew what was going on. See, look here," she instructed, as she turned around for him to read the label at the gown's back.

"An original—"

She interrupted him. "An original by *Tess*." She nodded knowingly. "That's Tess Bradley."

Carl Lee looked at her blankly.

"I thought I'd told you all about that mess years ago."

Carl Lee shook his head. "No. If you did, I done forgot it."

"Oh, you wouldn't have forgotten," Claire said pointedly. "You didn't go to our high school, so you missed out on all the gossip."

"Can you fill me in tomorrow?" Carl Lee asked, as he reached out to stroke her thigh through the silk fabric.

She idly patted his hand and went on speaking as if she hadn't heard him, caught up as she was in remembering the past. "It was our sophomore year, and it was plain as day to everybody—Vivian included—that Gabe Westin was smitten with Tess Bradley."

Carl Lee stared at her vacantly. "So?"

"*So,*" Claire replied, "Tess is black. Folks around here still have trouble accepting biracial couples, but what you think they said about it over twenty years ago?"

"Plenty, I'm guessing," he answered. "Mr. Will in particular, right? And Vivian—she must have been powerful jealous."

Claire shook her head. "She wasn't so much jealous as she was hurt," she said. "Truth be told, it just about destroyed her, is what it did. I sometimes think that year caused her depression every bit as much as her knowing how much Will regretted not having a son."

She moved from her spot on the bed to the dresser and picked up her brush. She began brushing her long hair while she went on talking.

"It was an accepted fact that Gabe and Vivian would marry one day. That's the way Will wanted it, and for once, Vivian was in perfect agreement with her daddy. She'd loved Gabe since they were little children, and the thing with Tess—it left her broken."

"But, two young teenagers," Carl Lee remarked hesitantly, "couldn't have been no more than puppy love. And besides, Gabe married Vivian."

"Oh, it was more than just puppy love," Claire assured him. "That boy was *crazy* about Tess. And—Carl Lee, don't you ever repeat this—but Tess dropped out of school early our junior year. There was talk going around that she got pregnant."

"Whatever happened to her? And the baby?"

Claire shook her head. "Tess moved away. That's all anybody ever knew."

Carl Lee frowned. "Why's all this coming up now?" he asked.

"Because, Tess came back to Antioch about a month ago. I knew it, but I never said anything to Vivian. She's a fashion designer now—opened a shop downtown. Anyway, Gabe come wagging his big dumb ass in today with this gown for Vivian that he'd bought from Tess."

"Uh-huh," Carl lee said, nodding his head knowingly. "That's why she gave it to you. Now I understand. But you don't think she believes there might be something going on between them now, do you? I mean, that was a long time ago, and they were kids."

Claire was silent for a time, and then said: "I know my best friend, and I know it doesn't matter to her nearly as much whether they actually did anything or if it was all just gossip. What mattered to her then and what matters to her now is that Gabe *wanted* those stories to be true. Vivian's fragile, Carl Lee, and just knowing that her husband loved somebody else could send her over the edge. And, to top it all off," she added, "Tess was unbelievably beautiful."

"Mmm," Carl Lee murmured. He reached out to draw Claire close to him. She fit him so good this way, her back nestled against his chest. His big hands stroked the soft skin of her arms before migrating to her small, firm breasts. As his thumbs gently caressed her nipples, he felt the buds spring to life through the silken fabric. "I bet she was never as beautiful as you," he whispered against her hair.

But the moment evaporated as Claire disengaged herself from his embrace, rose from the bed, and began nervously pacing the room. "I just can't think about anything else right now."

"Baby," he said patiently, "Vivian and Gabe are gonna be fine. Why, they're an institution. There ain't nobody could split them two up."

"You're right, I'm sure. I was about to say that I'm worried about my boy."

"*What?*" Carl Lee was exasperated. "You're doin' it again. Just now, you were talking about Vivian, and then you switch back to Leander. You need to settle down, woman, and come over here."

She stared into space as if she had not heard him. Finally, she said: "I can't shake the feeling that he's troubled about something. I know my son, and I'm afraid there's more to it than just 'growing pains', as Moam put it."

"Uh-huh. Well, seeing you in that gown has done give me a *growing pain.*"

"Huh?" Claire turned to him questioningly. When she saw the sheet over his lap move on its own, she turned away to suppress a giggle. "Carl Lee!" She turned out the lights and made her way toward their bed.

Their room was bathed in moonlight filtering through the sheer curtains. She shrugged the thin straps off her shoulders and felt the gown drift to the carpet as weightless as breath. "God, I wish Vivian and Gabe had what we have," she whispered.

Carl Lee reached for her. "It'll all work out, you'll see. Now, come here."

28

Vivian's body jerked as she woke suddenly. Her thoughts were muddled for a moment until she realized where she was. She had fallen sound asleep in an awkward position on the living room sofa, and now her legs tingled painfully. She yawned, stretched, and began to massage the feeling back into her extremities.

The grandfather clock in the hall chimed the midnight hour. Slowly, she stood up and, after assuring herself that her steps were steady, she picked up the dessert plate and empty brandy snifter and prepared to make her way to the kitchen. The instant before she reached to turn on the table lamp, movement through the window caught her eye. The living room was dark, and knowing that she could not be seen, she moved closer to the window to peer out at her husband.

Vivian was confused. Had he been unable to sleep and gone for a midnight stroll as he had been known to do in the past? Or had he left her dinner table hours ago and never even went to bed at all? She watched him trudge slowly across the lawn from the direction of the gazebo and The Bluff.

When Gabe stopped in his tracks and lifted both hands to his head, Vivian's first inclination was to meet him on the front veranda and make sure he wasn't ill. But that thought faded quickly as she saw him reach for his handkerchief and press it to his eyes. *He's crying!*

She continued to watch him with growing dismay. Had her rejection of him and his gift that afternoon caused this rare display of emotion? But no sooner had that thought entered her head, than she dismissed it. Vivian steeled herself against the knowledge of what she feared to be the *real* cause of Gabe's distress.

The click of the front door signaled his entry. Vivian remained motionless in the shadows of the living room until his assent to the top of the staircase was heralded by the creak of oaken floorboards. She made her way to the kitchen to deposit her dishes. As was her habit, she locked the kitchen door before turning off the floodlights.

She hadn't heard her father come in, but there was his car parked in its customary place under the carport. Vivian methodically switched off the lights in the kitchen and made her way up the back stairs to her room. Although she was comforted by the knowledge that all her family was home, safe and sound, she couldn't shake the uneasy sensation that something was very, very wrong. Their earlier dinner, tense and uncomfortable, came to mind.

"You were right, Gaby," she whispered. "Some homecoming party this has turned out to be."

* * * * *

How long has it been, now? Well, let's see: it's four a.m., so that's what, eleven, twelve hours, maybe? A better question would be how long before you can close your eyes and not see her lifeless ones staring back at you?

All the night's distractions didn't help, did they? You did what you thought earlier would be impossible, though—you survived the family dinner, a strained and miserable affair. And, you managed to engage in conversation and to dole out the appropriate smiles and hugs. You did all the things expected of you. But then, you always do what's expected of you, don't you?

So, how did it happen? How COULD it have happened? And, what was 'it' exactly—rape, murder?

NO, shhh, be quiet. That is NOT how it was! Get that straight in your head right now. First of all, she didn't scream. She was curious. She even giggled. Therefore, no rape. Second, you did not cause her death. Why? Because you tried to help her, that's why. You helped her to sit up, and you lifted her arms over her head, and you patted her back.

"Hold on, girl. Tawney, w-w-what's the matter? Calm down, now, everything's gonna be alright. We didn't do anything wrong. You know that, don't

you? Why, of course you know that! You're a real smart girl. You're practically a grown-up woman, anyway. Talk to me, Tawney. Why can't you talk?

"Hey, look here: let's get your clothes back on, and, and we'll walk around a bit. That'll help, trust me. Here, let me help you. I know what we'll do: you and me are gonna walk on over to that SnoBall stand at the forks of the road, you know the one. You'd like that, wouldn't you? There, there, see: you just needed to stand up. Feeling better, now? Can you get your breath? No, no, girl. Don't sit back down. Breathe, please BREATHE! Oh, God! Oh, God! Oh, Jesus!"

What could've happened to her, anyway? One minute she was fine, and the next she couldn't get her breath. Then, she started acting all crazy, shaking all over and couldn't even speak.

Then she died. A young girl died.

And you left her there all alone and lying on the ground! How could you do that? How could you just leave her in that sad and forsaken place?

Wait a minute. Just what the hell should you have done? It was an accident, pure and simple. Nothing to be gained by telling everybody, that's for sure. Think about it. How's that gonna look: you in the middle of the woods with your pants down, going at it with a twelve or thirteen-year-old black girl, and she ups and dies on you? Fuckin' media would turn that into a circus, for sure. I mean, you couldn't bring her back by ruining the rest of your life, now, could you? Of course, you couldn't. And, don't forget, there are a whole lot of other people to consider besides yourself.

It didn't even seem like you, anyway. It was more like somebody else was there with the girl, and you were looking down and seeing what was happening, but you weren't really there. What is that: one of those out-of-body experiences?

Nonsense! Think logically. Let's look at what we've got going on here. Bad judgment for starters. But you've got to think it through, just like you always do. Something snapped inside of you, and you can blame it on the heat, on your headache, or stress, conflicts, memories. How 'bout frustration, or just a goddamn lousy turn to your day—whatever.

And now? Well, you've got to keep your wits about you and take each day as it comes. You've got to focus on what's important. You cannot help her now, so get your mind on other things. You've got friends and family and work—especially work. Time heals, right?

Man, you are exhausted. But you've done well, you've rationalized the situation. Situation: is that what it was? Whatever you call it, bottom line is that really bad judgment resulted in an accident. An accident that no one witnessed and one that can never, EVER be traced to you.

Ruin the rest of your life? Not an option.

You'll be able to close your eyes, now. You've worked it out. You'll sleep.

Tomorrow's gonna be a big day.

29

Leander sat at the table, idly observing his parents as they prepared breakfast. Saturday mornings were a special time in their house since his daddy didn't have to go to work. This morning, however, the mood was particularly upbeat. Mama was trying her best not to laugh at Daddy as he danced around the kitchen keeping time to the radio while attempting to mix pancake batter. Every so often, he would bump into her or pause to nuzzle the back of her neck, only to be swatted with a dishtowel.

Leander had figured out quite some time ago that the soft moans and hushed whispers that emitted from his parents' bedroom late at night were the catalyst for their silly clowning around the next morning. He knew about sex—well, sort of. He had overheard his mama when she talked to his two sisters. "Messing" she'd called it.

"Now, messing is natural for men and women," she told them. But then her eyebrow shot up and her voice hardened. "But don't either one of you be bringing no woods colts in here for me to raise!" Leander had learned that *woods colts* were babies that got born when you weren't married.

Is that what had happened yesterday? But, if so, then how could he have called it an 'accident'?

These thoughts bounced around inside his head with no obvious direction as he continued to observe his parents' gaiety. Any other time, he would have joined in their antics, delighting in the knowledge that his world was safe and that nothing bad would ever happen. This morning, though, he knew that was no longer true, and the realization made him feel old and cheated.

"You ain't doing nothin' but making a big mess for me to have to clean up," Claire said, with mock seriousness.

Carl Lee froze, pretending shock. "*Ain't* doing nothing," he whispered loudly. "Such talk in front of the boy with the highest grades in the whole class! Shame, shame on you, Mama," he chastised.

"You are so right," Claire said, "shame on me. What I *meant* to say is, 'you *aren't* doing anything except making a big mess for me to clean up'. Am I forgiven, Professor?"

Leander studied his parents in silence for a long time. Finally, he said, "I'm not going today."

His parents stared at him in disbelief. Even Moam turned from her chair in front of the TV. "What did you say?" his mother asked.

"I said that I'm not going to the party."

Claire spoke sharply: "I *heard* what you said."

"Then if you heard what I said, why did you ask?"

"Oh," Claire bristled, "again with the mouth!"

"All right, now. Let's everybody take a deep breath." His father's voice was calm as he went on speaking. "Son, are you still feeling poorly?"

Leander answered, "I guess so."

"You guess so?" Claire questioned. "Leander, you are either sick or you're not sick. Which is it?" She gave him no time to answer, though, before firing another question in his direction. "Wait a minute. Did you and Gabrielle have an argument?"

"Of course not," Leander replied, each word deliberate, "I just do not want to go today." And with that, he stood up and walked into his bedroom, being careful not to let the door slam behind him.

Carl Lee watched his son leave the room. "I guess that's that."

"What's what?" Reva asked as she entered the kitchen, yawning and reaching for the coffee pot.

"Your brother says he don't want to go to the barbeque today, that's what," Claire said. "That boy has changed overnight."

Reva ignored her mother's words. "Hey, Daddy," she said, "it's okay if I ask Calvin to go with me today over to the barbeque, isn't it?"

Carl Lee stopped flipping pancakes and studied his daughter for a moment. "Calvin, who?" he asked.

"Calvin Owens," she said.

"Bubbie Owens' boy? Hell, no it ain't all right for him to go *anywhere* with you, much less to Mr. Will's house. That whole family's bad news, little girl, and you'd best steer clear of all of them." Carl Lee ended the subject as he and Claire began filling plates.

"Let's eat," Claire said. "Reva, I've got to get on over to the big house early, so you help Daddy with the dishes after we're done, please."

Reva dropped into a chair. "Calvin's nothing like his daddy, or the rest of his family for that matter. He's even trying to get in to trade school. He wants to be a plumber. So, why can't I ask him?"

"Because I said so," Carl Lee said. "Now, the subject is closed."

But the subject was far from closed. Reva's face contorted as she struggled to hold back the tide of tears. "It's not fair!" she wailed. "It's just not fair! I'm seventeen years old and I don't have no say in my own life! And Mama was already married to you when she was seventeen!" She stalked from the kitchen and let the back-door slam behind her.

Carl Lee rolled his eyes heavenward, and then followed his daughter outside. "Wait a minute, baby. Let's talk 'bout this," he called after her. "And your mama was practically eighteen..."

30

The gently sloping front lawn of the Remington mansion had been transformed into a park-like setting, complete with bouncy houses and clowns to entertain the toddlers, horseshoe pitching areas, a badminton court for the young people, and a bar with tables and chairs for the adults. Yes, the caterers had listened to Will when he had instructed them to provide something for everyone. This barbeque in Remy's honor would go down as the social event of the season.

"And why shouldn't it be a blowout?" Will had responded brusquely when Vivian had commented on the ballooning size of her son's birthday party. "It's not every day my grandson turns nineteen, and I want him to know how proud I am of him."

"Oh, he'll know it all right when he gets his present," Vivian said as she turned and walked toward the other side of the lawn to supervise the setup of the band.

"You haven't said a word about it, have you?" Will called after her.

Vivian called out over her shoulder: "Wouldn't dream of it."

She had abandoned long ago any effort to instill in her son a sense of accountability. However, thanks to Will, all she could hope for now was that Remy might meet a young woman who would steer him away from the materialistic world to which his grandfather had made him believe he was entitled.

But that was just another of her air castles. She felt certain that Remy was going to marry M'Lyn Olsen, possibly before the summer's end. What was it she found so distasteful about the girl? Claire had asked her that same question several weeks earlier.

"I have absolutely nothing against M'Lyn, Claire," she had replied. "Only that she is as needy and manipulative as my son. His marriage to her, I fear, would turn out to be as disheartening as…"

She hadn't finished the sentence. Claire had not pressed her to do so.

* * * * *

"I don't believe I've ever seen this many people in one place at one time, except at the state fair," Claire remarked to Vivian.

The two women sat at one of the tables, shaded by a large umbrella as they surveyed the grand scene before them. The front lawn was dotted with dozens of such tables. White-jacketed waiters wove their way among the crowd, offering glasses of champagne and mint juleps. The small band played selections to Will's liking as he moved from table to table, welcoming the guests, slapping backs, and doling out kisses and compliments to all the ladies.

Vivian knew she should be performing her duties as hostess, and she would soon begin to do so. But for a few more minutes, she was enjoying the company of her best friend. "Well, now!" she said. "Just look who came to the party, after all."

The two women watched as Gabrielle and Leander emerged from the path that led from the Washington home. The children walked hand-in-hand, Gaby grinning triumphantly and Leander walking with eyes downcast.

Vivian sighed. "My daughter can make *anybody* do *anything*, it seems. I do hope Leander's not truly sick. Most likely he just ate too many sweets. And look who else just arrived—my soon-to-be in-laws."

Claire looked at her. "Did I miss an announcement?"

"Not yet," Vivian replied. "But I don't think that it'll be very long. Just look at those two: can't keep their hands off each other. Mark my words, my boy will be a married man in no time at all. And I worry about him, Claire."

Claire remained silent for several minutes. She nodded toward Gabrielle and Leander, who had joined in a game of badminton with other children. "Your Gaby has the prettiest hair and skin I believe I've ever seen. And eyes, too. Her coloring is simply to die for."

"Yes, and how I envy her. She spends the entire summer outdoors and doesn't even get a freckle. And just look at me," Vivian shook her head and rubbed her arm. "I live under an umbrella, and I still get red and spotty."

"That's the price you pay for having that pretty red hair," Claire responded.

"Well, I'm just glad my children look like Gabe."

They enjoyed silence for a while before Claire said, "You say you worry about Remy, but do you ever worry about those two, Viv? Gaby and Leander, I mean?"

"Of course, I do," Vivian responded. "With all the crime and drugs nowadays, I worry about all the children coming up. It's so different than when you and I were young. Why, we didn't even know about drugs back then."

Claire turned to her. "What I meant to say is, do you ever worry that they might grow, you know, *too close?*" She hesitated before continuing. "Relationships are hard enough to make work without complicating things."

Vivian smiled. "Do I worry that their friendship might turn physical one day?" She shook her head. "No, Claire, that won't ever happen."

"How can you be so sure?"

Vivian's gaze wandered over the guests that had come to celebrate her son's birthday. She stood up and reached out her hand to her best friend. As the two women began to stroll across the lawn, she said, "Claire, Gaby and Leander are above anything physical. They each have what very few people in this world have, and that is one true friend."

Claire nodded. "Just like their mothers," she said. They watched as Gabrielle took a fall on the badminton court and Leander rushed from his position to help her up. "I just hope that nothing ever happens to tarnish that friendship."

31

✦ ✦ ✦ ✦ ✦

One step at a time. One hour at a time. Keep smiling. Keep saying all the right things. It's a party, so act like you're having a good time and you'll get through it. The day will end eventually, and then you can be alone. Tomorrow will come and the next day after that. The sun will still come up in the morning, and life will go on.

And this, too, shall pass.

Just look at all the folks that came. To be expected, though. Who wouldn't want to be included in the Remington and Weston family? Nobody, that's for sure.

Even Police Chief Beddingfield showed up to rub elbows with Antioch's elite. Hope you're not planning on driving home, Talmadge, seeing as how you've been tossing back the mint juleps ever since you got here. I wonder who's protecting the good citizens today, Chief. Oh, well, Antioch's not exactly the crime capital of the South, now, is it?

Nothing much happening outside of some slashed tires.

And a dead girl lying in the woods.

"Well, this certainly is a quiet group for a party. C'mon, Remy, let's go dance." M'Lyn tugged on his arm.

"I'm not up to dancing right now, sugar. Maybe later."

Her practiced pout emerged. "Alright, then. I guess Mason's the lucky guy. Let's liven this place up, Mason."

Mason flashed his dimpled smile and said, "My pleasure, darlin'. Let's show 'em how it's done."

Remy watched as the two of them walked hand in hand toward the band at the far end of the lawn. "Hey, you two!" he called out loudly. "No slow numbers!"

M'Lyn acknowledge him only with a tiny bit more wiggle in her walk. He felt his face flush as he shook his head and grinned. "Don't know what I'm going to do with that girl, Granddaddy," he said.

"How 'bout marrying her?" Will responded. "That would be my advice to you, son."

"Don't rush him, Will," Gabe admonished his father-in-law. "Remy's got plenty of time to settle down."

"You and my daughter didn't wait," Will flared. "Neither did I, come to think of it." He continued with his lecture. "Marry young, Remy, so you can enjoy your children and grandchildren." He chuckled and added, "And great-grandchildren."

Remy nodded. "I think I'll go rescue her right now from the evil clutches of my best friend."

When his son had left them, Gabe spoke quietly, "I really wish you wouldn't always do that, Will—challenge everything I say to him."

"Look who just got here," Will said, pointedly changing the subject. "I need to go talk with Kirby Marston. His company just bought Young's trucking and I want to make sure that the bank won't lose that account."

* * * * *

"I've been looking for you," Vivian said, entwining her arm with Gabe's.

He smiled at her but kept silent. Dusk was falling, yet plenty of light remained thanks to the landscape lighting and the dozens of colorful lanterns that had been strung from one end of the lawn to the other. "I've been mingling," he said finally. "The party's certainly a huge success. Are you having fun?"

"Oh, yes. And more importantly, Remy seems to be having fun."

Gabe inclined his head in the general direction of the wooden dance floor. "I'd say he's especially enjoying himself at this moment."

Vivian's gaze followed his. "Yes," she said wistfully, "our boy certainly seems to be smitten." They watched as Remy and M'Lyn, locked in a tight embrace, barely moved to the slow number the band was playing. "He was obviously depressed—almost angry—at dinner last night. It's good to see him smiling."

"We were all a little down last night," Gabe remarked. "Sorry about that."

Vivian turned toward him. "I'm the one who should be apologizing. Actually, I went looking for you yesterday afternoon to tell you how sorry I was." Her voice quivered. "The way I acted. Your gift was lovely, Gabe."

Gabe tensed up. "Looking for me where?" he asked.

"Rosie said she saw you walking toward The Ramble. I walked a short distance along the main path, but didn't see you."

"That's because I wasn't there. Rosie gets mixed up." Gabe's curt reply caused her to turn and look at him. He went on speaking. "Perhaps I should take you shopping for your own gifts from now on, my dear."

Vivian put her hand on his arm. "I love your gifts, Gabe. I'm sorry."

"Look, Will's about to make an announcement," he said. "Time for birthday cake and presents, I'm sure. What did you get for our son?"

"Ostrich boots," she answered. "And you?"

"A briefcase with his initials engraved on it."

"He'll be pleased."

Will stepped up to the mic on the bandstand. "Attention, everyone," his deep voice rang out. "Let's all move around to the patio at the back of the house and enjoy some of Remy's birthday cake." He paused, his smile now lighting up his entire face. "And, there might just be a surprise or two in the mix."

A chorus of shouts, handclapping, and even a rebel yell or two followed. As the crowd of partygoers began making their way to the back patio, Vivian turned to speak to her husband once more, but he was nowhere in sight.

32

Will urged the caterers to speed up the serving of cake and ice cream. Although there was plenty of artificial light, he didn't want darkness to fall completely before Remy's gift was brought out.

"Alright, people, let's speed it up! I want everybody done with their dessert and plates cleared in ten minutes," he snapped at the servers.

"We 'bout ready, Mr. Will?" Carl Lee asked.

"We are. Go on and bring her out." Will raised his hand and whistled for attention. "Don't worry, folks. I'm not going to make a speech," he said to laughter and a smattering of applause. "I just want to thank y'all for coming here today to honor my only grandson. Remy, come on over here."

Remy made his way through the cheering, back-slapping crowd to stand beside his grandfather.

Will motioned for the crowd to make room at the far side of the patio. "If you folks will move to your left, I'm going to ask Carl Lee to bring Remy's birthday present out." He paused briefly as the crowd shifted and an air of anticipation settled in. "I'm mighty proud of you, grandson," Will said with sincerity. "Happy Birthday!"

Everyone seemed to inhale at the exact same moment, only to explode with jubilation as Carl Lee slowly drove the gleaming, tangerine-colored Corvette from the shadow of the garage and into the circle of the cheering crowd.

* * * * *

Houston Crawford sat up in his makeshift bed, propped himself on one elbow, and listened to the latest round of hootin' and hollerin' from the direction of the big house beyond the trees. He had managed to drift off into a fitful sleep, but thanks to some fool setting off a bunch of fireworks, he was wide awake now. "Rich folks sure can carry on," he muttered under his breath.

He was hungry, anyway, and thanks to the contribution to his livelihood from a Good Samaritan who had passed him on the street earlier, Houston would now enjoy a veritable feast. He untied the plastic bag the cashier had handed him at the Majik Market a couple of hours earlier and removed his choice fare.

He popped open the now-warm beer and took half the can in one gulp. Next came the tin of smoked sardines, followed by a package of saltine crackers, surprisingly still fresh and crisp. A gooey cinnamon roll washed down by the remaining beer rounded out the menu.

Houston belched loudly, the thought coming to him that all those uppity folks at that party had not dined any better than he had tonight. He began to stuff trash and leftover crackers into his knapsack when his fingers met the smooth metal object. He flashed a yellow-toothed smile. "I 'most forgot 'bout the best part," he said. "An after-dinner drink, anyone?" He lifted his pinky finger and clowned a bit before removing the cap from the flask and taking a sip of the liquor. The half-pint of Maker's Mark that he'd lifted from a comrade in Hobo Jungle had lasted him a little over a week. That proved that he wasn't an alcoholic, didn't it?

As Houston sucked the last drop from the flask, the engraving on it caught his eye. In the dwindling twilight, he studied the words, tracing them with his finger: *To Corporal Houston McNair Crawford with deep gratitude. Capt. Merrill Hanson.* Captain had given all the guys in his outfit a little something when they had returned to the States from that hellhole—the few that *did* return, that is.

Houston treasured that little flask, just as he had treasured his time in the Army. He even had a few good memories of his stint in Viet Nam. After more than twenty years, he still did not understand the anger directed toward the soldiers who had fought in that war.

What was it the military doctors had said was the reason that he had to leave the Army? Post-traumatic stress or some such medical jargon. Some of the guys in his platoon had said he'd "acted up" right after that big battle, but Houston didn't remember acting any different than he always had. When he told them that he wanted to stay in the Army, they just shook their heads, gave him some pills, and said they were thankful for his service to America and that he could go home.

Home. Houston looked around him. He sat crossed legged on the piece of tarpaulin that afforded him meager protection from the dampness of the ground. His possessions—a blanket, his Army fatigue jacket, hat, and knapsack—lay nearby.

The densely wooded area into which he had wandered earlier to escape any human contact had grown completely dark. Since his flashlight batteries were weak and needed to be saved for an emergency, he decided that this was as good a place as any to lay his head for the night. The wadded-up blanket became a pillow, and soon he began to drift into sleep.

The sound of another round of firecrackers floated over him, causing him to frown as long-suppressed memories began to worm their way into his subconscious. The clamor that only a short time earlier had seemed so harmless was suddenly transformed into exploding mortars, illuminating a garish spectacle of carnage that polluted jungles and rice fields. The muted sounds of merriment that erupted occasionally from the party across the way had become distorted into the agonizing shrieks of his wounded and dying comrades.

Houston fought against the shaking that wracked his puny body. He no longer lay on his makeshift bed, but sat hunched into a ball, his back pressed hard against a tree trunk, his arms hugging his legs in an effort to quell the trembling.

"S-s-shouldn't have come here," his ragged whisper brought him back to the present. But the present offered no consolation. He thought of the countless nights spent in the same way as this—eyes wide open, yet seeing nothing in a night-blackened forest, ears straining to catch the sound of even one twig breaking.

Houston's eyes ached. He closed them and tried to shut off the memories. He was an old man now, and his war had been fought a lifetime ago. As the years passed, he had managed to put most of it behind him.

There were some days when he didn't think about being *over there* at all. Even so, he had never been able to exorcize the prickle of fear that would crawl up his spine whenever death was nearby.

He felt it now.

33

"How about it, good buddy? You up for the first ride?"

Mason studied his friend. He had never seen Remy so charged. And who could blame him? His Mazda paled in comparison, especially it its current state. Mason squashed the rising tide of envy that had begun to crest. After all, this was Remy's night, and Remy was his best friend. He smiled and answered, "Man, maybe we'd better wait 'til tomorrow. You've been hitting the sauce a little heavy all evening. We wouldn't want to have *both* our new rides in the shop, now, would we?"

"Good advice," Will said as he joined the group of young people circling the car, oohing and aahing but not daring to touch it. "I'd rather not have it smashed up on its inaugural trip—you boys either," he added.

Remy nodded. "You're absolutely right, Granddaddy." His mile-wide grin faded, and a more serious expression crossed his face. "How can I *ever* thank you? I-I never expected this." His voice quivered. "You're the best, Granddaddy!" As he grabbed the older man in a bear hug, his sobs were audible. "I don't deserve it."

Will was not a man to give in to emotion. Gruffly, he pushed Remy back and held him at arm's length. "What the hell are you talking about? Of course, you deserve the car, and a whole lot more than that."

Remy wiped his eyes with the back of his hand and reached out to embrace a smiling M'Lyn, who had just sidled up next to him. He sniffed and said, "What'cha think, babe? Is this good enough to chauffeur the prettiest girl in Antioch?"

"How about me, Remy?" Gabrielle asked, squealing and jumping up and down with excitement. "When can I go for a ride?"

134

Remy reached out and playfully tugged his little sister's hair. "Tomorrow, for sure," he told her. "Matter of fact, you'll get the second ride. How's that sound?"

"Great!" she answered, her face aglow with happiness.

At Will's direction, the crowd surrounding the Corvette began to wander away towards the bar and the table laden with brightly wrapped gifts. "Alright, folks," he said, "the party ain't over yet. Our birthday boy has got lots of presents to unwrap."

Mason tossed back the remaining bourbon in his cup. He jostled Gabrielle and winked at her, saying, "When my new car gets out of the shop, I'm gonna take you riding first thing. And," he bent down and lowered his voice, "I happen to think that *you're* the prettiest girl in Antioch."

Gabrielle felt the blood rise to her cheeks as she dropped her eyes to the ground. "Come on, Leander," she said to the silent boy beside her, "let's go find a good place at the gift table."

When the children had left, Remy motioned M'Lyn to go on ahead. He turned to Mason and said, "Look, man, I know you like 'em young, but Gaby's off limits."

Mason's brash little grin melted into disbelief. "You're making a joke, right?" Met with Remy's stoic silence, he shook his head. "First of all, I can't believe you'd even *think* I meant anything other than giving Gaby some attention. For God's sake, man, she's a little kid!"

Mason turned to walk away, then retraced his steps. "And secondly," he said as he reached into his shirt pocket and produced an envelope, which he slapped roughly against his friend's chest. "Happy birthday, dickhead."

Remy barely caught the envelope before it fell to the ground. He opened it and chuckled as he studied the contents. "Wow," he said. "I've been talking about going to a Braves game this summer—guess you finally got the hint."

Mason shrugged. "Yeah, I thought we'd do Atlanta one weekend." He pointed to the tickets. "That's supposed to be a really good game."

"Thanks, man," Remy said and held out his hand. "I'm sorry. I don't know why I said anything so fucking dumb. I guess I'm just a little overwhelmed right now with everything."

Mason nodded and grasped his friend's hand. "And you're a little drunk, too. No worries. By the way," he said as the two men began to make their way to the gift table, "when we go to Atlanta, you're driving."

"My pleasure," Remy responded, glancing back at his Corvette. As he turned back to his friend, a frown crossed his face. "Hey, wait a minute."

"What's wrong, now?"

"Where's your key?" Remy asked. "I never see you without it."

Mason raised his hand to his neck. His fraternity key on its gold chain was gone. "I-I don't know," he stammered. "I haven't even missed it. Oh, man, you know what? I took a dip in the creek yesterday on my way here. It must have come off in the water."

"Well, if you did lose it in Dalton's Creek, that's too bad," Remy said as they arrived at the table laden with his birthday loot. "'Cause you won't ever find it in that water."

Mason nodded his head mutely. *That had to be where I lost it.*

34

Talmadge Beddingfield sat behind his desk and stared blandly at his clerk. He had a headache—a hangover, actually—thanks to the open bar at Remy Westin's birthday party the night before. He didn't feel up to being in the office on a Sunday morning, and he certainly didn't feel like taking any phone calls, especially one as potentially distressing as this one.

"Well, Chief," Fran pointed to the blinking red light on his telephone and prodded. "Do you want to talk to Jerome Simpson or not?"

Talmadge closed his eyes and counted silently to ten. Then he took a deep breath, which usually worked in calming himself down before he bit somebody's head off. Usually.

"No, Fran, I do not *want* to talk to Jerome. I don't have anything to say to him that I didn't say to him Friday night, or that you didn't say to him yesterday: namely, that we wait forty-eight hours before considering somebody to be a missing person. Why is that? Because that gives the person time to come back home, which is the typical outcome."

He paused and took another deep breath. "However, since you've already told him that I'm in the office, I suppose I *have* to talk to him."

Fran raised her eyebrows. "Chief, it's his granddaughter. It's a kid."

Talmadge surrendered and picked up the receiver. "Good morning, Curley," he said. "Any news?"

"No news, Chief. But I got a list of her friends at school and the church. I was hoping you could start with that and ask maybe has somebody seen or heard from her."

Talmadge listened as the older man's voice broke. "I tell you what, Curley," he said, "you come on down here to the station and bring that list.

When my deputies come in this afternoon, we'll start a search. How's that sound?"

"Thank you, Chief; that sounds real good. I'll tell Tavish. She's about to worry herself to death, you know. That girl, she's everything to us."

"I know that. I'll see you soon, Curley."

"She probably just got caught up with some of her friends and lost track of time," Fran speculated as she turned and walked back to her desk. "Knows she's gonna get yelled at, so now she's too scared to come home."

Talmadge closed his eyes again and began to count. "Or not," he muttered to himself.

* * * * *

Vivian stepped onto the front veranda, closing the French doors behind her. "Good morning, Gabe. I just helped Rosie set up a breakfast buffet in the dining room, if you're interested," she said.

"Thanks," her husband replied. "I'm still stuffed from last night." He stood up from the chaise lounge and stretched. "I could do with some coffee, though."

"Stay here. I'll bring it out," she said. Her gaze fell to the floor beside the chaise, and a quizzical expression settled on her face. Her husband's shoes sat beside a half-empty bottle of bourbon. She suddenly realized that he was wearing the same shirt and slacks that he'd worn the night before.

"Gabe, did you sleep out here last night?"

"Yeah, I did. You know," he hesitated and shrugged his shoulders. "With the excitement from the party and all, I was a little keyed up. Just thought I'd sit out here a bit and relax. Dozed off, I guess. Rather pleasant, actually." He turned away from her.

"Well, then," she said after a brief silence, "I'll just go and get our coffee."

She wanted to ask him why he was being so evasive. And she yearned to know the reason he'd been out walking so late the night before last, and why it appeared that he'd been crying. She would give anything to be a part of his thoughts. If only he would just talk to her. But that would take effort on both their parts. Right now, it was easier—and much safer—to simply go and get the coffee.

Vivian returned to the veranda just as Remy and Mason came cruising up the driveway in the tangerine Corvette. Remy brought the car to a gentle stop. He sounded the horn for several seconds before shutting off the engine and nimbly hopping out over the closed door. Mason followed suit, and both young men jogged up the front steps, grinning from ear to ear.

"Ain't she a beauty?" Remy exclaimed. "I still can't believe it's mine."

"What I can't believe is that the two of you are up and about this early," Vivian said as she hugged her son. "When I went upstairs, it was after 1 a.m., and the party was still going strong."

Remy laughed. "Yeah, I'm thinking we're both gonna crash before long. Had to make good on my promise, though, that Mason got the first ride." He punched his friend playfully on the shoulder and added, "After all, I got the first ride in his new car."

"And here comes the honoree for the second ride," Mason exclaimed as Gabrielle came bounding and squealing around the corner of the house. Leander followed behind her sedately, carrying two fishing poles and a plastic bucket.

"Here you go, princess," Remy said as he lifted his sister over the door and into the convertible's front passenger seat. "How does that feel?"

Gabrielle was in awe. "Feels like I really *am* a princess," she exclaimed to everyone's delight. "C'mon, Leander, you can get in behind the seat, and Remy can drive us down to the creek."

Leander shook his head. "No, thanks. I'll just walk 'cause I've got these poles and the bait."

"No problem," Remy said. "That's the good part about a convertible. You just climb on in and hold the fishing poles straight up."

"I-I'd rather walk," the boy said. "I'll ride some other time."

"Nonsense," Mason intervened. "Here, let me help you, Leander."

Leander recoiled at the touch of Mason's hand on his shoulder. "I don't want to ride now," he said much louder than he'd meant to. He backed away a few steps, aware that all eyes were on him. "I'd just rather walk this morning. Thanks, anyway, Remy."

"Suit yourself," Gabrielle called out. I'll see you at our fishing spot in a few minutes."

* * * * *

Leander waved and began walking down the drive. He was embarrassed. Why hadn't he simply climbed into Remy's car and ridden in silence, instead of calling attention to himself? Because if he had, he might not have been able to keep his current nausea at bay. Throwing up in the new car was unthinkable.

He had endured another dreadful night, allowing his eyes to close only briefly in periods of sporadic and disturbing sleep. And he was starving. The mere thought of food in his mouth, though, caused his stomach to heave. He took a deep breath and decided to use the remaining time it would take him to reach Dalton's Creek to try and get a grip on his emotions.

So many questions plagued him. How long could he live with his terrible secret? How long would he be able to continue lying to his parents, to Mr. Jerome, to Gaby? Could he live with the fact that he was a liar? He considered his only other option. If he told them everything that he had seen and heard, he would have a clear conscious. But then, everyone would know what *he* had done to her, and the police would come, and Gaby's family would never be the same. *Because a young girl died!*

And what if Gaby were to blame him for telling and ended up hating him? Could he live with that?

He reached his destination and saw her sitting cross-legged on the stone bench beside the path that led to the creek.

"There you are. Let's go catch some fish," she said.

"Where are the guys?" Leander asked.

"They're off to M'Lyn's house," Gaby answered. She took the fishing poles from him and headed toward the creek.

"You didn't want to go riding with them?"

She turned to him, grinned, and reached for his hand. "Naw," she said. "I'd much rather spend the day right here with you."

It seemed to Leander that he had his answer.

35

"I cannot believe you would even think such a thing, Curley, much less say it to my face." Talmadge's tone had morphed from empathy to irritated disbelief. "I guess you done forgot that my daddy and yours worked alongside one another for twenty years, shoveling tar into potholes for the highway department. We go way back, and now you accuse me of being prejudiced."

"I'm not accusing anybody of anything," Curley interrupted. "Just sayin' that, if it was a white girl from a wealthy family 'round these parts, y'all would have done started looking for her." His voice broke, signaling another wave of grief—one that Talmadge feared might be warranted.

The brief silence in the police chief's office served to calm both of them. Talmadge spoke first. "You know me better than that, Curley. Fran!" he called out loudly, "Come get this list and make a bunch of copies, please."

"How many deputies you got coming in this afternoon?" Curley asked.

"Only two today, being that it's Sunday. But all five will be here first thing tomorrow morning. We'll start contacting her friends right away."

"And a search?" Curley prodded.

"And a search," Talmadge echoed. "Where we start that search will depend on anything her friends can tell us, where they saw her last, and so on."

Curley nodded his head and rose from his chair. "Thank you, Chief. I'd best get on back home. Tavish is by herself."

"You got anybody that can come stay with you and help?"

"I've got a niece over in Traveler's Rest. She supposed to be here tonight. I'll open the store tomorrow morning as usual," he voiced his thoughts aloud. He seemed to regain a measure of composure as he straightened his shoulders and met Talmadge's gaze squarely. "Tawney would not run off, Chief."

"We'll find her, Curley."

* * * * *

"Oh, Daddy!" Vivian gasped and raised a hand to her chest. "You startled me. What in the world are you doing sitting in here with the drapes closed? You can't see a thing." She moved to the tall windows and pushed back the heavy damask fabric, allowing the afternoon sunlight to permeate the room.

Will's expression held little pleasure as he watched his daughter's movements. He sat in the leather chair behind his desk, elbows resting on the padded armrests, his hands clasped loosely and lying on his lap. He had not moved from this position since before she had burst through the closed door and interrupted his thoughts. He cleared his throat and spoke quietly, with no emotion.

"This is my study, daughter. I believe that I have every right to sit in here whenever I wish and under any circumstances that I wish."

"Well, of course you do, and I'm sorry that I disturbed you," she apologized. "I thought you were meeting with a client down at the bank."

Still, Will did not move. "I'm meeting with him tomorrow," he said. "Did you want something?"

"As I said, I didn't know you were home. I came in to straighten up your study." She hesitated. "I can do that another time."

"The house is quiet," Will said. "Where is everyone?"

"Gabe went upstairs to lie down. The boys are, no surprise, out in the Corvette, and Gabrielle went fishing with Leander." She flicked at a speck of dust on his desk when her eyes fell on the empty watch case.

"Where's your pocket watch, Daddy? You always keep it in its case."

"Took it out a day or so ago," he replied. "Why?"

"I thought maybe you'd given it to Remy."

"I *said* that I would give the watch to Remy, Vivian, and I will. When I choose to do so."

Vivian hesitated. "Daddy, is anything bothering you?"

"Close the drapes before you go, please."

* * * * *

Deputy Fred Bell tapped on Talmadge's open office door, then entered without invitation. "Hey, Chief, we got a guy out here says he needs to talk to the man in charge. I'm guessing that'd be you." Fred jerked his head in the direction of the waiting room. "You're gonna want to talk to him."

Talmadge turned from the report he'd been writing in his log. "Yeah, who is it?" he asked. "And what's it about? Do you know?"

"Well, first off, he looks like one of those street people. Them that live under the old bridge, or wherever. You're gonna want to talk to him."

Fred's attention span was limited, Talmadge knew. "Okay, so he's homeless," the chief prodded. He craned his neck and tried to see around his office wall to catch a glimpse of the man. "How bad is he?"

Oh, you know," Fred answered, "they all smell like dirty socks and cheap booze. This one's not too bad, though. You need to talk to him, Chief."

"That three times that you've said that, Fred." Talmadge wondered how much longer it would take his young deputy to get to the point. "Suppose you tell me *why* I need to talk to him."

"'Cause," Fred replied, "he says he knows where there's a dead body."

36

Gabrielle had remained silent just about as long as she could. She began to fidget, and a frown creased her forehead. She and Leander had been sitting side by side on the creek bank for what seemed like an hour, and he had not spoken. Any other time, she thought, he would have been jabbering on and on about why moss grows on the north side of trees and why spiders are beneficial and shouldn't be killed and other such stuff that was in their science book, though she didn't remember reading about any of it. She drew a deep breath, then exhaled loudly.

"Is something wrong?" the boy asked.

Gabrielle shrugged. "I don't know. Are you mad at me?"

Leander turned to look at her in amazement. "I'm not mad at you," he said. "And why would you think that?"

"'Cause you ain't said a word since we got here. You're not still feeling sick, are you?"

His eyes left her face and returned to stare at the float on his fishing line. "I'm waiting for a bite. That's all."

Gabrielle stole a glance at her friend. *He didn't even correct me for saying ain't!* After several minutes passed, she said, "I guess they're not biting today. You want to go swimming?"

"Sure," Leander answered. He stood up and began to reel in his line when suddenly the end of the pole bent, and the float disappeared under water. "Look! I got a big one!" he shouted.

A short time later, she watched as he removed the hook and placed the brown trout in the bucket. "Wow," she exclaimed, "another one like this and we got ourselves supper."

Leander laughed. "You say that like we don't have anything else to eat. What about all the food left over from last night?"

"This is different," she answered. "Doing something for ourselves is important."

"Of course, it is. But what made you think of that?"

"Well, last night I heard Daddy and Granddaddy sort of arguing."

"Sort of?"

"Yeah, Daddy said that if Granddaddy kept on doing everything for Remy that he was never going to learn to do anything for himself. He was talking about the Corvette. Said that it was way too much, and that Granddaddy should have talked about it with him and Mama first."

"What did Mr. Will say to that?"

"He said it was none of their goddamn business."

"Gaby, you shouldn't talk like that!"

"Well, you asked me what he said, and I just told you. Anyway, I hate it when they argue. It makes me so sad when my family gets mad at each other. But," she added, "I'm glad *you're* not mad at *me*."

"I'll never get mad at you," he said reassuringly as he laid his hand on her shoulder. "Everything will be okay. I promise."

She sniffed. "How can you be sure?"

"Because," he boasted, "I'm your blood brother, and I'll make everything okay." A second later, he grinned and pointed toward the water as Gabrielle's float disappeared under the surface. "Now it's your turn to catch supper."

* * * * *

Talmadge counted himself lucky. During his fourteen years in law enforcement, he had not been weighed down by 'big city' crimes. Weekend bar fights, breaking and entering charges, and domestic spats were what he customarily dealt with. Even though the past few years had seen a growing number of drug-related incidents find their way to the small town of Antioch, all-in-all, his tenure as Police Chief could be labeled as uneventful. He now feared that his luck was about to run out.

After listening to Houston Crawford nervously recount his night spent in The Ramble, Talmadge had immediately telephoned his off-duty deputies to report to the station, pronto. He had picked up the phone three times to summon the coroner's office, changing his mind each time. No need to jump the gun. After all, he wasn't dealing with the most reliable of witnesses. Crawford even said it was just barely dawn when he saw it. Hell, what if the old bum had only seen a log or a dead animal and started hallucinating? But the gnawing in his gut had brought Talmadge and his men to their present location.

"Did you talk to Mr. Will, Fred?" the chief asked as he stepped from his car. He was immediately swallowed up in the afternoon heat and humidity, not to mention the cloud of dust churned up by other official vehicles that had converged along the gravel road.

"I didn't see Mr. Will, but I told Mrs. Westin that we would be on their property 'cause we were conducting a search for a missing person," the deputy repeated his memorized statement to the letter.

"You didn't say anything about what Crawford told us, did you?"

Fred shook his head emphatically. "I didn't say one word about what he said he seen."

Talmadge nodded. He had delayed long enough. As he stood gazing into the deceptively idyllic scene of The Ramble's entrance, the knot in his belly began to grow. "Let's get it over with," he muttered to himself. He waved his arm, and another deputy escorted Houston to the Chief's side. "Alright now, Houston," he said. "It's your show."

37

C at Morrison straightened up from her close examination of the body lying on the slab. Placing both hands on the small of her back, she massaged away the stiffness that had gotten worse since her fortieth birthday eleven months ago. If only the image in her mind were that easy to alleviate.

The young girl's body had been stripped, carefully examined, and photographed. She had then been covered up to her chin with a white sheet before being identified by her next of kin.

Cat reached for the retractable microphone that hung suspended from the ceiling in front of her and adjusted it to the desired position. After closing her eyes for a moment to gather her thoughts, she cleared her throat, switched the mic to *on*, and began to speak.

"This is Dr. Catherine Morrison, Medical Examiner, Antioch, South Carolina. The date is Monday, May 31, 1999, and the time is 9:45 a.m. I am about to begin my post-mortem examination of an African-American prepubescent female, age twelve, previously identified by…" She paused, switched off the mic and flipped through her notebook, then resumed her dictation. "By the next of kin, grandfather Jerome Simpson, as Tawney Theresa Simpson."

At the sound of the wide, stainless-steel double doors opening behind her, she stopped her dictation and switched off the mic once more. "Come on in, Talmadge. I'm just getting started," she said.

He hung his jacket and cap on the hook by the door, wiped a hand over his bald head and walked to her side. Cat noticed that his brown eyes were bloodshot as he looked into hers and smiled weakly. "Don't mean to bother you. I just got back from driving Curley and Tavish back home and wondered if you've found anything yet."

"How are they? The Simpsons?"

"Like you'd expect. Pitiful, just pitiful." He inclined his head toward the table. "She was their whole world. Tavish don't look like she'll make it another day."

Talmadge stepped closer to her, prompting Cat to sniff loudly and glare up at him. "Is it really necessary for you to stuff an entire jar of Vick's up your nose when you come into my lab?" she groused. "I've told you over and over that my job depends on the use of *all* of my senses, including my sense of smell which, thanks to you, is now totally useless because I can only smell Vick's salve!"

"Sorry. Only way I can get past the odor in here. What'cha got?" he said, brushing off her censure.

"It's a morgue—deal with it," Cat muttered before turning back to her exam table. "This exam," she said, "is just the prelude to the autopsy, which I don't believe will need to be very detailed."

"So, you think you know how she died?"

"Won't be able to say the *exact* cause and manner of death 'til the autopsy itself," she answered. "But I'm pretty sure I'll find an unusually high white blood cell count. Probably observe a significant amount of pus on the walls of the airways. I'm betting on asthma exacerbation."

"English, please."

She turned to face him. "More than likely, she suffered an asthma attack, and her airways became irritated and swollen. She would have felt like she needed more air, but the harder she tried to breathe in, the more swollen her airways became. Eventually, it became impossible for her to get enough oxygen to fill her lungs." She fell silent and shook her head sadly. "In English—this girl died by asphyxiation."

"What else?"

Cat turned back to her exam table. "Because of the extended amount of time the body was exposed to the elements, there's little trace evidence left. Animals, you know."

"Was she sexually assaulted?" Talmadge asked.

She hesitated. "I don't exactly know how to answer that, Talmadge," she replied, her voice faltering. "She had minor scratches, but those could have been gotten simply from walking through the woods. And as for the discoloration on her right abdomen, her grandfather said she bumped into a counter at his store on Friday. There are no defensive wounds, like skin under her fingernails or lacerations, but…"

"But?" he prompted.

"She had sexual intercourse shortly before she died. Cursory examination did indicate minor tearing in the vaginal area. Probably find semen during the autopsy. Don't quote me," she instructed, pointing a finger at him, "but it was probably consensual sex. That's statutory rape, nevertheless. I'm sure you're checking on a boyfriend." Cat shook her head sadly. "God, Talmadge, she was *twelve years old!*"

"We're checking on all her friends. Curley was certain she didn't have a boyfriend, but you know how that goes," Talmadge said. He patted her shoulder gently and turned to leave. "Okay if I come over tonight?"

"Not a very good idea," she replied. "I'm probably going to be lousy company after this."

"We could be lousy together. How 'bout eight o'clock? I'll bring pizza. Celebrate Memorial Day," he pleaded his case.

She grunted her agreement. He had almost reached the stainless-steel double doors when she called out: "I believe that someone else dressed her, possibly after she was already dead."

Talmadge turned around. "Yeah, what makes you say that?"

"Because her shorts were on backwards."

38

Tate Jones sat quietly and respectfully before him as Talmadge instructed him on how to conduct this morning's interviews.

"How come you want me to interview the whole family, Chief?" Tate asked. "Don't you think it'd be better if several of us deputies were to talk to each person, and then compare notes?"

"No, I do not think that would be better," Talmadge replied curtly. "And, you won't be interviewing the whole family. I'm going to be talking with Vivian Westin, and Deputy Carson will speak with the little girl, Gabrielle, 'cause she's a woman and has a daughter around the same age."

Talmadge straightened the stack of papers on his desk. He tried to hide the irritation that had crept into his voice, but it was difficult. "The reason I want you to interview the rest of the Remington family is because you're my Liaison Officer, and it's your job. You know these folks, so what's your problem?"

Tate shrugged. "I know Gabe and Vivian, since we all went to school together. Just know their son when I see him. I've seen the Carlisle boy over the years, but I don't believe I've ever actually met him."

Tate hesitated before he went on: "Chief, my dad used to work for old man Remington as a janitor down at the bank. When Pop got sick with lung cancer, that sonofabitch fired him. I'd rather not have to talk to him."

"I'm sorry, Tate," Talmadge said, "but you got to keep personal feelings out of this office. Like I said, you're my Liaison Officer. I'm counting on you to do your job."

"Yessir, Chief. Can you tell me what I'm supposed to ask them about?"

"You ask them the same questions that you would ask anybody else that had a dead body found on their property. Ask did they know the deceased or

"

her family. Ask did they see her last Friday afternoon, and if so, was she with anybody." Talmadge's level of frustration rose as he counted off the points of discussion on his fingers. "Unfortunately, you also got to ask everybody to account for their whereabouts between two-thirty and five-thirty on Friday afternoon. Now, you think you can do that?"

"Yes, Chief," Tate said. "I can do that."

"Good. Now, let's get the conference room set up. Be sure and inform everybody that you're recording their conversation." Talmadge stood up in preparation to leave his office when Tate stopped him.

"Chief, just what exactly is a Liaison Officer?"

"That's easy, Tate," Talmadge replied with a dry chuckle. "That's somebody who does a job that I don't want to do."

* * * * *

If there was one thing Tate Jones had learned during his years in law enforcement, it was to be prepared. So, when the time for his first interview of the day drew near, he was ready. At least, he was as ready as he would ever be. He wrote the name of the person he would interview first in his notebook, and then underlined it: <u>William Remington</u>. He stood up from his chair as the conference room door opened.

"Well, well," the old man greeted him. "If it isn't young Tater himself."

Tate made direct eye contact with Will, hoping the sardonic smile that he'd practiced in front of the bathroom mirror equaled that of the other man's smirk. "Morning, Mr. Will," he said. "I hope you're well today. Thank you for coming in. Our conversation will be recorded, and I'll make my questions as brief as possible." He removed the tape recorder from its case, set it on the conference table between them, and resumed speaking. "Our office realizes that you're a very busy man, and we appreciate your taking the time to talk to us."

Will's smile grew wider and his eyebrows shot up. "How professional you sound, Tater. I'm impressed."

"It's *Tate*, sir." His gaze did not waver from Will's face. *Just let me get through this without punching the old fucker's lights out!* He switched the recorder on and spoke into the microphone with what he prayed would be a voice free of its childhood stutter.

"This is Deputy Tate Jones, Antioch Police Department, conducting an informal interview with Mr. William Remington. This conversation is conducted strictly to determine if Mr. Remington saw anything or anyone suspicious on the afternoon of Friday, May 28, 1999, between the hours of approximately two-thirty p.m. and five-thirty p.m., that might shed light on the death of twelve-year-old Tawney Simpson, whose body was found in a wooded area on the Remington property, commonly referred to as 'The Ramble'."

Tate paused, folded his hands, and began his questioning. "Mr. Will, did you see the young girl that I just spoke about, Tawney Simpson, on the afternoon in question?"

"No, I did not. I do not know the girl," Will replied flatly.

"Do you know of anyone who might want to harm Tawney?"

Will stared at him blandly. "I told you that I do not know the girl, so no, I don't know anyone that might want to harm her."

"Did you see anyone, including members of your family, in the area of The Ramble last Friday?"

"No."

"Where were you last Friday afternoon, Mr. Will?"

"Me?" Will's eyes narrowed and he appeared insulted. "I was at *my* home. On *my* property."

Tate let the sarcasm pass. "Did you at any time go into the area of The Ramble?"

Tate noticed the other man's face redden slightly, although his expression remained closed. After several seconds of strained silence, he repeated his question. "Mr. Will, did you at any time last Friday afternoon go into the area of The Ramble?"

"No, I did not. Are we finished here?"

Tate realized that he had, in fact, relaxed during the brief questioning. He also realized that he was rather enjoying being the one in charge. "We're not quite finished, sir. Did you happen to see or hear anything suspicious later that evening, say around eleven p.m. or so, when you were driving home?" The reaction that he hoped his question would invoke did not materialize. Instead, Will seemed to take the deputy's knowledge of his whereabouts in stride.

Will struck a pensive pose, seemingly deep in thought. "Friday night, around eleven? Let's see. I don't..." his words evaporated, only to return with clarity. "Ahh, yes, now I remember. I left Belle Fontenot's house shortly before eleven that night. So, I guess I arrived home about fifteen or twenty minutes later." His smile grew wide, his manner and tone of voice conveying complete openness. "It was dark, but I know just about every foot of my property. I neither saw nor heard anything out of the ordinary."

Tate took a few moments to jot down unnecessary notes in his notebook. "Thank you again for coming in, Mr. Will. If you think of anything that might be helpful, please let us know."

Will nodded as he stood up, his smile still in place, and left the conference room without another word.

39

T ate turned the page in his notebook and wrote <u>Gabe Westin</u>.

"It's always good to see you, Gabe," Tate said as he met the other man at the door and extended his hand. "Sorry it has to be under these circumstances, though. Thanks for coming in."

Gabe slapped the other man on the back and moved to quickly sit in the chair across the table from him. "How've you been, Tate?" he asked.

The deputy dropped his hand to his side. *That's odd. I guess some people just choose not to shake hands.* "I'm doing fine, Gabe, thanks for asking." He took his seat and moved the recorder to the center of the table between them. "Our conversation will be recorded. Let's get started.

"As you know, the body of twelve-year-old Tawney Simpson was found in The Ramble Sunday afternoon. Were you acquainted with her or her grandfather, Jerome Simpson?"

Gabe shook his head.

"Would you give a verbal answer, Gabe? Please."

"Sorry. I didn't know the girl. I know where her granddaddy's store is, but I've never been there. Terrible thing."

"Yes, it is," Tate said. "Where were you, Gabe, on Friday between the hours of 2:30 and 5:30 p.m.? Approximate."

Gabe hesitated, then said, "I-I don't exactly know. I was around the house during lunch. I went for a walk." He was vague, and Tate waited. After a time, Gabe continued. "I might have been down at Dalton's Creek about that time, but I can't say for sure. Why?"

"That's the time frame that the Medical Examiner has given for the girl's death." Tate responded matter-of-factly. "Now then, Gabe, during your walk, did you happen to go into the Ramble?"

"No, I didn't."

Tate made notations in his book and purposefully kept silent. After a time, he looked up from his notebook and met Gabe's gaze. "You sure about that?"

"I might have thought about it, or maybe started to cut through The Ramble, but no, no, I didn't. No."

"Did you see anyone else during your walk?"

"No. There's usually a bunch of kids playing around there this time of year, but I don't remember seeing anybody on Friday."

Tate leaned back in his chair and smiled. "Thanks again for coming in, Gabe."

"That's it?" Gabe asked, seemingly surprised.

"Since you didn't go into the Ramble at all, you couldn't have seen or heard anyone, could you? If anything comes to mind, though, be sure to give us a call."

"Sure will, Tate. This is terrible. Any leads?"

"We're working on it."

* * * * *

"Good morning, Mr. Carlisle. Okay if I call you Mason?"

"Of course," Mason replied, extending his hand. His presence immediately conveyed respectful consideration. Maybe this interview could progress more positively than the earlier ones consisting of Will's arrogance and Gabe's puzzling detachment. Tate turned the page in his book and labeled it <u>Mason Carlisle</u>.

Mason spoke first. "What a start to the summer, huh?" he said, shaking his head. "What exactly happened to that girl, Deputy Jones?"

"We're still waiting on the medical examiner's official report," Tate answered. He cleared his throat and switched on the microphone. "Our conversation will be recorded. As you know, we're talking with everyone at the Remington house to see if anyone saw anything out of the ordinary last Friday afternoon. Did *you*, Mason?"

"Did I what?"

"See anything suspicious in the area of The Ramble?" Tate clarified.

Mason leaned back in his chair, narrowed his eyes, and pondered the question. After a few moments, he shook his head, "No, sir," he replied, "I didn't see anything or anyone that might be considered threatening. I took a swim in the creek on my way from town to the house, and I didn't see anyone at all."

Tate scribbled notes in his book and remained silent. He had the feeling that the less he talked the more Mason Carlisle would. His hunch proved correct.

"I did see that poor girl—Tawney, right? I saw her earlier in the day at her granddaddy's store. Of course, I didn't know who they were at the time. Seemed like real nice folks. I just stopped in to get a bite of lunch. Whew," he exhaled as a sad expression settled on his face. "Young girl like that. You just never know, do you? I mean, when a person's time is going to come—we just never know."

"That's right, Mason," Tate said. "We never know. "And, it's especially sad—brutal, actually—when a person's time comes at twelve years of age."

Tate changed the direction of the conversation. "I heard about your tires getting cut up. Man, that's a bad deal. You got any idea why that might've happened?"

"None," Mason said. "I didn't even report it. You know, nobody's going to talk, so what's the use? Mr. Jesse's putting new ones on, and it'll be good as new." He shrugged and smiled. "We get over things. We move on, right, Deputy?"

"Mmm," Tate mumbled, scribbling more notes. "I'm not so sure the Simpsons are going to be able to *move on* after this." Abruptly, he sat straight up in his chair, placed his elbows on the table, and locked eyes with the other man. "Tell me, Mason, exactly what were you doing in that part of town? When you went into Mr. Simpson's store, I mean?"

"Nothing in particular," Mason said. "Just driving around town, enjoying my new car, I guess. I dropped Remy Westin off at his girlfriend's house earlier for lunch. Killing time, you know."

"Killing time in *that* part of town? That could be dangerous." Tate paused and raised his eyebrows. "Turns out, it *was* dangerous, wasn't it?"

Mason smirked. "Like I said, we move on."

"Did you see anyone else while you were killing time last Friday?" Tate asked, getting back to the business at hand.

A shadow of a smile crossed the young man's face as he answered unabashedly. "I had a brief—how shall I say it—business encounter with a young lady before I stopped at Mr. Simpson's."

"What did she look like?"

Mason smiled wanly. "Hard to tell with all the makeup she had on. She was young, dark-skinned—rather pretty, I'd say."

"Did the young lady have a name?"

"I'm quite sure she did," Mason said, growing increasingly glib and relaxed. "But I failed to ask her name. You know how it is."

Tate reached over and switched off the recorder. The silence allowed him time to collect his thoughts. He had a handle on Mason Carlisle, alright. Here was a guy of many facets. He comes in here a serious, concerned college kid, only to morph into quite the smug rascal. *Hard to believe he's only nineteen,* Tate thought. *He projects the presence and self-assurance of someone much older.*

He continued to observe the other man in silence, hoping to unnerve him a bit. It didn't work, though. Mason's smile widened, coaxing dimples into view. His dark blue eyes, rimmed with thick sooty lashes that women would kill for, twinkled as he continued to meet Tate's gaze.

"Well, sir, do you have any more questions?" Mason asked.

Tate flipped on the mic once again. "You like young black girls, don't you Mason?"

The smile settled into a pensive expression as he answered. "I like girls in general, deputy."

Tate continued. "After you left the young lady with no name, you stopped at Curley's Gas 'N Go. Is that right?"

"That's right. I bought a sandwich and some cold drinks, and then I left."

"Did you see Tawney Simpson anywhere after you left?"

"Nope."

"Let's move along," Tate said. "After you had your car towed to the Shell station, you walked to the Remington home. About what time would you say you arrived?"

"Let's see, now," Mason said, pulling at his chin, "I stopped for a swim in the creek, like I told you earlier. Must have been around three, maybe closer to four o'clock, when I got to the house."

"Anyone at home when you got there?"

"Probably. I didn't go to the house, though. I wasn't feeling so good, so I went straight to the guest house. That's where I stay. I laid down for a while, took a shower, you know—just hung out 'til shortly after five. Then I went over to the big house and joined the family for drinks and dinner."

"Did you go into The Ramble on your way home?"

"Just along the main path. It's a shortcut from the swimming hole to Mr. Will's house." Mason shrugged. "Maybe a ten-minute walk. I didn't see anyone."

Tate abruptly stood up from his chair and held his hand out to the other man. "Thanks again for coming in, Mason. It was good to meet you."

Mason extended his hand. "My pleasure, sir."

Tate frowned. The young man's earlier firm handshake was now unpleasantly cold and clammy. The two men walked to the outer office together and said final good-byes, Mason exiting the building and Tate heading for the men's room to wash his hands.

40

T ate was tired, tired of endless conversation and tired of people in general. He was by nature a quiet and intensely private person. *So, how the hell did I get to be a Liaison Officer?* He wrote neatly at the top of the blank page, <u>William Remington Westin (Remy).</u>

Remy wore a somber expression—actually, "pained" was the word to describe his countenance. He entered the room and closed the door behind him, then followed Tate's gesture to the only other chair in the room. "Sit, please, Remy. Can I get you anything?"

"No, thanks, Deputy Jones. How can I help? This is just terrible. We've never had any violence or accidents on the property. I just can't seem to wrap my head around it!"

Tate responded sympathetically. "Yes, Remy, it's heartbreaking for that young girl and her family." He cleared his throat and took a sip of water. "Sure you don't want something?" he asked.

Remy shook his head. "Any suspects?"

Tate frowned slightly. "Why would you think of suspects this early, Remy? Why, we don't even know for sure what happened to the girl yet. Won't know 'til Doc Morrison finishes with her autopsy." He fell silent and jotted a few notes on the blank page. When he finished writing, he propped his elbows on the table, laced his fingers, and met Remy's gaze directly.

"Were you in The Ramble last Friday afternoon, say, from around two p.m. until five or five-thirty?"

Remy swallowed audibly. "I was at my girlfriend's house most of the day. Uh, that's M'Lyn Olsen. Then her daddy drove me home." He hesitated, and when Tate offered no response, he went on: "I guess it was around four-thirty when I got to the house."

"Anybody at home when you got there?"

"Maybe," Remy shrugged. "I went on up to my room for a while." He swallowed again. "So, I don't know."

"Hmmm," Tate grunted as he wrote more notes.

Remy frowned. "What?"

"Oh, I was just remembering how it was when I would come home from the academy. You know, I couldn't wait to see my mom and my sisters. As a rule, they'd be right there on the front porch, waiting to grab a hold of me." He chuckled, then waited for a response.

"I don't know exactly where everybody in my family was when I got home," Remy objected. "I had a lot on my mind, so I just went on upstairs for a while."

"What did you have on your mind?" Tate asked.

Remy crossed and uncrossed his legs and, after a brief shrug, said, "You know, school stuff, mostly. And M'Lyn wanting a diamond ring." He closed his eyes and shook his head. "Lots of stuff."

"I understand," Tate said. "Tell me, did you go into The Ramble at any time last Friday, Remy?"

Remy squinted before responding. "Now, let's see," he said thoughtfully, "Mr. Tom dropped me at the entrance to our driveway. I didn't want him to get his car all dusty, you see. I walked to the house."

"You walked along the driveway, or did you cut through The Ramble?"

"Well, uh, both, I guess. I walked up the driveway to the big stone bench at The Ramble's entrance and sat there for a while. Then, I walked a little way on the main path. But I-I cut through some bushes and walked across the lawn to the house." He stopped speaking, sniffed, and waited.

Tate wrote in his book.

"I didn't see anybody on my way home," Remy added.

Tate looked up from his book and raised his eyebrows in question.

"Isn't that what you were going to ask me," Remy inquired with hesitation, "if I'd seen that girl or anybody else around there?"

"I was," Tate replied. "But I guess you beat me to it. So, you didn't see Tawney Simpson or *anybody* else on your walk home last Friday?"

"No, sir."

Tate closed his book, stood up, and extended his hand. "Thanks, again, Remy. If anything comes to mind, please give us a call."

"Sure will," Remy said as he acknowledged Tate's outstretched hand with a fist bump. "Terrible thing, just terrible."

"Yes, it is," Tate said. "By the way, congratulations on your birthday and your birthday present. Chief Talmadge said it was quite a party Saturday."

Remy smiled briefly. "It sure was. Thanks, sir."

* * * * *

"Whew!" Talmadge exclaimed as he leaned back in his desk chair and stretched long arms upward. "This has been one hell of a day for sure. You got your notes on your interviews typed up, Tate?"

"Just about finished, Chief," Tate replied. He surveyed the sheets of hand-written notes and numerous drafts that lay in disarray on his desk. "I'll get it all finalized before I leave this evening."

"Well then, I'll see you bright and early tomorrow, Tate. Thanks."

"Chief," he added thoughtfully, "you know, the one thing that I've learned since being a cop is that you can just about always tell when somebody's lying to you."

Talmadge turned to face him. "Yeah? Who do you think was lying to you today?" he asked.

Tate didn't hesitate. "All four of them, sir."

* * * * *

You continue to do and say all the right things. Just like always. Not difficult, though, since you didn't do anything wrong. You simply made a bad decision. And bad decisions most times lead to accidents. That's what it was, too, just a terrible accident.

You have to put this behind you and move on. You're strong, so you can do that. And no more bad decisions, you hear?

Time. People talk a lot about time. The sands of time. End of time. Time marches on. Time heals. In time, we forget. What was that quote you read once? Something about we think we're killing time, but time is actually killing us? Ouch, bad comparison.

41

C at had sent over the results of her official autopsy performed on Tawney Simpson. Talmadge held the document in his hand as he read from it. "The cause of death is determined to be asthma exacerbation. That means that—"

"I know what it means, Chief," Jerome Simpson interrupted. "I took her to every one of her doctor's appointments. Tawney had asthma. Couldn't hardly get her breath sometimes. *Especially*," he emphasized, "when she was upset 'bout something. Or scared, maybe."

Talmadge drew a deep breath. He absolutely hated having to talk to grieving families, particularly when he could offer them nothing beyond sympathy. Not being able to give them closure left him at a loss. He cleared his throat and said, "We're still talking with her classmates and teachers at school, Curley, but as yet, we have no idea who was with her in the woods." *Damn, this is tough!*

"She was raped, wasn't she?" Jerome's shaky voice finished his thought.

Talmadge sighed. "Technically—legally, I should say, since she was underage—this would be statutory rape. Dr. Morrison, the Medical Examiner, did note that, uh, sexual intercourse had occurred."

"She was raped," Jerome repeated, his words this time making an emphatic statement.

"Appears that it might have been consensual, Curley." Talmadge hurried his words, attempting to put them behind him. "Now, we're concentrating all our efforts on coming up with a name. I'm sorry. That's all I've got for now. I wish it were more."

The older man remained silent, his eyes downcast. Finally, he nodded his head thoughtfully and asked, "You got kids, Chief?"

Talmadge shook his head. "No, the wife couldn't have children. When she passed, I just never got around to remarrying. Lonely, sometimes."

"Yes, sir," Jerome whispered, "it can get mighty lonely. When do you reckon we can take her? Funeral plans and such."

"Dr. Morrison will release the body to you any time."

Jerome stood and prepared to leave. "All right, then."

Talmadge hadn't been completely above-board with the grieving grandfather. Oh, he certainly hadn't lied to him—he just hadn't been able to look the old man in the eye and tell him that his team had already spoken to *all* the students in Tawney's class, to no avail. And, her teachers had all shaken their heads and said they couldn't remember the girl being in the company of any particular boy. The folks at the Simpson's church couldn't offer any names of possible interest either.

Antioch was a small town, with little remaining avenues of investigation for the police to explore. "Probably never know," Talmadge muttered as he reached for the telephone. He needed to let Cat know that the funeral home would most likely be sending the hearse either this afternoon or tomorrow. He popped two antacid tablets in his mouth, knowing that, even as he did, they wouldn't help the gnawing in his gut. Retirement was still several years away. *It can't come soon enough,* he thought.

* * * * *

Vivian couldn't remember when she had experienced so much vigor, certainly not anytime recently. Her uncommon spurts of energy had become more frequent over the past week, ever since the body of Tawney Simpson had been found. She recognized her actions as an attempt—albeit a futile one— to banish the cloud of guilt that hung over her.

As usual, Claire was right: she had no reason to feel guilty. So, why did she? Although there was never an iota of suspicion directed at her family, the police questionings had left her feeling vulnerable and exposed, *almost as violated as that poor child.*

Vivian shook her head to clear her thoughts and tried to concentrate on her morning's project of rearranging closets. But the distraction proved short-lived. Her hands busied themselves with sorting out old and rarely worn garments while her thoughts remained fixed on her family and their reactions to the tragedy that had hit so close to home.

Her father's blustery manner as he countered any and all questions with an air of annoyance was to be expected. In fact, he had seemed to take the police investigation as a personal affront to his reputation and standing in the community. Ridiculous, of course, but that was Daddy.

Remy and Mason had expressed the appropriate amount of disbelief, shaken their heads in sympathy, then appeared to resume their untroubled daily lives. Well, now, there was that time when she'd happened upon Mason sitting all alone by the fishpond. He had assured her that he was just fine, but she could tell that he'd been crying. She hadn't wanted to pry, so she just smiled and left him to his thoughts. Vivian had decided early on never to ask too many questions.

Gabrielle had taken the news of Tawney's death stoically. For once, though, she had seemed eager to listen to Vivian. She promised to heed her mother's warning to avoid strangers, to always be aware her surroundings, and to never again play alone in The Ramble. As she thought of her precious, trusting Gabrielle, Vivian's heart quickened in her chest and the familiar panic began to rise. "That could have been *my* daughter!" she whispered aloud as her hands began to tremble.

No, no. Not today! I will not let dark thoughts overtake me. I will not borrow trouble. Vivian took several deep breaths to calm herself. Besides, Gaby was much too spirited and smart to ever find herself in the sad situation that had befallen poor Tawney.

Vivian moved from the upstairs hall closets into Gabe's bedroom. The room smelled of his cologne, and she thought wistfully of their life together. While their relationship had never been one of continual cheerfulness and spontaneity, neither had it been one of isolation. For the last week, though, Gabe had seemed to be making a point of avoiding her.

Perhaps it was just her imagination working overtime again. But, if he were dodging her, it was her own damned fault. Her reaction at his gift— okay, her reaction to where it came from—was uncalled for. That door had closed long ago, and she knew that. So, why, then, was her husband being so evasive?

She busied herself by flipping through the clothes in Gabe's practically immaculate closet. She removed several items that needed to be ironed, a sport coat with a stain on the lapel, and a winter suit that he had not worn in a couple of years.

"This one can go to Goodwill," she muttered to herself. She gathered the garments, along with the laundry bag, and was about to exit the closet when another item caught her eye. She was about to reach for it when her husband spoke from the doorway.

"Hello, my dear, you're not throwing me out, I hope."

"Oh! You startled me," Vivian replied, laughing. "I'm cleaning out closets today. I'll send your laundry out and get rid of this old suit while I'm at it."

"Good idea. Here, I'll carry these downstairs for you," he said as he reached for the clothing she held.

"Thanks. By the way, I just noticed that your favorite shirt is missing one of its buttons. Those are brass, and there's no way we can match it. I'll pick up all new ones when I go shopping. You wore this shirt just last week—wherever did you lose the button?" Gabe leveled a cold stare at her as he spoke in terse, measured words: "If I knew where I'd lost it, Vivian, then it wouldn't be lost!"

* * * * *

Moselle Washington liked to keep busy. She had accepted the arthritis in her legs and back as a fact of life that made walking difficult, but her hands, though twisted and bent, were still nimble. This morning, she sat in her old wicker rocking chair in the shade of a large oak tree, along with her daughter-in-law. The two women worked at shelling peas, talking little while they enjoyed the summer morning.

Moselle halted her work, chuckled, and gazed skyward. "This oak tree, it just about as old and crooked as me."

"But it still serves a purpose, Moam," Claire said. "It gives us shade."

Moselle smiled as her fingers resumed their chore. "Where is everybody this mornin'?"

"Carl Lee left early to move some cattle to another pasture. Carleen and Reva are still sleeping, seeing as how they both got home late last night. Don't tell their daddy," she cautioned.

"What's our boy up to?" Moselle asked.

"I haven't seen him this morning," Claire said. "Heard him moving around in his room, but he hasn't come out yet." Her words held worry.

Moselle decided to let it go. They continued quietly with their task until Moselle nodded toward the front porch. "Here comes The Professor now," she said.

"Hey, Moam. Hey, Mama. What are y'all doing?" Leander asked as he sauntered down the steps. "Oh, you're shelling peas. I love peas."

His tone of voice was somewhat brighter than it had been over the past week. *I knew it all along—growing pains.* "Want to help us?" Moselle asked.

"I would," he said, "but I told Gaby I'd meet her at the SnoBall stand. I want to treat her, so may I have some money, Mama?"

"Of course, you may," Claire replied. "Just let me go and get my purse."

Claire went inside the house and Leander sat cross-legged on the grass. Rocking back and forth, he stared at the ground and remained uncharacteristically silent.

"What's on yo mind, child?" Moselle asked.

He shrugged but said nothing.

"Not like you to be so quiet. And what're you doin' hanging 'round the house this fine sunshiny mornin', anyways? You ought to be out playing with friends! 'Less of course, you'd rather sit here and shell peas all day long."

Moselle cackled as her gnarled fingers stopped their work and lay still on her apron-covered lap. The rhythmic creaking of her rocking chair stopped as she looked directly into her grandson's eyes. "What's the matter, boy? You ain't said half a dozen words all week long. You got somethin' you wanna talk about?"

The young boy took a deep breath. "Moam, what did you mean when you talked about the devil's back?"

"Huh? Oh, you mean las' night when your daddy and me was talking. What I said was: 'What goes over the devil's back is gonna come crawling under his belly.' It's what my pap always said. Now, what that means is that whatever you done, be it good or bad, it's gonna come right back around to you for sure.

"You see, child, if you walk hand in hand with the Lord, then good things be coming your way. But if you play leapfrog with that ole devil,"—she paused and lowered her voice to a whisper as her eyes locked with her grandson's—"well, then, the bad you done gonna keep coming back to haunt you."

Moselle shook her head and wiped a tear off her cheek with the back of her hand. "And whoever done harm to *that child*—the devil gonna be coming back around to him for the rest of his days!"

42

Every so often, dawn ushers in a day so incredibly perfect that it doesn't seem real.

When the previous night's gentle rain brings relief from stifling heat and transforms parched vegetation into plump mounds that bend under the weight of summer's fat, fragrant blossoms. When the air that is normally heavy, muggy and wrought with pesky insects suddenly undergoes a serious drop in humidity, so that when one steps outdoors, they do not immediately melt. When the air smells of jasmine and fresh-cut grass and sheets drying on the line. When even the birds seem to sing a happier song...

A day this flawless should be free from crime and hatred and sin. No one should feel unloved or underappreciated. There shouldn't be hunger in the world. A day this unblemished should not be tainted with death, Vivian thought.

She stood up from her rocking chair on the veranda, gathered her purse and gloves, and walked down the steps toward Claire's approaching car. She was smiling as she slid into the passenger seat, determined to hold back the tears this morning—until the funeral, anyway.

"Thanks for driving, Claire. It's been so long since I've driven a car, I'm not sure I even remember how."

"No problem. Let's have lunch afterwards."

Vivian nodded. "I'd like that. Today is too beautiful not to do *something* enjoyable."

"We certainly don't get many days like this one in August, that's for sure," Claire said. Ordinarily, her favorite black suit would be too heavy for a summer funeral, but today the jacket felt good against the morning chill. "My heart just breaks for Curley. Less than three months after burying his granddaughter, now Tavish. But Lord knows, that poor woman suffered enough. And I don't think anybody, Curley included, was surprised by her passing."

"While we're on the subject," Vivian said, "I heard that Talmadge brought a high school boy in for questioning about Tawney's death. Theron Jackson. Do you know the family?"

"I heard about that. The boy is in Reva's class, or I should say, he *was* in her class. She said he dropped out before the end of last school year. Word is that he'd been hanging around Curley's store a few months back, asking for work. Reva didn't say much about him, other than he was strange."

Vivian shook her head. "All we can do is keep our own children safe. I've told Gabrielle that she is *not* to go anywhere alone, and for once, I didn't get any backtalk from her. She didn't know Tawney, but this has really shaken her. How is Leander?"

Claire slowed the car in preparation for the turn into Anderson and Sons Mortuary. "Looks like we'll have to walk quite a way," she said. "Parking lot's full." After finding a spot, she switched off the ignition and answered Vivian's question.

"Honestly, Viv, I don't know what to make of Leander lately. I'm sure that the shock of a child being found dead in his favorite spot on earth had a troubling effect on him, but that boy has been like a different child for the past couple of months."

"Go on," Vivian prompted.

Claire shrugged. "Well, as I've told you before, it's been ever since *that* day—the last day of school when he came home sick." She shook her head. "He's been so distant. And sad, too. Leander's always been such a happy little boy. Oh, well," she looked at Vivian and shook her head, "I guess Moam's right—growing pains have got a hold of him."

Vivian patted Claire's hand. "He'll be fine. He's a very special boy. I feel certain that the dedication ceremony will help all the children deal with this."

Claire looked puzzled. "What dedication ceremony?"

Vivian leaned back in surprise. "Leander hasn't mentioned it to you? The school has scheduled a ceremony honoring Tawney's memory for next Monday, the first day of school. The students and teachers will gather at the entrance of the playground for the planting of a tree and flower garden. Gabe and I bought the tree, a magnolia, and the bank is donating a bronze plaque." She paused, seeing disappointment register on her Claire's face, and squeezed her friend's hand a bit tighter. "I'm sure Leander just forgot to tell you. Kids, you know, can't seem to concentrate on any one thing for very long."

"I suppose," Claire remarked, dismissing her bruised spirits for the moment. "The important thing is that the dedication will surely bring some closure to the students." As she prepared to exit the car, she smiled at Vivian and said, "It's so good of you to come today. It'll mean something to Curley for you to be here. After all, you didn't know the family personally."

"I *had* to come today, just like I had to attend Tawney's funeral. God, Claire." Vivian paused, her voice faltering. "Our home, my poor mother's beloved Ramble—it's all been defiled. It will never be the same, there in that once-perfect place. Oh, I know what the coroner said about an asthma attack being the direct cause of her death, but *somebody* was there with her to bring it on."

Claire nodded. "Most likely it was a classmate of hers—just a couple of foolish, curious kids slipping off to The Ramble, like so many have done before."

"Yes," Vivian said. "But this time, only one of them came back."

* * * * *

Sure would be nice if these windows could be opened—don't get many days like this one during dog days. Of course, you could always go up to the roof. On second thought, not a good idea, since there'd probably be a bunch of busybodies looking for you, asking you what's wrong. Why can't folks just let you be?

"*What's the matter, are you sick?*"

"*How come you look so glum?*"

"*You got something on your mind, a problem? Can I help?*"

Blah, blah, blah.

Of course, these windows can't be opened, stupid. You ever hear of a bank with open windows? Come on in, folks, help yourselves to some money. Bearer bonds? Right this way. And the safety deposit boxes are through that door.
STOP IT!

Three months. Almost three months…have to check the calendar. Anyway, three months and two funerals. Let's see, in another hour, and it'll be two funerals. You cannot continue to dwell on it. Do you understand? You cannot go back. You cannot undo what you—no, no. You cannot undo the accident.

Ahh, even with these plate glass windows between you and the outdoors, you can still sense this morning's cool breeze, still smell the clean air. A day like this, man, you ought to be on the golf course. Taking a walk, maybe. Second thought, you're exactly where you need to be. Work helps. And being around other people helps, too, even when their nosy questions piss you off.

Just keep smiling. Just keep saying all the right things. Just keep breathing.

"Excuse me."

"W-w-what? What is it? I didn't hear you come in."

"I knocked on your door. Everyone's waiting for you in the conference room. The meeting's about to start."

"I'm on my way."

"Are you okay? You look a bit pale."

Just breathe!

43

Gabe exited the bank building at exactly six o'clock. He was usually the last one to leave, but today Will had remained to put the finishing touches on their revamped retirement plan for the mill. They would be meeting the day after tomorrow with Tom Olsen to present the package.

Tom's predicted acceptance of the new plan would result in Remington Banking and Investments receiving a substantial commission. That fact alone would be cause for celebration, but coupled with the engagement party for Remy and M'Lyn, scheduled for next Saturday night at the Country Club, the soiree would be elevated to celebrity status.

Gabe reached the parking garage, unlocked his Lexus, and slid into the cool, leather seat. He started the engine and automatically switched the A/C to high before realizing that he didn't even need it. The day's cool, dry air had continued into dusk. He lowered his window and opened the car's skylight.

Traffic had thinned as Gabe pulled out of the garage. He waved at several folks he knew as he drove slowly down the length of Main Street on his regimented route home. The lights were still on in Tess' shop, signifying another bridal shower underway. This had been the norm on most evenings during the summer months, and Gabe was glad for her success.

They had not spoken since that day. A couple of times, he had seen her at the grocery store, once at the steakhouse. He'd nodded a time or two while passing her on the street. But no contact. Better that way.

He shook his head and grunted to himself. *M'Lyn's bridal shower will certainly be held elsewhere.*

Remy a married man. Gabe was still not comfortable with the idea. Sure, he and Vivian had married young—at eighteen, to be exact. And a full year remained before their son's wedding. But Remy was nowhere near ready for the responsibility of married life. Vivian knew it, just as he did. But, as usual, they had both managed to suppress their misgivings and surrender to Will's elation at the upcoming nuptials.

"He'll be twenty when they get married, and that's old enough," Will stated strongly when Gabe had voiced his concern. "That's how old I was when I married Lily. You and my daughter were even younger. She's a lovely girl, good family. You should be looking forward to becoming a grandfather, Gabe. Best part of life is having a grandson."

And so, the matter had been settled, like everything else in Gabe's life— by Will Remington. Sometimes, he hated Will. But, oh, how he loved him.

Gabe brought the car to a stop at the four-way and habitually flipped on his right turn signal in preparation for his turn onto the estate's gravel drive. He remained there for a full minute, listening to the cicadas and crickets through the open window as they ushered in the close of day. Confused by his own hesitation, he jumped as the horn blasted from the car behind him. Without a second thought, he cancelled the signal, waved an apology to the other driver, and drove forward toward the four-lane highway and away from his home.

Gabe couldn't remember exactly when the lapses in his memory had begun. *Black holes*, he had secretly named those confusing gaps when, without warning, he would find himself in a place with no recollection of how he had gotten there. These incidents had become more frequent over the course of the long, hot summer. Must have been why this evening's cool, dry conditions had enticed him to make this trip instead of going directly home.

Tonight, he was vaguely aware of having made the forty-minute drive to Greenville. The sign hyping the newest jazz club on Wade Hampton Boulevard caught his eye, but the exact route he had taken off the four-lane highway to get there was completely lost in space.

He sat, gripping the Lexus' steering wheel until his hands cramped. He massaged them and prepared to get out of the car. "Oh, well," he murmured aloud, "might as well have a drink and enjoy some music."

* * * * *

Remy swirled the amber liquid in his glass. "This is fine scotch, Mr. Tom. To you," he said, raising his hand in a toast.

"To *us*, son, and I've told you before, you can drop the *Mr.* It's just 'Tom'. The wife feels the same way, you know. We're just Tom and Lynn to you."

"Yessir," Remy said, grinning at his future father-in-law. "I sure do hope y'all are as happy about M'Lyn and me getting engaged as my family is."

Tom nodded thoughtfully. "All I've ever wanted was for my girls to be happy. Suzanne—hard to say about her. We've just never been that close. But M'Lyn, she's easy to read. You make her happy, so that makes me happy." Tom belched loudly, stood up, and walked to the bar in the corner of the living room. He poured himself another drink and held the bottle up to Remy. "You ready?"

Remy shook his head. "Not quite. Better take it slow since I'm driving."

"Good thinking," Tom said, moving back to his chair.

"About M'Lyn," Remy said, "I want you to know that I'll do my best to keep her happy. I love her, Tom."

Tom downed half his drink and studied Remy thoughtfully. "I know you do, son. The two of you are wrapped up in each other, just like me and her mama was. But," he punctuated his words with a raised eyebrow, "do you *like* her?"

Seeing Remy's quizzical expression, Tom went on. "You see, when the romance starts to fade—and it will—you're left with somebody that you damn sure better like to live with." He chuckled as he stood up and retraced his earlier steps to the bar. "Don't know how I got so lucky, but that lovely lady upstairs helping your future wife get dressed actually likes me."

Another belch, and Tom was back, facing Remy and expounding on his topic. "I eat too much, I drink too much, and I'm a loud-mouthed, red-neck mill operator that don't really belong at the country club. But I got too much fuckin' money for 'em to kick me out!" He laughed raucously, and Remy joined him.

"And still," Tom said, his voice softening and his eyes misting, "my Lynn likes me, and I sure do like her." He downed his third scotch, set the glass down, and smiled. "Back to my youngest daughter. She's spoiled rotten, and I ain't real sure that she's gonna be all that easy to like. But you got a year to work on that." He smiled. "There you have it, son—some fatherly advice whether you want it or not."

Remy remained silent, taking in what Tom had said and trying to come up with some appropriate response when he was suddenly saved by the women's entrance. "Sorry to keep you waiting, Remy," M'Lyn purred. "I just couldn't decide what to wear." She moved to his side and snuggled against him, the rose-colored silk dress accentuating her body as she walked.

"You're beautiful," Remy whispered. "Be the prettiest girl at the club, that's for sure. We'd better get going. I told Mason that we'd meet him and Connie in the bar at six-thirty." He checked his watch, then turned to extend his hand to Tom. "I sure enjoyed our talk, Tom. Thank you."

"Thank you, son. You kids have fun, now."

M'Lyn placed her hand on Remy's right wrist. As lightning bolts of color radiated from the three-caret diamond on her finger, she asked, "Baby, where's your gold ID bracelet I gave you last Christmas? I haven't seen you wear it in forever."

He swallowed hard but kept his expression serene. "It's in my room. Since Mason and I have been playing so much tennis and golf this summer, I took it off so I wouldn't lose it."

She smiled. "Good thinking, I suppose. Bye, Mama, bye Daddy. Love y'all. Don't wait up."

That went well, Remy thought as they walked to the car. He had no idea what could have happened to his bracelet, or even the last time he might have worn it. But he knew where M'Lyn had purchased it. He'd ask Granddaddy to take care of getting it replaced.

* * * * *

The music was good. In fact, it was some of the best jazz Gabe had heard in a long time. He smiled and sipped his second vodka gimlet of the evening, remembering the jazz concerts that he and Vivian had enjoyed back in the day. On his trips home from college, the two of them would seek out a concert, leave baby Remy in the capable care of Rosie—and Will, of course—and spend the evening together. *Why don't we ever do that now?* he wondered? They certainly had the time.

"Another one?" the bartender asked, breaking Gabe's train of thought.

"Sure, why not?" he replied. This was pleasant, and even though he knew he had to go home, it didn't have to be right now. He wouldn't be missed anyway. Vivian, had gone to the funeral and would spend the rest of the day with Claire, and then go to bed early. Remy and Mason had plans for the dinner-dance at the club, and Will was probably still at the bank.

The clarinet player's first few notes of *Fly Me to The Moon* coaxed chill bumps along Gabe's arms. He grunted with pleasure.

"Nice, huh?" the woman said as she slid onto the barstool next to his.

"I beg your pardon?"

"The music. It's very nice."

"Yes, it is," Gabe agreed. "One of the best trios I've heard lately."

She sipped her drink and said, "I wasn't sure you were enjoying yourself. You look lonely."

Gabe glanced her way and thought that she looked to be about his age, a little younger, perhaps. Her blond hair was cut short in a modern style, accentuating a face with fine bone structure and very little makeup. Her business suit was well tailored and expensive. "A person can be alone and not lonely, you know," he offered.

She wasn't dissuaded. "You look to be both. What's your name?"

He answered immediately, without thinking. "Gabe."

"Is that short for Gabriel?"

"It's just Gabe."

She drained her wine glass. "Well, 'Just Gabe', are you?"

"Am I what?"

She propped her elbows on the bar, rested her chin in cupped hands, and turned soulful brown eyes to his. "Are you lonely?"

This time, he hesitated before responding. *What the hell am I doing here?* "I'm fine, really," he said before turning back to nurse his drink.

"Well, excuse *me*," she said, her voice catching in her throat. "I didn't mean to bother you. I'm new at this, and I guess it shows. I'm sorry."

She practically leapt from the barstool and was halfway to the exit when Gabe caught up with her. Gently, he tapped her shoulder and was taken aback when she turned to face him with tears streaming down her face.

"Look, miss, if I said anything to upset you, I am truly sorry."

"No, no, you didn't," she said. She wiped away her tears with the back of her hand and tried to smile, but her chin kept quivering. Again, she apologized. "I'm sorry. It's me, not you. Goodbye."

"Wait just a minute. Please." Gabe hurried back to the bar, gulped the last of his gimlet and plopped down a twenty-dollar. When he turned around, she was no longer there.

Outside, the night air was cool and the sky full of stars, promising another picture-perfect day tomorrow. He saw her a few yards away, leaning against a shiny new Volvo, her head down, the toe of her right, high heel shoe drawing little circles in the gravel. He walked in her direction.

"Got my divorce papers today," she said in a well-modulated voice. "He was kind enough to have them delivered to me at my office."

Gabe leaned against the car alongside her. "Yeah, where do you work?" he asked.

She laughed—not a polite little chuckle, but a throaty, robust laugh. *A wonderful laugh,* Gabe thought. He grinned at her. "Well?"

"Okay," she said. "You win. You cheered me up. I work at a bank. I'm a vice-president, actually."

"You gotta be kidding," he said. "*I* work at a bank."

"Well, that just goes to show you that the old saying is wrong."

"What old saying is that?" he asked. The thought occurred to him that he was enjoying this entirely too much.

"That old saying that opposites attract," she said. Her eyes found his once more. "My name's Beth."

"Is that short for Elizabeth?" He could feel himself grinning.

"Formally, yes. But 'just Beth' is fine."

"Look, 'Just Beth', you've had a lousy day. And I've had a normal day, which for me is not lousy, but damn close to it. How about we start over?"

She sniffed, smiled a bit brighter, and asked, "What'cha got in mind?"

"Another jazz club would be nice, provided you know of one around here since I'm from out of town. And dinner, too. I'm starved. "How's that sound?"

She fell silent and seemed to be toying with an idea. Finally, she spoke: "I just happen to know where there's an amazing collection of the all-time jazz greats. And," she took a deep breath, "if you like pot roast, I can heat it up."

It sounded like someone else speaking, not his voice at all. "I'll follow you."

44

Mason was enjoying himself. The evening was cool, and the open-air bar lively with Antioch's elite—and he with the sexiest girl in the club. He sipped his drink, thinking that life was indeed good.

Connie Dunham sat beside him, her hot-pink mini dress riding high on her long, tan legs. She was either very good at ignoring the admiring glances that came her way, or she accepted them as her due. Mason thought it to be a little of both. Connie's coloring mirrored his own, except that her blue eyes were more of an aquamarine hue. Her dark hair always looked to be tousled, whether she had just stepped out of the salon or climbed from his bed.

Mason frowned as last night came to mind. Connie's passionate antics, and her apparent expectation of a repeat performance tonight, were going to make for an awkward parting of the ways. But the fact was that he and Remy would be heading back to college in a couple of weeks, and he had no intention of allowing a summer dalliance to advance into anything remotely resembling a relationship. He would wait, though, until after Remy's engagement party next Saturday. Then, he'd let her down as easy as possible.

While Connie's attention was caught up with the band and in speaking to everyone in the bar, Mason continued to assess the young woman by his side. She was a catch, alright. She came with a rich daddy and a socialite mama. *And,* he thought wryly, *she's only marginally dumb.* So why couldn't he make love to her without fantasizing about that mousy little Mexican girl bussing tables in the bar?

If Mason had ever held any illusions concerning himself, they had evaporated long ago. Not that his financial future caused him any concern since his summer employment at the bank had gone so well. He felt certain that, upon his graduation, he would settle into a cushy position within the partnership. And on the social scale, he was and always would be at the top.

And yet, his resolve to direct his personal life toward a higher standard seemed to have fallen by the wayside. The heated cravings that propelled him had not subsided, leaving him to wonder if the world was indeed stuck with the same old, self-centered S.O.B. that he'd always been. He turned to Connie, observing her more carefully. No one had to tell him that he was tossing a priceless coin into the wishing well. But what was it that he wished for?

MORE! That's what his sultry mistress by the name of Greed dangled in front of him, lulling him into justifying his actions as being simply ambitious. Oh, he knew better. He knew his paramour would continue to manipulate his thoughts and deeds until one day she would rule him completely. Just like she ruled Will Remington. But was that so bad? Where was the crime in following the path that led to riches and fame? As long as you caused no pain along the way.

"You're being mighty quiet tonight, sugar," Connie said above the music. "Somethin' troubling you?" Her hand found its way to his thigh, and her wet, full lips parted in a seductive smile, showing off perfectly capped teeth.

"Why would you think anything was troubling me?" Mason's words were sharper than he'd intended. He smiled slightly. "I'm fine, dahlin', just enjoying the moment." He recognized the dull pressure that had begun to build up behind his eyes to be a warning of another irritating bout of melancholy. He needed to get his thoughts back on track, and fast. Thankfully, he spotted his best friend across the bar. He gently removed Connie's hand from his leg and stood up to signal their location to Remy and M'Lyn.

"Here's the woosome twosome now," Mason said as he slapped Remy on the back and guided M'Lyn into her chair.

"Sorry we're a bit late. Daddy was having 'the talk' with Remy," M'Lyn said.

"Not to worry," Mason said, his mood becoming brighter by the moment. "Let's get you two a drink and toast a perfect ending to a perfect day."

* * * * *

Will stepped from the elevator onto the marble floor of the bank's lobby. He liked being all alone in the big old building. He had made sure all the lights were off on the upper floors, except for the indirect lighting that encircled the mezzanine. As was his custom, he paused for a moment to survey his surroundings. *Not a finer decorated bank lobby in the south,* he thought with pride.

His father's portrait hung on the wall between the two elevators, above the plaque denoting the elder Remington as the bank's founder. Will took out his handkerchief and polished the brass, letting his fingers linger briefly on the Remington name. As he made his way toward the front door, the ancient grandfather clock in the corner began to strike eight o'clock. He had told Belle that he would try to leave in time to have dinner with her and her friend from Charleston, but after the long day he had just put in, going home sounded a lot better.

As the clock finished striking, he thought for the umpteenth time that he simply *must* find the time to search his office at home for his daddy's pocket watch. "That's what I get for taking it out of its case in the first place," he grumbled under his breath. Will's number one fear—one that he kept from everyone, including Gabe—was a fading memory. He had always prided himself on being able to recall names and faces, as well as keeping his entire appointment schedule in his head.

Lately, though, he thought with more than a little trepidation, he couldn't even remember where he'd put his watch. He should chalk it up to having too much on his plate. The retirement plan that he had just put the finishing touches to for Tom's mill was just one of several that the partners had successfully placed over the summer months. Both he and Gabe had put in many long days, and Will was tired.

Remington Investments was indeed growing by leaps and bounds, thanks in no small part to the fresh ideas of the two young, soon-to-be partners. Mason Carlisle was a natural salesman, able to schmooze with the best of them, even outshining Will himself in that department. And Remy? Will could not have been prouder. His grandson's marketing ideas had succeeded in raising the eyebrows of several new investors. Although offshore banking and international reserves seemed far-fetched concepts to Will, he certainly was not opposed to exploration. He grunted pleasurably to himself. *Been a good summer,* he thought with satisfaction. Well, maybe not entirely good.

The grandfather clock's chiming of the quarter hour brought him out of his reverie with a start. He'd been standing in one spot for close to fifteen minutes and now felt totally spaced-out. "Whew, you *are* tired," he muttered. He set the alarm system and stepped out into a beautiful night. After locking the bank's door, he began to stroll down the practically deserted street to the parking garage.

He banished the shadowy images from his mind and directed his thoughts along a more pleasing path. Remy's and M'Lyn's upcoming engagement party would be the catalyst that would secure the continuation of his dynasty. Yessiree, in one short year, those two would be married and, if his advice to his grandson had sunk in, they would not wait to start a family. A great-grandson! Will's smile grew wider and he nodded to himself. *That's what makes life mean something,* he thought.

He had reached his car and decided that maybe he wasn't as tired as he'd previously thought. He drove the Mercedes slowly out of the garage and turned toward Belle's house. He would enjoy dinner with her and her friend. Then, he'd go home and find that damn pocket watch.

45

Three months had passed. Sometimes it seemed like only a few days since the sounds, sights, and smells of *that day* had taken hold of him and changed his life forever. Then, some mornings when he woke, the events were hazy and unreal, as if they had taken place many years ago. A couple of times in the dark of night, he would pretend that it hadn't happened at all.

Leander had not spoken her name for fear that she might come back to haunt him. He knew that kind of thinking was senseless, but he imagined that she would somehow slip into his room during the night and suck the breath from him. Maybe, he fretted, she would follow along behind him as he walked through the winding paths of The Ramble, becoming visible like the apparition of Miz Lily. Or, would she reach a spectral hand upward and ensnare him as he swam in the waters of Dalton's Creek?

He didn't believe in ghosts. And yet, he had not been able to speak her name. He whispered it now, though, in the pastel glow coming from his aquarium. "Tawney." As he did so, the familiar ache in the back of his throat brought stinging tears to his eyes. Leander blinked them away. *This is no time for crying,* he thought as he sat crouched on the floor, concealed almost entirely behind the aquarium. This was as close to being invisible as he could get, and right now he desperately wanted to be invisible. It was well past midnight, and everyone else in the household had gone to bed hours ago.

Earlier, Leander had retrieved his treasure box from the closet shelf and now held it on his lap. Mama had given the box to him the day he'd received the medal for reading in the first grade. He studied the box with trepidation. His small hand caressed its intricately carved, wooden lid as he lifted it.

Inside, the mute residents lay gleaming on the purple velvet just as he had placed them—his reading award, the little gold cross for reciting Bible verses in church, the first-place medal he'd won in the elementary school spelling bee, and his scouting badges. These and other mementos had once sparked pride, but now meant little to him.

He pushed the trinkets aside and lifted the latest addition, the one he had placed there on the night of Tawney's death. He had not touched it since then, and the thought occurred to him that he would feel something like a shock when he did so now. A chill, perhaps?

Nothing. It was only a thing, with no life of its own. But had *she* touched it? He wondered. Surely if she had, then he would be able to feel a connection. He turned the shiny piece over in his hand and thought about that horrific day. As he retraced yet again the events of three months ago, he realized that the once-traumatizing memory was now strangely invigorating. "Okay, then," he whispered.

Leander wrapped the object in tissue and placed it back into its velvet nest, closed the lid, and returned the treasure box to the closet shelf behind some old toys. As he climbed into bed, he heard Moam's old mantle clock strike two a.m. He closed his eyes and tried to relax but thinking about his plan for the following day made sleep elusive. Tomorrow would be a tough day. But he had endured worse.

* * * * *

Vivian smiled as she looked around the dining room table. "It certainly is nice to have all the family gather for breakfast. Seems like we're all too busy to share a meal together anymore."

"Thank you for the great buffet, Mama," Remy said around a mouthful of scrambled eggs. "What's the occasion?"

"Rosie and I thought it would be nice to celebrate Gabrielle's first day in the fifth grade," Vivian replied. "How 'bout it, sugar? Are you looking forward to this school year?"

After a long moment of toying with the food on her plate, Gaby answered, "I guess so. I'll be glad when today is over with, though."

"Why's that, dahlin?" Mason asked as he returned to the table after helping himself to another heaping plate. "What's going on today?"

"Well, for one thing, we're having the dedication ceremony for Tawney. That's going to be sad," Gaby said solemnly.

"I'm sure it will be," Gabe said. "But remember that all of the children will be doing something to honor her memory. That's important."

Attempting to cheer her daughter up, Vivian said, "Perhaps you and Leander can go fishing after school."

"Can't," Gaby responded. "I have to go to that stupid birthday party for Megan Sullivan. *Yuck!*"

Will put his morning newspaper down on the table and joined the conversation. "*Stupid* is an ugly word, Gabrielle. You shouldn't say it. And why would you not want to attend a birthday party for one of your friends?"

Gaby laid her fork down and met Will's gaze directly. "You're right, Granddaddy," she said without the least bit of sarcasm. "Stupid is an ugly word, and I'm sorry I said it. The reason that I don't want to go is that Megan Sullivan is boring. She can't throw a softball, and she doesn't know how to fish. She's a total sissy and no friend of mine. She only invited me to her party to get a present."

Remy hooted. "Wow, lil' sis! Tell us how you *really* feel!"

Will's expression hardened. "Young lady, you would do well to have the Sullivan girl for a best friend. Her family is one of the wealthiest in the county. Nice people."

A concerned little frown creased Gaby's forehead. "So, Granddaddy, are you saying that rich people are nicer than poor people?"

"I did not say that, Gabrielle." Will's tone of voice grew brusque, contradicting the set little smile on his face. "I only point out that you should keep company with other children who come from a family such as ours. And I say again, that the Sullivan girl would be a good choice for a best friend."

The puzzled expression had not left Gaby's face. "But, Granddaddy, I *have* a best friend. Leander is my best friend, always will be," she said sweetly. "Miz Claire is Mama's best friend, so I guess that means that their family is just like ours. Right?"

Will appeared to choose his words more carefully. "To a point," he said. "You are old enough, I believe, to realize the differences in people, are you not?"

Gaby leaned forward in her chair, her eyes never leaving her Grandfather's face. "Please excuse me, Granddaddy, but are you talking about black people and white people?"

"You opened *that* door, Will," Gabe said as he rose from the table. After a brief pat on Vivian's shoulder, he made his exit from the dining room.

But Gaby wasn't finished. "So, if I had a girlfriend that was black, that'd be okay? That would be like Mama and Miz Claire."

Will's face flushed. "I suppose," he snapped.

Vivian was finding it more and more difficult to stifle a grin as the conversation between her father and daughter continued. And from the downcast eyes and twitching mouths from Remy and Mason, she wasn't alone. *Oh, my precious daughter, you are so much better at this than I EVER was.*

Gabrielle was the only person Vivian knew who could use innocent-sounding phrases such as 'I'm sorry,' 'Yes sir, Granddaddy,' and 'Please excuse me' as weapons. Throughout the repartee, as Gaby's tiny daggers found their mark, it became crystal clear that whatever her daughter undertook in life, she would never be intimidated. She would never know the feelings of inadequacy. Nor would she be forced to swallow her tears or try to quell the bouts of anxiety that Will's biting words induced.

Gaby drew a deep breath, exhaled loudly, and said, "So, Granddaddy, you think that I ought to have a girl for my best friend instead of a boy. Right?"

Will seemed pleased with himself as he responded. "Yes, dear, you should have a girl for your best friend." As he prepared to leave the breakfast table, though, Gaby launched one more missile.

"Now I'm really confused, Granddaddy. *You* said that Cousin Betty wasn't invited to Remy's and M'Lyn's engagement party because she'd be bringing that girlfriend of hers! So—"

"Goddammit, Vivian Ellen! Talk to your daughter!" Will exited the dining room in a huff and slammed the kitchen door behind him, but not before the guffaws from Remy and Mason erupted.

Gaby looked to be sincerely perplexed. "What did I say wrong, Mama?"

"Nothing, my sweet," Vivian said, laughing. "You run along now and have a good day at school. You just made *my* day perfect."

46

The entrance to Antioch Elementary School had been for over thirty years little more than a wide expanse of cracked and buckled asphalt, its concrete curbing continually being chipped away by school bus tires. But today, that dreary patch of ground had been transformed with newly applied black-top, the planting of flower beds and a magnolia tree, and the addition of a brass plaque remembering Tawney Simpson. Even the somewhat antiquated and rusty playground equipment had been spruced up.

The children from all eight grades stood in silence as the principal and several teachers spoke of Tawney. It was a somber event, and being that she normally disliked any occasion of solemnity, Gabrielle was surprised to realize that she was actually enjoying the ceremony.

She had spoken little about Tawney to anyone, even Leander, during the summer months. But she had thought of little else. *Someone only a few years old than me had died on our property!* It was a sobering thought, as well as a terrifying one. At one point during one of the teacher's talks, she felt her heart begin to race and she almost teared up. But Leander's hand found hers, and all was well. She felt strong and safe once again.

A short while later, as the ceremony ended and the students began to make their way to classrooms, Gabrielle asked, "Hey, Lee, how come nobody ever gets honored before they die?"

"I guess that folks just never think about doing something nice for somebody 'til it's too late," Leander answered thoughtfully. "Moam says that we ought to tell people how we feel about them while we have the chance."

The old oak floorboards creaked under the footsteps of twenty-five students, and the walls resonated with shrill voices as the fifth-grade classroom filled up. As the already beleaguered teacher begged for quiet,

Gabrielle said, "Well, then, I'm telling you right now that you're my very best friend."

Leander grinned. "And you're mine."

* * * * *

Timing was everything. Leander had taken into consideration the day of the week, which being Monday meant less afternoon business at the bank. Fridays were the busiest days, because that's when the mill workers got paid. And people going out of town for weekends would usually stop by the bank on their way. Thursday afternoons were reserved for golf or tennis or whatever at the country club, and prayer meeting at the church occupied Wednesday evenings. Today was ideal also, because Gaby was at the birthday party.

Planning just the right *place* was important, too. No one ever came in through the formal front entrance except during parties and holidays, so that was out. The side door into the kitchen was the favorite entry, unless one of the family cars sat under the carport. In that case, the French doors at the back of the house by the swimming pool would be used as a direct access into the family room. He'd put quite a bit of time into deciding which entrance would be the most likely one today and had opted for the French doors. If his plan didn't work out, he could easily slip from view around the back of the big garage.

Everything Leander did was well thought out: this was no exception. Weeks of studying the comings and goings of Gaby's family had brought him to his present location. He sat stiffly on the curved brick wall that bordered the flagstone walkways of the Remington house's rear gardens. He looked at his watch and saw that it was four fifteen, six minutes later than when he'd checked it earlier. His mouth was dry as cotton, and he longed to sip from his water bottle. But he had already consumed one bottle, which resulted in his having to scurry into the bushes to pee several times.

Oh, how his stomach hurt! *Must be gas,* he thought. And that very thought was paralyzing. What if he had another attack of diarrhea? Well, he would just rather die, that's all. This might not be a good idea, after all. But backing down was not an option. He took a deep breath, straightened his shoulders, and checked his watch again: four eighteen.

To calm his queasy insides, Leander strolled over to the koi pond. The colorful fish immediately gathered at the pool's edge for morsels of food they knew would be tossed to them. *The simple life.* He watched the water churn with color as the fish gobbled up the bits of grain that he dropped. The ruse worked. For a few moments, his anxiety lessened, and he nearly forgot about his mission.

"Hey there, Leander. What's going on?"

His unexpected voice rendered the boy speechless.

"You looking for Gabrielle?"

Leander swallowed hard, shook his head, and eventually found his voice. "N-n-no."

"Oh, is your mama in the house?"

Slowly, the young boy began to walk toward his adversary. "No, sir." Leander's voice was a little stronger. *It's now or never.*

"Look like you seen a ghost, boy. What's the matter with you?"

The pain in his stomach had returned, worse than ever. He felt bloated and suddenly wondered if he shouldn't simply turn and run away. But then, if he did, he knew that he'd never be able to stop running.

One more deep breath. "I need to talk to you."

"Well, now, you sound mighty serious. Let's go on in the house where it's cool."

"Be best out here," Leander's voice broke, causing him to chirp like a little bird. He recovered. "This is serious. S-s-sir."

The heavy iron chair made a scraping sound as he drew it across the stone courtyard. "Hell fire, son, have at it. What do you want to talk about?" His demeanor was condescending, and his voice tinged with sarcasm, which made Leander more determined than ever to do this right. He stood in front of the chair and made direct eye contact.

"I was there."

Moments passed. An expression of complete confusion settled on his face. He said, "Okay, you were where?"

"There," the boy whispered, "there in the woods. In The Ramble."

"So, you were in The Ramble. I-I don't see where this is going. Whatever it is you've got to say, spit it out."

Leander's heart was pounding, but his gaze never wavered. "*That* day. I was in The Ramble."

Moments passed. Guardedly, the man asked, "What day?"

"She was there, too." Leander's words were less than a whisper.

"Who was there? What the hell are you talking about?"

The cramps in his stomach had lessened. But an even worse fate loomed—*Swallow hard, stay calm, do not start crying.* Leander coached himself and soon felt composed enough to speak again. "The day that Tawney…" he faltered briefly. "The day she died. I was there. You were there."

His voice was flat. "Boy, where the hell did you get such an idea?" Some of the color drained from his face and his eyes were aflame.

His countenance terrified Leander. The boy backed away a few steps and murmured, "You were crying. And, and you s-s-said that it was an accident."

He leaned forward in the chair. His eyes narrowed. "Are you accusing me of something, boy? If you are, then you've got some kinda nerve, I'll say that. Coming over here like this!"

Leander's next words silenced him. "You dropped something."

Deliberately, he stood up from the chair and began to advance on the boy. "You little mongrel! You spiteful, blackmailing little bastard!" Beads of sweat began to trickle down his face, and his hoarse voice quivered with rage. "Why are you here now? To threaten me?" His hands were shaking, and his voice dropped an octave as he asked, "What exactly is it that you want? What's your price?"

His hateful words wounded Leander more deeply than he would have thought possible. But he halted his retreat, met his gaze, and said, "I want for Gaby to never know. I want to make sure that nothing bad ever happens in her family."

Neither one spoke. Leander was relieved and quite surprised to realize that, after all the time he'd spent worrying, the confrontation had lasted only a matter of minutes. He had accomplished what he had set out to do. The tension between the two of them had found its spot and taken root.

The sudden sound of a car door closing and approaching footsteps penetrated the silence.

"Oh, you're just now getting home, too, I see. Let's get out of this god-awful heat. After today, I'm in bad need of a drink."

Breathe. Close your eyes, take deep breaths, and calm down. Not the end of the world. Close, but not the end. You need some time, but you'll figure it out. You always do. You can analyze the situation all you want, it ain't gonna change. Here's the simple, unavoidable fact: there will be a price. There is always a price. And it will have to be paid.

"You coming in, or what? Drinks are ready."

"Right behind you."

He scanned the courtyard one last time, but Leander Washington was nowhere in sight.

47

Vivian Westin had come to the realization that time passed more pleasantly for her when she thought about it in terms of special events rather than days on the calendar. At least that way she didn't dwell so much on growing older. Lately, the special event in her life was Remy's upcoming wedding. She shook her head, thinking that it didn't seem possible for an entire year to have passed since the engagement party.

She sat at her dressing table and carefully studied her reflection in the three-way mirror. Did she look thirty-nine? She snickered as a trivial question popped into her head. *Just what does thirty-nine look like, anyway?* She lifted her shoulder-length red hair and secured it with clamps. After turning from side to side, she decided to wear it up for tonight's rehearsal dinner. Gabe liked her hair up. In fact, he'd told her many times that he wished she would cut it short. But that would infuriate Daddy, *and we can't have that, now can we?*

Vivian's attention was drawn to another reflection in her mirror. The mint-green, formal satin gown hung on the rack behind her. That one was for the wedding next Saturday. Tonight, she would be wearing the strapless black lace cocktail dress ecstatically chosen for her by Gabrielle. Her daughter had good taste, alright. She had zeroed in on the most expensive garment at Bridal Boutique.

Her son's wedding to M'Lyn would be the social event of the summer, for sure. Lynn Olsen had been careful to keep Vivian updated on the plans. After the ceremony at the Antioch First Baptist Church, the reception and formal dinner-dance would be held at the country club. Vivian liked the Olsens. Both Tom and Lynn were down-to-earth, genuine people. And she wanted to like M'Lyn, to love her even, like a daughter. Perhaps that would come with time.

The night had been cool, and the open French doors beckoned Vivian. After pouring herself another cup of coffee from the breakfast tray that Rosie had brought up earlier, she stepped out onto her balcony just in time to see Gabe's car come into view. Vivian glanced at her watch: just past nine a.m. He'd obviously spent the night in Greenville again.

Ever since Remington Investments had purchased that small bank in Greenville, Gabe had taken its management upon himself. She had heard her father applaud him time and again, saying that it had been one of their more lucrative acquisitions. But why did he have to spend so much time there? Perhaps a better question was, had she given her husband a reason to come home at night?

But if Vivian were truthful—and she was, with herself—except for the rare social event that she actually enjoyed and the time she spent with Claire, she was quite content to remain alone. And Gabe knew it. There had always been awkwardness between the two of them from the time the shy, sad little boy had come to live at Remington Manor. Their relationship had been one of courtesy, with each child competing for Will's attention while trying valiantly not to hurt the other's feelings. Of course, there was never a doubt as to who had won her father's favor.

Vivian closed her eyes and saw clearly the two of them as they had been: two youngsters tiptoeing carefully around each other throughout their childhood and into an equally courteous adolescence, still with a curtain between them. And while the first couple of years following their marriage had held intimacy, they had never been—*what?* She frowned, searching for the word that would describe what was missing in her marriage. *Honesty.* That was it. She and Gabe had never been open and honest with each other. They never talked of their feelings, never expressed their needs or desires. Why? Did each one fear that they would hurt the other? Perhaps the truth was what they feared.

"Enough," Vivian said, scolding herself. She finished her coffee and went back into her room to begin preparations for the day. The more time she spent in self-analysis, the more depressed she became. The signs were clear: melancholy, regret, rapid heartbeat, sweating and, finally, a migraine. But not today, not this summer.

The tragic death of a young girl had overshadowed all else from last year and had cast a pall over her family that was just now beginning to lift. But this year, Vivian would be marking the time with joyous events… wouldn't she?

* * * * *

Gabe brought the car to a stop underneath the carport and switched off the ignition. He leaned his head back against the headrest and closed his eyes. The morning air was still cool, and sleep tugged at him. But how would he explain falling asleep in his car at 9:30 in the morning to anyone who might happen upon him? Absently, he rubbed away the twinge of pain in his temples as his mind replayed the previous sleepless night.

Beth had prepared dinner at her apartment after they left the bank. The evening had been pleasant and laid-back. They had settled on the terrace after dinner, sipping wine and listening to jazz. They spoke of music or of some insignificant incident at the bank when they spoke at all.

Gabe remembered taking several deep breaths but failing each time to launch into the speech he had so diligently—and sadly—rehearsed. Then, just as Tony Bennett had finished leaving his heart in San Francisco, Beth spoke.

"What will you miss most about me, Gabe?" Her voice was clear, but it lacked the musical lilt that he found so pleasant.

He turned to look at her in the dim light. "What do you mean?" he had asked, knowing full well what she meant. *She had known.*

"When you're gone," she whispered. "When you don't come back to me anymore. What part of me will you take with you?" Her voice, sinking from a whisper to barely a breath, had pierced his heart.

He had taken the remainder of the night to gather his thoughts, wanting to give her more than some trivial answer. *What will I miss the most?*

Her eyes were dark brown. That is, until the light caught them just right. Then, the most amazing thing happened: they turned green. Well, sort of green. They reminded Gabe of dropping a leaf into a clear stream and seeing the ripples gently expand into circles of tan and green with an occasional hint of blue. *Hazel eyes, maybe?*

He had reached out to touch her hair. It was the color of corn silks. He liked it short, liked the way it lay against her long, smooth neck. Her neck always smelled lightly of musk. Her hands had found his then, and he thought how pretty they were as he stroked them. She rarely wore rings, and she kept her nails cut short and unpolished—his no-nonsense lady.

There had been no complications with Beth, certainly a rare situation in his life so far. She never asked difficult questions of him, never put him on the spot with demands that they both knew could never be met.

She had a head for business, too. No doubt about it. Soon after Remington Investments had purchased the small bank, Gabe realized just how valuable Beth was. He had taken great satisfaction in getting rid of the good ole' boy regime who had made it a practice to quash her ideas.

What part of her would he take with him?

They had passed the night on the terrace with more of the music they loved and more wine. And as the sun crept above the horizon, Gabe had gathered his belongings and prepared to leave. Neither of them had trusted themselves to look at the other. With his hand on the doorknob, he had turned slightly toward her and answered the question she had asked hours earlier.

"Your laugh. I shall carry with me your wonderful laugh."

With more than a little effort, Gabe opened his eyes and blinked away a tear. Slowly, so as not to become dizzy, he got out of the car and walked up the steps to the kitchen. Sleep was calling him, but a more pressing need was a cup of Rosie's strong, black coffee.

48

Will leaned back in his chair, propped his feet on his desk, and closed his eyes. He dictated his morning's correspondence into his hand-held.

"You can be confident knowing that Remington Banking and Investments is on your side. By providing your company with an effective retirement plan, we will be helping you attract and keep the best employees, etc, etc, blah-blah. Okay, Ginny, tart these letters up a bit and get 'em in the mail on Monday." He reached out and turned off his recorder without opening his eyes. He grunted slightly as a feeling of disgust settled over him.

They had taken this week off from work—*they* being Gabe, Remy, Mason, and himself—in preparation for the wedding. But just because a man doesn't go into his office shouldn't mean that he *forgets* about it. *Hell fire,* Will thought, *it's only a little after nine a.m., and I've already read three morning newspapers, dictated five letters, and called one client. So what if that client wasn't out of bed yet? Lazy bastard should have been.*

And just what had his family members accomplished this week? Mason's days seem to have been spent in sleeping off the previous evenings' dalliances, while his beloved grandson lagged doe-eyed behind his soon-to-be wife. *Can't hardly blame him, though.*

And then there was Gabe. His son-in-law had rarely spent an entire week at home for close to a year now. Will had to admit, though, that their acquisition of the Greenville bank was a genius move. Gabe's handling of the transition had proved to be practically flawless. But Will feared that his involvement went beyond banking business.

"Hello, Will." As if on cue, Gabe spoke from the office doorway. "Got a minute?"

"Always, son. Sit down," Will answered brightly. "I looked for you at breakfast."

Gabe chose the chair closest to his desk. He sipped from his coffee cup before speaking. "It was late when the board meeting in Greenville broke up. I had a couple of drinks with some of the guys, then got a room."

Will laced his fingers together and rested his chin on them—his usual pose when pondering his next remarks. Several seconds passed before he spoke: "How's the transition going?"

"Quite well," Gabe replied. "I believe it's time that I stepped away and let the bank operate on its own. We've gotten rid of the dead wood, so to speak, and I'm confident that the newly appointed president will do an excellent job. We'll continue to see profits."

"Good, good," Will responded with seeming disinterest. He shuffled some papers on his desk and asked, "What's the new president's name? I can't seem to remember it."

Gabe cleared his throat. "Ms. Simon. Beth Simon."

"Ah, yes. Beth Simon. I met her, didn't I?"

Gabe shifted in his chair. "Yes, Will," he answered a bit sharply. "You've met Beth Simon on several occasions. In fact, you're the one who suggested naming her president of the bank."

"Of course. Now I remember," Will said. His sardonic little smile remained in place. "So, I guess that means you won't need to spend so much time in Greenville now."

"That's right. Now I can start looking for more acquisitions," Gabe responded as he stood up from his chair. "Got lots to do before the rehearsal dinner tonight. See you later."

Will took a parting shot. "Let's hope those future acquisitions won't take you away from the family quite so much."

49

Talmadge Beddingfield stepped out of the City Hall building's front door to an almost deserted Main Street. Like most Sunday mornings in Antioch, a predictable boredom hung over the town. The police chief relished the few minutes of peace and quiet.

Much as he cared about Cat—loved her, in fact—she was getting on his nerves this morning. He couldn't blame her, though. He had sprung it on her only a month previously: his decision to take early retirement and resign his position. She still hadn't been able wrap her head around it. Today, she had insisted on coming down to help him clean out his office. Talmadge shook his head, realizing that, after more than twelve years on the job, that objective posed a daunting task.

Cat stuck her head out of the door. "I wondered where you'd gotten to. If you want to get all those file cabinets cleaned out and packed today, you need to quit wandering off," she scolded him good-naturedly.

"Yes, dear," he said. "Just let me clear my head and I'll be back in."

"Humph," she snorted. "You'd better get rid of that damned cigarette and clear your lungs."

Talmadge ignored her last remark as he continued to wade through the quagmire of mixed feelings that leaving his job evoked. The catalyst, though, didn't need to be analyzed. The circumstances that had resulted in Tawney Simpson's untimely death remained a mystery. The realization that he was probably never going to bring closure to the case had made the past year as police chief intolerable.

Angrily, he ground out his cigarette butt under his boot heel but quickly bent to pick it up and toss it into a nearby trash receptacle. A bit of pride emerged as he studied the results of the past year's "Beautify Antioch" campaign. The town square's freshly painted and refurbished buildings, updated street lighting, and newly installed picnic tables and playground equipment were a source of pride. *Just goes to show what folks can do when they put their minds to it,* Talmadge thought.

Of course, the collection of granite and marble honoring the heroes of the Confederacy remained prominently displayed center stage. These silent vestiges of the south's divided past had defined the small town of Antioch for generations. But every so often, an unexpected and persuasive symbol of coming together would emerge. Talmadge smiled as he watched the two children approaching him, walking hand-in-hand.

The girl skipped along excitedly, tugging on the boy's hand and urging him forward. She prattled on and on in her usual effervescent way, describing something of apparently wondrous proportions. The boy responded with nods and smiles, captivated as he was by her every word. His mannerisms gave the impression of someone far beyond the age of almost eleven that Talmadge knew him to be. But of course, the police chief had always thought of Leander Washington as an 'old soul'.

"Good morning, Chief Beddingfield," Gabrielle chirped. "It sure is a nice day today, isn't it?"

"Yes, it certainly is. You two youngsters are playing hooky from Sunday school, I see."

"Yes, sir," the girl replied. "Everybody's sleeping late this morning 'cause of my brother's rehearsal dinner last night. It was some kind of fun. And, it was way past midnight when we got home. I was just now telling Lee all about it." She stopped to catch her breath, and then continued with her monologue. "You're coming to the wedding next Saturday, ain't you?"

Leander gave her hand a decisive yank. "*Aren't* you?" she immediately corrected herself.

Talmadge chuckled. "I sure am. I'm honored to be invited to Remy's wedding. Where are you kids off to this morning?"

Not giving Leander a chance to contribute to the conversation, Gabrielle answered. "Well, we was—were—going to go fishing. But then we decided instead to come downtown and try out the new jungle gym equipment in the park. Looks like fun."

"Sure does," Talmadge responded. "You kids have a good time."

"Oh, we will. C'mon, Lee! Race you."

Leander turned, smiled good-naturedly and said, "Have a nice day, sir."

Talmadge smiled and nodded in reply. Watching the children skip happily down the street made him feel a bit better about the future. As uncertain as it was, something told him that those two would see the tough times through together. Abruptly, he turned and made his way back inside the building to face the mountain of paperwork he still had to wade through.

Cat sat on a cushion in the middle of the floor, methodically packing thick file folders into boxes. Talmadge said, "Not those, babe. Those four folders go in my briefcase."

She leaned back, crossed her legs, and studied him. Her eyes narrowed, and a sly little grin spread over her face. "You think one of them did it, don't you?"

Talmadge walked to the row of file cabinets and began flipping through the top drawer's contents. "Who are you talking about? And what is it that *you* think that *I* think that *someone* did?"

Cat patted the stack of folders still sitting on her lap. "I'm talking about Tawney Simpson's death," she answered. "And, *I* think that *you* think that one of these four men did it."

"'Did it' is not accepted law enforcement lingo," he said. "Here, put these in that box." He handed her an armload of dusty spiral-bound notebooks. "Never know when a deputy's notes might come in handy."

Cat took the notebooks from him and dropped them into the open box without taking her eyes off his. "You *really* believe somebody in the Remington household could've had a hand in that girl's death?" Her tone of voice made it obvious that such a thought was incredulous. "Do you have any idea what a shit-storm that would stir up in this town?"

Talmadge looked at her for a long time before responding. When he did, his tone was official and not at all like the one normally reserved for his lady. "Don't put words in my mouth, Cat. You know I can't—and don't—discuss police business with civilians. Not even with you."

"Since when did the County Medical Examiner become a civilian?" she shot back crossly.

He took a deep breath and sat down heavily in his chair. Cat waited for him to respond. This was what he had needed for a long time. He needed to get at least some of the frustration off his chest. He lit a cigarette, leaned back in his chair, and closed his eyes. For once, she didn't complain about the smoke.

"Last month, I drove down Southside. Don't know why. Guess I just wanted to say something to Curley. You know, tell him that we hadn't forgot about his granddaughter. Reassure him that the department was doing all we could to get answers as to what actually had happened that day." Talmadge paused to collect his thoughts.

"Anyway, I went into his store, and there he was, doing exactly what we're doing today. He was packing up boxes, closing, he said. Told me he was going to live with his niece 'cause the memories here were just too much for him to bear."

Cat had moved from her spot on the floor to perch on the corner of his desk. She spoke quietly, "That's about the time you gave notice that you were retiring. Isn't that right?"

"Yeah," he answered. "Matter of fact, it was the next day. Seeing how sad and empty Curley was and knowing that life was all but over for the old guy just sort of soured me on the job. Understand?"

"Sure, I understand. I see the victims at their worst. Even though it's my job, sometimes I feel like I'm defiling their bodies all over again." She began to place the four file folders in his leather briefcase. One by one she slipped them inside, until the last one remained. It was thicker by far than the others, its corners dog-eared, its surface stained with spilled coffee and its spine reinforced with layers of tape. Cat lifted the folder up and peered at Talmadge over its top. Quietly, she repeated her earlier statement. "You think *he* did it."

Talmadge waited a few seconds before he responded. "I think—have a suspicion, I should say—that he saw or heard more than he told us. Could be he saw something or someone and dismissed it as not being important. It happens. Anyway, as I said earlier, 'did it' is not proper police terminology. I might call him a person of interest, though. Now, that's enough talk, and I don't have to remind you that anything I say to you stays between us. I'd like to get the office cleared out before the guys come in tomorrow morning."

Cat nodded. "Speaking of tomorrow," she said nonchalantly, "I thought maybe I'd drop by around noon and take you to lunch. How's that sound?"

Talmadge grinned. "Sure, come on over. You certainly don't want to miss my *surprise* retirement party."

Cat huffed. "Who told?"

"Nobody had to tell me anything. All the whispering and giggling going on, not to mention the phone calls between you and my secretary. Once a cop, always a cop, they say. I can still pick up on a clue now and then."

He stood up and hugged her. The earlier, somber mood lightened as the two of them shared a laugh. Talmadge was invigorated and ready to tackle the packing process in earnest. He fingered the leather briefcase containing the files in question, only to second-guess himself for the countless time. Did he really and truly believe *he* could somehow be involved?

Could a man of his position and background possibly be guilty of engaging in sexual intercourse with a child, and then after witnessing her death, coldly leave her lying alone in the woods? And, finally, could he calmly lie about it? Did personal integrity not come into the mix at all? What about conscience? Could he, an officer of the law, allow himself to believe the worst of another human being based entirely upon gut instinct and not one shred of evidence?

Talmadge snapped the clasp of the briefcase firmly closed, then placed it in the corner, away from the boxes. He began to whistle as he stacked boxes onto the dolly in preparation for their transport to the storage locker.

The briefcase would accompany him home, its muddled contents to be read and reread and agonized over throughout the years to come, with little hope for closure. *Goddamn right he did it!*

* * * * *

Can't hardly believe that a whole year's gone by. Actually, it's been three hundred seventy-nine days since you—since the accident. And you have survived. Of course, you have! You're the personification of survival. Each day gets a little easier, just like you knew it would. Tim heals. There are exceptions, though, like today when the weather's intolerably hot and, for some unknown reason, you've wandered down here to this path that you'll never be able to set foot on again. Then, it gets a little hard to take it all in.

Was it fate that put you and her in this same place at the same time? And how about the boy? Now, if fate put that nosey little shit there, then fate is a fucking bitch! It's obvious that he hasn't said a word to anyone. Hell, he hasn't even spoken to you since last fall. Of course, he's being quiet on purpose, so you'll wonder when the other shoe's gonna drop. When he does come around, what'll be the price for his silence?

How could you have let yourself get caught up in something that could ruin your life? Whoa, wait just a minute, now. It wasn't ALL your fault. What the hell was that girl doing in The Ramble in the first place? Truth be told, she probably saw you and followed you there. Asking for it! They all ask for it, then holler rape!

"WHAT? Shhhh."

No, no, that's not right—she didn't holler rape. Fact is, she didn't cry out at all.

She didn't even breathe.

PART II

Growing Pains
(Three Years Later)

50

Remy's butt had grown completely numb at least an hour ago, about the time that the Dean of the School of Business had risen to the podium and begun to praise the University's Business Department as being one of the top fifty in the country. And how this year's recipients of the "coveted" (yes, he'd actually said that) Bachelor's Degree in Business & Managerial Economics would become shining examples, leading the American business world to heights yet unattained. Dean what's-his-name's speech was punctuated with short breaks after every few words. He smiled his little Howdy-Doody grin and waited for the obligatory bit of handclapping that followed each pause.

The only good thing about the graduation ceremony was that it was being held at night. It was hot enough now, just after eight. He couldn't imagine having to sit here on the University's football field, sweating rivers underneath the heavy cap and gown, with the sun beating down. As if to punctuate that thought, another rivulet escaped from his cap, trickled down his forehead, and landed in his right eye. He couldn't retrieve his handkerchief without calling attention to himself, so he just blinked until the stinging stopped.

Remy was miserable. He hadn't even wanted to attend the graduation ceremony. What was the point, he'd complained earlier in the week to his family. "Our diplomas will be mailed to us anyway," he had said. "There's thousands of grads, you know. We don't actually walk across a stage, shake hands, and get handed a diploma."

"Doesn't matter," Granddaddy had affirmed. "I'm gonna be sitting right there in the family section, and I'm gonna holler and clap when I see my only grandson walk out in his cap and gown and graduate from college, goddammit! Understand?"

Oh, yes, Remy had understood. Everyone else in the family had understood as well, and they were all there. He felt sure that they were just as uncomfortable as he was. He shifted from one butt cheek to the other. The very least the University could have done for the grads was to find some folding chairs with padded seats.

The applause was louder this time, shaking Remy loose from his thoughts and signaling the end of another boring speech. Three more to sit through, then back to the apartment for the longest cold shower in history. He and Mason had packed and cleaned for the past week; tomorrow they would leave Columbia for good.

No longer a college man. The thought was depressing as he realized that, as far as the proverbial college experience was concerned, he'd never actually partaken. Regret nibbled as he thought of the multitude of missed opportunities that an all-American, red-blooded college man *should* have.

Of course, there had been the usual drunken escapades at the frat house—too many, in fact—during his freshman and sophomore years. But the past two years as a married man had all but ended those dimly remembered antics. Good times, with him and Mason being on their own and yet knowing that family was close by if needed.

Remy smiled. The mere thought of family brought back the last serious conversation he'd had with Granddaddy. The two of them had gone walking one morning during spring break, as they had done countless times during Remy's life. The rolling pastureland behind the Remington house had always been their preferred direction.

"Bet you're wondering what I got here in this knapsack, huh?" Will had asked as he came to a stop and sat down on a large boulder. They had been walking briskly for an hour, and the older man's breathing was as relaxed and normal as if he'd been sitting still all morning.

Remy plopped down on the grass, took off his t-shirt and mopped his brow with it. "I figured you'd tell me when you wanted to."

Will grinned. "Smart boy." He removed the knapsack from his shoulder, unclasped it, and took out several large, folded sheets of paper. As he began to unfold them, Remy recognized blueprints for a house. A *big* house.

After peering at the architect's renderings for several moments, Remy asked, "Whose house is this?"

Will's voice seemed to catch as he tried to answer. He cleared his throat and said, "It's your house, son, yours and M'Lyn's. It's for the two of you and your family." He paused and took a deep breath before continuing. "I hoped there would've been a great-grandson by now."

Remy shrugged. "It ain't from lack of trying. But what about this house?"

"Had Pratt and Pratt draw up these plans. You know, they're that pansy-assed bunch of architects that came to town last year. Well, everybody's raving about their designs, and after looking these over, guess I got to agree. We'll build it right here, son, right on this knoll. What'cha think?"

Another round of applause and the flashes from numerous cameras momentarily interrupted Remy's nostalgia. What had he thought of Granddaddy's latest gift? He was embarrassed that he couldn't remember much more of their conversation, or if he had actually thanked him or not. What he did remember, though, was mumbling something about not being deserving of such generosity, that he had not always made good decisions. And, he remembered bawling like a little kid. How could he ever forget that?

Will had smoothed everything over then, just like always. "Hell yes, you deserve it. You're my grandson, my legacy."

He went on to say something strange—something that still puzzled Remy. "Son, just remember that the past shouldn't cast a shadow on the future."

Remy had wanted to take something positive from his granddaddy's last statement. *But what could he have meant?*

The stirrings from his fellow graduates drew him out of his reverie and signaled the approaching grand finale. As if on cue, they all stood up, removed their caps, and hurled them into the air. A college graduate!

51

M'Lyn smiled as she looked at the saleslady. It was not her radiant, magnificent smile revealing perfectly capped white teeth that had aided in her being crowned in numerous high school beauty pageants. Nor was it the sweet, slightly sad little smile reserved for her friends who needed the occasional shoulder to cry on. And certainly, it wasn't the demure yet seductive smile reserved for her husband at bedtime—at least, on the nights when he wasn't too tired to respond to her. Remy had been putting in entirely too many hours at the bank and not enough with her. However, this latest purchase was going to change *that* situation.

No, her smile on this occasion was condescending in the face of the silent saleslady. M'Lyn cleared her throat and drew a deep breath, accentuating the fact that her patience was wearing thin. She made a point of looking closely at the nametag on the employee's lapel before speaking in her mockingly sweet tone. "Denesha—I do hope I'm pronouncing it correctly—please tell your supervisor that M'Lyn Westin would like to speak with her, please. That's Mrs. *Remy Westin*. Thank you, dear."

She drummed perfectly shaped acrylic nails on the marble countertop as she waited. She was furious but determined to remain calm. Imagine being told that her purchases exceeded the credit limit. Why, she'd never been so insulted in her entire life! Thank goodness, she had decided to come shopping alone. Had Carla been with her, it would have been all over the club by nightfall that M'Lyn Westin had a spending limit. Her fingers caressed the silken fabric of the mountain of designer lingerie that threatened to spill onto the floor. *These will bring Remy home early for sure.*

The velvet curtain behind the counter parted, and the woman stepped forward to greet M'Lyn. "Yes, ma'am. How can I help you?"

"I told the young lady that I wanted to speak with her supervisor," M'Lyn answered, her tone remaining unchanged.

"That would be me, then, since I'm the owner." The older woman smiled pleasantly and offered her hand. "I'm Tess Bradley. It's a pleasure to meet you, Mrs. Westin."

"Oh," M'Lyn responded, momentarily taken aback. She recovered her composure quickly and lightly brushed the extended hand. "This is the first time that I've been in your salon. I didn't realize that you had a credit limit."

"Denesha was simply doing her job," Tess said. "I do place a credit limit on new patrons but make exceptions, certainly in your case." She began to fold M'Lyn's purchases and place them among perfumed layers of tissue. "I'll be happy to assist you. Just fill out this card, and your bill will be mailed at the end of the month."

Tess watched her closely as she completed the customer information card.

"Thank you, Mrs. Westin," Tess said as she handed the large shopping bag across the counter. "I do hope we'll be enjoying your patronage in the future."

"Absolutely, Tess. I believe you'll be seeing quite a lot of me," M'Lyn said, casually using the other woman's given name. Her smile this time was one of pure contentment as she glanced around the showroom one final time and made her exit.

* * * *

"Hey, there, baby girl. You buy out all them stores today?" Roberta asked as M'Lyn entered the kitchen, struggling to maintain her balance while carrying an array of boxes and shopping bags of all sizes. She deposited her loot on the kitchen table with a groan.

"Just about, Roberta," she replied to the maid. "When you get time, can you come up to my room and help put everything away, please?"

"Sure thing, baby. Jus' soon as I get dinner started. Mr. Remy, he's home early. Most likely upstairs now."

"Really? I didn't see his car outside," M'Lyn said. "I thought he and Mason had a golf game this afternoon?"

"Mr. Mason dropped him off 'round noon. Said he'd be back to pick him up, but then I hears Mr. Remy on the phone telling him not to come. So, I don't know." Roberta's words faded as she turned her attention back to the dinner preparations.

M'Lyn gathered up her multitude of purchases once again and headed upstairs. *Strange,* she thought, that Remy would stay home for an entire afternoon. But when she thought about it, her husband had been acting a bit strange for several weeks now. It was obvious that his mind was somewhere else when it should be on her.

Mama had told her when she married that things would change, but she hadn't paid any attention to her. *It will be different with me and Remy,* she'd said. Their passion would never end, and he would certainly never lose interest in her. But he had, to some degree. Most of his time and attention, lately, seemed directed toward his job at the bank or studying the plans for their new house.

The house was going to be exquisite, of course, the envy of all her friends. But M'Lyn was in no hurry to leave the couple's current living quarters. Having the newly renovated suite in her parents' house, which meant keeping Roberta, was just fine with her. What was the hurry, anyway? The thought of the two of them rattling around in that big house was a bit gloomy. It was all Remy could talk about, though, coming home at night to his own home, *blah-blah-blah.* She would rather go out more, like they used to before they were married. Remy was much more outgoing then, certainly more attentive. Now, she got more compliments from—well, come to think of it, from Mason.

M'Lyn reached the top of the stairs and dropped some of her packages on the floor for Roberta to carry in later. She opened the door and crossed the carpeted floor, kicking off her shoes as she went, dropping the remaining items on the king-sized bed.

"Do you ever do anything besides shop?" Remy's voice was tight and cold as he startled her.

She whirled around to see him sitting in one of the chairs in front of the French doors, his long legs stretched out in front of him, his hands resting on his knees. His expression was hard to read as he stared intently at her.

"Hey, babe! What're you doing home in the middle of the afternoon? I thought you and Mason were going to the club today." She dropped into the swivel chair across the cocktail table from Remy's chair. "Just wait until you see the dress I got for the Member-Guest at the club. And since your mama's hosting this year's charity gala, I knew you'd want me to have something new to wear to that as well. And of course," she grinned seductively, her tongue flicking across her lower lip, "I did manage to buy a few things for your eyes only."

Remy didn't respond to her flirtation. When he spoke again, his tone of voice was unyielding. "I asked if you ever do anything besides shop. Why don't *you* try hosting an event, M'Lyn, or volunteer to help my mother? Maybe you might try showing a little interest in our new house. Have you even been to the site since the contractor started grading?"

M'Lyn studied her husband in silence for a long moment. Finally, she spoke. "What's the matter, Remy? Do I spend too much money? Is Granddaddy complaining? You've always liked the way I looked, the way I dressed, haven't you? Well, that look doesn't come from K-Mart, you know."

"I don't give a shit how much money you spend, and neither does Granddaddy. He does care about something else, though."

The pout was working full-time, but he didn't seem to be softening. Finally, spreading her hands, she asked, "What?"

Remy leaned back against the chair's headrest and closed his eyes. Quietly, he said, "Mason and I did have a golf game scheduled this afternoon. He dropped me here to change while he ran an errand." He stopped talking, opened his eyes, and stared at her.

This is getting tiresome, M'Lyn thought. "Okay, so what's wrong, Remy? Did something happen?"

"I decided to take a quick shower, but when I looked in my underwear drawer, it was empty. So, I go downstairs, find Roberta, and ask her about it. Seems like her hip was bothering her this morning more so than usual, so she gets her little granddaughter to bring up the laundry and put it away."

M'Lyn was losing patience. "So, what about it?"

"Roberta says that maybe the little girl put the laundry away in the wrong place. Says I should look in some of the other dresser drawers." Remy stopped speaking and reached into his shirt pocket, all the while maintaining eye contact with his wife. "And in my search, what to my wondering eyes should appear?"

Her mouth was dry and her heart skipped a beat as she watched her husband slowly remove the small, plastic circular case from his shirt pocket. Methodically, he leaned forward and with a flip of his thumb and forefinger, he set the object to spinning on the glass-topped table, just as a child would spin a top. Whirling on its smooth edge, it gradually slowed, began to wobble, and finally clattered to a stop, displaying the half-remaining circle of tiny pills and the prescription label for Ortho-Novum.

Silence hung between them like a curtain. Finally, M'Lyn spoke. "I can explain, Remy. The pills are to regulate my periods, that all. I've been having—"

"Bull shit!" His words made her jump. "You're a liar! You've been lying to me ever since we got married over two years ago. Telling me you didn't know why you hadn't gotten pregnant yet, making me think that maybe something was wrong with me." He stopped speaking and buried his face in his hands.

M'Lyn thought that perhaps it was time for tears. They came quickly. She murmured, "Remy, you know that I love you so much and I never wanted anything except to marry you and make you happy. But," her voice dropped to a whisper; "I-I don't know if I want to have children." She stood up and walked to the French doors across the room. Soon, she felt his presence behind her.

The edge had not left his voice. "Well, I *do* want children. As does Granddaddy. He wants a great-grandson to carry on his legacy, and I fully intend to give him what he wants. Is that clear?"

"Oh, it's clear alright," she said angrily, turning to face him. "It's clear that all you care about is pleasing your grandfather, and to hell with what your wife wants! That's what's clear to me."

"Is it equally clear to you that Granddaddy is the reason you spend your days in the shopping malls, your entire life in luxury?"

M'Lyn swallowed hard and wisely took a step backward. She was not ready to concede the argument, though. "Of course, that's clear to me, and I'm grateful to your Granddaddy. But he needs to understand that it's my body and my decision whether or not I give birth."

Remy's hands clenched and unclenched. His face was red and the big vein in his neck throbbed and pulsed. M'Lyn had never seen him so angry. In truth, she had never seen him angry at all. It was a stranger who faced her now, one who spoke with barely contained fury.

"*YOU* are the one who needs to understand something. Granddaddy wants a great-grandson, and that what he's going to get."

He moved closer now, and she realized that her back was against the wall, literally. Moving was impossible, sandwiched as she was between the wall and his rock-hard chest. His eyes were unfocused, and he was sweating profusely. Suddenly, his hands were around her neck. "*Now,* do you understand?" he hissed.

M'Lyn was dizzy, and she was terrified. She pulled at his hands, but it was no use. She thought about kicking out at him, but her body was in a vice. She managed to whisper hoarsely, "Please, Remy, I can't breathe!"

As quickly as he had grabbed her, he released her and stepped back. His face was ashen, and his eyes once more focused. "I-I'm so s-s-sorry," he said as he shook his head and met her frightened gaze. She simply nodded and turned away from him.

When he spoke again, his voice was calm and matter-of-fact. "I'll see you tonight," he said. He turned to leave the room. Passing the table, he retrieved the pill case and dropped it onto the floor. With one decisive stomp of his ostrich boot, bits of plastic and pills exploded into the pale blue carpet.

M'Lyn flinched This time, she didn't have to coax her tears. This time, they flowed freely.

52

Mason Carlisle lounged easily in the Adirondack chair in front of his dad's beachfront condo. Clad only in swim trunks, his toes snugly buried in the sand, he sipped his breakfast smoothie and pondered how he should spend the last week of his summer break before heading back to Antioch.

He was surprised to realize how much he had enjoyed the summer with his old man. They'd bonded for probably the first time in his life. Mason attributed that to the departure of the latest step-mommy, taking with her the drama that had defined the union. That, and Layton Carlisle finally reaching the other side of his mid-life crisis. And, just maybe, he himself had grown up a bit as well.

One thing he did know for sure was that he was eager to begin a new chapter of his life as partner in Remington Banking and Investments. With a contented little grunt, Mason marveled once again at the amazing direction his life was headed. Together, with his dad's graduation money and Will's generous signing bonus, one of the new upscale townhouses at the Antioch Country Club would be his new home. Equally astounding had been Will's insistence that he take the summer off and spend it here in Charleston, all the while on the bank's payroll.

Mason sat his cup in the sand and retrieved the bottle of suntan oil from his bag. He never bothered with sunscreen, fostering instead the dark tan that showcased his blue eyes. At least, that's what *she* had said last night. He leaned back in the chair, closed his eyes, and grinned broadly. Oh, life was indeed good.

But his idyllic fantasizing didn't last. "Damn it to hell!" Mason spat the curse savagely, despising himself for his inability to control his own thoughts.

His eyes flew open, and he sat bolt upright. He immediately regretted the sudden movement, as the morning sunlight brought with it arrows of stabbing pain. He was momentarily blinded by the bright, shimmering of the ocean, and he wisely closed his eyes and willed his heart to stop racing. *Why did this always have to happen?* Whenever he thought of his comfortable life, the 'yeah-buts', 'if-onlys', and 'what-ifs' reared their ugly heads.

Nothing is going to go wrong--nothing. Mason shook his head vigorously, managing to dislodge the menacing qualms, for the moment at least. Lifting his glass, he drank deeply of the now-warm smoothie. He idly watched the southwesterly breeze tease the clumps of sea oats. Rain would come later in the day, he predicted. Soon, high tide would all but cover these grasses, and the movement of the waves would deposit clumps of sand, sediment, and shells, known as beach balls, along the now-pristine stretch of sand. The unsightly remains would eventually be swept back to sea, leaving the shore clean once again.

Ah-ha! A metaphor, he thought. *Enjoy the good times and live in the light. The dark and ugly images will soon fade away.*

A snowy egret drew Mason's attention. Unmoving, the bird stood in a nearby tidal pool. After a time, his patient stance was rewarded with a morsel of food, and he slowly began to meander down the beach. Mason gulped the last of his drink just as the breeze shifted, bringing with it the distinctive marsh smell. He recognized the redolent odor of the surrounding paper mills and not sewage, as newcomers to parts of the low country would initially presume.

Mason wrinkled his nose in distaste as he swallowed what now tasted like the rotten-egg smell instead of orange-pineapple. "Ick," he groused aloud, tossing the plastic cup towards a nearby trash basket.

"Hey, sugar. Is somethin' wrong on this fine mornin'?"

Mason turned around at the syrupy voice behind him. His last night's date had been sleeping soundly amid the tangled bed sheets when he had risen hours ago. He'd been careful not to wake her—he wasn't in the mood for conversation. He still wasn't.

"Good morning..."*Jennifer? Jessica? Jen? Jess? ...* "dahlin. Sleep well?"

She gracefully lowered her bikini-clad body to the sand at his feet and began to massage the calf of his leg. "Uh-huh," she purred. "I slept like a baby. What's on the agenda for today?"

Mason stroked her thick, dark hair as he gently extricated himself from her touch. "You're welcome to hang out here as long as you want," he said nonchalantly. "I, on the other hand, have to get ready for a business meeting this afternoon." He shook his head slightly and hoped his expression was one of regret as he continued to spin his little white lie. "And, since I have to leave tomorrow for Antioch, I've still got packing to do."

"Oh," she responded, obviously disappointed. "I didn't think you were leaving for another week." She inched closer, making sure her scantily covered breasts caressed his thigh. "You're not gonna forget about me, are you?"

Mason studied Jen-Jess from the protection of his Ray-Bans. His initial thought was to remind her that, since she'd told him the night before of her recent move to Charleston from Baltimore, she should probably drop the irritatingly fake southern drawl. He also thought about telling the complete truth for once, which was that, since he couldn't even remember her name, it was doubtful that he'd remember much else about her in the days to come. But, then, the complete truth sometimes came with baggage. And Mason certainly didn't need any *more* baggage.

He lowered his face to hers and gently sucked her full lower lip into his mouth. "'Course I won't forget about you, dahlin," he whispered. He gently tweaked her erect nipple before rising and retrieving his beach bag. As he began strolling toward the condo, he turned and bestowed one more dazzling smile on her. "Why, you're unforgettable," he said.

53

Will Remington sat behind his desk, gazing trance-like at the wall of floor-to-ceiling plate glass. It was a rarity, indeed, when the time he spent in his fourth-floor office was not devoted entirely to the banking and investment business. Today was different, though. He rose from his chair and stepped closer to the windows, stretching away the stiffness in his back brought on by sitting still for much too long. With his efforts came the fleeting thought that he was aging. But, swift on the heels of pessimism, came a tingling of excitement that today's news was going to make him feel young again.

Despite his preoccupation, Will found himself rather enjoying the view of Antioch's Main Street, adorned on this uncommonly cool June day with blossoming cherry and peach trees and alive with people strolling from one trendy little shop to another. The thought came to him that the bank's sponsorship of the "Beautify Antioch" campaign a few years ago had been a stroke of genius, albeit someone else's idea and not his.

The publicity generated from the town's promotion had spread state-wide and had resulted in more than a dozen new lucrative accounts for Remington Investments. Yes, his son-in-law had been right yet again when he'd convinced Will to underwrite the initial cost of the campaign. It had been Gabe's recommendation as well that the new downtown park be dedicated to the memory of the Simpson girl. Bottom line: it had been a wise move.

Will shook his head to clear away what he considered to be inconsequential thoughts and to make room for more important matters. "Ginny," he called out loudly, "have you heard from my grandson this afternoon?"

The rapid clicking of high heels on the slate floor outside his office announced the secretary's arrival. "No, Mr. Will, I haven't heard a word since around ten o'clock this morning when Remy called from the doctor's office. Or," Ginny paused to suck in a breath before she prattled on, "I guess it wasn't the doctor's office, but maybe the lab. No, now, let's see." She paused again, closed her eyes, and tapped a bony finger to her forehead. "Oh, now I remember. Remy called from the *imaging* center. That's what they call it where you go and have MRI's and x-rays. I guess they still do x-rays, huh? Well, anyway, they were at the imaging center when he called, and he said that they were next to go in for M'Lyn's test. Oh, I can't think! What is it they call that test that she's having today? Don't say it. Don't tell me. Oh, I know, it's an ultrasound." Ginny took a deep breath, obviously pleased with herself. "They were next for their ultrasound. And that was at ten o'clock. When Remy called."

Will stared at her with wonder. "Ginny," he said softly, "I'm constantly amazed at how many words can come out of your mouth to answer a simple yes-or-no question." His sarcasm was not wasted. His secretary of almost forty years glared at him for a long moment, then sniffed loudly as she turned her back to him.

Her parting words coaxed a chuckle from him: "Well then, in answer to your question: No."

"Thank you," he called out sweetly. Where the hell *was* Remy, he wondered? Even allowing for lunch after the appointment, he should have been back by now. Will checked the clock on the wall: three-fifteen. Without warning, his stomach knotted up. *Could something be wrong?*

The matter of M'Lyn's pregnancy was not to be taken lightly. The young couple's first try had resulted in an early miscarriage. When she became pregnant again last fall, Remy had demanded that she not set foot on the tennis courts for nine months. Smart move on his grandson's part, Will reckoned. And with that thought, he heard the familiar whistling from down the hall.

"Hey, Granddaddy," Remy said as he swept into his office. "Whew, what a day. First off, the center was packed, so we had to wait over an hour. Then, M'Lyn wanted to have lunch with her folks at the club. After that, she was exhausted, so she went home with Tom and Lynn, and I went to the house for a shower." He removed his jacket and tossed it in the general direction of one of the leather chairs facing Will's desk as he collapsed into the other.

Will lowered himself slowly into his chair and spread his hands. "Well?" he asked with apprehension.

Remy shrugged. "Baby's moved since the first ultrasound, but still bashful. Had that little leg curled up right over the mid-section."

"So, what? We still don't know if it's a boy or a girl?" Will asked.

"Nope. We'll have to wait 'til the big day."

"Alright, then," Will replied in resignation. "That's only another couple of weeks. Right?"

"Doc said it could be a little longer, 'cause most first babies tend to be late. We could be looking at a July 4th baby." Remy yawned. "I'm exhausted. M'Lyn can't sleep, so that means that *I* can't sleep either."

Will began to flip through the stack of files on his desk. With his earlier eagerness to learn the gender of his great-grandchild tempered, business once again claimed top spot. "Everything else going okay with M'Lyn?" he inquired absently.

"Yeah, I guess. It's not like I know what to expect, though. One minute she's happy, then crying her eyes out the next. Her feet are swollen. She has to pee every five minutes." Remy closed his eyes and rubbed his temples. "She's miserable, Granddaddy. And I feel guilty as hell."

Will directed his attention away from the papers on his desk and back to Remy. "She'll be fine, son. All women feel the way she's feeling when they go through the birthing process. And all men tend to feel guilty. Just don't over-think it. You're tired, so go on back home and get some rest. Maybe first thing in the morning you could go over these numbers on the Madison Brewery account. I can't make heads or tails of their spreadsheets."

"Thanks, Granddaddy; I'll do that. See you tomorrow."

Will stared after his grandson. Out of the blue, he thought of Lily. Her pregnancy with Vivian had been a trying time as well, with severe mood swings that had mystified the guileless twenty-two-year-old that he had been back then. He closed his eyes and leaned back in his chair. He knew the distress that Remy was going through now, and he knew that it would pass. But guilt—now, that was a whole other animal.

54

"These ham biscuits sure are good," Leander said between mouthfuls. "Rosie must have gotten up early this morning."

"Nope," Gabrielle said. "Mama cooked 'em. She said to let Rosie sleep 'cause she was up late last night on account of Remy's and M'Lyn's anniversary dinner. Look yonder, Lee!" she suddenly squealed. "You got a bite. Looks like a big one, too."

Gaby dropped her biscuit carelessly on a patch of moss and jumped up from her seat on the ground. She bounced with excitement as she looked at the boy's bent fishing pole. "Hurry up! You gonna let him get away!"

Leander calmly laid his biscuit on a paper napkin and got to his feet. With fishing pole in hand, he began to steadily reel in his catch. He laughed and said, "Take it easy, girl. This one's hooked good."

Gaby breathed a sigh of relief as she watched him deftly remove the hook and place the large trout in his creel. "Biggest damn fish I ever did see," she announced. "Sorry," she added.

"He's probably the biggest fish that I've ever caught. Your turn, now," Leander said, retrieving his biscuit. "The fishing has been good so far this summer. Moam said it's because of all the rain we've had lately."

"Believe you're right," Gaby said as she began to reel in a slightly smaller fish. She quickly cast a newly baited hook into the swift-moving water and settled back to her spot beside Leander. Pensively, she asked, "Do you think that we'll ever get tired of fishing, Lee?"

"I doubt it. Why would we?"

"I don't know. Maybe since we're teenagers now we might want to do other things." Gaby turned to face her friend for guidance.

"True, we're thirteen," he replied, "but that's just barely a teenager. And, I still like to go fishing. Do you?"

"You bet I do!" she exclaimed, pointing to her fishing pole as it began to quiver.

"So, how was the anniversary dinner last night?" Leander asked.

Gaby shrugged. "It was okay, I guess. The food was great, especially the cake. But," she shook her head and sighed, "M'Lyn didn't seem to enjoy herself. She complained all the time, saying stuff like that she was miserable and how it seemed a lot longer than just three years since she and Remy had got married. I heard her tell Mason's new girlfriend, Sterling McKenna, that she hoped to God she had a boy. That way, maybe Remy wouldn't want any more babies."

"Sounds to me like she's having a tough time," Leander responded sympathetically.

Gaby turned to him with raised eyebrows. "Sounds to me like she's a sissy."

The children's idle conversation was suddenly interrupted by the sound of footsteps on the path behind them. Gaby turned around. With a questioning smile on her face, she said, "Hi, Mason! What are you doing here? Did you come to fish with us?"

Mason's expression was somber as he spoke. "Didn't come to fish, baby girl, came to fetch you back to the house. You, too, Leander."

Gaby didn't move from her crossed-legged position on the ground. She stared with huge, unblinking eyes at Mason, while Leander reacted with unquestioning compliance by reeling in both fishing lines and gathering their belongings.

After a few seconds, she swallowed hard and asked, "What's wrong?" Then, in the twinkling of an eye, her face exploded into a grin. "Oh," she gushed, "am I about to be an aunt?"

Leander had remained silent in his preparations. As the three of them turned toward the path, he looked up at Mason and indicated the remaining items on the ground with a nod of his head.

Mason stooped to retrieve them, and then extended his other hand to Gaby. "C'mon, baby girl. We got to go home."

* * * * *

Gabe Weston sat on the kitchen stool, elbows propped on the counter, a favorite spot of his. He was prone to reminiscing, and this morning was no different, with the memories—each one more vivid and more achingly precious than the one before—cascading through his mind.

He recalled his very first day as a member of Will's family, when indecision about where he was supposed to go and what he was supposed to do in the great big house had all but overwhelmed the little boy of seven. The house had been so quiet that he hadn't known for sure if anyone else was there. Hunger, and a bit of curiosity, had enticed him to creep down the stairs just as dawn was breaking. But then, he'd gotten turned around and had no idea how to find his way back to his bedroom.

She had found him, still clad in his pajamas, sitting stiffly on the sofa in the living room, trying valiantly not to burst out crying.

"Well, now," she'd said with mock formality, "who do we got here but the future gentleman of the house, sitting in the parlor." When she saw his brown eyes swimming and his chin begin to tremble, her teasing had stopped. Swiftly, she lifted him in her arms as if he were weightless, carried him into the kitchen, and sat him here, on this very stool.

"Now, then," she had said, giving him the kindest smile that he'd ever seen as she wiped away his tears, "this is where you and me gets acquainted. That is, right after I fix you some blueberry pancakes. You ever had blueberry pancakes?" At Gabe's assenting nod, she had responded emphatically, "Humph, you ain't had *my* blueberry pancakes!" She was right: he had never tasted blueberry pancakes that good. He still hadn't.

He couldn't begin to count the times throughout his childhood when a bad dream had prompted him to make his way down the back staircase and tap on her door in the middle of the night. The two of them would sit here on these stools with mugs of hot chocolate until his goblins had been replaced with giggles.

Gabe shook his head. Right here, on this same kitchen stool, he had sat with eyes downcast and confided to her with embarrassment that he had wet his bed—at thirteen years old, no less. That afternoon, when he'd gotten home from school, he discovered a new mattress on his bed. It was never mentioned. She had just taken care of it.

Then, there was *that* night, in another lifetime, when he had sat on this stool, all hunched over, head in his hands, and haltingly poured out his heart to her. And she had understood. She hadn't judged. She simply told him in no uncertain terms that a future with Tess could never be. And again, she had wiped away his tears.

He smiled now, remembering the happiness on her face when he had opened the velvet box to reveal the diamond he'd bought for Vivian. "You're the first person to see it," he told her. "Will hasn't even seen it yet."

It had been her turn to shed a tear, then. "My boy," she simply said. "I'm so proud of you!"

He had stopped confiding in her years ago, stopped taking his fears and anxieties to her, as all children stop running to their parents when they become adults. *Parent?* Yes, she with no children of her own had instilled in an orphaned boy who barely remembered his own mother and father what it meant to be a parent. And now, she was gone.

His Rosie was gone!

Vivian's hand on his shoulder brought him back to the present. "I called the doctor. He's sending the medical examiner. And…" her voice broke and Gabe patted her hand, "Claire's on her way over. I called Remy, too, but he doesn't want to leave M'Lyn."

"Will sent Mason to bring Gaby back. I saw him go out to the front porch a while ago to wait for them," Gabe said absently. "Do we know how old she was? I don't think I ever heard her say."

"Funny you should ask," Vivian said. "I was wondering the same thing earlier. I looked in her Bible, you know, the family record pages. Anyway, her birth is written there. She was eighty-eight."

Vivian was silent for a moment. "I found something else in her Bible," she said finally.

Gabe grunted questioningly.

"She had a sister, Mavis," Vivian responded. "There was a newspaper clipping: Mavis passed away last year, and Rosie never mentioned it. Her *family*. She never said a word."

"That's because *we* were her family. As soon as uh, they, you know, take her away," Gabe stammered, "I suppose Will and I should go into town and make arrangements."

"Yes, you should," Vivian said. "Oh—here's Claire, now."

The two women embraced as the sound of voices filtered in from the dining room. Will entered the kitchen, followed by Mason and the children. Leander walked solemnly to Claire's side as Gabe made his way to Gabrielle and knelt to her level. "Gaby," he said softly, "did Granddaddy tell you about Rosie?"

Gaby nodded, tight-lipped, then whispered, "He said Rosie died."

Vivian watched as her husband spoke in hushed tones to their daughter. Gaby stared straight ahead, willing herself not to cry as she watched Gabe swallow *his* tears. Vivian looked at her father—God forbid that the ever-macho Will Remington would shed tears. And she, herself, was no different. It was she who had found Rosie, lying in her bed as though she were only asleep. And what had she done? Suppressed her own grief by putting on a brave front—as well as her makeup.

What's wrong with this family? Vivian pondered sadly as she crossed the marble foyer to answer the doorbell. *Must we always be so damn valiant?*

55

"Remy, come here and help me!" M'Lyn hissed angrily. "I couldn't navigate these steps even if I *wasn't* pregnant! I do not see why you had to drag me out in this god-awful heat for a funeral. *A funeral!*" she repeated. "It's not as if Rosie would *know* if I'd been allowed to stay indoors in air-conditioned comfort instead of being subjected to an hour of torture—*pure torture*—sitting on that hard pew. My back, Remy, is killing me. I'm not supposed to sit on hard surfaces for long periods of time. You heard the doctor with your own ears, did you not?" She ground her words between clinched teeth, only to suddenly realize that it didn't matter one bit if her complaints were overheard or not. What did she care what these people thought, anyway?

She looked around disdainfully at the smattering of mourners, made up mostly of the aging membership of King David AME Zion Church, along with two out-of-town women introduced as Rosie's nieces, Carl Lee and Claire Washington and their children and the Remington-Westin family.

Her husband stood at her side, appropriately sad-faced and appearing to accept the dressing-down as his due. "Well," M'Lyn said, directing a withering look his way, "are you going to help me down these steps, or should I try it on my own?"

Taking her elbow and gently maneuvering her into a sideways position to make the steps visible around her ponderous belly, Remy instigated their slow decent down the rickety wooden steps of the small church. "Baby," he said, "I'm so sorry. I didn't know the service would last this long. And I've never been here before, so how would I know about the hard pews, or these steps, for that matter?"

"This is stressful and not good for me or for the baby," she said. Playing the baby card always worked: Remy looked more guilt-ridden by the second.

"Here, sweetheart. You're on the cement walkway now. It goes all the way 'round to the cemetery in back. Just a little while longer, and we'll be on our way home. I'm just so sorry."

Remy wondered how many times he'd uttered those words— 'I'm sorry'—during the past nine months. *Too many times, that's for sure.* He longed to tell her to quit her constant bitching, like she was the only woman to ever have a baby. But then the reality of the situation set in, and he chastised himself all over again.

She was the only woman to ever have *his* baby.

Gabe had stationed himself a few paces away from the other members of his family. He stood with his long arms clasped behind his back and his head slightly bowed in reverence. He tried valiantly to keep his eyes straight ahead and focused solely on the business at hand—that of saying his final goodbye to Rosie. It was impossible, though, not to cast a glance to the left, to where the smattering of sad little crosses, washed-out plastic flowers, and sun-faded teddy bears marked the section of infant graves.

He longed to wander there to gaze more closely at the little granite lamb that he'd seen from the corner of his eye earlier. But self-flagellation would have to wait for another time. Instead, he reached out to offer a steadying hand to his daughter-in-law as the young couple approached him at the graveside. His gesture was ignored.

"I don't want to go home," M'Lyn whispered to Remy as the old Reverend cleared his throat and prepared to speak one last time over Rosie's coffin, positioned over the waiting grave. "I want to go to my Mama's house."

"Of course, baby—whatever you want," Remy said. He placed his arm around her shoulders and she leaned against him, allowing herself to be comforted if only for a moment.

The afternoon heat was oppressive, and Remy could feel the steady stream of perspiration running down his back and soaking into the waistband of his shorts and slacks. He felt something else, too, but what was it? The strange sensation continued to permeate his consciousness until he became fully aware of what was happening.

M'Lyn was leaning more heavily on him now. Looking down, Remy saw that his pant leg and shoe were soaking wet. "Granddaddy!" he called out, interrupting the final benediction. "I-I think it's time!"

Claire was the first to move. She hurried to M'Lyn's other side to help support the soon-to-be mother. "Come on, Remy," she said. "Let's get her to the hospital. Her water's broke. Gabe, you go get the car and drive it as close as you can. Viv, you call the doctor and tell him we're on the way and to meet us at the hospital. Then call her parents."

Everyone fell in line, doing exactly as Claire ordered. They were no longer mourners, but excited family members, friends and strangers alike, walking with a spring to their step, expressions of sadness and loss melting into smiles of anticipation as the circle of life continued.

* * * * *

If hospitals are supposed to be the safest places to go when you're sick—or giving birth—then why do they always smell the worst? Makes you wonder, huh? Hospitals give you the creeps, always have. And the seating—do they try to see how uncomfortable they can make these chairs? Don't forget the fact that you're freezing to death! Makes no sense whatsoever, ninety-eight outside and it's a frigging meat locker in here! Guess that old saying holds true: if you're not sick when you come in here, you will be before you leave.

What a day! Everybody's here together, though. That's good. Like family— mostly. Death, life, death. Don't think about it. Just take a deep breath.

"Huh, w-what?"

"You were certainly zoned out. I said, 'Here comes the nurse.'"

"Good afternoon, everyone," the plump, pleasant-faced nurse Thelma, identified by her nametag, said. "Mrs. Westin is all settled in the delivery room, and it looks like it's going to be a *long* ordeal. She's doing just fine, though. Dr. Cope is in with her right now."

"How long, Nurse?" Will asked.

"Hard to tell, especially with these first babies." Nurse Thelma answered. "She's asking for her mama and her husband to come on back and be with her, now. So, y'all follow me, and I'll get gowns for both of you."

Thelma beckoned both Lynn Olsen and Remy to accompany her through the stainless-steel double doors and spoke over her shoulder to the remaining group in the waiting area. "The rest of you folks had best find a good book and make yourselves comfortable."

Claire stood up. "Viv, I'll take Gabrielle and Leander back to your house. I'll get some supper started, too, so you can stay here," she said. "You call me soon as that baby comes."

She had picked up her purse in preparation to leave when Gabrielle said, decisively, "I'm not going *anywhere* until I see my new niece or nephew."

"And I'm not leaving Gaby," Leander declared.

The two mothers looked at each other knowingly. "I guess that settles that," Vivian said.

"Well, then," Claire said, "I'll go pick up some take-out and bring it back here. That way, we can all eat together."

"Yeah, pizza!" Gabrielle decreed.

"And milkshakes, too, please," Leander chimed in.

"You stay here, Miz Claire. I'll go pick up the food," Mason said.

"Why, thank you, Mason. Are you sure you don't mind?" Vivian asked.

Mason smiled. "I'm sure, Miz Vivian. If I'm busy, the time will pass faster. Truth is, I could use some fresh air."

56

Leander sat stiffly on one of the plastic chairs that lined the walls of the hospital waiting room. It was impossible to get comfortable. He was tall for his age, but if he sat properly in the chair, his feet still wouldn't touch the floor, making his legs fall asleep. If he sat forward, his back hurt. Nurse Thelma had brought out blankets to everyone, but he was still cold. Sipping on the icy milkshake didn't help.

Perhaps he should stand up and walk around a bit to stretch his legs, like everyone else was doing. He didn't want to call attention to himself, though. The gathering tension that permeated the waiting room was unsettling to be sure, and every time Leander moved, he felt as though all eyes were fixed on him.

The door to the delivery room swung open. A distraught-looking Remy, clad in a green surgical gown and sweat-soaked cap, emerged. He held up his hand to quell any questions from the anxious faces before him. "Nothing yet, folks. Baby's taking its own sweet time. I just came out to, uh, well…" He gazed around the room with a look of chagrin. "Actually, I came out 'cause M'Lyn told me to get the hell out of her sight."

Several good-natured chuckles erupted as Gabe reached over to pat Vivian's hand. She nodded understandingly. "She'll forget all about it, son," she said, "the minute she holds that baby in her arms."

"That's right, Remy," Claire added. "Now you get yourself something to eat. It's all gonna be just fine."

"Come on, Lee," Gabrielle said, "let's have some more cookies."

"Sure. Then, we should probably gather up all the trash and take it to the dumpster. We could pack up the left-over food for later, Mama. Would that help?"

Claire smiled and gave her son a quick hug. "That would be a big help, Leander," she said.

Vivian moved to her best friend's side and watched as the two children began their chores. "Just a few years ago you were worried about Leander being so distant and moody. Remember?" She didn't wait for a reply. "I told you then that you had nothing to worry about. He's becoming a fine young man, Claire."

"Oh, I remember very well," Claire said. "I remember that *attitude* of his just appeared right out of the blue one day. It was like he was mad at everybody and sad all at once." She shook her head. "Then, just as quick, there was my sweet boy, back with me. Still, there's times, Viv, when I look at him and…"

"And what?" Vivian prompted.

"Sometimes he just looks so troubled. But I know that Moam was right after all when she said it's just growing pains."

With their tasks completed, the two young friends settled into a quiet corner of the waiting area. While Gabrielle occupied herself by flipping mindlessly from one boring TV channel to another, Leander pretended interest in an outdated issue of *National Geographic*.

The air of anxiety had lessened in the room, as everyone milled about and tried to boost Remy's spirits with reassuring tales of past births. Leander felt less self-conscious and continued his discrete people-watching over the top of the magazine.

Throughout the day, both during Rosie's funeral and at the hospital, Leander had tried not to look at *him*. Times like now, though, he found it impossible to take his eyes off him. *He looks normal,* the boy thought, quickly realizing that he wasn't sure exactly what *normal* should look like. The man laughed at jokes and appeared sad at funerals. Surely, those were indicators of normalcy. But so many other times, his expression was impossible to read, particularly for Leander, since the two of them had not spoken directly in four years except for brief greetings.

Reverend Solomon preached just about every Sunday about forgiveness. Leander had tried to forgive—him for the horrible deed, and himself for sheltering it. He hadn't been able to do so, yet. Perhaps if he could see into his mind and know that he was *truly* sorry, forgiveness would come.

Was he constantly tormented by the events of that day? Or, had he dismissed it years ago as simply an unpleasant accident? Did his actions haunt him, or did they pass as a fleeting memory? Leander wondered.

Was the man basically a good person? Leander knew the answer to that: of course, he was a good person. But no matter how often his thoughts hovered on past good deeds, they always came back to settle on the cold, hard fact that on *that day*, the man's actions had taken the life of a young girl.

The boy closed his eyes and drew a deep breath. It was impossible to read someone's mind, to know their innermost thoughts. Still, he wondered.

Nurse Thelma burst through the double doors. "Alright, folks, we're just about to have us a baby, any minute now, I believe. Remy, you come on back now. She's asking for you."

Everyone was on their feet now, hugging each other and grinning from ear to ear. Leander stood up and clasped hands with Gabrielle. She was beaming. How she loved her big brother, her whole family, Leander knew. Getting caught up in the excitement was easy for him. Perhaps one day the forgiving would come just as easily.

After more than twelve long hours, the curtain covering the window looking into the newborn nursery slowly began to open. Still clad in the shapeless gown and sweaty cap, an expression of rapture having replaced his worried countenance, Remy stood before crowd of onlookers. He didn't try to hold back the tears as he proudly introduced the blue-swaddled bundle cradled in his arms.

"Great-Granddaddy, Grandpa Gabe, Grandma Vivian, Aunt Gaby, Papaw Tom, Uncle Mason, and friends," Remy's voice broke as he gazed lovingly at his baby. "I'd like to introduce you to William Remington Westin, Jr. We're calling him William."

"M'Lyn?" Tom Olson asked as he wiped his eyes and blew his nose loudly into his handkerchief.

"She's fine, Tom," Remy answered. "Tired, but she did so good. Y'all can come on back once they get her in a room. Lynn's helping to get her settled right now. But I think she's gonna want to sleep for a *long* time."

"He's beautiful, son," Gabe said, hugging Vivian tightly.

"Almost as beautiful as you were," Vivian added.

"I want to hold him! When can I hold him?" Gabrielle was ecstatic.

"You'll be the first one to hold him, Gaby. I promise."

The family and friends chattered with excitement:

"I'm next."

"Who do you think he looks like?"

"Oh, you can't tell. He looks like a baby!"

"He's got a head full of hair; and blond, like M'Lyn."

"Well, I think he looks like my baby picture. I'll show y'all next time we're together. I'll bring that picture. Looks just like I did."

Mason moved closer to the glass and spoke to Remy. "Man, you guys did good. He's amazing."

"Thanks, dude," Remy responded. "Hey, you're up for Godfather, I hope."

Mason swallowed hard before nodding. "It's an honor, man."

Will had remained silent. "Granddaddy, what do you think?" Remy asked. "Is he a keeper?"

Everyone turned to look at their patriarch. Will spoke quietly. "I've never been prouder than I am right now. This family, this next generation," he held out his hand toward Remy and baby William and smiled, "is complete. The best is yet to come."

"Hear, hear!" Gabe said to another round of hugging and excited congratulations all around.

Gabrielle couldn't stand still, and Leander was amused at her antics. He hadn't seen her this excited in a long time. He was happy for her and for everyone in her family. He looked around the room at the circle of smiling faces and realized that he, too, was happy.

Then, for one electric moment, their eyes met. Locked within that gaze, Leander's awareness of the day's events was heightened. Could they both be sharing the very same thought: *Why does life take so long to begin, then end so suddenly?*

PART III

Coming of Age

57

Eight years! Eight years to the day, as a matter of fact. Does he realize that? Of course, he does. That's why the sonofabitch picked today for this meeting.

Eight fucking years, and he's spoke maybe half a dozen words to you. Now, he wants to meet with you. Why? You know why—today you're gonna find out what he wants. What his price is.

Haven't you paid enough already? The sleepless nights. The cold knot of fear that you'll be exposed? The revulsion when the anniversary of her unsolved death is recounted on the news channel as an act of rape, of cowardice?

BUT NO ONE KNOWS. Only him, that is. And he doesn't REALLY know. Who would believe him, anyway? Believe some colored kid over you? Hell, folks would just say he was making it up. Or, would they believe him and not you, and everything you've worked for and achieved would be gone and you'd be ruined and go to prison!

The tap-tap on the office door made him flinch. "Y-y-yes?" he stammered.

The door opened. "A young man here to see you," the secretary said.

You are better than this, better than HIM!

Uncertainty and fear fell away as he stood up and extended his hand. Once again, he was in charge, the master of graciousness and professionalism. "Come in, Leander," he spoke warmly. "Have a seat. Thank you," he said to the secretary, dismissing her.

Once his office door was closed, he sat back down in his chair—which was by design exactly two inches higher than the one his visitor occupied—rested his chin on his clasped hands, and studied the young man under hooded eyelids. He had grown tall and was well-built, a man most folks would describe as very good-looking. And his countenance? Nary a hint of the scared, nervous kid he had been during their last face-to-face.

He got down to business. "You asked to see me, Leander. What can I do for you?"

Leander gathered his thoughts for several seconds before speaking. When he did so, his voice resonated with a calm mellowness that surprised him. "Thank you for seeing me, sir. I know how busy you are, and I won't take too much of your time." He cleared his throat and leaned back in the chair.

"No problem at all."

"My future," Leander said.

His eyebrows rose slightly. "What about your future?"

"As you know, I will graduate next year. College will follow." Leander spoke matter-of-factly. "I'm requesting your assistance."

"So, you're here to ask for money?"

Leander met his gaze directly as he straightened in the chair. "May I finish, please?" he said, his tone suddenly cool.

"Sorry. Go ahead."

"I'm asking for your assistance with the application process to the institution of my choice. Perhaps you have some contacts. What I am *not* asking for is any money. My parents have managed to save some for my education, and I plan to work while in school as well. Additionally," he went on, managing to temper the edge in his voice, "with my grades, I believe scholarships will be offered."

He studied the young man for a time before responding. "Very admirable. What colleges are you looking at?"

"Only one. Harvard."

The eyebrows shot up again, higher this time. "Harvard!" He practically shrieked. "What the hell do I know about Harvard? What's wrong with Carolina? Or Wharton? I have contacts at both. As you well know—"

"Harvard," Leander repeated.

He didn't bother to hide his mounting irritation as he pushed his chair firmly back from the desk, stood up, and strode to the large windows. Keeping his back to Leander, he asked, "And your major?"

"Business. I'll be concentrating on investment banking," Leander replied. The young man rose from his chair and walked to the office door. "Thank you again for your time and your help," he said. "Goodbye, sir."

Lost in thought, he stood at the window until his intercom announced the long-distance call he was expecting. "Yes, yes," he responded irritably as he returned to his desk.

HARVARD! Jesus!

58

"Gaby, this is absolutely the worst idea you've ever had! We're going to get caught, I just know it. And when we do, there goes our futures, right out of the window," Leander whispered as he tried to talk his best friend out of her latest, crazy idea. "Come on! Let's leave now before somebody sees us, please!"

Gabrielle stopped in her tracks, took another swig from the flask she carried, and glared daggers at her best friend. "Lee, I'm going to do this with or without you. Besides, even if we do get caught, it won't be the end of the world. That shit-head Hadley's gonna pay for the way he cheated you out of being valedictorian. Fat sonofabitch is gonna pay big time!"

"Stop this, Gaby, please. And stop cursing," Leander continued to plead, although he knew his words carried no weight. Trying to change Gaby's mind when she was hell-bent on doing something was like trying to change the weather. All he could do now was go with her and maybe keep her from getting hurt. "And just how much vodka have you had?"

She stopped walking and turned to face him. Her tall slender body was backlit by the glow of the streetlight, transforming her into the golden angel of Leander's childhood. She tilted her head and bestowed a silly little intoxicated grin on him while extending a wobbly hand, holding the flask in his general direction. Her other hand awkwardly brushed the heavy golden tresses back from her face. "Want some?" she slurred sweetly.

Resigned once again to let her have her way, Leander reached out to steady her. "No, thank you," he whispered harshly. "I think you've had enough for both of us. If you are bound and determined to do this, then let's get it over with and get back home. It's after midnight." At that very moment, Leander realized for the countless time in his life that he would do *anything* for her. Even agree—against his better judgement—to 'roll' Principal Hadley's front yard.

"Midnight—the witching hour," Gabrielle said, barely coherent. She reached into the plastic bag lying at her feet and retrieved one of several rolls of bath tissue. Planting her feet wide apart for some measure of stability, she threw the roll of paper practically into the top of one of the stately live oaks that circled the large brick house. "For Hadley's witch of a daughter."

Leander shushed her again, even as he heard muted voices coming from their cohorts. Out of the shadows came the four other students, giggling and staggering to join their friends. "Backyard's done. What's taking you two so long?" Benny Lively asked. He had been disciplined by Hadley so many times he'd lost count and was thrilled to be included in the "lesson" Gabrielle had said they were going to teach the principal.

"What's taking so long?" Gabrielle grunted loudly as she hurled another roll over a crepe myrtle limb and watched as it became absorbed by clusters of pink blossoms and droplets from the recent rain. "My good buddy here, our rightful valedictorian, has been hindering my progress by trying to talk me out of this." She hiccupped loudly, evoking giggles and warnings from the others.

"Why, man?" Latrell Snelling asked. "Far as I'm concerned, the old fart deserves whatever he gets."

Leander, being the only sober one in the group, spoke in a whisper. "Look, I feel bad that you guys are doing this because of me. We all know how things work here and, yeah, I'm mad, too. But worse things can happen, like not getting to graduate next week. Now, we've done enough. Let's all go home and hope to God that we haven't been seen."

"Lee's right, as usual," Gabrielle grudgingly asserted. She reached for his arm for support. "See y'all tomorrow."

"Right. Tomorrow"

"Good work, comrades."

"Word, man."

Gabrielle stood for a time, watching the night breeze tease the strands of tissue even as the beads of moisture began to knead them into tiny, hardened clumps. Her expression was one of satisfaction.

"Okay, Lee," she said. "We can go home now."

59

Leander and Gabrielle walked arm in arm along the gravel road, their path barely visible in the circle of light. "You're always prepared," she said. "I never thought of bringing a flashlight."

"Watch your step, Gaby," he cautioned as he steadied her against a fall.

She stopped and took the final slurp from her flask. "Ahhh," she exclaimed, following up with a loud burp.

"How ladylike," Leander rebuked, giving her a rueful look.

She giggled. "You look just like your mama when you raise that eyebrow." She poked his shoulder playfully. "And, you sound like Granddaddy when you scold me."

"Sometimes you need scolding. But hey, let's change the subject. Who're you going with to the graduation dance tomorrow night?"

Gabrielle sighed. "Ned Worthy."

"He's nice, quiet. But you'll keep the conversation going, I'm sure," he teased her.

"He's the only guy that asked me." Her voice was flat. "Yep, me and Nerdy Ned."

They had reached the front of the Remington house, and Gabrielle dropped down to sit on one of the steps. Leander sat down beside her and remained silent. Being attuned to her moods as he was, he had noticed that, during the last leg of their walk home, Gaby's euphoria from their earlier mischief—not to mention the vodka—had faded. She looked sad. And that made him sad.

At last, she broke their silence. "Why do you think that none of the cool guys ever ask me out?"

As she turned to face him, her eyes locked on his. They shone golden in the dim porch light, and as always, took his breath away. Leander took her hand in his. "You frighten them, Gaby. You frighten everyone, even me sometimes.

"Frighten? How? What do I do?"

She was frustrated, and Leander knew that he had to make her understand how terrifyingly wonderful she was. "First of all," he began, "you are assertive, even bossy at times. But that's okay, because you are a natural-born leader, Gaby. You got that from both sides, Gabe and Mr. Will. The other kids see that, even though they might not know how to define it. And then there's your looks." He stopped and shook his head.

"My looks? Come on, Lee," Gaby said morosely. "I'm too tall, my left eye is weird, and I have *no* boobs!"

Leander laughed heartily. "Gabrielle Westin, when you walk into any room, you command attention without even trying. *That's* scary. Besides, boobs are overrated."

His humor was lost on Gaby. "What else?" she prodded. "I need to hear this, and nobody but you will tell me what's wrong with me."

Leander was quick to reassure her that absolutely nothing was wrong with her. He gently mentioned that she might want to speak a bit softer and urged her to tone down the cussing. She was occasionally a smart mouth in class. And at times, she came off as downright rude. Not to mention that most folks in town were in awe of her Granddaddy and might be wary of getting too close to the family. There was also the fact that she was rich.

"Jeez, anything else I should know?" Gabrielle asked. She was mildly annoyed, but Leander knew it would be short-lived.

"I would venture a guess that most of the guys in our class still remember the butt-whooping that Remy gave Kenny Bishop back in junior high. Could be one reason why you don't get asked out on a lot of dates." His laughter was contagious, and soon the two friends were holding their sides in merriment.

"Well, can you blame my big brother? He just happened to be picking me up from school that day when Kenny made the remark about why you were my best friend. He said I liked you 'cause black guys got big dicks. I thought Remy was going to beat the little bastard fuckin' senseless!" Her hand flew to her mouth. "Sorry."

Leander just shook his head. "Come on, girl. Let's get you in your house and me home to mine. We got a big day tomorrow and a big night tomorrow night." He reached out a hand to help her stand. The two of them began to walk to the back of the house, where Gaby always entered.

Suddenly, she froze, a pained expressing crossing her face. "I-I think I'm gonna be sick," she said forlornly.

With one arm around her waist and the other holding her hair back from her face, Leander bent her over and held her steady until the retching stopped. "Better now?" he asked, handing her a wad of tissue from the bag they carried.

With trembling hands, she pressed the tissue to her face. "Sorry," she murmured. "You forgot to mention that I drink too much."

"That, too. Feel better?"

She nodded, took a deep breath, and focused on trying to walk straight. "Hey," she said, stopping to face him, "you didn't tell me who *you're* taking to the graduation dance."

"Mikayla Reese."

"Oh, Miss Cheerleader Captain. I'm impressed," she teased. "That's how many dates you've had with her?"

"Tomorrow night will be four, if you count church last Sunday with her folks."

"Sounds serious."

"Not serious," he said. "When you think about everybody going off to college in the fall. All of us heading in different directions…" His voice trailed off.

"You would have to bring that up," Gabrielle scolded him. "I don't know how in the hell I'm supposed to get along without seeing you every day."

Leander hugged her. "You'll be fine, Gaby." He held her at arm's length and spoke with sincerity: "Believe me, you are going to do great things."

She nodded and blinked away the beginning of tears. "Thank you, Lee, for telling me the truth. You'll always be my best friend."

"And you'll be mine. G'night sister."

"Night, brother," she answered as she began to climb the stone steps. Suddenly, she turned and skipped back to Leander's side.

Her eyes were aglow, and she was once again the impish, nosy Gaby of their youth. "So," she asked excitedly, "have you and Mikayla *done it* yet?"

Leander looked at her skeptically. "Done what?"

With hands on her hips, Gabrielle matched his expression. "This is me you're talking to! No secrets between us. Remember?"

"That subject is private. Therefore, it doesn't constitute as a secret," he said. "Good night."

"Oh, you and your big words. Guess I got my answer," she chirped.

Leander parted the bottlebrush limbs and shone his flashlight along the familiar trail that led to his home. His own words about everyone going in different directions came to mind.

He still found it hard to believe that he was actually going to Harvard. It had been his dream for as long as he could remember, ever since he had seen the pictures and read the lofty descriptions in the school library. For months now, even though he had the acceptance letter in his possession—framed, no less, and sitting in a place of honor on the mantle at home—he'd been afraid to dwell too much on the fact. Afraid to speak of it as if the dream would be dispelled.

The announcement in Assembly today, though, had served to bring his dream to fruition. *"Leander Washington: Harvard Law School and Harvard Business School."*

He had applied to both Law School and Business School, never really believing that a joint degree in law and business could be his. But the independent reviews had resulted in his acceptance.

Oh, he had brushed off Gaby's worry about the two of them being separated, but in truth he didn't see how he could endure the next four plus years without her. They would have their summers, though. And, McDaniel College was only a few hours' drive from the Boston Area.

Leander knew that Gaby was smart. She just had not applied herself during high school. Her senior year had seen a marked improvement, though, and with McDaniel's high acceptance rate, she had gained admission.

Gaby was excited about the prospect of college in general and spoke with enthusiasm about her chosen major of Political Science. Leander chuckled to himself as he recalled Will pontificating loudly at last Saturday night's dinner at the club that his granddaughter would perhaps one day make a fine state senator. He had fallen silent when Gaby had rather flippantly informed him of her differing political stance.

Leander reached his home and noticed the porch and kitchen lights were still on. Mama was most likely sitting in the parlor, waiting for him. The lump rose in his throat as he thought of Moam's empty rocking chair. "I'll make you proud, Moam. I promise," he whispered.

He had to admit that, aside from his earlier trepidation, the evening had been fun. And, he had handled Gaby's complex questions satisfactorily, he thought. That girl could still put even him on the spot, though.

Leander's smile faded. *No secrets.*

60

Hamilton Hall couldn't have been farther from where Leander's assigned parking spot was located. Nor was it any closer to the several classroom buildings that he visited daily. Days like today, though, his long trek was pleasant. It was Sunday morning, and even he was glad for a day with no classes. His room in the ancient residence hall was huge in comparison to his bedroom at home, but today its walls seemed to be closing in on him. His exit was marked with a spring in his step.

Mid-October in Boston was breathtaking. The fall foliage, the warm sunny days, the nippy nights were brand new to someone who had grown up in a climate ranging from periods of hot and sticky to not so hot and sticky.

He spied his car just ahead. He slowed his pace and retrieved the keys from his pants pocket. *His* car! Leander had not wanted to accept the shiny new Ford SUV. He had not wanted to accept any gift from *him*, but the huge card attached to the car's windshield had made his refusal impossible. "To an amazing young man with a bright future, from your friends at the Bank."

His dad had been so proud during the presentation, and his mother had never smiled so brightly. "Thank you, sir," Leander had managed to say as the two men shook hands briefly.

And then there had been Gaby's reaction to further his acceptance of the car. "I get the first ride," she had exclaimed brightly.

Of course, she had no inkling that her words had unearthed his suppressed memories of another celebration with another new car.

"Wrong car?" The voice at his back startled him, so much so that he dropped his keys. Quickly, he stooped to retrieve them, then turned to see who was responsible for whisking away his unwanted recollection.

Leander dropped the keys back into his pocket. "Hello. What did you say about the car?" he asked. And then, he smiled and said, "Oh, my goodness! You look just like that movie star!"

"Yeah, I've heard it before," she replied. She smiled back, and it was the most beautiful smile Leander had ever seen. "People say I look a bit like Halle Berry, but I don't see it. I'm Michelle Daily." She extended her hand and stood waiting for his response. After a few moments, a puzzled look crossed her face. She lifted her hand a bit higher and said, "And you are?"

Leander felt like a complete idiot. Grinning sheepishly, he grasped her hand in a firm handshake. "I'm Lee Washington. It's a pleasure to meet you. And you *do* look like her." He hoped his composure had slipped back into place but soon realized that was not to be.

"Uh, may I have my hand back now?" she asked sweetly, her soft brown eyes shining.

"Oh," Leander said, dropping her hand as if he'd been holding hot coals. He swallowed audibly. "Are you a student here?" The question was miserably lame, but it was all he could manage. The guy with the best vocabulary in high school, and he was at a loss for words.

She seemed to take his awkwardness in stride. "Yes," she replied. "I'm a third-year law student. And you?"

"First year law school and business school. I'm still learning my way around. And getting lost quite often in the process." *Okay, I'm doing better.*

"Getting lost is easy. It's a big place. Say, I'm on my way to Otto's for early lunch. Care to join me?"

Leander hesitated only briefly. "Sounds good. I'll drive us."

"So, this *is* your car, then?" Michelle asked.

"Yes. Why did you ask?"

She laughed lightly. "When I first noticed you, you were standing still as a statue, keys in your hand, and staring at the car like you'd never seen it before. I thought maybe you were lost."

"Actually, I *was* lost — lost in thought. It's my car," he repeated. "Hop in."

"Let's walk, if you don't mind. Otto's is close by."

They walked and talked practically nonstop through burgers at Otto's. They walked to the nearest library and sat in silence reading, their eyes meeting often over the tops of their books. The dry and dusty *Comprehensive Leadership* could not hold Lee's attention, and he noticed that she had not turned a single page of the current issue of *Law Review*. He had noticed something else, too—the modest diamond solitaire on her left ring finger.

Although Michelle had invited him to lunch, Lee had insisted on paying. As they left the library at dusk, he vaguely wondered how he would manage to afford food for the remainder of the week. But that thought fled from his mind, as did the diamond ring, when she mentioned dinner the following evening.

She took him to Russell House Tavern and paid with her Gold American Express card. Two nights later, she used the card at Legal Seafood. And on the last night of their first week together, she served him clams and champagne in her Boston townhouse. After dinner, she introduced him to the symphony.

With the echoes of Shubert igniting his senses and her clever, captivating dialogue, they walked arm-in-arm back to her townhouse, where she introduced him to pleasures far greater than classical music.

The following morning, they sat in easy silence at her breakfast table, Lee in his boxers and Michelle in an oversized t-shirt. They sipped coffee, nibbled at a plate of scones, and occasionally commented on this or that from the Sunday *Globe*. He looked up from his paper and reached for her left hand. Her ring had disappeared sometime during their night together. The faint indention remained, though, and he stroked it.

"Did I complicate things?" he asked.

She shook her head. "No, you didn't. You made things clear."

They smiled at each other and went back to their newspaper. Leander marveled at how comfortable life was at that moment.

61

"*Comfortable?*" Gabrielle practically shrieked into her phone. "You did *not* say that to her, did you? Please tell me that you did not tell this woman that she's *comfortable.*"

"Well, uh, n-n-no. I don't think that I actually *said* the word," Leander stammered. He was befuddled by his friend's response. "But what if I did? What's so terrible about being described as 'comfortable'?"

Gabrielle sighed expressively before responding. "Lee, Lee, Lee," she spoke pointedly. "A blanket is comfortable. An old chair is comfortable. How about a mossy spot by the creek: now *that's* comfortable. A woman wants to be described as beautiful or sexy. Or, maybe—let's see now," she rambled, thinking aloud. "I know! *Intoxicating;* that's a good word. Tell her that she's intoxicating."

Leander smiled. He had wasted no time in calling his best friend to tell her about his new girlfriend. Before he could respond, though, Gabrielle's tone of voice changed dramatically, and her exuberance waned. "Who the hell am I to give advice on romance. I've never even had an actual boyfriend," she bemoaned. "So, what do I know. Anyhow, Michelle sounds terrific. Sorry I yelled at you."

He let the silence settle in for only a moment, then responded gently. "Hey, sister, maybe you're right. And, for your information, I *always* need your advice. Don't worry, I won't tell her she's comfortable. Now," he tried to sound upbeat, "I want to hear about your first month as a coed."

"It's been okay," Gabrielle said. "The apartment is super. Of course, Granddaddy only buys the best. My classes are hard, but I'm studying. Got a B on my American History test yesterday."

"That's great. Made any new friends yet?"

"A few. One girl, Rachael, my partner for debating, seems nice. She asked me to go with her to The Boar's Head tonight. It's some sort of sorority thing. But you know me. I ain't one to mix with a bunch of silly, giggling girls."

"Go!" he ordered. "You hear me, girl? Go to the party and meet people. And join clubs."

"Okay, okay," Gabrielle said. "I give up. I'll go to the stupid party! Happy now?"

"Happy," he replied. "Now, when can you come to Boston for a weekend? After all, Michelle has to have your blessing. Next weekend?"

"Uh, let me check my schedule. I'll get back to you, but probably. I'll take the train, and you can pick me up."

"Sounds like a plan. I can't wait to see you, sister."

"Me, too, brother. Bye, now."

Leander leaned back in the leather recliner, absently taking in the view through the bay windows in Michelle's living room and reflecting on his conversation with Gaby. Throughout their lives, she had been the one who came to him with questions, needing direction, asking for advice. But today, she had schooled him.

He readied himself for a day of exams on corporate law by glancing over last night's reading: passages he practically knew by heart. He donned his heavy coat in preparation for a cold, windy day, exited the townhouse and locked the door behind him. The short walk to the parking garage gave him time to think about his best friend's words. Michelle was all the adjectives that Gaby had mentioned. She was beautiful, sexy, and smart—bordering on brilliant, actually. Leander started the car and turned on the heat. And then, he accepted the fact that, most of all, Michelle was comfortable.

* * * * *

"Okay, Buffy my sweet. Show me the young ladies that you consider worthy of my attention." Christopher Braxton spoke in his midwestern drawl. He sounded bored. He *was* bored. He hated these mixers, and his companion knew it. So, why was he here?

"Come on, Chris. Drinks are on the sorority tonight," his ex-girlfriend, Buffy Addison, had told him earlier. "Plus, hot freshman babes with rich daddies."

That had settled it for Christopher. The hint of wealth rarely missed its mark with him. "Another Bud Lite, beautiful," Chris said to the drab girl standing behind the bar taking drink orders. She moved away without a word or a smile to comply with his request. He turned his bar stool around, braced his long legs on the floor, and began his inspection in earnest. He let his gaze wander over the several groups of students who stood around, conversing with one another amid the smoke-filled bar.

"I'm actually glad that I came tonight, Buffy. It's time for some new blood. Time to retire the wore-out sophomores," he added glibly. There was a tiny flicker of either sadness or regret in Buffy's eyes as she bit her lower lip. But his last-year's flame was much too chic to admit to a broken heart. She bounced back admirably.

"Let's see now, whom might I choose to be my successor?" Buffy said, basking in the attention of the trio who had joined them at the bar. "I see two brunettes at that table near the dance floor."

"Nope. Lesbians," Christopher decreed.

"Aha," their friend Janet exclaimed brightly to a chorus of chuckles. "See you guys later."

Pete McConnel spoke up. "Do you know that girl in the red sweater, Buffy? Looks like she's dressed for Sunday School."

"I was just about to point her out, Pete," Buffy replied. "But I don't think she's Chris' type."

"I noticed her earlier when she walked in," Chris said. "You're talking about the tall girl with the Barbra Streisand thing going on, right?" He motioned back and forth with his index finger between his eyes. "What makes you think she's not my type?"

"She's in the debating club. Southern belle from South Carolina," she mocked, batting her eyelashes. "Of course, she *is* from one of the richest banking families in the south."

"Yeah? What's her name?" Christopher asked.

"Gabrielle Westin—she's the granddaughter of William Remington," Buffy added with a hint of reverence in her voice.

"Who?" Pete asked.

"Not *the* William Remington?" Buffy's best friend, Ramona Honore, played along. "That's Remington Banking, Pete. Surely you've heard of him?"

"I think she's rather pretty," Chris said thoughtfully to no one in particular.

"I agree," Buffy said.

"I don't think I'd describe her as pretty, but I'd kill to have her hair," Ramona said.

Christopher nodded. "Let's grab that table over in the corner. And Buffy, go ask Miss Westin to join us."

62

Gabrielle decided that the gathering wasn't half bad, especially since Rachael had managed to procure two drinks from the bartender who hadn't bothered to ask for IDs. But then, even bolstered by the vodka, uncertainty began to rear its ugly head. She wished that Lee was there, for he would admonish her for doubting herself. He would gently coax her back to the effervescent, confident person that she wished she truly was. She missed her friend.

Her upbringing should have reinforced at least some measure of self-assurance, but at this very moment, Gabrielle felt too tall, over-dressed, and totally conspicuous. Her thoughts of inadequacy, she knew, mirrored those of her poor mother's. The glib words of comfort she had directed to Mama over the years flitted through her mind. She had meant well, of course, but now saw that her attempts to cheer Vivian had missed their mark miserably. Was she destined to fall into the same inert melancholy that had claimed— well, *both* her parents? *Oh, why did I agree to come tonight!*

Gabrielle flinched at the gentle tap on her shoulder. She turned around.

"Sorry, I startled you. The damn band is so loud, I guess you didn't hear me." The girl smiled brilliantly, showing perfect white teeth. The sparkle in her pale green eyes matched the smile, suggesting that her greeting was genuine. "I'm Buffy. You're in the Debating Club, right?"

"Uh, yes, I am. I'm Gabrielle Westin. Call me Gaby," she replied. "Nice to meet you."

"Likewise," Buffy said. "Why don't you come join us at that table in the corner?" She didn't wait for Gabrielle to respond, instead taking her hand in a welcoming gesture and leading her in the direction of her waiting friends.

The band took a much-appreciated break just then, and Buffy continued her monolog in a whisper. She said, "The guy with the blond hair and bedroom eyes thinks you're hot. He said he wants to meet you."

"Oh," was all an anxious Gabrielle could say.

* * * * *

"Okay, now. You've told me all about your home back in South Carolina. And," Christopher punctuated his words by casually placing his arm around her shoulders, "you've given me vivid descriptions of your family. I'm impressed. But what I *really* want is to know all about you. Tell me about Gaby Westin." He pulled her a bit closer as they walked along the narrow sidewalk that led to her apartment building.

The night wind was chilly, but Gabrielle hadn't noticed. What she had noticed as they were leaving the bar was the time: two a.m. Where had the time gone? She had fully intended to stay only an hour or so to appease Rachael and to fulfill her promise to Lee. But now, she'd never known time to pass so quickly. Or so pleasantly.

"There's not much to tell, actually," she said. "I'm a bit of a tomboy, I suppose. I like to go fishing, swimming. Just being outdoors."

Christopher's arm slid from her shoulders, and his hand clasped hers warmly. "And you were, undoubtedly, your high school's beauty queen."

Gabrielle chuckled. "Hardly. I never cared for that sort of attention. It's a good thing—I can be loud, even obnoxious, at times. And, I drink too much on occasion. I'm usually ill at ease in formal social settings because I speak my mind instead of smiling and agreeing with people whom I don't agree with. At least, that's what my best friend, Lee, and I talked about just last month." She fell silent for a few moments before she added, "That's why I wasn't very popular in high school. That's Gaby Westin."

"Well, when I meet your friend, Lee, I'll be sure and tell her that you are both wrong. I think that you're just about perfect," Christopher responded.

"Lee's a guy."

Christopher arched one eyebrow. "Should I be jealous?"

Gabrielle looked at him, smiled and shook her head. "Lee's like a brother to me. In fact, we've been blood brother and sister since we were nine years old. His mom and mine have been best friends all their lives, and he and I were inseparable until college. He's at Harvard now."

The couple continued to walk, hand in hand, without further conversation until they reached her building. Gabrielle punched in the security code and the door opened. Christopher said, "If you were trying to scare me away earlier, it didn't work. We all drink too much on occasion, and I happen to like women who speak their minds." As he spoke, he gently turned her to face him, cupped her chin in his hands, and brushed her lips with his. The tip of his tongue flicked along her lower lip as he whispered, "I want to see you again."

Gabrielle couldn't move. She couldn't speak. When she finally managed to open her eyes, she was looking into his. She swallowed audibly and weakly whispered: "Okay."

He stepped from her and began backing away. "I'll call you," he said.

Numbly, she nodded. When he reached the street corner and was out of sight, she finally exhaled. On shaky legs, she managed to make her way through the lobby and into the elevator. In her cozy apartment, she collapsed on the sofa with a glass of wine and a wistful smile.

The evening had seemed more like a dream than an actual experience. For the first time in her life, Gabrielle had felt marginally at ease in a social setting of her peers. She marveled at the effortlessness of Buffy and the other girls as they glided through the flirtatious tête-à-tête between the sexes. She'd even picked up a couple of pointers from the coeds.

One thing she did find quite shocking, though, was Buffy's introduction of Christopher as her "ex-lover". Gabrielle was wide-eyed for second while the others took the remark in stride. She rallied and tried to appear nonchalant, thinking it must be a mark of sophistication.

63

Christopher Braxton had many strong points, patience not being one of them.

"I'll be ready soon, Chris," Gabrielle called from her bedroom. "Make yourself at home."

"No problem, hon," he responded, trying to modulate a tone of voice that belied his current level of stress. Chris had never been one to, as his mother would say, "court" a young lady. Tonight marked his fourth date with Gaby, and still he hadn't bedded her.

"What's wrong, baby?" he had whispered urgently on the several occasions when his hands had wandered skillfully to her breasts. "I know you want me, and I'm dying for you!"

Her response was always the same: "I'm just not ready."

"Okay, Chris," Gabrielle announced as she entered her living room, "I'm ready. Sorry you had to wait."

His practiced charm was evident as he stood up, smiled, and said, "Baby, you're worth the wait. You look fabulous. Can't wait to show you off to my folks. They're gonna love you."

Dr. and Mrs. Braxton were in town for an obligatory early Thanksgiving dinner with their son before heading to New York to celebrate the actual holiday. Gabrielle was nervous but excited to meet Chris' parents.

"His mom and dad are coming here this weekend, Lee," she had related to her friend a few days ago. "Chris says he's told them so much about me that they're dying to meet me. Oh, Lee," she gushed, "he's wonderful!"

Leander had responded with his usual caution and a bit of apprehension. "Listen, little sister, go slow. After all, you've only had a few dates with him. And, what do you really know about him?"

Her best friend's comments had taken the wind from her sails, even though she knew his concern was genuine. "I'll take things easy, I promise," she had responded.

Shut up, Lee. I love him.

* * * * *

Gabrielle snuggled against Chris' shoulder during the cab ride from the restaurant to her apartment. *The evening went very well,* she mused.

While Mrs. Braxton extended no meaningful act of friendship toward the younger woman and talked mostly of the events they had planned in New York, the good doctor certainly made up for his wife's lack of graciousness.

He had immediately dubbed Gabrielle as "the girl with the golden eyes" and was quite attentive, even to the point of making her feel self-conscious. But, as the evening wore on and the wine flowed, she had relaxed and warmed to the attention. She'd even remarked that it was evident where Chris had gotten his charm. Her remark had drawn beaming smiles and chuckles from both men. Mrs. Braxton had gone to the ladies' lounge without comment.

"Your dad is a great dinner companion, Chris," Gabrielle said as they walked from the cab to her apartment building. "He would get on famously with Granddaddy." She punched in the security code and waited as Chris opened the door for her. The fact that he had dismissed the cabbie after paying him did not escape her.

"Well, we'll have to make sure the two of them get a chance to meet soon. *Real* soon," he said, pressing her against the elevator's wall as the door slid silently closed. "I need to meet your family. All your family. Tell them how absolutely *crazy* I am about their Gaby." He whispered his words between kisses brushed on her lips and nibbles on her neck and ears.

Gabrielle could barely breathe. Her legs were weak, and she leaned heavily on him as they walked from the elevator to her apartment door. Chris took the key from her trembling hand and unlocked it.

The dark living room gave way to outdoor lighting on the terrace, which normally drew one's attention to the view of a picturesque street below and stately buildings of the college campus in the distance. Tonight, that view went unnoticed.

Tonight, the young lovers tore themselves apart only long enough to step over their clothing carelessly being shed and dropped on the carpeted floor. Gabrielle's coat, the gold cashmere sweater dress that Buffy had insisted she purchase for the dinner, Chris' blazer, shirt, and tie, trousers, all marked their hushed and heated journey to the bedroom.

Chris' eyes never left hers as he gently eased her down to the bed. He removed his remaining clothes and went to her. As he gathered her in his arms, he whispered his question: "Gaby?"

She nodded and pressed her body to his. Her fingers stroked the hard muscles of his chest before they tentatively explored foreign places. *This is it!*

Gabrielle had wondered how it would be. She had dreamed of this moment from his first, brief kiss. But, no one, not even her mother had prepared her for what to expect. *What am I supposed to do?*

The chorus of thoughts, fears, and doubts were erased from her mind as Chris guided himself inside her. The initial shock and pain were soon replaced with warmth and longing. She wanted the feeling to last forever. She moved in rhythm with him, needing to make the journey alongside him. *Take me with you, Chris,* she silently pleaded.

But he left her behind.

With a shudder, he fell heavily on her, then rolled away. "Oh, wow! Great, huh?" he said after catching his breath. He pulled his shorts on and stood up from the bed. "Want a beer, babe?"

After a moment, he walked back to the bed, turned on the lamp, and sat down. She had drawn the sheet up to her chin and blinked back tears.

"Gaby," he whispered as he gently stroked her arm, "what's wrong? I-I thought you wanted to."

"Oh, Chris, I did, I did! And there's absolutely nothing wrong." She smiled and flicked away a lone tear. "I don't know what I expected, but I know it'll get better. I just want to please you."

He studied her face for a long time, until realization hit. "Oh, Jesus, Gaby. Are you telling me that this was your first time?"

She turned to stare at him. "Well, *of course* it was my first time, Christopher," she said, not yet deciding if she were angry or embarrassed. Or both. "I don't go around having sex with someone that I don't—well, that I don't care about." *I will not say the 'L' word 'til he does!* Her speech was punctuated with a pillow to his face.

"Gaby, Gaby," Chris cooed as he pushed the pillow away and hugged her. "I didn't mean to upset you. It's just that I never made love to a virgin before. He caressed and nuzzled her until her tension lessened. "I guess tonight's a first for both of us. And, I promise you, it'll get better."

His kisses began once again, slowly this time, his tongue exploring her mouth until Gabrielle felt herself responding. She watched through half-closed eyes his hands as they began to lightly stroke her body. The earlier sensation of floating on water left her now, as his caresses pulled her under, stripping her of breath. But she didn't care. In fact, if the earth had exploded at that very minute, she wouldn't have cared. She closed her eyes as his hands and lips continued their deliberate progress, coaxing her deeper and deeper until her cries of ecstasy brought her to the surface.

Hours later Christopher lay quietly on his back and listened to Gaby's steady breathing. They were both exhausted, but sleep eluded him. His mind played over the events of the evening, causing him to frown. He wondered if, in fact, he was actually beginning to care for this one. Now, that *would* be a first.

64

Gabrielle woke early, before six a.m. Her normal Friday schedule would be no different, even though today was the first day of Christmas break and no classes would be held. She would shower, dress quickly, then on to the kitchen to start the coffee pot, turn up the heat, and leave the apartment for her morning jog. All this would be done on her tiptoes and with a minimum of lighting so as to not disturb Chris.

Throughout his college experience, Chris had managed to *never* have an early morning class and rarely got out of bed until at least nine o'clock. She, on the other hand, rejoiced in the early dawn. Witnessing the beginning of each day excited her as it had since early childhood—a joy that she wished she could share with Chris. That was not to be, though, as she had learned in the beginning of their relationship that waking him early resulted in his being in a horrid mood for the remainder of the day.

Gabrielle exited her apartment building to several inches of fresh snow and began a brisk walk. The bitter cold of the northern winter had hit her hard at first, but she soon found it invigorating and looked forward to her customary three-mile walk/jog, which usually ended at her favorite coffee shop for hot chocolate and some time on the computer.

Chris didn't like her absorption with e-mail and social media. She only spent a few minutes chatting online, but it made him cross. She avoided a scene by taking advantage of the coffee shop's in-house computer service.

It was just easier that way.

Never had Gabrielle been one to make concessions. In fact, she had always met head-on any obstacle—or person—who might present a challenge to her beliefs. Acquiescing was something that she left to her mother. *How is it possible that I've changed so much?*

She knew the answer. A frown crinkled her forehead and her gait increased. She tried to block the negative remnants from last night's tiff with Chris from her mind. But they lingered still.

"Why do you have to stay on that goddamn computer all the time, Gaby? You must think I enjoy sitting here all by myself," Chris had shouted at her for the umpteenth time over the past month since he'd moved in with her. "Hell, I might as well go down to the bar. At least I'll have somebody to talk to," he muttered, grabbing his coat and hat and heading for the door.

Her words had stopped him. "Don't go, Chris, please. I was just e-mailing Lee to find out what time he thinks he'll get here tomorrow. I-I'm sorry. And I'm not *always* on the computer." Her apology had ended with a bit of self-defense, which had drawn an icy stare from him.

But he hadn't left. She fixed his favorite dinner, and they watched an action movie that he liked on television. They talked and laughed before going to bed.

Gabrielle reached her destination. The aroma of coffee and fresh-baked muffins made her smile as she entered the shop. After ordering her usual, she found a corner table and quickly logged on to one of the computers. She grinned as she read Lee's response to her e-mail. He should arrive the following evening around six, barring any traffic problems. She couldn't wait to see him. She was also anxious for him to meet Chris. Then, he would see how much in love they were and stop harping on "being careful".

After catching up on e-mail, Gabrielle phoned her friend, Rachael. "Time to rise and shine, sleepyhead."

"Oh, hey, Gaby," Rachael said. "How come you didn't return my call last night? Some of the girls met for drinks and burgers, and we wanted you to join us."

Perplexed, Gabrielle asked, "When did you call?"

"Must have been around six. Chris said you were taking a shower, and he'd tell you to call me."

"He just forgot. You know, he's been studying so hard lately."

"Sure," Rachael said. "We missed you. When are you leaving for home?"

"Lee's driving over from Boston tomorrow. We're planning on leaving the next morning. Hey, if I don't see you before, have a Merry Christmas."

"You too, girlfriend. See you next year."

Gabrielle sat for several minutes, ignoring her food and lost in thought. Had Chris simply forgot to tell her about Rachael's call? She wanted to believe that had been the case, but she knew that Chris didn't like Rachael. He had never said so directly, but his off-hand remarks made his feelings quite clear.

"She's okay, Gaby—just not one of us. Besides, you've got Buffy, Mona, Jo-Jo—they're your friends. They talk to you all the time."

"No, Chris," she had tried to explain, "they talk *over* me. They talk *around* me. They do not talk *to* me."

"Yeah, wonder why that is," Chris dismissed her complaints every time. "Could it be that you constantly disagree with their views? Look, Gaby, if you have an opinion that differs from everyone else's, it's best to just keep it to yourself."

Gabrielle accepted his rebukes because she believed that things would change for the better the longer that she and Chris remained together. This past month was simply an adjustment period, that's all. Getting to know one another's moods, likes, and dislikes.

And so, when in the presence of their group and talk turned to politics or social concerns—practically any subject for that matter—she swallowed her words and kept her views to herself.

It was just easier that way.

65

Chris idly watched Gabrielle as she prepared a tray of elaborate hors d'oeuvres. She was animated and chatted practically non-stop about growing up with Lee and their antics as children. He thought briefly of his own childhood, which had been far different.

He was the only child of a mother who doted on him but did not actually like children and a father too busy with attending to other people's kids to pay him any attention. Chris had never experienced a close friendship like the one Gaby shared with Lee. He didn't know whether to be jealous, curious, or simply entertained by her stories. He opted for the latter.

"Obviously, the two of you were inseparable," he said. "Never boyfriend and girlfriend?"

Gabrielle laughed. "Heavens, no. I've told you before, Lee's like my brother. Actually, we're even closer than Remy and me 'cause we're the same age. You're going to really like him, Chris. He's super smart, but he can talk to anybody about almost anything."

"So, he can talk to me even though I'm not super smart?" His voice was thick with sarcasm.

She bit her tongue. "That's not what I said or meant," she said calmly, silently begging him not to spoil the evening with one of his moods.

Chris studied her for a long time before his expression softened into a dimpled smile. "I know that, babe," he said. "Just kidding you." He moved around the kitchen island and hugged her. "While we're still by ourselves, Merry Christmas." He removed the slim black velvet box from his back pocket and laid it in her hands.

"Oh, Chris!" Gabrielle exclaimed as she opened the case to a diamond tennis bracelet. "It's beautiful! I *love* it!" Her eyes were shining as she watched him place it on her wrist. "Love you, too," she whispered.

"Me, too, babe. Hey, that's Lee now, I'll bet," he said as the doorbell sounded.

The oven timer pinged at the same time. "Go let him in," she said, "and I'll be there in a minute."

"Sure thing." Chris whistled as he made his way to the door. This would be an enjoyable evening, he decided. It would be good to meet Lee, and Gaby was thrilled with the bracelet. He was glad that his dad had thought to send it.

Chris' expression froze momentarily, then grew quizzical. "May I help you?" he asked after opening the door.

"Hello. You must be Chris," Leander said, extending his hand to the other man.

"I must be. And you are?" came his cool reply.

"I'm Gaby's friend, Lee Washington."

After several seconds, Chris responded. "Oh, of course. Lee, come in. Welcome. Gaby," he called out, "Lee's here."

Leander's face broke into a beaming smile as she bounded from the kitchen. Shrieking with delight, she jumped into his arms and wrapped her legs around his tall body, almost toppling him in the process.

Laughing and talking at once, they both staggered to the sofa. "I've missed you so much," Gabrielle said.

"And I've missed you, little sister." He disengaged himself from her embrace, stood up, and once again offered his hand to Chris. "Please pardon our display, Chris. Gaby and I still act like wild kids from the country occasionally. She talks of you so much that I feel like we're already friends."

After a subtle pause, Chris shook his hand. "Same here. Hey, Gaby, how 'bout a couple of beers?"

The threesome sat in the cozy kitchen, enjoying drinks and snacks. "Gaby, the apartment is great," Leander remarked. "Mr. Will made a good investment."

"It's nice, but sometimes I wonder if I'm missing out on the actual college experience by not living in the dorms."

"Well, from my perspective, you're not missing *anything*. With my class load and jobs, I wasn't getting much sleep in the dorm. Michelle's townhouse is paradise."

"That's right," Chris said, pausing to retrieve another beer from the fridge but failing to offer refills to anyone else. "You're a law major. Right?"

"Law *and* business," Gabrielle announced proudly. "A double major at Harvard, no less." She quickly realized her mistake as she saw Chris' mouth tighten into a thin, hard line. She hastened to make amends by adding, "Chris' degree will be in marketing. We all know that's the secret to success in business. Right, Lee?"

"Marketing has certainly been key for the bank's success," he responded.

But the damage had been done. She had compared him to Lee, finding him lacking.

"We should get down to the Boar's Head before all the tables fill up," she said as she began to gather up empty bottles and plates.

"I have another idea," Chris said. "I'll go pick up a pizza for us. You two can catch up while I'm gone." He pulled on his heavy coat and hat as he walked to the door.

"But I thought that we'd take Lee to the bar, introduce him to the gang, maybe show him around campus a bit," she said with obvious disappointment.

Chris was already at the door. He turned and smiled. "A supreme okay with you guys?"

"That's fine, Chris. Actually, that's a good idea, since Gaby and I will be leaving early in the morning. We don't need a late night."

The door closed decisively.

* * * * *

"I wish you'd change your mind, Lee, and just crash here on the sofa," Gabrielle said several hours later. "Then, you wouldn't have to drive back here in the morning."

"That's okay. I've already set it up with Michelle's friend. He's got an extra bed in his room and he's expecting me," he said. "Besides, that will get me more of the 'college experience'."

"Have a good night, man," Chris said. "We enjoyed it."

"It was good to meet you, Chris. Merry Christmas. Sister, see you at seven in the morning."

Gabrielle hugged him once more. "I'll be ready. G'night, brother."

After locking the door, she turned and put her arms around Chris' waist. "Tonight sure was fun," she said. "Thanks for getting the pizza. Good idea."

She began to tidy up the room but soon realized that Chris had not moved from his position by the door. She looked at him, only to see his eyes wide but unfocused, his brows arched questioningly, a puzzled expression on his face.

"Chris, what's wrong?"

He didn't speak for a long time. Eventually, he blinked his eyes and focused on hers. He shook his head slowly, as if coming out of a trance. "You could have told me, Gaby."

She was mystified. "Told you what?" she asked.

He held out his hands, palms up, and spoke louder. "Come on, Gaby! You've got to know what I mean. You never referred to him by anything but 'Lee'. Just maybe, if you'd told me his name was *Leander Washington*, then I might have guessed. But, no. You gave no clue whatsoever."

He stalked to the kitchen and jerked the fridge door open to get another beer. Gabrielle followed. She felt like screaming at him, but she didn't. Calmly, she asked, "Are you referring to the fact that Lee is black?"

"Ding, ding, ding, the lady wins the prize," he said, a scowl darkening his face. "I'm going to bed. Don't wake me in the morning."

No more words were spoken. Gabrielle quietly finished in the kitchen, then packed her bags for the trip. She pushed everything from her mind as she brushed her teeth, got a blanket and pillow from the hall closet, and settled on the sofa for the night. She twirled the diamond bracelet on her wrist, swallowed the lump in her throat, and went to sleep.

66

Leander stepped on the SUV's gas pedal, bringing the speed up to just over the posted limit. He set the cruise control. "Finally, we're off the ice and snow-covered roads," he said to Gabrielle. "Good to be heading south, huh?"

A cloak of silence had swathed them during the trip so far, with Leander's eyes glued to the road and Gaby's staring, unseeing, out of the car's side window. Now, she only grunted a reply to his question.

He shot a quick glance her way. "You want to stop for food, bathroom break, anything?"

Another wordless grunt.

"So," he went on, "I've been thinking about buying an airplane. Learn how to fly. Trips home would be a lot quicker. What'cha think, Gaby?"

She exhaled loudly and answered, "That would be good."

Leander shook his head sadly. *She hasn't heard a word I've said.* Perhaps the drastic change he'd seen in his best friend was partly his fault. After all, wasn't he the one who told her to not be so caustic with her words, stop the cussing, drink less, go to parties, meet new people? Hadn't he, in fact, told her not to be herself?

Damn! Was he to blame for the transformation from the carefree little spitfire that he'd grown up worshipping to the anxious young woman who walked on eggshells last night? A woman who teetered between who she was and who she thought she should be?

He stole another glance at Gabrielle. She was fingering the diamond bracelet on her wrist. "The bracelet is beautiful," he said. "Looks great on you."

She looked at him and smiled. "Thanks, Lee. Sorry about last night. He really loves me, you know."

"I know. And last night was fine. I like him, Gaby," he lied.

He wanted to spare her any embarrassment—God, picture the two of them *ever* being too embarrassed to speak their minds! He imagined the conversation between her and Chris practically word for word following his departure last night. And, his heart ached for her.

But now was not the time to speak of the reality that he feared would hit her all too soon. Instead, he said, "The two of you should come to Boston for a weekend in the spring. Michelle and I would love it." Just maybe, he could coax the brash and confident in-your-face Gaby back from whatever troubling vortex held her.

"We will. Chris wants to come and meet my family, too. Maybe spring break."

"Uh, yeah," Leander said. "I was going to talk to you about that. I won't be coming home for spring break. Actually, Gaby, I'm not planning on coming home for the summer either."

She gasped aloud as she turned to face him. He knew that his words had shocked her, and he went on talking quickly before she could interrupt.

"I'm going to work during spring break and put the money toward summer school. If I do that every year, I believe that I can finish with the dual degree in three years."

"Wow," she said after taking in what he told her. "But, what about our summers?" Soon, her words returned in volume. "Shit, Lee! Why do things have to change?" She crossed her arms and stamped her feet on the car's floorboard. "I frigging hate change!"

And miraculously, his Gaby was back, however briefly. Leander laughed heartily, playfully punching her shoulder. "Not everything changes, girl. You're still my best friend. Hey, this looks like a good exit. Let's stretch our legs and get a burger."

Leander filled up the SUV's gas tank, then parked in front of a pleasant-looking diner. As they began to walk to the door, Gabrielle said, "I'm actually glad you stopped, 'cause I'm starving." Suddenly, she stopped in her tracks and looked intently up at him.

"What's wrong?" he asked.

"What the hell was that about an airplane?"

67

+ ✦ ✦ ✦ +

They celebrated Christmas Day in the same manner within the Remington-Westin household that Gabrielle remembered throughout her childhood.

Lavish presents, gaily wrapped and stacked high, surrounded the eight-foot Christmas tree in the mansion's living room. A live tree, of course, cut and installed to Granddaddy's precise instructions. No fake greenery in this house!

Following the traditional family Christmas breakfast, everyone gathered around the tree for the gift-giving. Gabrielle sat cross-legged on the floor beside the tree, handing out one gift at a time, and allowing each person to unwrap their gift before proceeding to the next.

One day, young William would have this honor, but for now the precocious six-year-old was too busy being the center of attention. He gleefully opened present after present, shrieking with delight as Remy and Granddaddy vied with each other to see whose fabulous toy could top the other's. Gabrielle smiled at the child's excited antics, all the while sharing her parents' concern that young William would grow up to value only what money could buy.

Gabrielle studied her family members. *Nothing has changed,* she thought. And yet, everything had changed.

"You're thinking of your young man, aren't you?" Vivian spoke quietly as she gathered more crumpled wrapping paper and handed it to her daughter. They had been cleaning up the living room for half an hour—in silence.

"I guess so," came her glum reply. Christmas night always seemed to be a bit of a let-down, especially when everyone went their separate ways. Granddaddy had gone to Belle's house for dinner, Remy and M'Lyn to her parents', Mason to God knows where and Daddy upstairs to bed. Gabrielle sighed. "I thought Chris would call today. Probably busy with family."

Vivian wanted to ask all about Chris. She yearned to talk with her daughter about being in love. And if it was, in fact, love, then why was she so sad? But then, Gabrielle might ask her the same question. So, all she could manage to say was: "Your bracelet is lovely. He must care a great deal about you."

"He does. Thanks, Mama." Gabrielle smiled as she gathered an armload of trash bags and headed towards the kitchen.

And the two strangers said goodnight.

* * * * *

But Chris *had* called, the day after Christmas and almost every day thereafter. Everyone noticed the dramatic change in Gabrielle's demeanor from morose to practically giddy. Leander had noticed more than anyone and had commented to his mother. "If he makes Gaby that happy, I suppose I'll have to make the effort to like him."

"You just need to spend more time with him, that's all," had been Claire's advice.

More time. There didn't seem to be enough hours in the day as it was, Leander thought. Upcoming classes, juggling two jobs, trying to find a few minutes to spend with Michelle—it was all beginning to tighten around him. He wondered once again if he'd bitten off more than he could chew. But, as panic began creeping toward him, he knew he could and would always make time for Gaby.

"Did you ask Chris when the two of you can come to Boston?" Leander broke their easy silence as they neared Westminister and the exit to McDaniel College.

"He says maybe spring break. We might drive over and then on Antioch to meet the family, if things work out."

Maybe. Might. If.

"That would be great." He brought the car to a stop in front of her apartment building. "Gaby," he said as he reached for her hand, "I think I'm going to miss you more than ever. We had a great Christmas break, huh?"

"We sure did. I still can't believe Granddaddy paid for us to stay in DC for New Year's. That's got to be my favorite city."

"Yeah, that was special. You need help with your bags?"

"No, I can get them," Gabrielle answered as she opened the car door. "But why don't you come in for a while?"

"I'd better keep going. Feels like more snow on the way." He paused, then said, "Hey, Gaby, you call me if you need *anything*, you hear?"

"I will, Lee. Love you, brother."

"Me, too, sister."

* * * * *

At first, the apartment looked dark and deserted. As her eyes adjusted, though, Gabrielle saw the faint glow of candles—lots of candles. And roses, perhaps two dozen of them, filling a vase on her coffee table. Slowly, Christopher rose from the sofa and made his way toward her.

Her eyes sparkled. She took the glass of champagne he offered as candlelight flickered across his face. The cold expression he had worn on the last night they had been together was gone, replaced by one she couldn't quite put her finger on. Wordlessly, he raised his glass to hers. The clinking crystal was the only sound in the room until she could remain silent no longer.

"I missed you so much," she whispered.

"Show me."

68

Gabrielle walked rapidly through the poorly lit alleyway. Her footfalls echoed, undoubtedly sounding much louder to her than they were. The thought crawled through her mind once again: *Why in God's name did I decide to come this way?*

But she knew why. Chris had said it was a shorter route to the Boar's Head. "Park my car at that old warehouse building," he had instructed her earlier that afternoon. "Then, go around the east side of the building and take the alley. It's a short walk, and you'll be at the club before you know it. I'll meet you there."

She couldn't remember the last time she'd been scared of anything, but an uneasy feeling had dogged her steps from the onset of her journey. Nervously, she gripped the tiny can of pepper spray a bit tighter and increased her steps to a near trot. She hadn't even wanted to go out tonight, but Chris had insisted. They "needed to talk," she'd said.

"Babe, we talk," he had responded. "We'll talk to the group tonight at the Boar's Head. Besides, I've got a present for you."

"No, Chris," she said, trying to convince him to stay home. "I don't need presents, and I don't want to talk to anyone else. You and I need to talk." But he'd simply dismissed her with a quick kiss, a curious shake of his head, and instructions of where to park his car.

Gabrielle shoved her uneasy feelings to the back of her mind as she mentally rehearsed what she would say to Chris later on that night. That is, if he happened to end up in a state loosely resembling sobriety. Experience told her that their evening would play out as always, with Chris holding court and expounding on the merits of capitalism and its resulting growth of wealth as the only form of government worthy of consideration. And while his loyal subjects—their group of sophisticated hangers-on—would heartily toast their leader with pitcher after pitcher of dark ale, Gabrielle would sit quietly by his side. Her Chris was a brilliant orator who could occasionally persuade even her to agree with his political stance. But not very often.

The narrow alley's exit loomed just ahead, and Gabrielle breathed a sigh of relief. *Chris may have been right about this being a shortcut,* she thought as the faint sound of guitars and drums reached her ears. *But I won't be making this trip again.*

She nimbly stepped around a pile of questionable garbage and wrinkled her nose at the stench. A rusty, three-wheeled shopping cart sat beside a foul, overflowing dumpster. The cart was stacked precariously high with what looked to be sacks of old clothing resting on a foundation of crushed soda cans. A slight rustling at the rear of the dumpster identified the *property* as that of a homeless person seeking some measure of shelter from the cold March night. Gabrielle crossed her arms in an attempt to snuggle a bit deeper into her parka and quickened her pace. In her rush to reach her destination, she failed to remain aware of her surroundings.

A streak of black materialized from the corner of her eye before she could catch her breath, much less cry out for help. One strong arm encircled her waist and the other flattened her against the brick wall of an abandoned building. With her face pressed against the rough wall and the breath momentarily knocked out of her, she managed only a pitiful whimper.

His voice was threatening, yet mesmerizing. "Drop the spray, or I'll hurt you!"

She froze.

"Did you hear me?"

She nodded her head a fraction and did as he had demanded. The metal can fell from her trembling fingers and clattered to the broken pavement. It rolled slowly away, coming to a stop in a pothole.

His low voice came to her as pure evil, yet somehow entreating, causing the skin along her arms to prickle. "Don't move. Do as I say, and you'll walk away."

She remained motionless, trying to squelch her initial panic—racing pulse, pounding heart and ragged breathing. Not to mention the sudden urge to vomit.

His right arm released its pressure, allowing a gloved hand to brush her hair aside and expose her neck. His mouth floated along her skin, causing her to hold her breath for what seemed like several minutes but in reality, was but seconds. She felt his tongue, barely discernable, begin to trace a path. He stopped all movement then, his mouth hovering over the exposed hollow behind her left ear. Suddenly, he bit down hard on the tender skin. She cried out.

"Shut up!"

Now, both powerful hands shoved her roughly back against the brick wall, scraping her cheek and drawing blood from her cracked lips. He moved closer, and she felt him harden as he pushed himself against her backside. He growled low in his throat, the sound mimicking a chuckle. He lessened his pressure only long enough to reach under her skirt and pull her panties down. Then, he kicked her booted feet apart and pressed his body against hers once more.

"Don't! Not, not like this, please!"

Viciously, he grabbed a handful of her hair and jerked her head backward. "I said to shut up!"

But then, his tactic changed. His leather gloves landed silently on the pavement, and the hands that had hurt her earlier now began a slow and gentle massage along her shoulders and upper arms.

"So soft, smooth," he whispered. "You're perfect."

She held her breath. Movement was impossible.

He lifted her skirt and pressed his bare flesh against hers. His vice-like grip on her had lessened and his arms now supported her as he began his slow and oh-so-familiar rhythm. She fought against the unexpected response that his assault evoked, her mind screaming: *NO, NO, NO!* But her body had a will of its own and would not listen.

The filthy brick wall that had initially been her prison now gave support to her open palms as she pressed against it and arched her back.

And it was over soon. Ecstasy claimed control over her as fear and pain were washed away in a rush that she had never known before.

For several seconds, neither of them could speak. When Gabrielle broke the silence, she did so by clenching her teeth and allowing the stream of angry words to erupt. "Damn you to hell, Christopher! You scared me half to death!"

He leaned heavily against her until his heavy breathing subsided. He chuckled once again. "Told you I had a present for you, didn't I?"

She pushed him away. "Some present. You hurt me," she said, staggering slightly as she retrieved her underwear.

"C'mon, babe," Chris responded, his voice recapturing its teasing inflection. "You gotta admit that was the best ever! Besides, you know that old saying: 'No pain, no gain'."

"*Not* funny!"

He straightened his clothes and studied her in the dim light cast by the one yellow bulb that remained in the nearby streetlight. "I'm sorry, Gaby. You're not really mad at me, are you?" He drew her close and nuzzled her hair. "I just thought we'd liven things up a bit."

She exhaled. Forgiveness, even under the current circumstances, came easy where Christopher was concerned. She closed her eyes and allowed him to dab at the scratches on her cheek with his handkerchief.

He can be so gentle. Maybe I should tell him right now.

She reached out and took his hand. "Chris, do we have to go to the bar tonight? Let's just go back home. Look at me. I'm a mess, and I really need to talk to you."

"We'll talk, babe. I promise," he said. "And you look just fine. Who's gonna notice, anyway?"

69

"Darling, what in Heaven's name happened to you? Why, you're an absolute wreck!"

"I'm fine, Buffy," Gabrielle said. Her voice had grown calm and her image in the ladies' room mirror reflected a much-practiced smile. As she finished washing her hands, her gaze met Buffy's in the mirror, and she was taken aback by what appeared to be a look of genuine concern in the other girl's eyes.

"Here," Buffy instructed as she gently turned Gabrielle to face her. "Let's see what we can do about covering those scratches. This, by the way, is *the* best cover stick that I've ever used." She tapped the enamel case with a perfect pink fingernail and went on speaking. "Never a blem, zit, or dark circle with this stuff around."

Buffy only needed a minute to cover Gabrielle's scratches and her cut lip. "Now, for some mascara," she prattled on as she retrieved a makeup bag from her Gucci purse. Lipstick was the final touch. "*Voilà!*" she said, turning the silent Gabrielle to face the mirror once more. "Better, now?"

"Much better. Thank you, Buffy."

"No problem, sweetie. Hope you feel better." She began to replenish her own already perfect makeup, then asked nonchalantly: "What happened to you, anyway?"

Gabrielle shrugged her shoulders. "Just clumsy, I guess. I'm always running into things." After months of not really knowing Buffy and not liking her at all, she was surprised to wonder if she had perhaps misjudged the girl. There just might be more to the campus gossip queen than met the eye. Buffy had reached out to her with kindness, so maybe the two of them could become friends after all.

She gathered her parka and purse and headed for the door. "Thanks again, Buffy. I really appreciate your help."

When no response came, Gabrielle turned around and met Buffy's gaze once again. No concern shown in those eyes this time. No warm smile and no wrinkled brow of anxiety appeared either. Buffy slowly crossed her arms across her chest and took several steps, closing the gap between the two of them.

"W-what's wrong, Buffy?" she asked, recognizing that the sinking feeling in the pit of her stomach was reality—the *real* Buffy was materializing before her very eyes.

A condescending little sneer crept into Buffy's expression as she continued to study Gabrielle. Finally, she spoke. "You are aware, are you not, that Chris and I were—how shall I say it—*together* last year?" Without pausing for reply, she continued: "So, you see, *Gaby*, I know a great deal about his tastes, shall we say."

"What's your point?"

"Oh, I'm not trying to make a point. Just an observation," Buffy answered coldly. She elbowed her way towards the bathroom door, deliberately brushing her firm breast against Gabrielle's arm. Before making her exit, and true to her hallmark, she tossed one last cutting remark. "Walking alone through dark alleys can be quite dangerous."

"Ahh, here's my girl!" Chris said brightly as he stood up and placed an arm around Gabrielle's shoulders. "Sit down, babe. I'll get you a daiquiri."

"Make it fruit punch instead, please." Gabrielle sat down and smiled politely to the three guys at their table. She was keenly aware of Buffy and the other two girls in their group standing at the bar, talking. Occasionally, one of them would glance her way, then continue with their whispered conversation. *How could I have thought for even a second that Buffy could ever be my friend?*

"Here you are, babe," Chris said as he sat the frozen daiquiri—complete with a cherry and tiny umbrella—in front of her with a flourish.

Gabrielle looked at him in amazement. "Didn't you hear what I said? I told you that I wanted fruit punch." Her tone of voice was harsh. She knew it but for once didn't care. The tumultuous beginning of their evening had taken its toll.

Chris shrugged, immediately dismissing her as he took his seat and resumed what had apparently been a good-natured dissecting of the state's current budget. "Sorry, I didn't hear you. Damn band's too loud, I guess."

But he made no attempt to remedy the situation. Gabrielle sat quietly, staring at the slowly melting frozen cocktail in front of her. Buffy's melodious laughter drew her attention back to the trio of girls still at the bar. They were enjoying the attention and free drinks from numerous admirers. Their dates, more interested in Chris' monologue and the pitchers of beer that he kept ordering, seemed oblivious.

The band certainly was too loud, she thought, rubbing her sore forehead. Her eyes searched the room for a friendly face, someone she might want to talk to. Perhaps Rachael would show up tonight. But no one garnered her interest. *Just a crowd of sad people trying to act happy…*

"I don't belong here," Gabrielle whispered under her breath. She had grown to dread coming here nearly every night, choking on the fog of cigarette smoke, trying to overlook the cool dismissal of the other girls and pretending interest in the political deliberations with which she could not agree.

But she *did* belong with Chris. Didn't she? Ill-equipped as she had been to deal with the ferocity of love and desire, realization had eluded her at first that she was always the one to give in. Not calling the shots was new territory for Gabrielle, but she had explored it willingly. But was she still willing to relinquish her ideals, her opinions? Was it enough to remain by his side if she had no voice of her own?

Buffy and her two friends returned to the table, loud and giddy, with attempts to provoke their dates into a show of jealousy by relating one pickup line after another that they had received. The interruption spurred everyone's decision to call it a night, much to Gabrielle's relief.

"Ready?" Chris asked, taking Gabrielle's hand as he prepared to stand.

"Whenever you are," she answered.

He smiled at her and leaned over to gently kiss her swollen lip. "Let's go home, then," he whispered.

With just a touch, just his eyes looking into hers, Gabrielle felt the wrenching power that he had over her. But a relationship is always two interconnecting stories. She only knew hers. She gathered her parka and purse and prepared to leave the bar. Her gaze drifted to the untouched daquiri now sitting in a puddle of water on the table. Chris hadn't even noticed.

Tonight, she needed to find out *his* story.

70

"Wow, I didn't realize how late it was. Good thing neither of us has early classes tomorrow," Chris said as the couple entered the apartment and began removing coats and boots. "Turn on the fireplace, babe, and I'll get us both a nightcap."

"None for me, thanks," Gabrielle said as she made her way to the fireplace. After igniting the gas flames, she settled into her favorite corner of the sofa and drew a cashmere throw over her feet. Wordlessly, she patted the sofa beside her.

Chris' look was quizzical. "You okay?"

"I'm fine. Just need to talk to you. Fix yourself a drink, then come back."

"Sure thing, babe." He yawned, stretched, and headed for the kitchen.

Gabrielle closed her eyes and listened to the sounds of him whistling as he puttered around the kitchen. *He's not even the least bit curious about why I want to talk to him.* She remained motionless until she felt his presence beside her on the sofa and heard the clink of his glass on the coffee table. He settled into his corner and lifted her legs onto his lap.

"What's on your mind?" he asked as he began to massage her feet.

"Spring break, next week." She opened her eyes and made a conscious effort to keep her tone light. "I wanted to talk to you about our trip home. Meeting the family."

"Yeah, I'm looking forward to it." He chuckled and reached for his brandy. "From what you've told me about your granddaddy, I'll bet he and I are gonna hit it off big time."

"No doubt." She took a deep breath and reached for his hand. "So, sometimes things happen and change comes, uh, and situations and people change." Frustrated, she paused to gather her thoughts. "Chris, things are going to change for us, so I need to know that we're a team. That I can count on you."

He interrupted her speech. "What are you talking about, Gaby?" He sat erect and for the first time during the entire evening, seemed to actually be paying attention to her words. "What kind of change?"

She spoke calmly and quickly, before she lost her nerve. "I'm pregnant, Chris." The clock ticked. The gas logs hissed. Christopher was a stone. After a full minute of silence, she continued. "I know it's a shock and I know it's not what either of us would've planned, but it happened. So, I thought that we could make some plans while driving to Antioch. What we'll say to my folks. Of course, our lifestyle will change, but we can handle it."

Again, Chris spoke, this time with palpable emotion. "How come?" he asked. Abruptly, he stood up, causing her legs to fall from the sofa and hit the coffee table. The snifter of brandy teetered on the glass-top table. He stood with his back to her, his hands on his hips and his forehead gently banging against the wooden fireplace mantle. He repeated, "How come?"

"W-w-what do you mean, *how come*?" Gaby asked. "Chris, we've been together for months, now. And before you ask me if I'm sure, I did the test. Twice."

He did not look at her. His voice was shaky as he asked, "You haven't been on the pill?" Before she could reply, he answered for her. "Of course, you haven't. My God, Gabrielle, what the hell were you thinking?"

"Well, I guess I *wasn't* thinking," she shouted angrily, then stopped, swallowing words that could not be taken back. She softened her tone. "Maybe neither one of us was thinking. But, but we love each other, Chris, and everything will work out. We just need to calm down and make plans."

The sound she heard was something between a sad little snicker and a soft sob. It was a forlorn sound, one that Gabrielle couldn't immediately tell whether it was coming from him or from herself. She waited.

As quickly as he had moved away from her, he now walked back and gently pulled her to her feet. She struggled against the crushing need to reach out to him, to *make* him want what she wanted. Bewildered that she could not, she remained still.

Tentatively, he touched her cheek, his fingers caressing her bruised lip. "Oh, Gaby," he whispered, "you talk about love like it's the simplest emotion in the world. It isn't. I don't even know what love is, but I do know that our definitions—mine and yours—they're, they're worlds apart. Like, different kinds of love." He moved away from her, then, toward the door. "I need some space. I'm going to the dorm."

Betrayal and loss closed in, threatening to choke her. He turned around then, and hope sprung, but only for a moment.

"I need you to understand. I didn't sign up for this, Gaby." He shook his head. "I'm not going to insult you by offering money. I know you don't need it." He turned toward the door again.

Finding her voice, she asked woodenly, "Money for what?"

"To get it taken care of." His hand was on the doorknob. "I'm sorry, Gaby. I'm so sorry. But family? Not now. I can't do this." He was still talking, more so to himself than to her, when the door firmly closed behind him.

71

The sun's rays radiating from a brilliant blue sky streamed in through the glass doors, bathing the living room in a golden glow and bringing teasing thoughts of springtime. Gabrielle knew better. Last night's weatherman had predicted a beautiful clear day, but one punctuated by a frigid north wind.

She rose slowly from the sofa where she'd spent the night. *Their bed—she couldn't.* Straightening her shoulders, she fought against impending nausea and tears. And, in usual Gaby fashion, she won.

"I absolutely *must* get at least a B on that exam today," she announced as she steeled herself and marched stoically into the bathroom. "Block it out. Just think about the test and nothing else. You know the subject matter because you studied. Concentrate, pay attention, just like Lee says."

Her self-coaching continued through a long hot shower. After bundling up against the cold, she walked from her apartment building and, after a stop at the coffee shop, continued on to the Science Building for the most important test of her freshman year.

Resilience: where had it come from? Was Lee right when he told her she was stronger than she knew? She settled into her desk chair, removed her coat, and smiled weakly at the professor as he handed her the exam. "You've got this, Gaby," she whispered.

Some things you just know. And Gabrielle knew that she had gotten an A on the exam that day. *Imagine that, Lee! Me getting an A on a college exam!* She had agreed to dinner with Rachael after the exam not because she had wanted the company or the food, but because she hadn't wanted to go home. Now that dinner was over and Rachael had left for her dorm, there was no place left to go *but* home.

She wasn't surprised at all when she opened the apartment door to silence. No music, no television, no click of computer keys, no "Hi, babe" ushered her inside. Only silence. His key lay conspicuously on the table by the door. She removed her coat and hung it in the closet beside empty hangers. More empty hangers stared at her from the bedroom closet. His razor, toothbrush, cologne, books, laptop—everything that was *him* had vanished.

And yet, he remained. The echo of his laughter at one of his own jokes. The feel of his arms around her. The flicker of candlelight dancing in his eyes. The smell of him on her pillow. Her hands dropped to her belly. She marveled again at this new-found strength that had overtaken her during the past twenty-four hours. No tears. No hysterics. No panic. Perhaps because it didn't seem real to her. Nothing seemed real at the moment.

She squared her shoulders and walked purposefully into the kitchen and poured herself a glass of wine. *One couldn't hurt.* She sipped the wine while staring intently at her image in the hall mirror.

"You are a survivor, Gabrielle Westin," she said with determination. "You are strong. You are alright."

Until she wasn't.

72

You are an amazing fellow, indeed. And quite the orator to boot. Three new accounts in as many days. None of the other partners can boast this level of success, no sir. All those weeks of writing and rehearsing—and what a delivery—had 'em eating out of your hand. Couldn't wait to invest. Golden, that's what your presentation was! Hell, everybody benefits, not only the partners, but the investors as well. See, you're making money for everybody, you're doing good, you're helping people.

So, why did you have to ruin the day by coming here? It's getting close to the time of year, that's all. Don't even remember walking from the house, but here you are, the last place on earth you ever want to be. Invoking some sort of self-torture? Atonement, perhaps? The new equipment for the children's' wing at the hospital should have taken care of that. But still you come here, can't seem to help it. You come here to sit on this bench, bury your face in your hands, and wish to God you could go back in time. Back almost ten years. But that's impossible, so you go on. You just keep on keeping on.

"What's the matter, Mister?"

"W-What?"

Oh, God, no! I do NOT hear your hushed whispers! I do NOT see your lifeless eyes! I cannot be here in this place that lures me with the hope of peace and quiet, only to stab me with painful memory!

"Stop it!" Stop being so fucking weak, because you are not weak! Get up and leave this wretched place right now. It's growing dark, and you'll be late for dinner. Celebration dinner, everyone together at the house, toasting our success— your success. The good that you've done this week, that's what's important. Hell, every week you do good for the bank, the investors, the family. Doesn't all the good make up for one—accident?

That's it, stand up and walk away. Walk away and leave it behind. You can do that, can't you?

"I can help you, Mister."

* * * * *

"It's yours," Michelle mumbled as she elbowed Leander from an exhausted slumber. Two jobs and mid-terms had crushed him, leaving only one night over the past week to get more than four hours of sleep.

"What? Time is it? Jesus, my phone, where?" He was incoherent as he wrestled his way out of the cocoon of blankets, finally managing contact with the bedside lamp. "Three o'clock! Who the heck calls at three in the morning?"

"Make it stop," Michelle pleaded as her head disappeared under the pillow.

"Yeah, hello!" Lee was irate.

"H-h-hello, Lee."

"Gaby, what's wrong? Do you know what time it is?"

"Sorry to be calling at this hour, Lee. I need to talk to you." Her voice was flat, devoid of emotion, and sounded far away. He was suddenly wide awake.

Michelle sat up, her expression questioning. "Gaby. Something's wrong," he whispered. "So, what's up, sis?"

She was silent for several seconds, then sniffed and said, "Had my big exam today. Positive I got an A. Can you believe that?" She sniffed again.

Leander already had coffee brewing. He sat down at the kitchen table. "It's me, Gaby. What's wrong?"

"Can't fool you, now, can I?" Her attempt at humor failed. She took a deep breath. "I really need to talk to you. I just don't know where to begin." Leander remained silent, allowing her time to sort out whatever it was that she needed to say. Instinctively, he knew that it would not be good.

"Chris and I, well, we had an argument. Actually, more than an argument. It's over, and I..." Again, she faltered. And again, Leander stayed silent.

"I don't know what to do, Lee. I'm in trouble."

With the coffee poured into a thermos, Leander hurried back to the bedroom and began tossing items into his duffle bag. Calmly, he addressed both women. "Michelle, can you take my shift at the coffee shop for the next few days? Oh, and ask Arty if he'll take lecture notes for me. He won't mind, he owes me big time. Gaby, pack your bag, and I'll be there in about three hours. We'll head for home and drive 'til we get tired."

Michelle nodded in silent agreement as she added items to his bag and zipped it up. "Do not worry," she then spoke loud enough for Gabrielle to hear. "I'll handle everything at the coffee shop and the library, too. Your exams are done with, so you're good to go. Gaby, he's on his way."

Leander paused, bag and thermos in his arms and phone still to his ear. "You understand, right?" he said to Michelle.

She smiled. "Of course, I understand. Be careful and call me."

"Will do." He blew her a kiss and was out the door. In the span of twenty minutes, his plans had been abruptly altered, to what extent he did not yet know. But that didn't matter. Neither did he know the details of Gaby's problem, and that didn't matter, either. All that mattered was that she needed him, and he would always be there for her.

"Okay, I'm on my way. See you soon."

"Oh, Lee! I feel so bad," Gabrielle said. "You weren't planning to go home at all for spring break."

"Plans change."

73

"You always know what to do, how to help me, what to say to make things better, Lee. I can't imagine what I'd do without you."

"You won't ever have to worry about that, lil' sister," Leander said as he slowed the car in preparation for the Antioch exit. "I'll always be right beside you."

And he had stayed beside her, except for restroom breaks and the one phone call that he'd made, she hadn't been out of his sight for the entire trip. They had taken turns driving, but neither one of them had been able to sleep.

He glanced at Gabrielle and hoped she didn't feel as bad as she looked. She was unusually pale, and the dark circles under her eyes spoke volumes. Her demeanor worried him as well. She was too calm, especially for Gaby, and he found himself wishing for one of her infamous temper fits. *Scream, cuss, cry—anything, Gaby!* But her control remained steadfast—not one tear.

"Home at last," she said as she smiled weakly and stretched.

"You want to stop anywhere before we go in?"

"No, this is good," she said.

"Okay, then," he said as he put the car in park and shut off the engine. He glanced in the rear-view mirrors and, seeing that no one was in sight, opened his door. "I'll get your bag."

They walked hand in hand from the quiet street to the brick walkway lined with tulips. Gabrielle's question came from out of nowhere: "Does Michelle love you, Lee?"

He hesitated briefly, then answered, "Yes, she does. And we're good together. Michelle's a wonderful person. She's probably one of the most thoughtful people that I've ever known. She's smart, too—she'll be a very successful attorney." Leander realized that he was already trying to justify his answer to what he knew would be Gaby's next question.

"And do you love her?"

They had reached the top of the steps, bringing them to the elegant veranda. He said, "I guess I haven't given a lot of thought to it, Gaby. There's, well, there are different kinds of love."

"So I've been told," she said remorsefully. And with that, she reached forward and pulled the brass chain to announce their arrival.

The door opened to the faint strains of jazz, the smell of vanilla, and the warm smile of a still beautiful woman. "Come in, you two, and let me look at you. Leander, you're just the best-looking young man I ever saw." Belle fell silent and gently drew Gabrielle into her arms. "Gaby, darlin'."

Their embrace lasted for a full minute. Gently, they parted as Leander spoke: "Miz Belle, you look wonderful. Thank you for your help."

She hushed him with a wave of her hand. "Now you just drop that *Miz*. I'm just plain Belle. We're all family, and family doesn't have to thank each other." She flicked a tear from her cheek and led the couple by their hands into the spacious living room.

"You two make yourselves comfortable while I get some snacks and a bottle of wine. How's that sound?" she asked as she hurried into the adjoining kitchen, high heels clicking on the polished oak floor.

"Sounds great, Belle," Leander answered. He settled Gabrielle into a comfortable chair, moved the ottoman to accommodate her feet and tossed her a throw pillow.

She hugged the pillow to her chest in her customary pose and rewarded him with a smile—her first in days.

"Alright, kids, here we are," Belle announced as she set the tray of hors d'oeuvres and crystal wine glasses on the coffee table. "Let's have a toast to being together again."

"Here, here," Leander said, raising his glass.

"To friends and family," Gabrielle said. "And to those who are both."

Belle studied the young woman. In less than a year she had passed from a lighthearted, spirited child without a care to someone who, the older woman feared, might not be capable of coping with this next step in her life.

She drank deeply of her wine and then sat the glass down and folded her hands in her lap.

"Gaby, sweetheart, when Leander telephoned me, he told me of your problem. Let's talk a bit about it." She paused and made eye contact. "But before we do, your granddaddy must *never* know of this. Do both of you understand? I-I would lose him, and I cannot lose him."

"Of course, Belle," Gabrielle said. "No one can know. Not ever."

Belle nodded as silence fell on the threesome. After allowing time for everyone's thoughts to settle, she went on: "Tell me, Gaby, when was your last monthly cycle?"

"Six weeks ago, I believe. No more than seven."

Belle nodded. "Very good." Her tone became businesslike as she refilled her wine glass and continued. "Let me tell you what *could* happen this evening. Then, you can decide if you really want to spend the night here with me or leave with Leander."

"Go on," Gabrielle replied.

"Very well. After Leander takes his leave, you and I will get into our PJs, open yet another excellent bottle of wine, and have ourselves a girls' night." She became animated, drawing grins from the young couple.

"Honey, I can tell you stories 'bout your granddaddy that you just won't believe! I tell you, that man was something in his day—hell, he still *is* something."

"Hey," Leander said, I just might stay for some of the storytelling."

"No, sir. Girls only," Belle responded good-naturedly. She then grew serious. "Around ten o'clock or so, Gaby, I'm gonna give you a dose of medicine that will be the most horrendous thing that you *ever* tasted. Now, I'll give you some chocolate to kill the awful taste, and about an hour later, you'll get another dose."

Belle moved to the ottoman and began to gently massage Gabrielle's bare feet, never taking her eyes off the younger woman's. "Along about one, maybe two o'clock, you're gonna get a terrible stomachache—think you're about to die, but you won't. I'll be with you the whole time."

"And then what?" Gabrielle whispered tentatively.

Belle closed her eyes and drew a deep breath. When she began to speak again, her words seemed to be born of fragmented memories.

"You'll be in the bathroom for half an hour or so. And then, my sweet, it will all be over. Then, I'll fill the tub and you'll have a long, relaxing bubble bath. Afterwards, we'll get you into bed, and I'll give you a backrub and a little something to help you sleep." She reached for Gabrielle's hands and drew them to her cheek for a caress before releasing them and standing up.

She began to clear the coffee table. "Leander will come for you tomorrow. By the way," she directed a pointed finger towards him, "I'm not an early riser, so a good time should be around one. Thirty." She walked briskly into the kitchen, leaving the young couple alone.

Leander stood and took Gabrielle's hands in his, pulling her to her feet. "You're sure?" he asked simply.

Her voice rang clear as she answered his question. "I'll see you tomorrow. And don't worry, Lee. I'll be just fine. Belle's going to take good care of me."

"You bet I am, sweetie," Belle answered as she returned to the living room. "Oh, before I forget, Leander, when you come back tomorrow, drive around back through the alley. My neighbors are old and spend entirely too much time looking out their windows."

"Yes, ma'am. I love you, lil' sis. I'll be at the Comfort Inn on the four-lane. Tomorrow, then."

74

"Y'all watch your step on these flagstones," Belle cautioned. "I keep meaning to have them reset, but then I forget all about it until I stub a toe. Or worse, break a high heel."

Gabrielle nodded silently, then turned and enveloped the older woman in her arms. "How can I ever repay you?" she whispered.

Belle held her at arms-length and spoke with seriousness. "Repay me by not letting this time in your life define the remainder of it. You," she gently shook Gabrielle's shoulders for emphasis, "are more beautiful than you see yourself. You are stronger than you feel, and you have talents that you have yet to discover. Spend your life with someone who deserves you."

"Yes, ma'am," Gabrielle said.

"Get lots of rest this week, and take the vitamins I gave you. I'll see you two later." As she turned back to her door, she barked a final order: "Now, go enjoy this beautiful day."

"Hungry?" Leander asked as he pulled onto the quiet street.

"No. Belle made a huge breakfast."

"So, you want to go home?"

"Not just yet," she said. "You know where I want to go. Please."

* * * * *

The weak blue of the spring sky had held the sun longer than most days this time of year. For that, Leander was glad. He stood up from his seat on the creek bank and stretched his long, lean body. "We're just about to lose the daylight, sister—almost four o'clock," he said. "You about ready to head home?"

295

Gabrielle grunted contentedly. "Soon," she said. "It's so perfect here, I think I dozed off. Being back at our special place makes the rest of the world seem far away."

"Sure does," Leander agreed. He jogged in place for several seconds, then resumed his seat on the blanket beside her. "Tell me, now, are you okay?" he asked.

She met his gaze with clear eyes. She was no longer pale, and the tiny smile that played at the corners of her mouth gave him hope. "Yes, Lee. I'm okay. I've been thinking about the past seven months."

"And?" he prompted.

She shrugged. "It's like it all happened to someone else. Someone else's life." The easy silence lingered between them for several minutes until Gabrielle stated adamantly, "I don't want to end up like Mama. Loving a man who doesn't feel the same must be such a lonely life."

"That's not true, Gaby," Leander tried to reassure her. "Gabe loves your mama."

"Yes, I know," she said. "I know all about those *different* kinds of love."

He thought it best to say no more on the subject. A big trout chose that moment to jump from the rushing waters of Dalton's Creek, bringing smiles from the couple.

"We need our fishing poles," Gabrielle said lightly. She laid her head on his shoulder and spoke matter-of-factly. "He never loved me at all, you know. Christopher. Not ever."

Leander's heart broke for her. Softly he whispered, "Then, find one who does. One who deserves you."

She didn't respond, and he began to gather up jackets, soda cans, and snack wrappers. "We'll get to your house just in time for cocktails. Tell everybody we drove straight through. They'll understand why I won't stay for dinner, and you can say you're tired and want to go to bed early." He chuckled. "That's true. My folks will most likely be at church, so I'll crash in my room and deal with all the hugging, kissing, and catching up tomorrow."

Leander stopped his random one-sided conversation as his ears picked up the strange sound. At first, he thought it was someone calling in distress.

A second later, the fate of a wounded animal crossed his mind until he realized exactly what he was hearing.

Never had he witnessed this. Not when she had fallen from the jungle gym and fractured her ankle. Not when the softball had struck her directly in the face and blacked her eye. Not when Rosie had died. He could not remember a time when his precious Gaby had cried.

And now, all he could do was cradle her against his chest as the sobs shook her thin body. He held her until the sobbing was reduced to weak little snubs. Eventually, she sat erect, wiped her face and retrieved her makeup bag from her purse.

The gathering dusk followed the couple as they walked hand in hand through the tall bulrushes and trees that had grown to camouflage their special spot.

"You hold all of my secrets, Lee—no one else." Gabrielle said.

"And I will keep them safe, Gaby, I swear."

Secrets!

PART IV

Allure

75

"It is time, child. We must go." Elsaneth spoke softly and with no emotion. She laid her hand gently on the young girl's shoulder as she walked past her. But she did not embrace her. She did not look into her daughter's eyes. She dared not.

"Why must I go, Manman? This is my home. I do not want to leave you!" The young girl dissolved into tears as she had done for the past three days. Ever since she'd been told that she was to board a ship alone and sail to a far-away place—a place where she knew no one. A place from which she would not return. Not ever.

Elsaneth shut her eyes tightly, fighting against the flood of emotion that threatened. She swallowed her tears and said, "Because, Maffi, you are not safe here. You have no future in Haiti."

"But, Manman, you are here and you will protect me! I don't want to go."

Elsaneth's voice rose and her demeanor changed dramatically as she silenced her daughter. "No, I cannot protect you, not anymore. There is no guarantee of safety for anyone. The soldiers, they come to our villages every day. They plunder, they rape. They take young girls, especially the ones such as you who are so beautiful." She fell silent for several minutes before straightening her shoulders and saying, "There is more."

"W-w-what is it?" Maffi asked timidly.

"At the ceremony last week, the spirit *Loa* entered me." Elsaneth's words caused her daughter to gasp. "Yes," she continued speaking in a whisper. "The *Loa* rode me for hours and told me of the danger you are in. It is not my will, child, but the will of the spirits."

The young girl's posture changed from fearful defiance to calm resignation. "It will be so, then," she said.

* * * * *

The full moon reflected off the gently lapping waves, making the night seem like midday. Elsaneth and Maffi, both dressed in black, sat huddled together on the deserted dock. The older woman gazed at the position of the moon. "We will see the ship at half past the midnight hour."

Maffi no longer believed that her mother was sending her away voluntarily. She knew that there was no such thing as free will and personal choice. That was for non-believers. All life and all choices were determined by the spirits. She laid her head on her mother's shoulder. "Will you tell me about Gran-Grann once again?"

Elsaneth chuckled. "Of course. Your great-grandmother was called Sanité. She was born a slave in Haiti. But her owners were kind people. They took her to their Catholic masses and taught her their prayers. But her manman—whose name I do not remember—gave your Gran-Grann *proper* instruction in the voodoo. And this, my child, assured her to receive the *Loa's* assistance throughout her life. She was a great healer here in Haiti, and she lived to be very old. She had one daughter, my manman, Allu, who died birthing me. That was because she fought the possession of *Erzuli*, the great mother spirit. You must *never* fight the spirits, Maffi! Do you understand?"

Maffi nodded. "Yes, ma'am. I will always heed the spirits."

"And if you do, you will be rewarded in your life," Elsaneth said. "You will meet a man who will adore you and give you a daughter, just as I met your father. But never let that man change who you are. You are destined to be a priestess, just as your great-grandmother, Sanité, was a priestess. Always remember this, Maffi. And remember how much I love you."

"W-w-where will the ship take me, Manman?"

"You will sail to the west to a safe island," Elsaneth answered. "The ship's captain will take you to a man who will give you lodging and work."

"Will this man be my husband?"

"No, my child. He will only keep you safe." Elsaneth drew a deep breath and rose to her feet. "The ship nears, Maffi. Your journey begins." Seeing her daughter's tears begin anew, she counseled her further.

"You are a woman now, a woman of fourteen years. Cry no more. The spirits go with you on your journey. Sanité goes with you. I go with you, as well."

Elsaneth watched as the ship slipped further and further away from the dock and became swallowed up in the sea's blackness. An unknown future awaited her only child, but a future far more promising than the repression from which she had saved her. How many years she herself had left in this life Elsaneth could not know. She would be sure to make a proper sacrifice so that she might be ridden again by the *Loa*. Perhaps she would be allowed a glimpse into the future her daughter would find in her new life.

But for now, she would go back to the loneliness of her meager shack. For once, she was thankful for her poverty. All that she had owned in this world was the small bag of coins that her Carlos had left for her before he had gone to fish and was found three days later with his throat cut. Those coins and her prized beads had been given to the ship's captain to pay for Maffi's passage. Her dire situation afforded her a small measure of safety. Since the evil *attachés* had no use for her possessions, she had no fear of being terrorized nor forced to abandon her home.

Elsaneth was tired, her energy spent, and all she wanted now was to sleep. She knew, though, that sleep would not come easily. As she collapsed on the straw mat in her hut, she feared that this night would be no different than the many other nights before. She closed her eyes and conjured the spirits to impart peace to her amid the constant barking of street dogs, the pitiful cries for help, and the sporadic bursts from machine guns that defined life in Haiti.

76

Gabrielle paused as she exited her apartment building and prepared to walk the short distance to the coffee shop to meet Rachael. Gingerly, she touched the real estate sign posted on the brick wall beside the front door. It read: *Luxury One-Bedroom Apartment with Fantastic View for Sale – Sale Pending.*

She turned away and began her walk, suddenly a bit sad. The apartment had been her home for four years. Good times. Bad times. But her first venture on her own. For a brief moment, fear knotted her stomach. *What do I do now?* But her anxiety soon passed. Whatever the future held, Gabrielle knew that she could face it. And of course, Granddaddy was right to sell the apartment. She had no use for it now: she was soon to be a college graduate.

The spring morning was a day of sunshine, cool breezes, and the scent of daffodils in the air. Gabrielle realized just how much she was going to miss Westminster. "What a day, huh," she happily exclaimed as she joined Rachael at one of the sidewalk tables. "No rain on our graduation day."

"It wouldn't dare," Rachael decreed. "I've already ordered for you. Thanks again, Gaby, for last night. Dinner was great, and I loved seeing your family again."

"Yeah, it was a fun party. I still can't believe *everyone* came. Even my sister-in-law made the trip!" Gabrielle paused to sip her coffee. "I'm sure Remy insisted, but for once, M'Lyn didn't try to make everything about her."

"And Mason—that's only the third time that I've seen him, but I swear he gets better looking every time," Rachael said.

Gabrielle smiled. "Mason's great. He's family, too, you know." She grew serious as she studied the only real friend she had made in college. "I'm going to miss you, Rachael," she said simply.

"Me, too, Gaby, but we'll never lose touch. Hey, it's only three months 'til my wedding, and you'll be flying up for a week."

"Looking forward to it, for sure," Gabrielle said. "Who wouldn't just *die* for a week in The Hamptons in August." She shook her head and laughed. "It's a freakin' fairy tale, Rach: you're marrying the boy you've loved since the fourth grade. That doesn't happen anymore. Anyway, I'm thrilled to be your maid-of-honor."

"Only problem with that is that I'm afraid that the maid-of-honor is going to outshine the bride." Rachael had been in awe of her friend since the two had met early in their freshman year. Gabrielle was tall and willowy with hair and eyes the color of burnished gold. She turned heads everywhere she went and was all the things that Rachael was not. But there was no jealousy on Rachael's part, only love. The love of a sister, and that made it all the more difficult to tell her what she knew she must.

She cleared her throat. "What are your plans for this morning, Gaby?" she asked.

"Well, later on, I'll drive out to the inn and hang out with the family 'til time to go to the auditorium and get our caps and gowns." She paused to finish her coffee, then continued speaking. "Right now, though, why don't we go over to the Alumni Office and make sure they've got our correct addresses. I'd like to stay in contact with some of my professors; they've been so much help to me. Sound good to you?"

"Uh-huh," Rachael replied. "Actually, I stopped by there on my way over here this morning." At a sudden loss for words, she fell silent.

"What, you signed up? I thought we were going to do that together. No matter. You can walk with me now, and I'll sign up," Gabrielle said.

Rachael hesitated. "Uh, Gaby, there were a lot of alumnae there this morning." When her friend did not respond, she took a deep breath and said, "Gaby, Chis, uh, Christopher was there. He's there."

Gabrielle digested her friend's news. Of course, Christopher came to graduation. He came last year as well. After all, he was president of the McDaniel Alumni Association. After a time, she said, "I hadn't thought about it, but it's no surprise."

"Gaby, Chris didn't come alone—Buffy is with him."

Gabrielle chuckled. "That's no surprise, either. When you think about it, the two of them deserve each other."

"They made an announcement this morning," Rachael spoke rapidly now, deciding to get her news over with as quickly as possible. "They were with his parents last week in New York. Buffy and Chris—they got married."

* * * * *

"Here's to our girl!" Will Remington's booming voice silenced the others that had gathered in the Antrim Inn's elegant reception room. Will raised his glass. "My granddaughter, Gabrielle, you've made us all proud. Just as your brother did on his college graduation." He paused, lifted his glass to the chorus of voices all around.

"Speech, speech!" Mason and Remy said in unison.

Gabrielle stood up slowly, smiled, and said, "Thanks, Granddaddy, and thanks to all of you for coming. I love you guys. You're probably just as surprised as I am that I actually did it. Hell—sorry, I mean, heck— *I'm* surprised that I even managed to graduate high school!"

She sat down amid echoes of laughter and head shaking.

"No one is surprised, Gaby," Leander's deep, calm voice subdued the laughter. His gaze locked with hers. "I remember someone once telling you that you were stronger than you realize, smarter than you think, and more beautiful than you know. Never forget it." His speech ended in a whisper.

Gabe lightened the moment as he lifted his glass and said, "And a toast to Leander, as well. Dual degrees in business and law—an accomplishment earned by few. I believe that Will has an announcement at this time?"

The older man waved his hand. "You go ahead, Gabe."

"Very well. Lee, the partners sincerely hope you will be joining us at Remington Banking and Investments."

Leander stood up once again and, when the clapping ceased, said, "It will be my honor. Thank you all."

Remy, who had been rather quiet up until now, asked, "So, when is the bar exam?"

Leander smiled. "Not for a while, Remy. Thank you. I still have a couple of tests before graduation in two weeks." He added, "I'll be sure and keep you up to date."

Laughter, more champagne, and music carried the happy family into the late evening. Midnight found the two best friends curled comfortably on sofas in the hotel's lobby.

"When did you last see Chris?" Leander asked after hearing the news.

Gabrielle sighed and closed her eyes. "I ran into him at the Boar's Head right after my sophomore year started. First week in September, year before last." She exhaled loudly. "His senior year had just begun. The usual crowd was there. I had gone in to pick up my pizza, and there he was, talking above everyone else, like always. Drinking. Showing off."

Her voice grew faint, and Leander prompted. "What happened?"

Gabrielle shook her head slightly and uttered a sad little snicker. "He saw me and for a minute he stopped talking. Just looked at me. I-I could actually see his eyes drop down to my stomach. Then, he just turned away. Went right back to talking, like it was nothing." She laid her head on Leander's shoulder, and the two of them sat quietly for several minutes.

When she spoke again, it was barely a whisper. "Like he didn't even know me."

77

+ + + + +

The gravel road leading from the Remington-Westin estate into town had recently received a new topcoat of brightly colored gravel and had been widened considerably to accommodate the installation of an updated drainage system. But it remained exactly what it had always been: a hot and dusty country road on this June morning.

"You just *had* to walk, huh!" Leander berated himself aloud.

As he entered the town, he noticed that the "Beautify Antioch" campaign had grown in scope over the past several years with more flowerbeds, park benches, and fountains added to the town square. Leander gazed in amazement at the trees towering over his head. Some of them had been saplings that he, Gaby, and other kids in their school had planted.

But change? Not so much after all. All those lovely amenities still centered around a monument honoring the Confederacy.

Leander continued to reflect on his hometown and his decision to return here instead of taking the position at Michelle's law firm in Boston. *Michelle*—he missed her. He missed her warm, comforting presence in his bed. He missed their stimulating conversations and her sensible advice.

"Your roots are in Antioch," she told him. "Go home, at least for a while."

The analytical side of his brain took over as he concluded that Antioch had not changed one iota. But what was a town anyway? A town was made up of people, and the people here comprised two distinct groups: old money and the working poor. Oh, there were a few, of course, who fell in between, in the category of upper middle class. But those folks, like Tom Olsen and other supervisors at the mill, business owners, attorneys, doctors, and the like were all dependent upon the old money group. If that ever gave out, then they would be demoted to a level nearing that of the working poor.

Leander decided that he had engaged in quite enough mental anguish for the day. He checked his wristwatch: he was twenty minutes early for his scheduled appointment. He took a seat on one of the park benches, placed the new leather briefcase that his parents had given him on the bench beside him, and blotted his brow with his handkerchief. As a rare cool breeze fanned the magnolia leaves shading him, his thoughts flowed to this morning's approaching meeting with the partners of Remington Banking and Investments. *Now, there's something that represents real change.*

When he entered the bank building this morning and took the elevator to the executive floor, he would not be doing so as the once self-conscious child whose only acceptance lay in his friendship with Gaby. Nor would he be entering *his* office as the composed yet terrified high school student who had practically demanded help in gaining admission to Harvard. No sir, not today.

Today, he would enter those high-level offices with the self-assurance of an honor graduate from Harvard University. Today, he would accept whatever position was offered to him. He would succeed in that position. He would work tirelessly and rise in the ranks of the firm to earn the respect of all the partners. And, he would deserve it.

"Good morning, gentlemen. Thank you for this meeting."

* * * * *

"So, you think Lee's the one to handle the offshore division?"

"That's what I said. You see any problem with that?"

"He's young, green as a gourd. Just out of college, and hell, we only formally hired him today!"

"Well, I agree that Lee's the one. Now, I'm not saying he's the smartest guy in the world—he's just the smartest guy *we* know."

"Bullshit! I could write a prospectus on offshore banking."

"That may be true, but with all due respect, you didn't. Lee wrote it, and I found it enlightening. I have to agree that he is our man."

The clock chimed two. "I've got a tee time. What's the consensus? Do we send Lee Washington to Grand Cayman to set up an office?"

"I say yes."

"I agree. He's the obvious choice."

The clock struck the quarter hour.

"It's two-fifteen, and we need a decision. What do you say?"

"Okay, okay."

"Good. We're in total agreement. Who's gonna give him the good news?"

You played that well. Smart, acting like you had doubts. Of course, you always know how to play it, don't you? Yeah, taking the lead comes easy. Been hard, having him back in Antioch, having to see the son-of-a-bitch, being forced to say 'Good morning, Lee. How you doing, Lee?' Now, though, he'll be miles away, on an island. You won't have to speak to him at all.

You haven't thought about 'things' for years, but since he's been back, it's got all confused again. Can't stop the whispers, the headaches. Get rid of him, and life will get better again. That's it—you know how to handle problems.

What a hoot, YOU get to be the one to give him the news. 'A cushy assignment right off the bat, Lee. Congrats. We know you'll do a bang-up job for the partners.' Translation: Get the hell out of my sight, you fucker!

You just THINK you're the winner—Harvard, Grand Cayman—but I'M the winner. I'm getting you out of my life.

"Gettin' rid of him ain't gonna help you none, Mister. I can help you, though."

"SHUT UP!"

78

The Cayman Islands has one of the highest standards of living in the entire world. Their strong economy is the direct result of not only robust tourism but is driven by a strong financial sector. Even though a U.S. government crackdown on off-shore banking hurt the economy of the Caymans by causing many companies to resign their registration there, it remains a trustworthy banking center. That fact, thanks in part to Great Britain's 2010 decision to step in to help, will reestablish the Islands as the best *off-market* in the world. And so on, and so forth, blah, blah, blah…

Leander grew bored with reading and rereading his own prospectus. He closed the portfolio and returned it to his briefcase, which he placed under the seat in front of him. He stretched his long legs, thankful for the extra room first-class afforded him, and accepted a Perrier from the flight attendant.

He reclined his seat back, his thoughts playing on his new position. He had done extensive research, and although he firmly believed in the prospectus that he'd written and presented to the partners, he was wise enough to know that he'd stuck out his neck. If their venture failed, he would not only be looking for another job, he'd be a laughingstock.

But that won't happen. He would make this remarkable opportunity work—for himself as well as for Remington Banking & Investments. He would do so by working day and night and by meeting with and taking the advice of all the right people in the banking environment. Above all, he would never mislead clients as to the possibility of taxation from their home governments, even as he dangled the proverbial carrot of amazing financial gain.

The sudden slowing and banking of the aircraft jolted Leander out of his daydreaming. "Please fasten your seatbelts and return all seat backs and tray tables to their upright and locked position in preparation for our landing at Owen Roberts International Airport, Grand Cayman Island." The flight attendant's words directed his attention to the airplane's window.

The brochures inked in vivid color, friends' photographs, nor Hollywood's movie scenes had prepared Leander for his first breathtaking sight of the Caribbean. The pristine white sands melted into the many-hued brilliance of jade, turquoise, and sapphire. Goosebumps rippled his arms and his pulse quickened as apprehension faded and all yearning for the familiar bosom of the Carolinas slipped away.

* * * * *

"I'm glad I caught you before you got away this morning, Gaby," Vivian said, hurrying down the stairs as her daughter paused at the front door. "I'm just dying to show you my latest scrapbook. Do you have a few minutes to sit with me?"

"Wish I did, Mama, but I don't want to be late for this interview."

"Oh, I didn't know you had an interview! Tell me all about it."

"That's right," Gabrielle responded. "You weren't at dinner last night, so you missed my news. Executive Director for the Town Council—pretty small-time stuff. But if I get the job, it's a start."

She retrieved her purse from the entryway table and prepared to leave. "Hope the headache's gone, Mama."

"Much better, thank you dear. Perhaps we could have a drink this afternoon when you get back and you could tell me all about the interview?"

"Sure. No, wait. I promised William that I'd go to his baseball game this afternoon. Why don't you go with me, Mama?"

"Oh, I don't think so. It's so hot, and my skin, you know."

"I-I'm sorry, Mama. We'll spend a day together soon. Promise." Her words were punctuated with a quick kiss on Vivian's forehead.

The door closed behind her daughter, leaving Vivian alone. The previous four years seemed to have passed in the twinkling of an eye, and she could not remember a single, meaningful conversation with her daughter. Was that because she did not make the effort, as Claire so often pointed out? Or, was it simply because the two of them had nothing to say to one another?

Vivian knew the answer. As she slowly climbed the staircase back to the seclusion of her rooms, she fully admitted that it was easier for her to interact with those she loved through the many scrapbooks that she had so lovingly arranged. Photos, notes, pressed flowers, from the time that she and Gabe had been young children together to depictions of their lavish wedding flowed into more volumes detailing the children's accomplishments. Her latest project had recounted Gaby's last four years, from high school graduation to her completion of college two months ago.

Slowly, Vivian placed the scrapbook—seen only by her—on the bookshelf beside all the others. She sat in her chair and studied them. *A life in pictures. A life not lived.*

79

Leander stood amid other travelers, most of them tourists, and slowly began to absorb his surroundings. He tried but found it impossible to discern which one of his senses piqued with the highest degree of response.

The brilliance of hibiscus, orchids, and flowering vines completely unfamiliar to him shimmered in the mid-day sun, causing him to reach for his sunglasses. He closed his eyes and breathed deeply, taking in the aroma of the blossoms and other scents around him. He heard the happy sounds of squealing children, the rustle of palm fronds in the breeze, and the honk of taxi cabs zipping along the road.

Opening his eyes, he realized that he'd been standing in the middle of the rental car lot, grinning from ear to ear. He walked toward the blue Chevy pointed out to him by the friendly clerk with the delightful British accent. He chuckled as he remembered that the Customs officials hadn't been quite so amicable.

Thanks to Will's forewarning, though, Leander knew that the Cayman Islands were not a place that visitors traveled to indefinitely, and that employment was a requirement for one to remain here. Undoubtedly, questioning would have gone on for much longer, had he not politely handed the officer his business card.

"Oh, yes, Mr. Washington. Welcome! Mr. Remington has informed Customs that you would be arriving. We are most happy to have Remington Investments establish an office here."

Leander put all thoughts of business and legalities out of his mind. The goosebumps returned, and his belly tightened at the most purely sensual place that he'd ever been. Michelle's image came to him in a flash.

He took his phone from his jacket pocket and began to snap photos of his surroundings. He would send them to her tonight before he called her.

He placed his luggage in the car's trunk in preparation for his drive into the center of town. He adjusted the seat so he could fit his long legs behind the steering wheel, thankful that it was on the "correct" side. Now, if only he could manage to drive without incident on the "wrong" side of the road.

PAPA JACK's ISLAND PARADISE: The sign was impossible to miss, but the driveway leading to the establishment wasn't. Leander almost drove past the left turn and waved an apology to the vehicle behind him. He drove slowly down the narrow, shell-covered drive, coming to a stop in front of Papa Jack's. The sprawling, one-story building boasted a long veranda across the front, covered with a profusion of flowers, potted plants, and baskets loaded with ripe, wonderful-smelling fruits.

The side entrance sign read: "Bait & Fresh Fish", while the main entrance directed visitors to the "General Store & Cottage Rentals". Stepping from the veranda, Leander was immediately drawn into another world. The dark and uneven wooden floor groaned under his steps, and the large fans hanging from the exposed rafters moved the musty air around with the creak of old bones.

As his eyes gradually adjusted to the dark interior, Leander spied the registration desk to his left and the well-stocked general store beyond. But that would have to wait, though, as the scene directly in front of him beckoned. The back wall of the ancient building had been opened up, providing a view like none other. *Another photo op for Michelle.*

Stone steps made walking easy from the building's back deck through white sand to the Caribbean's edge. In a flash, Leander had rolled up his britches to the knees, discarded loafers and socks, and was a laughing boy once again. The gentle surf tickled his ankles as his toes buried themselves in the silken sands.

"Ahh, 'tis your first time to the islands, yeah?" The old man's voice startled Leander, and he turned at the sound.

"Yes, sir," he answered. He wiped his hand on his shirt and extended it to the older man, studying him as he did so. He was much shorter than Leander and well advanced in age. His skin was coal black and his hair snow white. "You must be Mr. Jack. My company has arranged for me to rent one of your cottages. I apologize. I should have registered before walking out here."

The old man laughed as he finished Leander's thought. "But the sea called to you, I know." He flashed white teeth and shook hands with a strong grip. "It calls to me as well. Please call me Papa Jack—everyone does."

"And I am Lee Washington, Papa Jack. It's a pleasure to meet you. Your island is beautiful."

The old man gazed at him for a long time. So long, in fact, that Leander became slightly self-conscious. "Well, then," he said, "shall we go inside and let me get registered?"

Papa Jack's silent perusal went on for another moment or two before he replied. "You may do that another time, my young friend. You are most probably tired, or you may wish to explore further. Your cottage is the one on the end there," he said, pointing to the larger of four dwellings. Painted bright blue with white shutters, the bungalow was surrounded by a charming, white picket fence as well as the normal array of flowering vines and bushes.

Leander smiled. "It's perfect."

After several more minutes of quiet observation Jack spoke, almost as if to himself. "Yes, Lee, we are glad that you have arrived. I will have your car brought to the cottage. You may walk over, and I will have my girl meet you with the key." He turned and began to walk back to the store, obviously expecting his directions to be followed.

"Uh, thanks, thank you, sir. Jack. Papa Jack," Leander stammered after him. He gathered his shoes and socks and began to stroll down the beach to his new home. The old man's demeanor had perplexed him.

"Do I look that different from other folks here?" he muttered to himself.

Leander took his time making his way to his new home. He walked a fair distance past the bright blue cottage toward denser vegetation and tall palm trees. He now carried more of his clothing than he wore and continued to direct his feet to the turquoise water's edge. Several yards up ahead, he spied a hammock—quite a few, in fact—each one of them secured between the palms. They swayed gently in the sea breeze, summoning him.

With coat, necktie, and dress shirt joining his footwear in a pile on the sand, the newly-ordained banking executive collapsed with a sigh in the nearest hammock. *Ahh, Gaby, my new happy place!* The image of his best friend and the golden memories of their childhood flashed across his mind.

"I miss you, lil' sis," he whispered.

Regretfully, he rose from the hammock, stretched, and began to make his way back down the beach to his new home. The gate swung silently open at his touch, revealing a small garden space with flowering bushes and vines that all but covered the ground. Rounding the corner, Leander saw that his car had been brought around and his luggage placed on the front porch.

"Hello," he called to the young Caymanian boy. "Thank you." He retrieved his wallet from his pants pocket, but his attempt was quickly waved off.

"No problem, sir," he said. "Welcome to Grand Cayman Island. We very glad to have you here, sir," he called out as he skipped backwards toward Papa Jack's, smiling all the while. "The missy, she is inside, and she brought your supper. Welcome, sir."

"Thank you," Leander called and headed for the open door of his cottage.

The furnishings were simple and tasteful, consisting of woven chairs padded with large, white cushions and an array of painted chests and tables. The bedroom and bath were visible through open French doors to the right, and the kitchen straight ahead. Someone was rattling pots and pans.

She stood with her back to him, softly humming to herself as she stirred a bubbling pot on the stove. She was short—five-two, he guessed—and tiny. He watched silently as her perfectly proportioned body began to sway to the tune that she hummed. Her hair, a light brown, hung in thick ringlets down her back, almost reaching her full hips. Her bare feet tapped a gentle rhythm on the wood floor. The white lace sundress she wore complemented the café au lait color of her arms and shoulders. Leander leaned against the door frame. He didn't want to startle her. More than that, he didn't want the moment to end. He cleared his throat, and she turned at the sound.

"Hello," he managed to say.

She stood quietly for several seconds before parting her lips in a smile and slowly approaching him. Extending a small, smooth hand, she responded, "Welcome to Grand Cayman Island."

Her hand was cool to the touch. Leander held it a bit too long. "Thank you. I'm Leander Washington. Please call me Lee—everyone does."

She continued to study him intently. *What is it with these island people?* "Whatever it is that you're cooking—it smells delicious," he asked with a nod toward the stove.

Leander stopped feeling self-conscious, as it now became his turn for close scrutiny. Her faint, floral scent reminded him of Michelle, but the similarity ended there. No hint of sophistication registered in the face before him. No shy curiosity, either. Rather, her expression strangely conveyed familiarity, as if she had known him forever. Her smile grew wide, revealing perfect, white teeth. He found himself wondering if those dark, full red lips tasted like they looked—like cherries, wet and sweet.

"Turtle soup," she said.

"Huh?" He was momentarily confused but soon recovered. "Well, as I said before, it smells wonderful. I've never had turtle soup, but I know it's quite popular here. I'm sure I'll like it. Thank you very much."

"No problem. I like to cook. Papa Jack taught me." She turned back to the bubbling pot, extinguished the heat, and once again spoke to him as if they were old friends. "Tomorrow, Leander, I will take you to visit the green sea turtle farm. They are raised there, some for food, and some released back to the sea."

She walked past him and into the living room. "I will come at ten o'clock tomorrow, and we will tour the island. Yes? Then, perhaps I will take you to Hell."

"Uh, wait, w-w-what?" His reaction caused her to laugh, and it sounded like tiny bells.

"Hell is on the west side of the island. Tourist place. Black limestone. You will see."

"Whatever you say," he replied good-naturedly. "And, yes, ten will be good. I'll look forward to seeing you. Wait—you haven't told me your name."

She turned back to face him, her luminous gray-green eyes hypnotic. "I am Allure."

Leander sat at the small kitchen table, gazing out the open doors at the rapidly fading daylight. The sun had long ago slipped beyond the horizon, and the waves breaking against the sand now shown silver. The second bowl of turtle soup had tasted even better than the first and, coupled with the red wine included in his welcome fruit basket, had left him stuffed and mellow.

He would sleep soundly tonight, he thought, as he cleared the dishes and made his way to his bedroom. It had been a good day, the first in what he looked forward to as a new beginning. After stripping down to his shorts, he stretched out between cool, fresh smelling sheets and was immediately asleep.

He hadn't thought to call Michelle.

80

Leander nodded his head. "Yep, I do believe this is what Hell might look like. But I hope I never find out."

He was rewarded with another pleasant laugh. "Come," Allure said, taking him by the hand, "you should send your family postcards from Hell."

The touch of her hand sent a shudder through him. He recovered and said, "I'm not sure my mother would appreciate that, but Gaby will love it."

She stopped and looked up at him, her eyes searching. "Gaby?"

"Gabrielle Westin, my best friend since—well, since all my life, actually. I call her Gaby. We're like brother and sister," he explained.

The couple continued to stroll hand in hand along the wooden walkway that served as a viewing platform overlooking the field of rough black limestone that poked out of the ground. The stark contrast between the bare rock formations and the lush surroundings was not lost on Leander. However, he found his companion far more interesting than the local attractions.

She broke their easy silence. "I hope you have enjoyed the day, Leander."

"I have, very much so," he said. "I especially liked the turtle farm. You should call me Lee."

"I will call you Leander," she said. "It is a strong name."

He chuckled. "Now, you sound like my mother. She's the only one who still insists on using my full name." They had reached the car, and he checked his watch. "It's nearly five o'clock. I'd like to take you to dinner."

She nodded silently, holding his gaze. "There's a wonderful place nearby."

They strolled across a picturesque bridge that took them from the parking area to the restaurant where they were greeted by a large, brightly colored parrot sitting atop his perch. "Welcome," he squawked shrilly.

Leander was amazed. "What a beautiful bird!" he exclaimed.

The parrot's limited repertoire of "Thank you", "Beautiful", "Welcome" followed the couple to their table overlooking the water.

After the waiter had set fruit-filled rum cocktails before them, Leander raised his glass and said, "Here's to you, Allure. You have the most beautiful eyes that I've ever seen." The crystal clinked, and he added, "Your mother must have beautiful green eyes as well."

She smiled. "Thank you. But I have my father's eyes."

"Your father? But, Papa Jack—"

Her laughter cut his words short. "Oh, no. Papa Jack's not my father. Everybody calls him *Papa*. My father is a white man from America." She sipped her drink. "My father came from Weeming. He came here for vacation, fell in love with my mother. The rest is history, as they say."

Leander looked puzzled. "Weeming? Where is that?"

"A state in America," Allure said. "He's a cowboy."

He couldn't help but laugh at her delightful pronunciation. "I believe you mean *Wyoming*," he said.

"Yes, yes, that's it."

"And do your parents still live here?"

She took a deep breath before answering. "My father went away when I was very young. I can remember him swinging me around and hugging me. And laughing. He laughed a lot. But that is about all that I remember."

"I-I'm sorry," Leander said.

"Don't be. I asked my mother why he went away, and she said only that he had too much of paradise."

"And your mother?"

Allure sipped her drink. Leander could tell that she was making her way through a difficult memory.

"Manman—my mother—she went away as well. When I was twelve, she left me with Papa Jack and went away." She nodded her head as if to convince herself. "I think that she went to find my father."

Leander cleared his throat. "How old are you, now?

"I am twenty-two."

"That's sad, Allure. I can't imagine my parents not being there for me. It must have been hard for you to deal with."

"At the time, perhaps. But she taught me what I needed to know before she left. And Papa Jack took care of me. He took care of Manman when she came here, as a young girl."

"Where did your mother come from?"

Allure looked past his shoulder. "Here is our waiter. We should order the fish and vegetables."

*   *   *   *   *

"I will walk from here," Allure said as Leander brought the car to a stop. "Papa Jack's house is beyond those trees, but you cannot drive there."

"I'll walk with you, then," he responded as he opened the car door. "Perhaps tomorrow you can go with me to return this car and look for one to buy."

"Of course. I will ask Papa where you should go."

They had reached the dimly lit porch of the small, two-story house. He had no idea how to end their day together; he only knew how he *wanted* it to end. She seemed to read his mind as she stepped close to him and placed both hands gently against his heart. His physical reaction was immediate and a bit embarrassing. Did she even know of such things, he wondered? He moved to embrace her, but her words stopped him.

"Soon," she whispered, looking up to study him intently. "One day, you must tell me of the darkness that you carry inside of you, Leander Washington."

"W-w-what?"

She said no more as her fingers burned a trail from his chest down his belly. She stepped back from him, her lips mouthing "Tomorrow."

He collapsed on his bed, exhausted, exhilarated, aching. "Sweet Jesus," he whispered aloud. At some point during the wee hours of the morning, he managed to fall asleep, his thoughts in a whirl.

81

"MONEY! Goddammit, Lee, *that's* what you're supposed to be thinking about: making money! That's what we sent you down there for. Just what in the hell have you been doing for an entire week? Huh? Well, tell me, for heaven's sake!"

"Calm down, Will," Leander kept his voice respectful, albeit firm. "I've gotten settled in, bought a car and things are moving along."

"Settling in. To a furnished, one-bedroom beach cottage." Will's voice took on a syrupy, condescending tone. "That should have taken all of one day. What've you been doing for the other six? You're not on vacation, you know. How long does it take to open an office that I've already paid the rent on for a year?"

Leander had had just about enough. "*We*, Will," he said sharply. "*We* paid the rent on the office here. The partners, for whom I work, paid the rent. And," he abandoned any effort to soften his words, "for your information, I have hired a receptionist and have a meeting scheduled with the CEOs of three of the largest banks on the island for Monday morning at ten o'clock. Now, if you would kindly check your e-mail, you'll find that I have also arranged for a conference call with all the partners for Monday evening, providing, of course, everyone will be available. I suppose Gabe didn't tell you that he and I talked last night."

Silence. "Until Monday evening, then."

Leander shook his head and listened to the dial tone before placing the receiver back down in its cradle. He had been completely truthful with Will, but what he *hadn't* revealed was that he had accomplished all of his business dealings in just one day. The remainder of his week had been spent in the spellbinding company of Allure.

Thanks to his beautiful companion, he knew his way around the island and had gained a first-hand knowledge of local restaurants. But today had been the best day of all—perhaps the best day ever. Papa Jack's catamaran had carried them to Stingray City. Leander, a novice at snorkeling, was as animated as a kid at Christmas when the peaceful, underwater world of Grand Cayman enveloped him and the graceful stingrays glided over the colorful coral beds to actually brush against him.

The day had ended with dinner at Papa Jack's home. The old man was a fantastic cook, and Leander had walked home with his belly full and his body exhausted from hours spent in the water. He fixed himself a rum cocktail and sat on his back porch to watch wispy clouds scuttle across the sky and far distant lightning dance on the water.

"Mmm," he murmured contentedly as he sipped his drink, replaying the day all over again. Was he becoming an islander for life? Or, would he one day find that he, too, had had too much of paradise? His brief phone conversation with Will flashed through his mind as a more pressing question begged to be answered. Would he be able to concentrate on business at all, when all he could think of was *her*?

* * * * *

The rum and a hot shower had completely done him in. Leander fell asleep instantly after lying down and turning off the light. When the sound came, though, he was wide awake and alert. What had he heard? The wind, perhaps? A rumble of thunder stalking the earlier lightning? No, it was definitely the sound of a door closing. He sat up in bed, preparing to do what? He had no idea how to deal with the knowledge that he was no longer alone in his house.

The French doors slowly opened, and as his eyes adjusted to the twilight, he made out her shape. Tiny, perfect, she floated toward his bed. As she grew closer, he caught the heady aroma of her perfume that had intoxicated him over the past week. Another smell, too, assailed him: the pungent scent of smoke.

Without speaking, she sat on the edge of his bed, her luminous eyes never leaving his. Trance-like, she reached out to him, and he noticed for the first time that her hands held an ornate goblet. She touched the cool rim to his lips and nodded.

The liquid smelled fruity and a bit spicy. "Wine?" he whispered the question.

Again, she nodded. "Drink, my Leander."

Her words sounded so far away, and he wondered vaguely if this were only a dream. Never in his life had a dream been so overwhelmingly erotic. She lifted the goblet to her own lips, drained the last sip, and placed it on the nightstand. As she stood up, the thin dress that she wore fell to the floor. She stretched out beside him and began stroking his bare chest.

"Allure," he whispered, "are you sure? We can wait."

Her answer came with her full red lips pressing against his. Their kiss, long, exploring, and delicious, seemed to extend into eternity. When last their lips parted, she said, "I have waited for you my whole life. Now, it begins."

Leander was dizzy. *Was this really happening?* He sought for breath to speak, but instead found himself swimming in delirium. Her lips joined with his once again, and the hard points of her breasts pressed against him. He hardly knew what was happening until suddenly, he was inside her.

From somewhere in the back of his mind, he heard her cry out. Then, he felt her body join in rhythm with his as if they had been together forever. A rhythm that united the two as one, with one heartbeat and one breath— and one explosion.

He heard her soft moans of pleasure until suddenly it was over. But only briefly, as the sensations that flooded his body began to build again. His release was exquisite, but satisfaction eluded him. He was only faintly aware of his surroundings, as throughout the night, their bodies, sore and exhausted, joined together again and again. Finally, as the dim light of dawn stole across a purple sky, he slept. But not before reality crept in. *What was in the wine?*

Leander swam through the fog of one caught in that neverland between sleep and wakefulness. They lay with their bodies entwined atop the damp, rumpled sheets. He lifted his head from its pillowed spot on her belly and began to nuzzle her soft places. She still smelled faintly of perfume—and of him. She whimpered and he raised up on one elbow to gaze at her beautiful face.

She opened her eyes and studied him in silence. *She looks into my soul,* Leander thought with a shiver.

"What did you mean," he asked, "last night when you said that you had waited your whole life for me?"

She didn't answer. Instead, she parted her legs and drew him close once again. As her lips renewed their tantalizing exploration of his, all questions were forgotten.

* * * * *

Leander woke with a start, his mind clear of delicious yet muddled memories. The bedside clock registered five o'clock—in the afternoon! He had slept the entire day. "Whew," he exhaled loudly as he began a cursory inspection of his body. He rubbed his belly and gingerly examined his privates. He was sore—raw, in fact. And, despite sleeping all day long, he still felt exhausted. And ravenous.

Tentatively, he rose from the bed and made his way to the bathroom to wash his face. Revived by the cool water, he donned loose-fitting pants and followed the wonderful aroma of food.

He leaned against the door for a long time, drinking in the scene before him. She stood at the kitchen stove, stirring the pot, humming to herself. It was a scene that he would never tire of. "Turtle soup?" he asked.

She turned toward him, smiling. "Conch chowder," she said. "Come and taste."

He closed the gap between them and sipped from the spoon she held out. "Delicious," he said. He reached out to her, cupping her face gently between his hands. "Allure, I am so in love with you."

"Yes," she whispered her response. "You were told to me. Our love was told to me long ago."

Again, her words brought a shiver along his spine. "What do you mean? Tell me."

"Sit," she directed. "First, we eat. We will talk later."

82

Vivian sat at the corner table on the country club terrace and listened to her best friend praise her son's latest accomplishments. And with good reason, Vivian knew. Will and Gabe had been bragging on Leander's early achievements with their offshore office for over a week, now. Even Mason, with his obvious jealousy of the younger man's success, had grudgingly praised Leander at dinner the previous evening.

"I know that I'm repeating myself, Viv, and of course, I'm partial, but that boy of mine is really something," Claire gushed. "I keep remembering what Moam used to say. She'd say: 'That boy's going to shed his rags one day.' Not that he *ever* wore rags, mind you," she prattled on, "but you know what she meant."

Vivian laughed and reached out to clasp Claire's hands. "You have every right to brag on Leander. As a matter of fact, Daddy said last night that they're going to make him a partner very soon. I don't follow business, but he said that in the two months since Lee went to Grand Cayman, the firm's new accounts have almost doubled over all of last year. Or, something like that." She paused to sip her wine. "Anyway, if he keeps that up, he'll be a partner before the year's out."

Claire's grin widened. "And to think, there was a time I worried about that boy."

"Now, didn't I tell you that you had nothing to worry about?" Vivian said. "All our children have done well, Claire. And, I still marvel at what a sweet and pleasant boy young William has become." She shook her head thoughtfully. "The way Remy and Daddy have spoiled him, it's a wonder he hasn't turned out to be—well, just like the two of them." She ended with a chuckle.

"Hmm," Claire muttered. "I just wonder if I'll *ever* get to be a grandma. Those two girls of ours have married well, but they don't seem to be in any hurry to start families. Speaking of our children, Gaby's job going well? And, does she have a boyfriend?"

Vivian shook her head. "She seems to like the job—already got a raise. But she doesn't go out very much, and I never knew what happened to her college boyfriend. Gaby's never been one to have many friends, and she really misses Lee. I'm glad she went up north to her friend's wedding. She'll be back next week."

"Why don't we have a party, then?" Claire asked.

Vivian felt her body tense up as she frowned. "I-I don't think so, Claire. I don't feel like socializing right now. And a party is so much work. No, I don't want to have a party."

Vivian pushed her half-eaten lunch aside and reached for her purse. Time to return to her cloister and her wall full of scrapbooks…

* * * * *

After the usual vague promises to make their lunch a weekly event, Vivian left Claire and retreated to the sanctity of her rooms. She undressed and sank into a perfumed bubble bath to ponder—*things*.

Valiantly, she tried to salvage the positive aspects of her life, but they kept getting mixed up with all the broken pieces. Resurrecting happy memories was hard work, but she made the effort: another promise to Claire. It was an exercise, her friend said, that would help to banish depression. It brought about headaches, though, and eventually Vivian gave up. Climbing from her bath, she found comfort in an over-sized terry cloth robe and in her favorite scrapbook. And one of her pills.

Nestled in her rocking chair on the balcony, she watched in silence as the members of her family began coming home after their workday for their customary Friday night family dinner. Remy and Mason arrived in Remy's convertible first, with M'Lyn and young William following closely behind. Gabe was next to drive up. Alighting from his car, he held the cell phone close to his ear and seemed to be lost in somber conversation. He was always on the phone, and Vivian wondered with whom. But she never asked. Gabrielle's car followed. And, as usual, Will was the last to arrive home. This afternoon, his mood seemed jubilant, and that could only mean money…

The family members made their way to the kitchen door, talking among themselves. A word or two drifted up to her ears before they rounded the house and out of sight. No one had looked up to her balcony. She had not called down to them. The gentle tap on her door signaled the arrival of her evening cocktail. "You may bring it out here, Hazel," she spoke to the housekeeper. "Thank you. I won't be joining the family for dinner tonight. You can bring me a plate later on, please."

"Yes, ma'am. Enjoy your evening."

* * * * *

Vivian's dinner plate—untouched, along with the empty martini glass and shaker—sat on her writing desk. Hazel would collect them tomorrow. She dressed for bed, then paused. With the prized scrapbook held tightly against her chest, she left her rooms and made her way down the hall to Gabe's room. She had heard the creak of the stairs earlier and hoped that he hadn't gone to sleep yet. She wanted to show him the book. That wasn't exactly true: the book was only a ruse. She needed to be with him tonight—just be near him.

She tapped lightly on his door, and at his answer opened it, almost shyly. "May I come in?" she asked.

"Of course, you may, my dear. Please come in," Gabe said, smiling broadly at her. "You were missed at dinner."

Vivian wondered by whom, but she refrained from making the caustic remark. "I had a headache, but it's much better now. I-I brought something to show you," she said, holding the scrapbook out toward him.

"Oh? Well, then, come sit by me. Let's have a look." He made room beside him on his bed. "Come. Sit," he repeated.

"You're not too tired, I hope?" she said, feeling a slight blush rise to her cheeks. *For God's sake, why am I so shy and embarrassed by the man I've been married to for years?*

He smiled warmly. "I'm never too tired to spend time with you, Vivian."

Her heart sang, but only for a moment. *He doesn't mean it. He's only trying to be kind.* She swallowed hard and said, "I've organized all of our family photographs, but I do believe this album is my favorite."

She made herself comfortable beside him on the bed. His arm went around her shoulders as he propped her up with pillows. He smelled of spice, and she allowed herself to lean against him. Her hands trembled slightly as she opened the scrapbook to the toothless grin of a beautiful baby boy.

Gabe laughed heartily. "Just look at Remy!" he exclaimed. "He was such a happy baby, wasn't he?"

"Oh, yes," Vivian agreed. "And Gaby was so serious," she added, turning the pages to reveal the solemn little girl with the beautiful hair who refused to smile for the camera.

"They soon became just the opposite, though," Gabe said. He continued to turn the pages, remarking how Gaby soon grew into the happy-go-lucky little daredevil, while Remy gravely followed his granddaddy from the time he could walk. "Our son became quite the serious one, didn't he?"

"He became what Daddy wanted him to be," Vivian remarked flatly. "He became just like him."

By the time they had reached the last of the pages depicting their children's early years, Vivian had drifted off in the comfort of her husband's arms.

83

Leander leaned back in his rattan swivel chair, stretched his long legs, and propped his shoeless feet on his newly-purchased mahogany desk. His grin was wide and genuine as he spoke into the receiver. "You know something, Gaby girl? I remember way back when *I* was the one who kept *you* grounded. Now, it's the other way around. I've probably bored you to tears going on and on about Allure." He paused and laughed. "But I love her so much. And, I've never felt so…"

Words failed him, and the brief silence that followed was palpable. Gabrielle finished his sentence softly. "Complete, Lee. You feel complete with her. I know. I remember."

"God, Gaby. I sound heartless, selfish. I'm sorry."

"Don't be sorry, Lee. Be happy. And what you sound like is someone truly in love for the very first time. Just make sure she deserves you, 'cause if not, then I'll have to step in and kick me some ass," she joked.

"I hear you," he said, laughing. "Allure is wonderful."

"Then, what's the problem?" she asked, reading him so well.

"Oh, no problem. Different upbringing. Places. Family and religious sorts of things. You know."

"Hey, dude," Gabrielle said firmly, "no secrets."

"No, no, no," he assured her. "No secrets, just, you know, adjustments. That's all. Hey, I miss you," he added, attempting to lighten the conversation.

"And I'm lost without you around. When are you coming home?"

"Not for a while. Can't leave when business is this good. Probably for Christmas, though. We'll talk again next week."

"Okay, and remember to make that phone call, Leander Washington!" When she used his full name, he knew she meant business.

"I'll do it right now. And you're right, Gaby, I should have done it weeks ago. Love you, sis."

"Love you, bro. Later."

Leander ended the phone call. He did miss his best friend. He missed the easy camaraderie that they had been born into, missed their carefree childhood. *No secrets.*

He shook away the sudden shiver. He checked his e-mails and tidied up his desk in preparation for the weekend. Friday afternoon, and he was putting business behind him. He allowed himself a moment to bask in the week's success. What was it that Will had said in his earlier phone call? He had brought in more new clients in the months he'd been in the Caymans than the partners had during the entire last year.

They praised him as if he were the second coming, but Leander held no illusion. His employers were vipers, just waiting for him to falter. And if he did, all his early success would be forgotten. But he would not fail. He would rise to the tasks at hand, both professional and personal. He picked up the telephone and punched in the number he knew by heart. He had delayed this particular responsibility far too long.

Her voice was cool and professional on the other end. "Daily and Washburn Law Firm, Michelle Daily speaking."

He swallowed the lump in his throat. "Hello, lady."

* * * * *

Leander took a longer route home today, hoping the sights and sounds of the bustling market would cheer him up after his phone call to Michelle. The distraction was only partly working, though. How had she put it? *I always knew that you would find your place, Lee. I also knew that it might not be with me.*

Of course, he had not mentioned Allure, but otherwise he'd been completely honest with her concerning his feelings. So, that made him an upstanding guy, right? "No, that makes you a heel," he berated himself aloud.

He drove slowly, his convertible allowing him to feel a part of the smiling tourists and islanders alike who strolled among the colorful shops. Whenever anyone from back home asked him what it was that he loved so much about Grand Cayman, Leander always found himself at an immediate loss for words. Countless images would race through his mind, vying to be his first response, but if pushed to give an answer, he could only describe it as a *feeling*. The island, with its barefoot elegance, had become a place that he could not imagine ever leaving behind.

Find his place? He exhaled deeply. *Yes, my sweet Michelle, I have found it.*

His spirits began to lift as his thoughts traveled to a favorite spot of his: the Queen Elizabeth II Botanical Gardens. He and Allure were going there tomorrow. He was going to ask her to move in with him. He had spoken to Will earlier about finding a larger house in the quaint capital of George Town.

"Why the hell do you need a larger place?" Will had asked gruffly. "You're at work practically all of the time. At least, you should be."

Leander had remained quiet, hoping that the older man might realize that he himself had once resided with only two small children and a housekeeper in a sixteen-room mansion.

Finally, Will gave in: "Oh, alright. Live wherever you want."

When he arrived at the cottage, the open front door told him that Allure was already there. Alighting from his car, he plucked an orchid from a nearby tree and took the three front steps in one graceful leap. He found her on the back porch, grilling fish.

Wordlessly, he took her in his arms for a long kiss. "I missed you today," he whispered. He placed the orchid in her hair and stepped back to take in the sight of her. "Did you have a good day?"

"Yes. I caught fish for our supper," she said, pointing at the grill. "And I missed you as well. I'm glad the weekend is here."

He nuzzled the back of her neck. "The fish looks delicious. I'll fix us a couple of rum punches after I change clothes," he said. "Be right back."

"Thanks," Allure called back over her shoulder. "No rum for me, though."

84

The fishing boat that carried Maffi away from Haiti and toward the unknown of her new home was beyond dilapidated. Its tattered sails were useless, and the antiquated engine sputtered and smoked, causing the captain to curse the sea, the weather and all the gods he could think of. Maffi was terrified, but she was determined not to collapse into tears. Instead, she spent her time huddled under the leaking lean-to that had been roughly constructed in the bow of the boat.

For the most part, she stared straight ahead to avoid the sickening nausea that had plagued her for the entire first night and day of the voyage. The captain was a gruff but seemingly kind man. He had brought her cups of weak tea and slices of dry bread to help with the nausea.

Maffi did not talk to the captain other than to offer her thanks in a shaky voice. The only other person onboard was the mate, and she certainly didn't speak to him. He was young, filthy, and could not completely close his lips over a mouthful of protruding, rotten teeth. His eyes were sunken and glassy, and he stared at her with an intensity that made her want to jump overboard. His attention towards her was reminiscent of the soldiers back in Haiti—the ones that her mother had tried to shield her from.

Elsaneth had sacrificed what pitiful possessions life had given her to send her beloved daughter away in search of a better life. Maffi knew this, and that knowledge was what kept her sane throughout the miserable days at sea. And just where was she going? She had no idea of what awaited her or even if she would reach her destination alive.

The final night of the voyage was the worst. Captain had insisted that Maffi go below deck to the rancid smelling, leaking cabin. Huddled on a dirty mattress, she rode through a squall that she was sure would capsize their run-down vessel. Throughout the night, the young girl fought nausea as she offered prayers to the spirits. Of course, she believed firmly—as all practitioners of voodoo believed—that everything happens at the whim of spirits, be it good or bad. The spirits must have been very angry with her to bring about this time of misery, she thought.

But just as Maffi had given up hope, the final morning of her trip dawned glorious. Captain had come below deck with bread and tea and motioned for her to follow him to the deck. Never in her life had she seen such a beautiful sight. Their boat limped its way between coral beds nestled in jade-colored waters toward snow-white, sandy beaches. Captain seemed to know exactly where he was going, and soon a lone pier jutting out into the sea came into view.

Maffi's legs were weak as a kitten's as she made her way down the rickety plank from the boat to the dock. Her woven basket, completely soaked and containing her meager belongings, was tossed down to her by the hollow-eyed mate.

"Good luck to you, girl," was the most the captain had spoken to her at one time for the entirety of her nightmare voyage. He tipped his hat and retrieved the plank as the ancient engine coughed to life. The boat slowly began to back away, leaving an exhausted and frightened young girl quite alone.

"That's the saddest story that I've ever heard," Leander said. He was nearly in tears after hearing Allure's recounting of her mother's perilous journey. "I can't imagine how terrified she was. And, I can't imagine having to leave my home and my parents."

The couple sat together on the smooth sand of the beach where they had walked after dinner. Leander was happy when Allure began to speak of her mother. Even with their time spent together, this woman whom he loved remained an enigma. Sometimes, he felt that he did not know her at all, especially when she spoke of voodoo so casually.

He yearned to know everything about her. At the same time, he dreaded knowing. In contrast, she seemed to know him so well. Like tonight, for instance, when she looked at him it was as though she were reading his innermost thoughts. *As though she knew my secrets.*

She laid her head on his shoulder, and he drew her closer. "What did Maffi—your mama—what did she do then?" he asked.

"Very soon, a man came to get her. He had known of her coming, you see. That man was Jack Dubois, Papa Jack. He took my mama to his home and gave her work. He kept her safe. She was very happy, especially when my father found her."

Leander hesitated. He did not know how to ask the questions that he knew he must ask. That is, if they were to have a life together.

"I want to spend my life with you, Allure," he said quietly. "You've said that you waited all your life for me." Words failed him. H tried again: "You talk of *spirits*, of, of…" Again, he faltered. He turned to face her. "You speak of *voodoo* as if it's a reality. I, I don't understand—"

"It is *my* reality, Leander," she interrupted him. "The spirits are my world, and they determine what happens in that world."

Her voice was calm, almost reassuring. *Almost.*

Only the waves brushing the shore and the night wind rustling the tall palms invaded the quiet. Finally, Allure whispered, "The spirits told me of you, that you would come for me. I can teach you, my love." Slowly, she began to stroke his thigh as she cuddled closer to him. "I can show you how to talk with them, and more important, you will learn how to listen to them."

Her words and her closeness were mesmerizing. Leander was once again in that vortex where nothing was real except the feel and the taste of her. But he needed to break the spell. Desperately, he wanted to know more, but right now he had to get away from her and try and clear his head.

"Stay here, babe. I'm going to get another drink. I'll be back."

The full moon made a light unnecessary as Leander made his way back to the beach. She had not moved from their spot, although it was apparent that she was speaking faintly under her breath.

He spoke to break the spell. "I brought wine for us." The glasses clinked together as he steadied them in the sand and prepared to pour the dark red liquid from the jug.

"None for me," Allure said.

"Really? This is your favorite. Since when do you not want wine?"

"Since last night," she answered.

He gazed at her. "What? Wine was bad last night? Made you sick?"

Her eyes locked with his and he gazed into their gray-green depths.

"Last night, my Leander, we made our child. We made our daughter."

His head was spinning. Her words, simply spoken, reverberated over and over, filling him with awe and wonder. And dread.

"W-w-what? You can't know so s-s-soon," he stammered, shaking his head. He realized that his heart was pounding as his confused words continued to pour out. "How can you know? I mean, Allure, no one can be sure *one day later*! Can you? You, you'd need a doctor, or a test…"

Her throaty little laugh stopped his rambling. "The spirits, my love," she whispered, "they tell me. Last night, we made our daughter."

Gently, Leander pushed her back at arm's length. "But even if you are pregnant, you certainly can't know whether it will be a boy or a girl." Valiantly, he tried to instill a bit of common sense into the moment. The expression in her eyes, though, told him his effort was useless.

She spoke as if she were explaining something to a child. "My great-grandmama, Sanité, had one daughter. She was named Elsaneth, and she gave birth to one daughter, my mother, Maffi. My mama had only me. Now, I will have my daughter. Our daughter. It has been told."

85

The wedding ceremony was quick and secular. It wasn't in the church, and none of their friends had been invited. Only Gabe and Vivian, Gabrielle, and she and Carl Lee had been in attendance.

There had been no prayer and no blessing, and Claire Washington was deeply disappointed. But she had tried her best not to show it. After all, her beloved son was married to the sweetest and most beautiful girl she'd ever met. He was happy, and that was the most important thing. Leander's happiness, and her a soon-to-be grandmother.

"I wish you could stay longer," Claire said as she hugged her daughter-in-law.

"We will see you soon, Mama Claire," Allure said. "You will come when our daughter is born."

"I need get back to work, Mama," Leander said as he loaded their suitcases into the rental car. He laughed. "With a new house and a baby on the way, I can't lose my job."

"No danger of that, Lee," Gabrielle chimed in. "Granddaddy's toast to you at dinner last night should have told you that you're on solid ground."

Leander nodded thoughtfully. "Yeah, last night was special. Allure loved it. I don't think she's ever been honored in her life. Not like last night, anyway. Hope everyone knows how much I appreciate it, Gaby."

"They know." She hugged him tightly and whispered: "Everything's moving so fast, Lee. I-I'm not losing you, am I?"

"Say what?" Leander held her at arm's length and studied his best friend's face for several seconds. "All you ever have to do is call, and I'll be here, Gaby. You're never gonna get rid of me, little sis."

339

"Oh, I know that," Gabrielle said. "It's just that, you and I never seem to have time for each other. Not like we used to." She dropped her head down and absently began to scuff the gravel with the toe of her shoe. She laughed. "Remember back when we were kids? We saw each other every day."

Leander nodded. "Oh, yes, I remember. Life, Gaby—life gets in the way sometimes."

Allure gently tapped his arm. "Leander, we had better be on our way."

Claire had noticed early on that Allure used her son's full name. She was pleased, as she thought that his preferred shortened name lacked character. She hugged them both again. "We will see you in May," she said.

Carl Lee had hung back during the good-byes. He came forward now to embrace his son. His normally robust, baritone voice shook a bit as he spoke. "I'm awful proud of you, boy," was all he could manage.

Group hugs, smiles, and a few tears ushered the newly-wed couple on their way to the airport. Claire waved until the car disappeared down the driveway. She folded her arms and looked at her husband: "I think I'd like to be 'Nana.' How 'bout you, Carl Lee? Paw-Paw? Gramps? What?"

"Whatever that baby wants to call me is just fine."

"Well," Gabrielle said brightly, "I think that Aunt Gaby and Nana need to go baby-stuff shopping. What do you say, Miz Claire?"

"Right behind you, sweetie."

* * * * *

Nothing you could put your finger on, just a feeling. Maybe feeling's not the right word, more like a warning. But a warning of what? Oh, hell! Stop with the psycho-babble. You were uneasy around the girl, that's all.

From the moment you shook her hand and your eyes met hers— uncomfortable, that's it. Just, just something different about her. Well, leave it to HIM to bring home a weirdo. Goddamn beauty, though, you gotta give him that. Yessiree, just about the best-looking gal you ever saw.

You handled it perfect, like always. You were your charming self, and nobody noticed. No sir, you were gracious, polite, everything a southern gentleman should be. Like always, of course.

God, when she looked at you during dinner, your insides were jelly. Hey, calm down. It's okay because nobody noticed. Stop your pathetic blubbering, you weak simpleton!

Wonder if anybody else thought that the girl was strange, or was it only you? Just something different about her, that's all.

86

It was well past midnight, and the spring night was warm. The full moon cut a silvery path through the dense growth of Spanish cedar, sandbox and royal palm trees. The heady scent from shoulder-high flowering bushes accosted him as he made his way carefully and, he hoped silently, along the trail that had summoned him from the narrow, shell-covered road to—what he did not know.

Leander had followed her tonight, from her barely discernable exit from their bed to this spot, a little over a mile from their house. He hadn't even known that the back road existed. Now, with the heady, pungent air clogging his lungs and the hair on the back of his neck prickling, his thoughts raced back to a time long ago.

Back to a childhood that had been devastated by one spring day. In a forest. Where curiosity had gotten the better of him. Where his life had forever been altered…

…Leander pressed on, as the green tunnel seemed to swallow him. He walked more slowly now, not only due to trepidation, but because the thick, sweet air made breathing a chore.

Rivulets of sweat ran from his head down the center of his back, making him itch. He thought of tiny spiders, like the ones he and Gaby had seen earlier emerging from their egg and flying away on silken threads. He backed up to a sycamore tree and scratched his back on its curly bark.

…Leander froze. The sudden noise made his heart skip a beat. For an instant, he couldn't decipher it. There it was again—the unmistakable sound of footfalls. Someone or something was walking just beyond the thick wall of bramble briars to his right…

A twig snapped under Leander's foot, bringing him to a standstill and jolting his thoughts back to the present. He took a deep breath and closed his eyes. The sobering thought occurred to him that what he was doing tonight could very well jeopardize his marriage. Possibly even destroy her trust. Her love.

Could he live without her? He could not. But the part of her that he could never share was eating him alive. It was the *not knowing* that had convinced him to take this risk tonight. The path was leading him toward the beach, and when it veered to the right, the thick grove of trees ended. The faint odor of smoke and the shaft of moonlight on white sand drew him forward.

Leander was sweating, but the sea breeze instantly refreshed him. Unseen by the four people who were gathered around the bonfire, he crouched behind a fallen log. And once again, that frightened little boy of years past resurfaced…

…He did not want to see, but he could not look away. He thought that he would never stop screaming, until he finally realized that his screams were only in his mind. He was unable to utter a sound.

Leander shut his eyes tight and counted to ten, praying all the while that the fall he'd taken had momentarily addled his brain. He prayed to Jesus that when he opened his eyes, the scene before him would have vanished and all he would see would be an abandoned garden with a silly, over-imaginative boy sitting on the ground all alone…

But as before, any prayer that he might have sent up went unanswered.

The scene before him branded itself into his brain. Papa Jack sat with a small drum between his legs, his hands caressing it, coaxing a spellbinding rhythm to life. A razor-thin girl who looked to be about fourteen chanted softly and with much emotion words that Leander could not understand. A woman, bent with advancing age, methodically cast something into the bonfire—powder or dust. And the flames from that fire leapt upward, illuminating his beloved Allure. Her body, nearly nude and swollen with his child, swayed gracefully as she threw her head back and held both arms toward the sky.

Leander could not look away. The scene was surreal, like a dream, entangling him in a web of emotions that ranged from revulsion to eroticism, distorting the difference. Weakly, he fought against it, but it called to him, playful and teasing, promising the ecstasy that his sudden erection demanded. For one terrifying moment, he very nearly moved to become one with them, one with the fire, the rhythm, and the chanting. One with *her* and his desperate need to possess every part of her.

How long he sat motionless in the shadows, enraptured by the scene before him, he did not know. At war with his emotions, Leander was finally able to close his eyes. By breathing deeply, he succeeded in relaxing his taunt muscles. He welcomed saneness once again as he wiped away the tears that had mixed with droplets of sweat to drench his cheeks. Nimbly, he rose from his hiding place and began the trek back down the path toward his house.

Exhaustion and confusion weighed him down. He felt—what? Guilt, perhaps, for spying on her? Would he confess to her what he'd done? He shook his head sadly, for he knew the answers. And as before, he would keep *the secret.*

Leander lay still on his side of their bed, facing the wall. He had heard the click of the front door, signaling her return home hours after his. He felt her body lie down and her hand reach for his under the covers. She squeezed his hand. He squeezed back.

"You are awake?" she whispered.

"Mmm, just now," he lied. "You okay?"

She drew his hand gently toward her body. After placing it on her belly, she said, "Can you feel our daughter? She is lively."

A thrill swept over him as he felt the urgency of his child inside her. "Yes," he said excitedly, "I can. Oh, Allure, I love you so!"

"I know, my love. I have been thinking," she said as she propped up on one elbow and looked at him. "My people give a name that translates to a quality. Like my grandmama was called *Elsaneth*, which means 'rare'. And she named by mama *Maffi*, or 'my girl'."

"Your mama certainly named you right," he said, caressing her smooth cheek. "You are enticing."

She smiled and snuggled against him. "I think, though, that we will name our daughter after your mother. What do you say?"

He turned his head on the pillow so she would not see the lone tear that slipped slowly down his cheek. "I think that's a wonderful idea."

Leander woke the next morning to the smell of ham and French toast. He found her in the kitchen, humming to herself as she prepared breakfast. *Just a normal day in a normal family household*, he thought to himself. *No different from any other day in their lives.*

Not so! Everything was different, and he had to know more. This was one secret that could not be hidden away in a box in a young boy's closet.

87

Leander slowly threaded his way through the crowd at Miami International Airport. He arrived at the appointed lounge and moved to an empty table in the corner.

He had no idea what Dr. Bertrand looked like, but the woman approaching him now certainly did *not* meet the mental image he had concocted of the learned professor and lecturer.

"You are Mr. Washington," she greeted him. It was not a question.

Leander was taken aback for a moment. The woman stood all of four feet tall and was dressed in a long, black cape. Her frizzy white hair stuck out from underneath an incongruous red pointy hat, making her closely resemble a garden gnome. Her dark eyes sparkled and took in her surroundings with quick darting movements. She sat down immediately in the chair facing him before he had a chance to stand.

"I'm Lydia Bertrand," she said, extending her hand across the table.

"It's a pleasure to meet you, Dr. Bertrand," Leander responded, hoping his initial surprise was not conveyed in his facial expression. "Thank you for agreeing to meet me today."

"Certainly, Mr. Washington. I regret that you had to fly here for our meeting. But, as I told you on the telephone, this is the only free time I will have for several weeks." She checked her watch. "My flight to Jamaica leaves in two hours, and from there—island hopping." She smiled at him, her bright eyes studying him intently.

"Work or vacation?" Leander asked as he signaled the server.

"Both," she answered his question simply and with no further explanation.

"May I get you something to drink, Doctor?"

"Tea would be nice. Iced."

"Two iced teas, please," he said to the waiter.

She continued to make eye contact for several seconds. When their drinks arrived, she spoke. "Tell me about yourself, Mr. Washington."

She made him feel self-conscious. *As if she already knows all about me.*

"Very well," he said. "I was born and raised in a small town in South Carolina. I attended Harvard and now live and work on Grand Cayman. I'm an investment banker."

Her gaze did not waver as she lifted her glass to her lips. "Where you were born and educated as well as where you now reside tells me nothing about *you*, Mr. Washington. I want to know why you seek information from a professor of occult studies."

She had caught him off guard with her directness but he soon recovered. "Of course, Doctor. I've spent the past month or so researching experts in the field of the occult. Your name appeared at the top of almost every list. I've read several of your published articles, and I believe that you're the one who can help me understand."

Her brow furrowed a bit as she continued her direct assessment. "We all carry a burden, Mr. Washington," she said. "You must let go of yours, or else it will bury you."

She seemed to sense his hesitation. She smiled kindly and rescued him. "Alright, let's talk about my burden first."

"Y-y-your burden?" Leander stammered.

"As I said, we all carry one." She sipped more tea. "I was born in Savannah, Georgia. My burden was growing up the only child of a surgeon who did his best to avoid his wife by putting in twenty hours a day at the hospital until a fatal heart attack relieved him of his marital duties, and a mother who never forgave me for being short, studious and not at all pretty."

She raised her eyebrows in anticipation and pointed a stubby finger at Leander. "Your turn."

He nodded, taking a deep breath as he began: "My turn. I want—I *need* —to know more about the practice of voodoo. If you knew where and how I was raised, you'd understand. It's conflicting. It's terrifying, actually."

"Mr. Washington, you grew up attending church, probably the Protestant faith, correct?" At his nod, she continued: "All religions and all forms of worship involve the same thing—faith. The belief in what cannot be seen, the hope of what is to come. We all call upon the spirit from time to time. Don't you agree?"

Leander was thoughtful. "Yes, I suppose that's right," he said. "Tell me more. Please."

"As I like to point out in my lectures, we all have a choice in the direction that we choose to walk. One path is toward the light. The other leads into darkness. So, it is with *Ewe vódũ*. We can choose to allow the spirit of light to gcrk one."

"Is the practice of voodoo dangerous, Doctor Bertrand?"

She laughed softly. "Perhaps for the chicken that sometimes gets sacrificed."

His gaze narrowed as he tried to interpret her expression. "Are you mocking me, Doctor?"

She sighed. "Please forgive me. My life spent between the covers of books has ill-prepared me for social chit-chat." She folded her thin hands and grew thoughtful. Leander waited.

"I've told you about my parents, Mr. Washington. Now, allow me to tell you about the woman who raised me. Astrid was my nanny and the dearest person on earth to me. It was she who cared for me. She who gave me my love of books and my desire to become a teacher. I learned to speak Creole French from Astrid. She told me of the spirits and the practice— rather, the mystique—of voodoo. You see, Mr. Washington, she was a native of Haiti. She was a *believer*."

"My wife's mother was from Haiti," Leander said. "I suppose you could say that I'm having some difficulty accepting the differences, Doctor."

"Then do not dwell on the differences." Her words were emphatic. "Is your marriage a happy one?"

Leander's response was immediate. "Oh, yes. We are very much in love. And, we're expecting our first child very soon. My wife, Allure, she's my whole world." Almost as soon as the words were out of his mouth, a smile lit up his face. He chuckled. "I don't actually have a burden at all, do I, Doctor Bertrand?"

She joined him in a hearty laugh. "No, my good man, I don't think that you do." She checked her watch again and prepared to stand.

"I should be getting along now. It's been a pleasure visiting with you, Mr. Washington. I hope I've been a help to you, and I hope you will reach out to me from time to time."

"I will, Doctor," he replied. "You've been a great help to me, and I thank you again for meeting and talking with me. Enjoy the remainder of your travels." They prepared to step from the lounge to their separate gates. He clasped her hand warmly and turned to walk away.

Her voice followed him. "Congratulations on the approaching birth of your daughter, Mr. Washington."

Her words stopped him in his tracks. He turned around. "How did you know that we are having a dau…?"

His question dissolved. Lydia Bertrand was nowhere in sight.

88

Compartmentalizing came easily to Leander where business was concerned. Things were much more difficult when it came to self-analysis.

He had tried without success to focus on the client portfolio he had brought with him for reading on the airplane. But as the "Fasten Seatbelt" sign flashed for their landing in Grand Cayman, the words on page one stared back at him. He did not know whether it was Dr. Bertrand's intelligence or her aura itself that had prompted his brooding. Probably a little of both.

He had traveled all the way back to childhood in his mind, finding it difficult to separate the young idealistic boy from the grown, idealistic man. Did he even still *know* that boy? The image of his parents flashed before him. Sure, they had been strict, but not overly so. No, it had been he, himself, who had set the firm boundaries for his life. *He* had been the one who had devised rules to be obeyed and the principles that would direct his actions. But instead of leading him along the path of glory and achievement, had those lofty principles gotten in the way of life itself? Had they simply fostered a cover-up? A trail of lies? *Secrets?*

The plane skidded to a stop on the wet runway, churning up a thick cloud of humidity that rose to greet the travelers. It was dusk, and Leander knew that the night breezes would soon begin to cool the island. Sweat beaded on his forehead as he prepared to deplane and drive the approximate one hour to his home.

He shoved his reflections to the sidelines and began to mentally itemize his to-do list, of which studying for and taking his bar exams was at the top—right behind getting home to Allure.

* * * * *

Leander walked through the courtyard to the front door, taking in the new flowerpots and baskets. Even in the settling darkness he could see that his wife had been busy during his day trip. Strange, though, she hadn't left the porch light on for him. He fumbled with his keys and, after locating the right one, unlocked the door.

Exhausted, he tossed his briefcase and jacket on the entry table and made his way to the small bar across the room. A drink sounded good right about now; a cool shower and a solid eight hours sounded even better. His hands, one holding the glass and the other touching the decanter, froze. Suddenly, he was no longer tired.

The skin along his bare arms prickled and his mouth went dry. There were no sounds. *Faint calypso rhythms that pleased her and made her sway to their tempo.*

There were no smells. *She was always cooking something.*

"Allure!" he called out, his heart racing. *Don't borrow trouble. She's probably lying down.* Trying to remain calm, he hurried through the dining room and down the short hallway to their bedroom. He turned from the empty room in a near panic when he saw the figure walking toward him.

Grabbing his chest in momentary fright, he said, "Good God, Tikki! You scared me to death!"

The young housekeeper giggled. "Oh, sorry, sir. I did not mean to startle you."

"It's okay," Leander said. "Where is my wife?"

Tikki put up her hands. "We try to call you, but could not reach you."

Leander shook his head. "I turned the damn phone off for my meeting and forgot to turn it back on. W-w-where is Allure?"

"The missus Allure, she is at the hospital." The young girl grinned broadly. "The baby is coming."

Leander was beyond panic as he raced back through the house and out the front door, shouting, "No, no, no! It's not time yet. It's weeks too early!"

Tikki stared at the door for a moment, then began to tidy up and turn off the lights. "Humph," she muttered to herself. "That baby say it's time."

* * * * *

Leander looked down in amazement at his hands. They looked huge to him, probably because of the tiny bundle they held—all four pounds, twelve ounces. A pink cap covered the brown silken hair and paled in comparison to the bright, reddish-brown hue of the baby's cheeks. Her ear-piercing cries terrified him.

"W-w-what's wrong with her?" he asked. "What should I do?"

Allure and the doctor both laughed at him. "Mr. Washington, you should hold her against your chest so that she can feel your heartbeat," Dr. Calle Idris instructed. "That way, she will know that she is safe."

Leander obeyed the doctor, and soon the softly-lit hospital room grew quiet. "Oh," he whispered in amazement. "It worked. I did it!"

Allure smiled. "You are a natural. I think that our Clarissa is going to be a daddy's girl."

Silence fell on the room, giving Leander a chance to take it all in. Holding her at arm's length again, he gently removed the blanket and counted fingers and toes for the third time. *Clarissa.* "So tiny," he marveled, "and so perfect. Would you just look at those little fingernails! And those long eyelashes!"

Lost in his own paradise, he barely heard the doctor's words: "Most early babies need the incubator, but this one has lungs as strong as mine."

"Obviously," Leander agreed as another loud wail erupted. He handed the baby to the doctor and she placed her beside Allure. He watched in hypnotic wonder as the tiny mouth found her breast. "When can they come home, Dr. Idris?"

"The day after tomorrow, I think. Now, Mr. Washington, please come with me to the desk to sign some paperwork. Then you can come back to your family."

When he reentered the room a short while later, his daughter had fallen fast asleep. Allure gently stroked the tiny face as she whispered unintelligible words. He remained in the shadowed doorway until a young nurse appeared. "I've come to take her back to the nursery, now," she explained.

Leander nodded, went to his wife's side, and took her hand. "Allure, I am so proud of you. I'm so sorry that I wasn't here for the birth."

"Oh, no, my love," she answered sleepily. "Do not feel badly. You are here now. Our little girl, she came so fast and so easy."

She blinked slowly, her eyes growing heavy as she gave in to sleep. "I'll see you tomorrow. I love you," he whispered to her smile and faint murmur. He paused at the door, Dr. Lydia Bertrand's words echoing. Had his questions been fully answered and his worries assuaged? Hardly. Could he possibly manage to temper his own principles and allow his beliefs to blend with those of his wife? Maybe. After tonight, Leander vowed that he would speak of it no more. He turned back to her bed, and at the sound of his voice, her eyes opened wide.

"Allure, you will raise my daughter—our daughter—to walk in the light."

As his wife slowly nodded, he left the room, closing the door behind him.

PART V

"Hell is empty and all the devils are here."

William Shakespeare

89

M'Lyn Westin checked her image in the foyer's full-length mirror. The Botox had worked wonders. Not that she'd developed any of those ghastly deep wrinkles that had befallen her older sister, but the tiny lines around her mouth had become a bit noticeable. As long as the dreaded liver spots remained at bay, another treatment might not be necessary for some time to come.

The body was still to die for, she mused, as she turned to study her profile. Flat stomach, tight ass, and still-perky tits, although they did grow a bit flabby after William's birth. A boob job just might be the next step to maintain the level of perfection she had known since her teens.

Well, she *should* look good, considering the strenuous exercise program she had adhered to for the past year. And having a personal trainer didn't hurt, either. It was even worth having to listen to Remy whine about the cost, especially when Raul's hands worked their magic on the massage table.

Enough delaying. She placed her hands on her hips and checked her image one more time before voicing the final assessment: "Not bad for thirty-six," she said. M'lyn turned from the mirror and made her way to the front door, the wheels on her overnight case clicking in time with her high heels on the marble floor.

"Just where are you going to be staying, M'Lyn?" Remy's voice stopped her with her hand on the doorknob.

Dammit, I almost made it out of this miserable place without his everlasting questioning.

"Like I told you last night, baby, I just don't know." She turned to face him, the practiced smile in place. "Anita and I will decide when we get to Charlotte. We shouldn't have any problem—it's not the season."

"And just what the hell am I supposed to do? And William? You ever think about your son, or just your goddamn shopping trips?"

She took her time before answering. "It's *one weekend*, Remy. My best friend and I are going on a weekend shopping trip. How many girls' outings do I have? Huh?" She saw his facial expression began to change from petulant anger to embarrassment. She struck again. "Just how many trips do you, Will, Gabe, and Mason go on?"

"That's business, and you know it. That's how I pay for your shopping trips."

"Thank you," M'Lyn purred throatily. "You can pay for this one, too." She turned, gathered her bag, and had almost made it out the front door when he spoke again.

"No goodbye kiss? By the way, how come you slept in the guest room last night?"

She went to his side and acted like she enjoyed the lingering kiss she planted on his lips. Turning back to the door, she explained, "You were tossing and turning all night, and you started talking in your sleep again."

"W-w-what did I say?"

"Nothing that made a bit of sense. Mumbling—just enough to keep me awake. See you Sunday night. I'll call you." And she was out the door.

Remy trailed along behind her down the walkway toward her car like a whipped pup. "What about William?" he asked sulkily.

"Oh, for heaven's sake!" M'Lyn said, her patience worn thin. "Take him to work with you. Gabe and your granddaddy practically raised you in that bank. You never take William anywhere."

"He doesn't like to go to the bank," Remy whined. "All he wants to do is play baseball."

M'Lyn started the engine, fastened her seatbelt, and spoke tersely through the open car window. "Then take him to play baseball!"

Driving down the winding drive from their house and past the Remington mansion, she wondered for the countless time what had gone wrong with her dream of the perfect life. She barely remembered the starry-eyed girl so in love with her handsome Remy. It did no good to reminisce, though—those young lovers were gone forever, and the empty space left behind could only be filled now with stolen moments, moments that brought no happiness, only a brief respite from the loneliness.

She turned onto the four-lane and headed south. Retrieving the cell phone from her purse, she hit speed dial. At the immediate answer, she said, "Hey, Anita. It's me. Listen, girlfriend, lay low this weekend. Remember that you're supposed to be shopping with me in Charlotte."

* * * * *

Will was a firm believer in the old adage, "If it ain't broke, don't fix it." But, dammit, things were simply not progressing to suit him. The partners were making money hand over fist. In fact, the offshore banking was making more than three times what Lee's initial prospectus had indicated. In the five years since he'd left for Grand Cayman, Remington Banking and Investments had amassed a fortune for the firm as well as for their growing number of clients and investors. Making Lee a partner early on had certainly been a smart move, Will grudgingly admitted to himself. Swallowing his personal dislike of the man had been made possible by the steadily growing earnings reports. But the realization that he was head and shoulders above his own grandson in the professional world of investment banking stuck in Will's craw like a fish bone.

Oh, Remy had his talents, no doubt. He could identify with the entitled rich boys who never had an original thought of their own. And, the wealthy maidens who lacked both beauty and brains fawned all over him in their haste to hand over Daddy's money. While the accounts he'd brought in over the years were worthwhile, it was Remy's lack of drive that made Will want to shake him sometimes. He seemed resigned to let Claire Washington's boy one-up him all the damned time.

"Hey, Granddaddy; what's up?" Remy ambled into the office at the zenith of Will's mental volcano.

He studied the young man long and hard before speaking.

"What's up is that you come dragging your sweet ass in here at three o'clock in the afternoon, dressed like a fuckin' hippy. Now, *you* tell *me* what's up!"

"Chill, Granddaddy," Remy responded.

Will scowled, annoyed.

"I'm sorry. Didn't mean to sound like a smart-ass. M'Lyn left this morning for a weekend shopping trip in Charlotte. Left me with William, so I guess I'm still a little pissed off."

Will studied his grandson. "So, where is William?"

"Downstairs getting a Coke. We're on our way to the ballpark for a little batting practice." Remy yawned and leaned back in the chair, stretching his lanky body. "M'Lyn's right, I guess. I don't spend enough time with the boy."

Will managed to swallow some of his ire before he spoke again. "Young William is nearly fourteen years old, son—way past the age when I and your daddy *and* you were brought to this office. The boy needs to see firsthand where his livelihood comes from. He needs to learn how to carry on when all of us are gone."

Will's voice had grown increasingly firmer as his speech progressed. He held up his hand to forestall Remy's attempt to interrupt. "Now, none of us work more than four days a week, but you barely make two. That is going to change." He paused once again for emphasis. "One day, you will be President of this bank. And after you, your son will take the reins. Both of you had better know what the hell you're doing!"

Will's tactic changed. "You ever wonder just how many hours Lee puts in at the Cayman offices? I'll bet he doesn't show up for work in the middle of the day."

"Hell fire, Granddaddy! I'm sick of hearing about Lee and how great he is."

"Then you get your ass in gear! You hear me?"

The kid gloves had come off. Meekly, Remy nodded his head. "Yessir, Granddaddy. I—*we* won't let you down. I'll have a talk with William."

"School's out for the summer. Bring him to work with you on Monday morning," Will directed decisively. He turned away from his grandson and picked up the financial report he'd been reading, signifying that their conversation was over. "Go on to the ballpark but remember that it's Friday night. Don't miss the family dinner."

90

Vivian Westin prepared to make her way downstairs for the customary Friday night family ritual. Tonight, she wanted to be surrounded by the people that she loved. She wanted to look into their faces, listen to their voices, and to believe, if for only a brief time, that her presence was actually important to them.

Life under Will's ever-critical and watchful eye had left Vivian with the self-confidence of a centipede. Unlike her father, she had wanted a life of structure and calm predictability. Now, though, a little chaos would be a welcomed respite from the loneliness that claimed her. But she knew that the loneliness holding her prisoner was of her own making. Admittedly, it was *she* who had removed herself from the family's history book, to never have a chapter of her own, to be little more than notes scrawled in the margins of the pages.

She gazed at the array of books on the shelves before her, thoughtfully fingering their leather spines before choosing one. She nodded to herself as she held it against her chest for several seconds before placing it on the table beside the door. She would share its contents with Gabe tonight after everyone had left and they had gone to bed. He did seem to enjoy the times that she found her way to his room with one of the photograph albums. But he was probably just being kind.

Vivian was tired. She was *always* tired. She breathed in and put a smile on her face as she checked her image in the mirror. She had taken extra care with her hair this evening, putting it up the way Gabe liked it and adding a bit more makeup than usual. Pleased for once with her appearance, she selected an emerald green silk wrap to brighten the beige dinner dress that she wore and left the solace of her room. The sound of laughter drifted up the staircase as she made her way slowly down to join her family.

Perhaps a sense of belonging would come to her tonight. Tonight, after all, was special.

* * * * *

The handsome waiter set the fresh cocktail on the table in front of M'Lyn, his dark eyes lingering on her cleavage. He smiled—a knowing, flirtatious smile—a bit unrefined, yet deliciously erotic in its familiarity. She delighted in his attention, as well as in the audible whispers when she had strolled into the courtyard lounge earlier, owning it in the red cocktail dress. Friday night, and the hotel's elegant night spot was filling up.

Earlier in the day, she'd been furious when told that she would be spending tonight alone, because *no way* could the written-in-stone Friday night schedule be avoided. But now, with her little temper fit behind her, she was actually enjoying being by herself. The glances, the toasts, the smiles being directed her way and the knowledge that she could have her pick were as intoxicating as the gin.

She crossed her legs, the red dress inching higher, and suppressed a grin as she accepted another drink from the distinguished-looking gentleman at the bar. God, she was mellow. She could wait one more day. After all, she had waited years for this. It would be worth it.

* * * * *

"Mama, you look beautiful tonight," Gabrielle exclaimed as Vivian stepped from the staircase.

"You certainly do, my dear," Gabe added, taking her elbow and escorting her into the living room. "Will, doesn't your daughter look lovely?"

Will stopped his monologue directed at Remy and Mason and studied Vivian for a moment. "Yes," he remarked, "very nice—except for the hair. Looks like an old-maid schoolteacher."

The rapid heartbeat, the ringing in her ears, the dazzling lights and stabbing pain in her head...FIGHT IT!

Vivian steeled herself against the familiar, rising panic. Despite her resolve, the crystal jigsaw puzzle that was her life cracked yet again. Each time this happened, she would somehow manage to pick up the fragile shattered pieces—but not quite all of them could be found. And the dark and gaping spaces in the image grew larger and larger.

Purposefully, she walked to the bar and accepted her martini from a silent and obviously embarrassed Remy. "Thank you, son," she whispered.

Turning toward the group, she lifted her glass in a toast: "To you, Daddy, for suffering through all of my faults." She downed the cocktail and held the empty glass out to Remy for a refill.

The room was quiet. She took a sip from her second cocktail and moved to Gabe's side. She took his arm, smiled up at him and said, "My husband likes my hair up. Don't you, Gabe?"

"That I do," he said. "Shall we go in to dinner?"

Breaths were expelled and conversation returned as the family members made their way into the dining room.

Will began to pour the wine as Vivian's headache vanished.

91

Claire Washington paced the floor, back and forth in front of her living room fireplace. The old mantle clocked chimed midnight. The oak floorboards creaked slightly under her bare feet. She rubbed her forearms briskly, but the goosebumps would not go away. She could hear from their bedroom Carl Lee's deep breathing as it morphed into sporadic little snores. The sound was comforting to her, but not enough to dispel the feeling of dread that had been building since early evening.

She had placed several calls to Leander, one to his office and more to his cell phone. *No answer.* Of course, if anything were wrong, he would call her. *Wouldn't he?* Her daughters were both okay. And her lunch with Vivian had been pleasant.

What is wrong with me tonight?

Carl Lee snorted loudly. Claire chuckled and shook her head. "Just having a bad night, I guess," she murmured aloud. She went back to the bedroom and gently prodded her husband to turn onto his side. She lay down and closed her eyes, trying to ignore the chill that would not leave her.

* * * * *

Gabe was caught in the dream. It was one of those dreams where he knew that it wasn't real, yet in a strange way, it *was* real. He struggled through bed covers and muddled images until he was finally fully awake.

He remembered last night and the awkward family dinner that had somehow turned out to be rather pleasant. He also remembered drinking a great deal more wine than usual and being groggy when Vivian came to his room. He vaguely recalled making room for her beside him in the bed and telling her that he was glad that she'd come. He must have passed out shortly after that, as his last memory was of her opening the photo album to a picture of the two of them: their engagement party.

Or, had it been Senior Prom? Wait, maybe it was their wedding photo. *Wow!* He couldn't remember anything after that first picture. *Blackout?* Gabe rubbed his eyes against the early morning sunlight that knifed its way through the partially opened blinds. When his vision cleared, he checked the bedside clock: nine a.m. Perfect time to get up on a Saturday morning. He sat up in bed, not surprised at all that he was alone, as Vivian never stayed the entire night. Her photo album lay open on the foot of his bed, drawing his attention.

So long ago. The beautiful girl smiled at the camera. Gabe remembered taking that picture himself immediately after he had given her the engagement ring. How happy she had been. And he—had he been happy?

Of course, he had. He chuckled as he recalled how the two of them had strolled hand-in-hand from the mansion that evening to the gazebo, her favorite spot. He'd even gotten down on one knee.

Gabe sighed. *Memories.* He yawned, stretched, and prepared to get up. After a shower, he would go find Vivian and apologize for falling asleep last night. He enjoyed having her come to his room at night, and he needed to tell her so. Perhaps one day that happy young girl might find her way back to him.

As he stood up, the album slid to the floor, exposing the folded sheet of paper. With a quizzical look on his face, he picked it up and began to read.

Gabe clattered down the back stairs to the kitchen. He had skipped his intended shower, choosing instead to splash his face with cold water, swish mouthwash, and dress hurriedly. He filled a mug with steaming coffee as he addressed the housekeeper: "Hazel, have you seen the missus this morning?"

"No sir," she answered. "I knocked on her door a while ago, but she wasn't there. They's breakfast in the dinin' room, though. Everybody else is in there, Mr. Remy and lil' William, they spent the night, so—"

"Thanks," Gabe absentmindedly cut her off as he walked to the adjoining room. "Morning, everyone. Have any of you seen Vivian?"

Will looked up from his morning newspaper. "No. Why?"

Remy turned from the breakfast buffet. "Haven't seen Mom. You, Gaby?"

"Not since we said good night after dinner last night. I've got a tennis game this morning," Gaby said, preparing to leave the room. "Remy, don't forget to get William up. He's got a baseball game at one o'clock. See y'all later."

Gabe's voice stopped her in her tracks. "We need to find Vivian. She, she wasn't…" his voice faltered. He drew a deep breath and retraced his words, slower this time. "She wasn't in bed when I woke up this morning."

He waved aside the raised eyebrows and surprised looks all around. "Look, I-I woke up and there was this note on the bed and, and we need to find Vivian," he repeated.

Everyone's attention was drawn to voices coming from the kitchen. Gabe called out, "Vivian, is that you?"

"It's just me," Claire said, coming through the door. "Where is she? Where's Vivian?" she asked.

"We were just wondering the same thing," Gabe replied.

"No, *we* were not wondering," Will blustered. "*You* were looking for her, Gabe. For heaven's sake, she never goes anywhere! She's around here someplace!" He grumbled, burying his face in his newspaper once more.

Claire turned on the group frantically. "I'm afraid that something's wrong. I found a note on my door this morning."

"A note?" Gabe asked, his hands shaking as he held out the note that his wife had left for him. Claire did the same, and neither of them could speak as their eyes scanned the notes written in Vivian's handwriting.

"Claire…Daddy," Gaby's voice shook with uncertainty.

Will was frozen, his face ashen.

"W-w-what?" Remy whispered.

Gabe's eyes locked on Claire's. His voice was hoarse. "Where?"

Claire was calm, determined. "I know where."

The two notes fluttered to the floor. Gabe's heart was racing as he staggered hastily to the front door. "Oh, God. I know, too."

Hazel had entered from the kitchen and began to wail. "Lordy, Lordy! Where's Miz Vivian?"

No one said a word as they hurried after Gabe, making their way through the front door and down the veranda steps. Will strode sluggishly after the group as they began to trot, then run across the wide expanse of lawn toward the gazebo, his words falling on deaf ears. "What in the sam hill is going on?"

Vivian Westin sat on her favorite chaise, shaded from the harsh sunlight. Gabe took the gazebo's three steps in one bound and knelt beside his wife, grabbing her hand. The sound from his throat was somewhere between pain and fear. The scene was paralyzing to everyone except Claire. Retrieving the cell phone from her pocket, she punched 911, handed the phone to Remy, then sprang forward to her beloved friend's side. Firmly, she pushed Gabe away and began mouth-to-mouth, all the while rubbing Vivian's arms.

Gaby shushed the wailing Hazel as Remy frantically repeated instructions to EMS.

Gabe knelt as close to Vivian as Claire would allow, willing her to breathe, and staring all the while at the crystal glass and the pill bottle on the floor beside the chaise. Both empty.

92

M'Lyn sipped her coffee in the intimate little coffee shop located in the hotel lobby. She had a clear view of the entrance and wouldn't miss him when he arrived. She wore a stylish new tennis ensemble that showed her long, toned legs to full advantage. She glanced from time to time over the top of the morning newspaper, basking in the satisfaction that last night's admiring glances had not waned in the light of day.

He had texted her three times already that morning. She hadn't responded to any of them, choosing instead to play the wounded lover. Well, actually, *lover* wasn't correct. Not yet, anyway. Their liaison had been building for a long time, and they both knew it. But this weekend would be their first time together. Oh, they had flirted, teased, and had quite a hot little encounter in the parking lot of the club last month. But this weekend would be their first time together.

Go ahead and admit it: the first time to cheat on the husband and the best friend.

Lost in thought, M'Lyn didn't see him when he entered the lobby. His hands on her shoulders brought her out of her trance, and his lusty kiss made her whimper with pleasure. "Damn," she whispered. "I thought you'd never get here."

"Hurried as fast as I could, dahlin," Mason said, taking a seat across the table and signaling to the waiter for coffee. He studied her for a long time, his eyes taking in her pink, slightly swollen lips and slowly moving down to rest on her breasts. He grinned knowingly as her nipples hardened under his gaze, pressing against the thin cotton fabric of her blouse. "You are some kind of fine, baby," he whispered.

She decided to keep the game going for a bit longer. "How about we take a walk? There's a lovely park not far from here."

She matched his grin as he began to shake his head. "Walking ain't what I got in mind."

"Oh," she responded, a practiced expression of mock innocence highlighting her face. "Just what *did* you have in mind, sir?"

His cell phone rang at that moment, and Mason plucked it from his jacket pocket. "Hmm," he muttered, shaking his head. "Remy's been calling me all morning. I told him I was going to Greenville to check with clients today. I'll tell him I had my phone turned off."

"He's been blowing up my phone all morning, too," M'Lyn said. "Ignore him."

Mason frowned and shook his head. "Yeah, but it's not like him to keep calling over and over. Why doesn't he just leave me a message? Or, better yet, text me. He should know I'll get back to him."

"How 'bout you forget everyone else and concentrate on *me* this weekend?" M'Lyn spoke sharply.

Mason continued to grin devilishly. "You're the one wanting to go walking in the park." He stood up from his chair and reached for her hand before he rolled his eyes at the sound of his phone ringing again. "Might as well get this over with," he said. "Hey, man, what's up? I had my phone turned off for my meeting with—"

In the span of a few seconds, Mason's countenance morphed from mild annoyance to one of alarm. "When? How?" His hand flew to his forehead and he bent double as if in pain. "I'm on my way, man! Heading home now! Oh, dear God, I-I'm there for you, man! I'm there!"

M'Lyn made no attempt to hide her panic after he had ended the phone conversation. "W-w-what's happened? What's wrong?" she practically screamed.

As she grabbed his arm, Mason turned to her, his face ashen. Before he could speak, her phone began to ring. She picked it up from the table, knowing the caller. Mason was already at the front door. He called over his shoulder, "Answer it!"

* * * * *

The rear doors of the ambulance stood open. The driver had backed at near top speed from the driveway of the house to the side of the gazebo. Gabe sprinted to the vehicle and loudly informed the personnel that yes, he *would* be riding in the back, to hell with their policies. Gaby had been the one to see William running from the house, still clad in his pajamas, demanding to know what was wrong. Quickly, she took him by the hand and, after calming the moaning Hazel, led both of them back to the house. Remy ran beside Claire to the first available vehicle to follow the ambulance to the emergency room.

Will Remington, standing ramrod stiff, his eyes unfocused, his perpetual smile nonexistent, marveled in bewilderment at the strange thought that occupied his mind at that very moment. *What a beautiful day it is,* he mused, looking up to see a jet stream trailing through a cloudless blue sky. He exhaled as a sudden breeze freshened to cool his brow. Idly, he watched a trio of crows bickering loudly with one another over territorial boundaries, and he wondered how Mother Nature could decorate such a morning as the gurney clattered past him: the gurney carrying the daughter whom he loved with all his heart.

93

The lighting in the hospital room was at its lowest level. Periodic noise from beyond the closed door drifted in from the outside world. Otherwise, the room was quiet except for the faint beeping of the machines that recorded blood pressure, heart rate, oxygen level and everything else that monitored life.

Gabe sat by the bedside, leaning in as close as possible and gently stroking his wife's hand. His eyes never left hers, willing her to open them. No one spoke as they waited. Gaby sniffed. The machines beeped.

Doctors' pages became louder over the intercom as the door opened slowly and Mason entered. Remy immediately embraced him, burying his face against his best friend's shoulder as the sound of his sobs pierced the silence. Quietly, the two men slipped from the room.

Claire tiptoed in with coffee for everyone. Gabrielle reached into her jacket pocket as her cell phone pinged. She smiled slightly as she read the text aloud. "William has calmed down a bit, Hazel says. Didn't go to his game, though." She sniffed. No one responded. The machines beeped.

Will exhaled audibly. When he spoke, he sounded tired. "Why didn't we see it?"

"We didn't want to," Gabe whispered.

The hours crawled by. Occasionally, one of the nurses would come in to check the IV or to jot something down on the chart. They eased Gabe away from her side momentarily as they removed the tube and gently washed her face, all the while smiling and nodding as they had been taught to do to reassure worried family members.

Remy and Mason returned sometime later to sit quietly along with the others. A few minutes later, Vivian stirred. Her husky whisper startled the room.

"Mmm, water, please."

Gabe fetched the cup, held it out to her, and placed the straw between her lips. "Here, my darling, drink. Be careful. That's good," he said. Setting the cup back on the nightstand, he gathered her hands in his. "Oh, Vivian," his voice broke. After a few moments, he regained his composure. "When I read your note, my heart stopped. Have I never told you what you mean to me?"

Slowly, Vivian opened her eyes and gazed around at the worried faces hovering over her bed. A sad little smile tilted the corners of her mouth as tears spilled from her eyes. She took a ragged breath and turned to Gabe. "Can you ever forgive me?" she asked.

His response was immediate. "There is nothing to forgive, Vivian. But you must know that my life could not go on without you. You are my *wife*. You are the other half of me!"

The tense and emotional atmosphere eased up a bit as the doctor entered the room. "Good evening, everyone. I'm Dr. Morris. I see that you have regained consciousness, Mrs. Westin," he said as he checked her chart. "Your vitals are very weak. However, that's to be expected with an accidental overdose such as this." He cleared his throat, replaced the chart on the end of the bed, and looked at the strained faces before him.

"Now, I am going to keep you overnight, Mrs. Westin. What you need is another IV and rest." Not allowing for any comments, he went on. "I suggest that all of you go home and get some rest yourselves. I'll be back at nine tomorrow morning."

"I'll be staying right here with my wife," Gabe said, "but the rest of you should go home."

Dr. Morris turned from the open door. "Very well, Mr. Westin. I'll have a cot brought in for you." He hesitated, as if an idea had just occurred to him. "I'd like to speak with you for a moment, if that's agreeable with you."

"Of course, Doctor," Gabe said as he rose from his chair. He patted her hand and spoke gently, "I'll be right back, my dear."

An embarrassed silence permeated the room after Gabe and Dr. Morris left. Finally, Vivian spoke. "Please, everyone, go home and rest. And please know how sorry I am."

"Oh, Mama!" Gabrielle laid her head on Vivian's chest. "I love you so much. We *all* do."

Will's blustery voice rang out: "Well, I'm just not sure that I completely approve of that Dr. Morris. What she needs is to be at home."

"You rarely approve of anyone, Daddy." Vivian's words were icy, and her voice stronger. "I like him. And, I'll take his advice. Now, please go and get some rest. I'll be alright." She closed her eyes. Her voice fell to a whisper. "Gabe will be here."

* * * * *

Accidental? That's what the doctor said, right? But was it? Was it just another accident, like, like the other one?

Oh, stop it! Stop dwelling in the past. And stop imagining that one unfortunate event has a damn thing to do with the other! For God's sake, man, YOU didn't do anything to cause the accident. Not this one, anyway. But you did nothing to prevent it, either. Wait just a minute—you're thinking that whatever happened years ago could have led to today?

Well, that's just bullshit! Why? Because no one knows, that's why. So, stop these absurd thoughts that keep crawling through your mind. Crawling like worms, making you hear voices. Making you want to squeeze your head in a goddamn vice. Crush the memory of the ACCIDENT. Crush the whispers.

"Let me help you, Mister."

94

Will parked his car curbside, turned off the headlights, and sat for several minutes, playing the events of the day over and over in his mind. With much effort he emerged from the car and made his way up the veranda steps to Belle's front door. As was his custom, he rang the doorbell. How often had she admonished him to use his key? But he chose to respect her house as her own private property. He waited until the sound of the television muted and the porch lights came on.

A mask of sadness and worry clouded Belle's usually smiling countenance as she opened the door. "Come here, Will," she said, drawing him to her. Their wordless embrace lasted a long time. When at last they parted, she closed the door and led him by the hand to his favorite chair. "Sit," she instructed. "I'll get you a drink. Are you hungry?" She headed toward the kitchen.

Belle soon returned with a decanter, two glasses, and a plate of sandwiches, which she placed on the coffee table before taking a seat next to him on the sofa. He had not answered her but nodded and helped himself. When he had eaten, he leaned back and drunk deeply from the whisky. He gazed at her for a long time before finally speaking. "I need to talk to someone, Belle—a confession of sorts, I suppose."

"I'm here for you, Will. You know that," she said. "I'll always be here."

After a minute or two, he looked into her eyes. "Are we entitled to our secrets?"

Belle leaned back, frowning. "Will, you're worrying me."

* * * * * *

Mason had driven Gabrielle home to care for William and, he hoped, to get some rest herself. She looked exhausted, as did the entire family. He had refused her offer to stay in his former residence in the guesthouse, using the excuse that he had things to attend to at his home. But he did not go home.

The night was warm. The red fingers of sunset had long left the sky, giving way to a full moon. Mason inhaled the smoke from his cigarette and sipped from his flask. The concrete bench on which he now sat was only a tiny bit more uncomfortable than those hideous hospital chairs. He grunted, rubbed his lower back, and squatted down to settle himself into a more agreeable position on a thick patch of moss. A familiar sense of belonging enveloped him as his eyes adjusted to the shadowed images of the Ramble's entrance. This was his chapel, the doorway to exorcising his demons. Or so he had once thought.

The warm brandy went down smoothly, drawing a contented murmur from him. But, as usual, no pleasant moment was ever allowed to linger. Without warning, that idiotic phrase popped into his mind: functioning alcoholic. Where'd *that* come from? "Nonsense," he scolded himself aloud as he polished off the contents of the flask, crushed the cigarette butt into the earth, and tried to find a suitable way to begin his prayer.

Mason loved the night. Loved the sounds of the owl, the crickets, and the peaceful feeling that always seemed to descend with darkness to erase the brashness of the daylight. He closed his eyes and searched his soul for words to direct to the Almighty. But he failed miserably, as the wretched actions of his past were replayed again and again in his mind like a bad movie. He shook his head sadly and wished for more brandy.

Soon, he got to his feet and began to make his way to his car. He had found no solace. Directing his vision upward to the starry, sapphire-blue of the night sky, cynicism again became his master. "Forgiveness? Redemption?" He scoffed as he whispered the words. "Good joke, God!"

* * * * * *

"Now, Remy, you go home and get some sleep. Thank you for driving me home," Claire said as she prepared to exit the car. "She's going to be alright, you know. We must trust the doctor, *and* the Lord."

"Yes, ma'am, Miz Claire," Remy said. "I-I still can't believe it—"

"I know, son," Claire interrupted, reaching out to grasp his hand. "Your mama needs our help and love. She needs professional help too, Remy. You know that."

He nodded. "Yes, I know that. I also know that you saved her life today." He swiped tears from his cheeks with the back of his hand took a ragged breath. "Thank you."

Claire squeezed his hand and smiled. "Son, your mama and me has been best friends all our lives, since babies. We've been blessed with you children and our grandchildren. We've laughed together and cried together, and we'll get through this, too."

"Yes, ma'am. Goodnight, Miz Claire."

"See you tomorrow, Remy."

After leaving Claire at her home, Remy drove slowly along the winding driveway that led to his house. He thought about stopping to check on William, but he knew that Gaby had everything taken care of when it came to the child. He wouldn't know what to say to the boy, anyway. He found it awkward to talk to his own son about routine matters, much less address his grandmother's "accident". That needed to change, Remy realized. A lot of things needed to change.

He entered the cavernous foyer and called out to M'Lyn. His voice echoed against the marble. She had texted him when she had gotten home and asked if she should come directly to the hospital. He messaged that he would see her later

"Remy?" She hurried from the kitchen to embrace him. He returned the embrace, hugging her body tightly against his. Gently, he held her at arms' length, studying her. She had been crying, and she looked tired and pale. And vulnerable.

"How can I help you?" she whispered.

"Mama's gonna be alright," he said. "Well, 'alright' is probably not the right word. Everyone keeps saying it, and I guess it comforting." He studied his wife for a long time. "You can do something for me, though."

M'Lyn sniffed. "What's that?" she asked.

He took her by the hand and led her to the staircase. "You can go upstairs, fix your makeup, and put on that black dress that I like so much."

"Whatever for?" she asked.

Remy took a deep breath. "We need to celebrate *life*, M'Lyn. We need to celebrate *us*. What do I want you dressed up for? Well, 'cause it's Saturday night, and I happen to want to go dancing with the prettiest girl in the county!"

* * * * *

Vivian watched as Gabe arranged the sheets and pillow on the cot beside her bed. He had removed his shirt and shoes and was preparing to lie down. "You know it would be fine if you went home and got a good night's sleep in your own bed," she said. "It would make me feel less guilty. Less of a burden."

Gabe sat on the bedside and reached for her hands. He drew them to his lips as he searched his heart and mind for words that might possibly reach that dark place that held her prisoner. "Vivian, you have a husband and a family who cherish you. Somewhere inside of you, my dear, is a bright and happy place. I know this, and you and I are going to find the path to that place. Do you believe me?"

She nodded silently.

"How you must have suffered, Viv. I am so, so very sorry." Gabe cradled his head in frustration.

"You have nothing to be sorry for, Gabe!" Vivian exclaimed. "Why, you could do *nothing* that would ever require an apology."

"Thank you, my sweet wife."

If you only knew.

95

Vivian lay perfectly still on the hospital bed. She had been awake for some time, listening to the sounds around her. Although the door to her room moved with barely a whisper of sound, she could always tell when someone entered by the level of noise coming from the busy hallway beyond. She even knew when the person standing over her bed was the doctor or one of the nurses. Or Gabe.

Throughout the night, he had gotten up from his cot to stand beside her bed. Vivian had been aware of each gentle touch, every little straightening of blankets and unnecessary pillow-fluffing. She had pretended sleep, not wanting to keep her husband from his much-needed rest. Or, had she spent the night in mute stillness to avoid talking? And where was Gabe now, she wondered, for she could tell that she was alone.

She opened her eyes only a small slit at first, knowing that the morning sunlight streaming from the window would momentarily blind her. Gradually, she became used to the daylight and began to take stock of her room for the first time. Yesterday remained a dismal blur, with the faces of her loved ones having been transformed into shapeless images who pulled at her and shook her, all the while shrieking unintelligible words.

Gingerly, Vivian sat up, positioning herself on the edge of the bed. A hospital robe and slippers lay on the nearby table: she reached for them. *How weak I am!*

With slow and deliberate steps, she made her way to a chair by the window. From here, she could see people walking from the hospital parking lot and into the visitors' entrance. Seeing Gabrielle striding briskly across the concrete brought a smile to Vivian's face. Her daughter carried a bag that she was sure contained street clothes, hairbrush and make-up. When the rest of her family came, they would see her looking much better than yesterday. That pleased her, eased her guilt just a bit.

And when the rest of the family did come—what then? The silence would be dispelled by everyone talking at once. Talking, yet saying absolutely nothing.

"Hey, Mama." Gabrielle dropped her bags on the bed and went immediately to Vivian's side and into her arms. "How are you feeling this morning?" she asked, searching her face for—what? *An explanation, perhaps?*

"I'm much better, my darling girl," Vivian said. "What have you brought for me?"

Gabrielle began to unpack the tote bag. "I have your favorite lounging pants and top," she said. "Also, some shower goodies, perfume, your makeup bag…"

* * * * *

An hour later, Vivian examined her reflection in the mirror. "Thank you, Gaby," she said. "I feel so much better just knowing that I look better. By the way, where's your father? I haven't seen him this morning. Perhaps he went home to shower and change."

"Oh, no," Gabrielle replied as she put the finishing touches to Vivian's hair. "He didn't leave the hospital at all. I saw him in the doctor's office when I came in. He'll be back soon." She smiled and kissed her forehead.

At that moment, Will's distinctive voice boomed, seeming to penetrate the very walls themselves. "Ahh," Gabrielle whispered in mock alarm, "the enemy advances!"

Vivian laughed, an unfamiliar yet melodious laugh, one that had not been heard for a very long time.

"Well, now," Will said as he entered the room. "My daughter seems in fine form this morning. Looks very pretty, I might add."

"Thank you, Daddy. I-I'm much better. My goodness," Vivian sputtered, as the room filled with her family. "The entire clan is here."

"More than you know, Mama," Gabrielle said, answering the ping of her cell phone and putting it on speaker.

Leander's deep voice resonated. "Good morning, Miz Vivian. I do hope you're feeling better. I miss you."

"Oh, Lee! How sweet of you to call," Vivian said. "When are you coming for a visit?"

"Soon. Very soon. Rest well, and we'll talk more later."

Indeed, Remy, M'Lyn, Mason, Claire, and Gabe stood in line to bestow hugs and kisses on her and, as she'd predicted, everyone began talking at once.

Will took his turn, awkwardly patting Vivian's shoulder. "Now, just as soon as that doctor makes an appearance, we'll be getting our girl back home where she belongs."

"Just a moment," Gabe said. Silence overtook the room as he cleared his throat. "Vivian is not going home right now. I—"

"What the hell are you talking about, Gabe?" Will demanded. "Of course, she's going home."

Gabe kept his voice clam and even. "Yes, Will, she *will* go home. But not today." He knelt beside Vivian's chair. Taking her hand in his and looking into her eyes, he went on speaking as if to her and her alone.

"My wife needs help to deal with some troubling feelings that she has. Feelings that are not her fault and certainly not of her making. Now, Dr. Morris has suggested a wonderful retreat only about an hour's drive from here. He tells me that the counseling and therapy program offered there is the very best."

"See here, now," Will argued, "we'll certainly have to check out this so-called retreat before making any decisions."

Gabe gave Vivian's hand a squeeze, smiled at her, and stood up. "Will, Dr. Morris and I have already checked out the facility. I would not think of recommending that my wife receive treatment *anywhere* that was not first-rate." His tone had grown brusque "Dr. Morris believes that her therapy would only require a stay of one month."

Vivian closed her eyes and listened to the voices of her loved ones as each and every differing opinion was expressed. After several minutes, she silenced the room.

"It is a frightening life to be a prisoner of one's own imaginings, to see only negativity in every situation." She paused, shaking her head. "When I awake each morning and see a beautiful day and hear birds chirping and people laughing, I want to be a part of it. But the idea of actually being happy terrifies me."

Her family remained silent as Vivian flicked a tear from her cheek and stood up. Taking her husband's arm, she said, "Gabe is right. I have felt alone and invisible for far too long."

96

Gabe Westin whistled gaily as he finished dressing. He had taken extra care to look his best, believing that Vivian would approve of his new sport coat. She had remarked before that he should wear more color. He picked up the two suitcases—the one he had packed for himself and the one he had asked Claire to prepare for Vivian. He coached himself to stay positive that his wife would also approve of the surprise he had planned.

"Good morning, everyone," Gabe said cheerily upon entering the dining room. Setting down his bags, he headed for the breakfast buffet.

"What's with the suitcases?" Will asked nonchalantly. "Not deserting us, are you?"

"Not likely," his son-in-law answered. "I'm picking up my wife at noon today and whisking her away for some much-needed time with just the two of us." He chewed his eggs rapidly, adding, "But we'll be back for someone's baseball game on Wednesday." He winked at William, whose young face crinkled into a broad grin.

Lowering his newspaper, Will frowned. "Have you forgotten the investors' meeting on Monday? You will *certainly* be back for that." It was a statement and not a question. "After all, business comes first."

Gabe finished his breakfast and stood in preparation for his departure. He smiled and said, "No, Will, I won't be at the meeting simply because my wife needs me more than the investors do. You and the other partners will manage just fine without me." Retrieving the suitcases, he headed for the back door. "Have a good weekend, everyone. Vivian and I will see you when we see you."

There could be no mistaking Will's mood at that moment. The hard, thin line of his mouth and the reddening of his cheeks belied his calm words.

"Today being Friday, I feel *certain* that the rest of this family will be here at five o'clock for cocktails and dinner."

"Well, I *was* going to be here to celebrate Mama's homecoming," Gabrielle said thoughtfully. "But since that's to be delayed, I think I'd like to go prowl art galleries in Greenville. Maybe I can rope Mason into going with me. Sorry, Granddaddy. I doubt that we'll be back by five," she added. "C'mon, William. I'll drop you at your friend's house."

"Thanks, Gaby," M'Lyn said, rising from the table and planting a kiss on Remy's forehead. "Since I'm going shopping, I'll take him."

Remy prepared to leave as well. "I'm off to the office, now. M'Lyn and I are going to the bar-be-que at the club tonight, Granddaddy. Next Friday, though, for sure." He sprang for the door to avoid any reprimand.

Will sat for quite some time in the silence of the dining room. When Hazel came to clear away the remnants of breakfast, not a word passed between them. He could not stop dwelling on Gabe's rare display of exuberance, and it irked him. His son-in-law had always been the epitome of calm, quiet predictability. But of late—to be precise, since Vivian's episode—he had exhibited the characteristics of behavior otherwise foreign to him. He'd become rather headstrong. He had begun to act *young*!

During the past month, Will had thought often of Gabe's outright defiance of him regarding Vivian's treatment. Oh, they had had their disagreements before, mainly concerning banking issues, but he'd never actually taken a stand against him. And, when pressed on how his daughter's therapy was progressing, Gabe would simply remark, "Very well."

And now, he was blowing off the investors' meeting. Will continued to work himself up into a near frenzy. He stood up from the table, almost knocking his chair over in the process. "Goddammit!" he cursed under his breath as he headed for the door. "So much for my loyal family!" He continued to fret over their casual dismissal of his Friday night ritual.

But Will was losing more than his patience, and he knew it. He was losing control. And Will Remington did *not* like to lose.

* * * * *

"You say that you feel like a failure? Why?"

"Because my father wanted a son, that's why."

"And, you feel unloved? Why?"

"Because my husband married me only to please my father, that's why."

"You feel unnecessary? Why?"

"Because I am. Unnecessary. No one really needs me, that's why."

"And, are you happy?"

"I should be happy, right? I mean, I've never wanted for anything. I have a life of privilege. I have children. Children are supposed to bring us happiness. Right?"

"Are you happy?"

"Yes. No. I don't know. I'm afraid to be happy. Okay?"

"Why are you afraid to be happy?"

"I'm tired. I don't want to talk anymore. I need to lie down. My head hurts. Take this thing off of me!"

"That *thing* is measuring your heart rate, which happens to be racing at the moment. Why do suppose that is?"

"How should I know? You're the doctor."

"You have begun to perspire, as well. And your hands are trembling. Is this how your headaches start?"

"I guess so. Yes."

"You are experiencing a panic attack. Do you know what triggers them?"

"No."

"Then, let's find out. After all, that's what you're here for, Mrs. Westin."

Dr. Karen Epstein reached across the coffee table that separated the two women and switched the recorder off. Sitting back in her chair, she smiled. "Well, Vivian, tell me how you feel after listening to your very first session with me only a month ago."

Vivian returned the smile. "I feel as though I've been listening to a stranger. I sounded so frightened. Numb."

The psychiatrist remained silent, allowing her patient ample time to express her thoughts.

"It's an old cliché," Vivian said, "but I now feel like a different person. Before my overdose, I believed that life held nothing for me. I didn't think that I had a purpose." She paused, shaking her head, then added, "I did not believe that I mattered to anyone."

"And now? Have there been any dark thoughts, any sad scenarios building in your mind? Any palpitations or headaches?"

"None of the above," Vivian responded, laughing. "Thank you, Doctor."

"You've responded well to our therapy. And having the proper antidepressant medication has certainly helped." Dr. Epstein frowned. "Those pills that you were taking before were doing you more harm than good. They simply dulled the pain of your headaches. And they should *never* have been taken along with sleeping pills."

She stood up and reached out to Vivian. As they embraced, she said, "I will want to see you on a monthly basis for the next few months to see how you're coping. But as of today, the next phase of your therapy begins." Gently, she took Vivian's arm and turned her toward the glass door—where Gabe stood smiling.

97

Their embrace lasted far longer than Vivian had ever remembered. Her husband's kiss thrilled her, but best of all was her response to his words that he had missed her terribly and that he loved her. Blissfully, she realized that she actually believed him.

So, it came as bit puzzling when Gabe turned to her when they were seated in his car a short time later. His expression was serious, as was his tone as he began what seemed to Vivian to be a very well-rehearsed speech. She loved his deep baritone voice, the way he accentuated his words with hand gestures, and the crinkling little lines around his eyes. But the best feeling of all, she suddenly realized, was that she was listening to his words with interest and expectation and without anxiety.

"Vivian, even though we have failed in the past to talk things through, we will do so in the future. We won't simply dismiss a subject because it might be difficult to speak of."

Vivian nodded. "Of course, Gabe."

"And when we do disagree, well, then, we'll have an argument. That's what married couples do—they argue from time to time."

"Yes, they do. As we will, I'm sure," she agreed.

"And, and when we do argue, we just might yell at each other." Gabe's voice grew louder. "We might even tell each other to piss off!"

She nodded sagely. "Uh-huh."

His hand gestures became more pronounced with each word. "As of now," he directed, "we will stop tiptoeing around each other. If we argue, then we'll make up. 'Make-up sex', that's what the kids say these days. My God, how long has it been since we made love?"

"Too long, my dear, and you are exactly right," Vivian replied.

"Another thing…" Gabe's voice trailed off and his eyes narrowed as he studied his wife's face. "Wait. You said what?"

She laughed at his confusion and leaned closer to kiss him. "I am in total agreement," she said when their lips parted. "I'm sorry for the miserable person that I have been for so long, but I am so much better now. This *new me*—I want her to stay."

"As do I," Gabe said softly. "Now, let's get going."

With her head resting against Gabe's shoulder, Vivian luxuriated in contentment as the retreat's winding drive brought them to the main highway.

Vivian sat up. "Dear, I do believe that you've made a wrong turn. We're going north instead of toward home."

"So we are," he said, chuckling. "Doesn't look like we're going home."

She played along. "Oh, and just where are you taking me?"

Gabe set the cruise control and glanced at her. "Do you remember the last part of our honeymoon? When we drove up into the high mountains and—"

"My goodness!" Vivian said "You don't mean that wonderful little cabin perched on the side of the mountain? Is it still there?"

"It had better be," he replied. "I have it rented for three nights."

"But what about our clothes?"

"Suitcases all packed, in the trunk," he responded, obviously pleased with himself. "So, you do remember the cabin."

Vivian closed her eyes, her face beaming. "I remember everything about that wonderful place. I loved sitting by that big window, watching the sunset behind the mountains. And those lovely walking trails. Do you remember when we came across the resident bear on that trail? Oh, I was so frightened, but she just looked at us and lumbered out of sight."

"Yes," Gabe said, sharing in the memory. "We sure hightailed it back to the cabin."

"The days were so warm and sunny, but the nights were freezing. We burned up all the firewood." Vivian continued reminiscing. "Golly, I remember how cold those nights were."

Gabe drew her hand to his lips. "And I remember how we kept warm."

98

"What a great day this has been!" Mason said. "I cannot believe how much I enjoyed the art galleries." He squeezed Gabrielle's hand. "The painting that you helped me choose—I mean, I love it. It's gonna look great in my living room. Thanks, baby girl, for making me go with you today."

They held hands as they strolled along the flagstone path from his car to the front of the mansion. "I had fun," Gabrielle said. "Thanks for going with me and for dinner." Midway up the steps, she paused and turned to face him.

"Thank you for *everything*, Mason." Her voice conveyed noticeable emotion. "This past month—well, I couldn't have gotten through it without you. With Lee a world away, Daddy thinking only about Mama, Remy a total basket case, and Granddaddy biting everybody's heads off, I don't know what I would have done."

"Hey, c'mon now, baby girl," Mason said, attempting to lighten the mood. "I haven't done anything special. Besides, I've enjoyed your company more..." he hesitated briefly, "more than you know."

"You've been a saint, that's what," Gabrielle replied. Leaning back against the banister, she studied him thoughtfully. "Almost losing Mama has made me realize just how alone I am. I've isolated myself, just like she has done." She shook her head, losing her words for a time. "I never had close friends, except for Lee. Never even *tried* to make friends. Do you ever feel that way, Mason? Like you're all alone?"

He thought about his answer for a long time. "Yeah. Most of the time, in fact," he said. "Hey, now, let's not put a damper on such a fine day. Tomorrow night's the big summer kick-off dance at the club. How 'bout you and me going together?"

Gabrielle perked up. "Like a real date, huh?"

He grinned. "Yeah, like a real date."

Gabrielle looked at him intently, her gaze unlocking from his and dropping to his lips. Slowly, she reached for his hands and placed one on either side of her waist. Mason complied, saying nothing. "Do I have to wait until tomorrow night for a good-night kiss?" she asked.

Answering was impossible. Spellbound, he stood still as her hands stroked his arms, then began their enticing upward trek to join behind his head. Tilting her head, she pressed her lips to his. She kept her eyes open, making him a prisoner of their smoky, topaz depths. Mason could not move. He felt weightless, dimly thinking that, if he released her, he might float away.

Toe to toe, Gabrielle was taller. Ever so slowly, she increased her hold on him and lifted her feet from the step. Easily, his muscular frame supported her slender one. Now, she did close her eyes as her mouth parted against his. Her hold on him relaxed, allowing her body to slowly slide down his until she was standing on a lower step.

Mason's head was exploding. His trembling hands gently pushed her from him. "I s-s-should, I should go now, baby girl," was all he could manage.

"I'm not a baby girl any longer." Her honeyed words lured him into another deep and delicious kiss.

They finally parted, and Mason steadied his breathing before replying. "Don't I know it!" Weakly, he began to back down the remaining steps away from her. "But I should go. I-I can't stay."

She continued her hypnotic control, reaching out her hand to him. "You don't have to go," she whispered. "Mama and Daddy won't be back for days. Granddaddy's at Belle's."

Although her words dissolved, her eyes, glistening in the glow of the porch lighting, conveyed her desire.

He smiled weakly. "Oh, but I do have to go." His steps were unsure as he ran towards his car. He fumbled with the car door handle. Her voice stopped him.

"Mason Carlysle!"

He turned to look at her. "What is it, baby g…" He caught himself, chuckling. "Sorry, old habits. What is it, dahlin?"

She lifted her chin slightly, a demure smile teasing the corners of her mouth. "Will you marry me?"

There are moments in every life when clarity presents itself, wiping away the fog of regret and illuminating that which is truly important. For this family, Mason believed it was Vivian's frantic attempt to end what had seemed to her to be a painful existence. Her reckless action had saved him as well, saved him from making one of the worst mistakes of his life.

The flash of reason was sudden, revealing itself in that very moment. With reason came the awareness that his past actions—some brazen and others to be forever held in secrecy—did *not* have to define who he was. The haunting subject of forgiveness was still to be litigated between him and God. But just *maybe* the road to redemption was right in front of him.

If ignored, clarity could fade just as quickly as it appeared. Mason's voice was clear and strong, free from the mildly mocking tone that he so often hid behind. His thoughts were lucid.

"Why, yes, Gabrielle Westin. I will."

99

Leander sat in his favorite chair, studying the drawing that he held in his hands. "Hmm," he murmured, pretending deep interest as he stroked his chin and nodded. He turned his gaze to the beaming child standing beside him. "I do believe, Clarissa, that this is the most beautiful drawing that I have ever seen."

"Really, Daddy?" His daughter squealed in delight. "I colored it all by myself!"

"Oh, this is truly a work of art. And," he said with a flourish, "I fully intend to have this framed and hung on my office wall. What do you think of that, my princess?"

Her little face exploded into unbridled delight. "But Mama said she's going to put it on the refrigerator."

"Absolutely not," he said sternly. "My office wall."

Her tiny hand covered his mouth as she giggled conspiratorially and whispered, "Okay, you win, Daddy."

Leander leaned forward and cupped his daughter's face in his hands. Gently, he planted a kiss on her forehead. He looked into her huge, hazel eyes and stroked the silky waves of light brown hair. "I love you, princess."

"I'm not really a princess, am I?" Clarissa asked with seriousness.

"Well, you're *my* princess," he answered. "Isn't that enough?"

Thoughtful for a long moment, the child finally said, "Mama says that one day, I will be a queen."

Leander closed his eyes. After a time, he put his secret thoughts at bay. "Clarissa, do you know what tomorrow is?"

She grinned. "Yes, it's my birthday!"

"And, how old will you be?"

She held up two fingers on each hand, causing Leander to laugh. "That's right. You will be four years old. And what happens tomorrow?"

"A party with cake and ice cream."

In the blink of an eye, her attention shifted. "I'm going to go and find Mama," she announced, turning away from him and walking purposefully out of the room.

Leander smiled and leaned back in his chair, his thoughts on the child. He marveled at their good fortune, especially after listening to friends recount the sleepless nights associated with their newborns all the way through the "terrible twos". Clarissa's behavior had mirrored perfection from the time they had brought her from the hospital. No colic, no temper tantrums, no misbehaving; simply the perfect miniature of her mother.

Leander worried, though. His daughter brought no friends home, nor did she ask to play with other children. Her pre-school teachers praised her as being one of the kindest children in the group, never exhibiting selfish behavior. But still, Clarissa had no playmates. He believed that a sibling was the answer and had told Allure of his desire for another child. "No, my love," had been her simple reply, ending the subject.

The brief moments that his daughter allotted to him in the afternoons were, Leander knew without a doubt, borne out of love. He also knew, though, that she longed only to be with Allure. Did he feel jealous or angry? Of course not. A bit sad, however, that he stood just outside that invisible circle that held only the two of them.

Laughter from outside drew his attention. He turned his chair toward the window to watch his wife and daughter in the garden. The little puppy that he had brought home for Clarissa was running circles around them, disrupting their planting of flowers. He chuckled as he watched the scene. Clarissa reached down to the pup and began to stroke him into quiet submission. Leander once again reflected on his daughter's gentle nature.

The phone's ring interrupted his thoughts, and he smiled broadly at the caller ID. "Well, well," he answered. "I see that you've finally found time to answer my calls."

"Sorry, Lee," Gabrielle said. "You just can't imagine how busy I've been."

Leander knew immediately that something was—what? *Different.* Like so many times throughout their years together, whenever a subject was difficult, her voice would become high-pitched. Anxious. He allotted her a few moments to gather her thoughts. When he heard her exhale, he spoke. "Tell me what's going on, Gaby."

"You do know me so well, don't you?" A nervous little giggle escaped her. "I've got the most wonderful news ever, Lee! I hope you'll be as happy as the rest of the family."

After a full quarter hour of Gabrielle's scattered ramblings, with his occasional grunts and murmurings in reply, she finally ran out of words. "Are you still there?" she asked.

"Is this some kind of a joke, Gaby?" He hadn't meant the harsh sarcasm that his voice conveyed. But he made no attempt to soften his tone. "You and Mason Carlisle are, are getting *married*? What in God's name are you thinking?"

"Ouch," she said after a moment. "So much for the blessing of my best friend."

"It's not a matter of blessing," he responded bleakly. "Mason is a, a cad!"

Gabrielle spoke softly. "Lee, trust me, this is right. Over the past month, I've seen a different Mason. We all have. The time that we've spent together has made me know that he and I truly belong together."

Leander closed his eyes and said, "Gaby, you, you *think* that you know him. But you don't. Please don't open yourself up to another heartache." Words now became impossible, and he could almost see the wall rising up between them. Incredulous as it seemed, the thought presented itself: *Did she actually love Mason?*

"Lee, I'm almost twenty-eight years old."

"And he is thirty-eight!" Immediately, he regretted his petulant attitude and, after several seconds passed, tempered them with a question: "When is the wedding?"

"In a few weeks. It'll be very simple and quiet," she answered before repeating her earlier words. "I'm almost twenty-eight years old. I have been head-over-heels in love once, and I do not want that feeling ever again."

Her voice grew stronger. "What I do want is a partnership with someone that I *know*. And, yes, Lee, I do know him. I know all about his reputation, his affairs, his smug self-absorption. But he isn't like that with me." She paused. "Look, Lee, I know that you and Mason have never been close and that, as a child, you never liked him. But, do you honestly think that he and I haven't talked about everything? About how both of our lives will change? Do you think so little of my ability to choose how to live my own life?"

Her words cut deep. "I'm sorry, Gaby," Leander said. "Of course, you are more than capable of making your own decisions." He could think of nothing more to say. Oh, he could perhaps stop this marriage. But then, would she hate him? Was he capable of destroying multiple lives to keep her from making what *might* be a mistake? He had no answers to the questions that had plagued him for most of his life.

He could sense tears in her voice as she asked, "Why can't life be simple, like it was when we were kids?"

"Because it can't," he replied solemnly. "But I'll always be here for you, Gaby."

"I know that, Lee."

Leander gradually resurfaced from the depths of his self-induced trance and back to the present. Dusk was gathering as he stared through the window into the garden. His wife and daughter were no longer there, and his house was quiet. He felt a slight movement at his feet, and looking down, he saw the little pup curled into a sleeping ball. Gently, he bent to scratch the warm, chubby belly. The pup whimpered contentedly and rolled over on his back. *Why can't life be simple?*

100

"You are our only daughter, Gaby," Vivian said as she clutched her daughter's hands. "Are you sure that you don't want a formal wedding? You know that your father and I would love to do it." The two women had strolled to the gazebo on the late May morning to admire the blooming azalea and, as Vivian put it, "to complete my healing."

"No, Mama," Gabrielle replied. "Mason and I talked about it, and we both want something quiet. Private, you know, with just the family."

"Well, then, you shall have it," Vivian said happily. "How about we have the ceremony in the courtyard on Saturday evening, then a dinner at the club?" At Gabrielle's eager nod, she chose her next words carefully.

"Gaby, I know that you were in love with your young man in college." She paused, allowing her daughter time to digest her words. "Do you feel the same—how do I say it—intensity for Mason?"

Gabrielle grew thoughtful as they walked across the lawn. "No Mama," she replied finally, "I don't. And I don't ever want that feeling again."

Vivian nodded. "We are all very happy about this marriage, not only your granddaddy. I've always thought of Mason as part of our family. I will admit, though, that some of his actions have given me worry over the years."

"When I was a little kid," Gabrielle said, "I had this *huge* crush on Mason. Oh, I never admitted it, but Lee knew. Maybe that's why he never really liked Mason." She grew pensive. "And, you know, during our teenage years, that dislike seemed to intensify. Lee was always so critical of Mason's lifestyle. I know that he was cocky and arrogant, but I've come to see that a lot of that was just a cover-up. He's actually a bit insecure."

"I believe that our Mason has changed," Vivian said.

"I know he has," Gabrielle replied. "Mama, I wouldn't marry him if I didn't believe that he and I belonged together. I just wish Lee could see it. I can't believe that he's refusing to be happy for me."

"Leander will come around, my darling," Vivian said. "I remember that, even as a little boy, he was always so serious." Wanting to express herself clearly, she soon gathered her thoughts. "Gaby, the men in our family are, at times, weak. In the business world, they perhaps cut corners and make excuses. They even cheat. Leander sees everything as either right or wrong, no gray areas. He keeps everyone on the straight and narrow. That's the only reason that he's critical of Mason. I'm sure of it."

"Thanks, Mama. Of course, you're right. Now, let's go shopping for my wedding dress."

Vivian beamed. "You are going to be a beautiful bride," she said. "And you and Mason will make beautiful children."

Gabrielle's face clouded. "When I said that he and I had talked about *everything*, I meant it. William's going to be your only grandchild."

* * * * *

The weather had cooperated, ushering in a perfect evening. The courtyard lay bathed in the afterglow of a magnificent sunset, and an uncommonly cool breeze teased the many candle flames. No extra seating had been brought in, as the few guests milled about enjoying the casual atmosphere.

Gabrielle checked her image in the hall mirror. The pale gold of her floor-length gown was the perfect color, and the tiara of yellow rose buds that Claire had laced into her hair made her look almost pretty. *For once in my life, I actually feel pretty!*

She smoothed the silken fabric of her gown and knelt to adjust the strap of her beaded sandals. She took the single rose from Vivian's hand and hugged her. As her mother left to join the others in the courtyard, she turned to Gabe.

"This is it, Daddy," she said as she took his arm and looked into his smiling eyes. The French doors stood open, beckoning. Not wanting to rush the moment, she hesitated, drinking in the scene before her. Mason stood flanked by Justice Cooper and a beaming Remy—her groom was looking at her like no one had ever looked at her before. Slowly, he lifted his arm and held out his hand. She nodded and stepped forward amid the smiles and murmurings of her loved ones.

When the tall figure stepped from the corner of the house and into view, Gabrielle gasped. Barely believing her eyes, she whispered, "Lee, you're here!"

"I couldn't miss your big day, little sis.," he whispered, his eyes misting over. "I wish you all the happiness in the world."

Gaby swallowed tears. "My wedding is perfect now," she said.

101

He just HAD to spoil yet another happy event, didn't he? Bastard just had to show up to her big day, a family day! Bad enough you have to look at him at business meetings, talk to him on a regular basis, but to be forced to sit at the club and have him staring at you, daring you, mocking you.

Why the hell can't he stay on his goddamn island, out of sight? And look at her, fawning over him! 'My best friend this, my best friend that'. It was HER big night, Gaby's wedding, for God's sake! And she's making him a hero. Talking about all their happy childhood days together! Just how much can you take, huh?

"Oh, my goodness, are you alright? Why, that glass just shattered! Your, your hand—are you cut?"

"Not a scratch. I must have been a bit overzealous with the bubbly. Sorry, everyone. Uh, waiter, another champagne and a clean-up, please. C'mon, everyone, no harm done. Let's have another toast."

After years of wallowing in memories and longing, Gabrielle realized that, as the night worn on, the scars inflicted by pain and loss were indeed beginning to fade. The exchange of their vows, the passionate kiss of her new husband, the love-filled speeches by her family members, and especially the presence of her best friend, ushered her into an evening filled with much emotion.

She was more than ready to leave behind her years of doubts, unspoken insecurities, and guilt. Well, perhaps not guilt, as she had grown so accustomed to carrying it around, she would feel lost without it. One day, though, she might be able to set it down and walk away as she'd done with her other baggage.

Looking around the room at the glowing faces of everyone she loved, Gabrielle Carlysle rejoiced in being the center of attention. She returned smiles and danced the night away, giving nary a thought to what might lay ahead.

* * * * * *

It was well past midnight when Vivian, clad in a robe and slippers, made her way down the staircase in search of her husband. Ever since returning from the treatment center, she had made a concerted effort to spend more time with him. Her attentions pleased Gabe, that much was evident. And, yet, he had appeared so distant at the wedding dinner tonight that she thought perhaps he was ill.

The door to his study was closed, but a voice from within drew her to tap gently before entering. Gabe stood with his back to the door. "I heard voices," Vivian said, looking around the room. "Were you on the phone?"

He turned to her, his serene smile in place. "No, my dear. Just reminiscing, I guess. Our daughter's wedding was perfect. You did a beautiful job."

"Yes, it was lovely. I'm so proud of her, Gabe, but I'm also a bit sad."

"Oh, why is that? Surely you're not worried?"

"I'm not worried at all. I'm a bit sad because my Gaby is gone, and we only recently began to know each other."

Gabe moved to her side and gathered her into his arms, rocking her gently. "I have an idea. Why don't you go pour us each a brandy, and I'll join you in the living room?"

"I have another idea," she called over her shoulder as she turned away from him. "I'll pour the brandies, and you can join me in my room."

"Even better," Gabe responded.

Alone again, Gabe stood with eyes closed, lost in thought for several minutes before coaxing himself out of his daze. He reached for the note pad on which he'd been writing, slipped it into his desk drawer, and locked it. He mustered a smile as he left the room to join his wife.

* * * * *

Mason emerged from the hotel room's bathroom and leaned against the door frame. He folded his arms and gazed at the scene before him. She sat cross-legged on the king-sized bed, propped against an array of satin pillows—his Gaby, his baby girl! Clad in a white lace gown, she removed the tiara from her hair and shook her flaxen locks free. She chuckled, seeing the grains of rice fall onto the pillows.

"What took you so long?" she asked.

He began to walk slowly toward her. "Just trying to find the words to tell you what you mean to me."

As he drew near, she noticed how brightly his cobalt eyes sparkled. "You could start by telling me that you love me," she said.

"Of course, I love you," Mason responded. "I've always loved you, ever since you were a little kid. Loved your entire family. But *love* is a misused word, Gaby. Everybody says it. We say it when we leave parties, when we end phone calls. We say: 'Bye, see you later, love you.' We've made it a casual phrase that's no longer special."

He was thoughtful for a time. "There's a reason I never married," he said, "never committed to anyone. That's because those vows were only words, never meant anything before." He joined her on the bed and began to stroke her long, smooth legs.

She moved her body closer to his. "Tell me more," she said.

The gown slipped easily over her head. "Well, for one thing, you're my savior. You've saved me from myself. And those vows? They mean everything to me, now. It's no longer just about me." Mason barely voiced the words as his fingers traced imaginary patterns along her breasts.

Gabrielle moved her body to accommodate his. "So," she whispered, "what word have you come up with that's better than 'love'?"

Their slow rhythm began, evoking the sensation that they had always been together. Mason held her gaze. "Adore," he said. "I absolutely *adore* you!"

102

✦✦✦✦✦

Leander placed the final items in his suitcase, fastened it, and turned to his wife. "Allure, I wish that you'd change your mind and go with me," he said for the third time that morning. "The banquet is in my honor—although for the life of me I don't know why—and I would be so proud to have you beside me."

She sat on their bed, her gray-green eyes watching him intently. She smiled slightly and shrugged. Her action caused the thin strap of her sundress to slide from its place and down her arm, exposing that tender hollow between her shoulder and breast, where his lips would cause her to gasp.

"Whew," Leander whispered. His reaction caused her eyes to brighten and her lips to part knowingly. But she directed her head with a nod to their daughter, who sat on the floor across the room. She was absorbed in gentle teasing of the litter of kittens that mama cat had ceremonially bestowed in the laundry basket only last week.

"I miss you when I only go to work for one day," Leander said. "How can I survive without you for a whole week?"

"And I shall miss you as well," Allure said. She rose from the bed and stood by her husband. "I have been to your home in Antioch twice. While it is lovely there, and I do so enjoy your parents and Gaby, I am uncomfortable there."

"Yes, you've told me that. But you've never told me exactly why."

She looked into his eyes for several moments. "Leander, there is a darkness there. I feel it. Something that you cannot speak of, that you cannot share with me. It is best that I do not go."

Her words brought a chill. He turned away. "I-I don't really know what you mean."

"Hmm," she murmured, dismissing his response. "I don't belong there, Leander, but it is your home. You should go. And the honor? Why, of course you deserve it!" She wrapped her slender arms around him from behind and laid her cheek against his back. "And I am so proud of you."

He searched his mind for an appropriate response. Finding none, he simply said, "*You* are my home, Allure." As a way of brightening the mood— and to avoid a subject he could not address—he gently freed himself from her embrace and crossed the room to sweep a giggling Clarissa into his arms. "You and this pretty little girl are my home."

"And the kitties, Daddy?" she squealed.

"And the kitties, and Bobo, too," he answered as the dog yipped delightedly while running circles around their feet.

A perfect family scene, Leander thought. One that he would carry with him back to his childhood home. And back to childhood memories.

* * * * *

Will Remington sat at his desk, reading the speech that he had just finished writing. He nodded approvingly, deciding that his words would convey praise where praise was due without laying it on too thick. The very last thing he wanted to do was invoke bitter feelings, but he knew that the announcement he planned to make at the banquet was the right one.

He had known many men who had risen from the ashes of disappointment to achieve success on their own. Remy would not be one of them. The future he had envisioned for his beloved grandson had not come to fruition. Oh, Remy was a good man with a bright mind but, unfortunately, no head for business. Gabe, on the other hand, possessed the shrewd reasoning required of an investment counselor. He simply had not passed it along to his son. And, Gabe reminded Will regularly that retirement was in his not-to-distant future.

Mason, the one most like Will himself but without his blood, had settled into a life that seemed not at all befitting—that of a happily-married man. Who would have thought it! During their year of marriage, Mason had doted on Gabrielle to the point of whisking her off for one exotic trip after another and prompting his clients to call Will for attention. *Women!* Only good at being a distraction.

Will leaned back in his chair, closed his eyes, and mentally laid out his plans. While the individual banks more or less ran themselves, it was their exploding investment business that concerned him. He would *not* see the financial empire that had morphed from his daddy's modest beginnings dwindle and fall apart. But Will had grown tired. It might be a bitter pill to swallow, but he knew that the time had come to hand the reins to the only man worthy of being named "Managing Partner".

As with so many times during his eighty years, answers and needed solutions had come to Will in solitude. With his business decision made and his speech confirming it finished, he took a fresh sheet of stationery from his desk drawer and began to pen a more personal message. He hardly knew how to put the unspoken words on paper, but gradually they began to flow.

Sometime later, Will heard the clock strike midnight. He needed to get some sleep before meeting the busy days that lay ahead. He read over his writings again before placing them in his desk drawer. He would read them a final time tomorrow, in the naked light of day.

103

Oak branches, adorned heavily with Spanish moss beards, stood sentinel over smaller trees and grasses that grew in profusion along the banks of Dalton's Creek. The swollen rivulet gurgled loudly as it rushed over its bed of rocks. Leander had almost forgotten how the hypnotic sound of the rushing water, coupled with and sights and smells of home, were so deeply rooted in his very soul. The sun, exhausted from its day's relentless assault, slipped below the tree line, bringing the occupants of this idyllic spot relief from the day's heat. Leander sighed and grunted pleasantly.

"Nice, huh?" Gaby said, ending their comfortable silence.

"Oh, yes," he replied. They sat back-to-back, leaning against one another on fat, moss cushions. They hadn't moved for some time. After several more minutes had passed, Leander said, "My butt's numb."

"Mine, too," Gabrielle responded. "You want to get up?"

"No." They chuckled and fell silent once again.

Finally, she groaned, stood up, and began rubbing her backside. "Why don't we ever think to bring lawn chairs down here?"

"No way," Leander said, following her lead. "That would spoil the ambiance."

"You're right. We never needed chairs when we were kids. C'mon, lets get our feet wet." She kicked off her sandals and bent to roll up her pant legs. "You're coming for dinner tonight, right?"

"Yes, I've been instructed. After all, we can't forget about Friday night family time."

"I need to get home, change clothes, and see if Mason has finished his speech for tomorrow night." She turned to smile at Leander. "You *do* know that Granddaddy told all the partners to prepare speeches for tomorrow night's banquet, don't you?"

Leander closed his eyes, a mildly pained expression on his face. "He's making way too much of this, Gaby."

"No, he isn't," she said sharply. "Granddaddy's honoring you for transforming Remington Banking and Investments, and he's right to do it. Mason agrees." She elbowed him playfully. "Now, don't you feel bad for not liking my husband?"

Leander's tone was noncommittal. "I like Mason just fine." He draped an arm across her shoulders. "He's good to you. Made you happy."

Gabrielle smiled. "Oh, yes. Mason has made me very happy. Simply put, he and I belong together." She dried her feet and slipped them into her sandals. "We—well, we rescued each other from some unfortunate episodes in our past."

"Hmm," Leander murmured and nodded his head in agreement as they began to walk away from the creek bank. *Unfortunate, indeed.*

* * * * *

Gabe sat on the side of his bed, still clad in his bathrobe. His tuxedo hung on the closet door, waiting. The blank sheet of paper he held in his hand stared back at him. He raised his head at the light *tap-tap* on his door. He shook his head slightly. *Forty years of marriage, and she still knocks on the bedroom door!* But his serene smile was back in place as he called out, "Come in, my dear."

"You're not dressed," Vivian said. "Is everything okay?"

"Of course. I won't be late. I just want to make sure my speech doesn't need any fine-tuning." He folded the sheet of paper and placed it on the nightstand. "Are the kids on their way?"

"Yes. Remy just called. William decided not to go. He's having some friends over to the house."

"That's not surprising," Gabe responded. "I can't imagine any teenage boy wanting to spend his Saturday night at a banquet, listening to a bunch of old farts praise themselves."

Vivian laughed. "You're right. Anyway, Remy and M'Lyn will be here any minute so you'd better get a move on."

"Uh, you go on with them. I'll finish getting dressed and rehearse my speech one more time. I'll be along soon."

"Alright, then," Vivian said, preparing to close the door.

"Wait," Gabe said. "You look lovely tonight, Viv." He took a step towards her, then stopped. "I love you, you know."

Caught off-guard, she laughed nervously. "I do know that, Gabe."

* * * * *

The lobby of Remington Banking and Investment had been transformed into a palatial banquet hall. The original, red marble floor had been cleaned and shined to brilliance. The oak wainscoting and long counter had been waxed and buffed to near mirror reflection, and each teller's window held a large bouquet of flowers. The old brass handrails, newly polished, gleamed in the glow of the crystal chandelier. A small combo was setting up in the far corner beside the bar as folks mingled and gradually made their way up the staircase to the mezzanine, where tables and chairs had been set up for the catered dinner.

"Impressive, to say the least," Leander said under his breath.

Claire Washington squeezed her son's arm. "And in your honor! We are so proud of you, Leander."

"Yes, we are, son," Carl Lee added. He had finally stopped fidgeting with his bow tie and accepted the confines of his rented tuxedo. He stood a bit taller each time someone stepped forward to shake his son's hand and pat him on the back.

Leander smiled, not trusting his voice as the whirlwind of emotions churned. Not until he had arrived at the banquet tonight had the true implications of the occasion come home to him. He would be named Managing Partner of Remington Banking and Investments this very night, and everything would change.

His status within the organization would rise. His relationship with the other partners would morph from that of colleague to one of superiority.

But, why? Because it's what Will Remington wants. But a vague answer such as that had never been enough for Leander Washington.

"There's Vivian," Claire said, waving to her friend and bringing her son out of his reverie. The two women hugged. "Where's Gabe?" Claire asked.

"Oh, he was still working on his speech," Vivian answered. She smiled and patted Leander's arm. "He told me to come on with Remy and M'Lyn, 'cause he wanted to get his speech *just right.*"

At that moment, they were joined by Remy, who lifted his hand to Leander for a high five. "Congrats, man," he said. "I'm heading to the bar."

"Of course, you are," M'Lyn replied caustically. She flashed her beauty queen smile and left the group with a "Y'all enjoy."

After a few moments of mild embarrassment, Vivian said, "Remy's disappointed, Lee, but he'll get over it. Deep down, he knows that Daddy made the right decision."

Leander nodded and smiled warmly, but in truth he doubted that Remy would *ever* get over having someone else—especially him—hand-picked by his own grandfather to manage their partnership. But he said nothing. Instead, his eyes searched the room, trying to locate Gabrielle. Just then, he heard a raucous whistle. Looking up, he spied his best friend, Mason at her side, leaning over the mezzanine railing and waving to him. He grinned and waved back. She motioned for him to come upstairs, then prepared to take her seat at the table. Mason remained standing, his hand resting on the bannister. Then, with an expression impossible to decipher, he lifted his arm in a stiff salute to Leander.

"Everyone should go up now," Vivian directed. "I'll wait down here for Gabe. Oh, there he is."

Gabe hurried over, gave his wife a quick kiss on her cheek and shook Leander's hand. Wordlessly, he nodded to the other members in the group, then guided Vivian toward the stairs. His face was flushed.

The band began to play dinner music as the lights dimmed to a golden glow. Waiters, clad in white tuxedos, stood at the ready as the remaining attendees made their way up the staircase. Everyone smiled and chatted gaily. The evening was shaping up to be a gala event. And Leander wished to high heaven that it was all over with.

104

For two weeks now—to be precise, ever since Will had announced this event would be held to mark his promotion—Leander had been experiencing periods where everything seemed slightly unreal. He would feel a bit out of it, like the few times in his life when he'd experienced a high fever. As the final speech came to end in a standing ovation, the very same feeling that none of this was real sparked fear that his mind was in danger of buckling under its own weight.

But as always, sensibility returned. "I am humbled," Leander began, "by this honor and by the kind words spoken here tonight." He paused, smiling, then continued speaking. "I have been fortunate to have had these four men as my mentors, partners, and friends for my entire life. Thank you, Will, Gabe, Remy, and Mason for the trust you have placed in me. I will work diligently to not let you down."

It was nearly ten o'clock when the waiters began their hurried clean-up. The diners stood and began their descent to the lobby floor, where the music increased in volume and tempo and the clinks of glasses assured all that the party was far from over.

Another round of handshaking, back-slapping, and congratulatory hugs trapped Leander at the head table. He had wanted to catch up with him before the party became too boisterous, but he seemed to have vanished.

While the speech he gave was entertaining, even eloquent, the part about *"Lee has over the years proven himself to be a true confidant"* had given him pause. Apparently, he wasn't the only one who zeroed in on that one statement: Gaby's eyebrows had shot up questioningly. Perhaps, Leander considered, it might be time for the two of them to sit down and wade through the painful past that they had pretended for so long did not exist.

* * * * *

Oh, you're the Illusionist, alright. There's not a damn thing real about you! If there WAS anything real, you'd have had the balls to stand up down there and say what you wrote in this letter. Say that there's not been a day—not one day—in twenty years that it hasn't been in your thoughts. That you haven't wished—wait a minute—wished for what, exactly? That he'd run home to his mama, maybe to the police? And if he had, then what? You would've had NO life at all.

Maybe no life would be better than this life, constantly seeing her, hearing her. No, that's not right. Life's been great for you. You're a star. So, maybe if the two of you could sit down and talk. That might make it better. Yeah, you and him together, talking. Get it all out and stop dancing around each other. Or not.

Enough! Get your ass back downstairs before you're missed. No talking, no note writing, nothing is ever going to make life any better. Get used to it, once and for all, that this is as good as it gets!

"I can make it better, Mister."

Do not start!

"I can help."

No, no, no, no. Nobody can help!

"Shhh, just take my hand, Mister."

* * * * *

"What a wonderful evening!" Claire exclaimed. She was having the time of her life, and it showed. She hugged Leander. "Dance with me, son. I can't seem to find your daddy anywhere."

Vivian practically shouted over the music: "And I'm looking for Gabe. Maybe they both stepped outside."

"Granddaddy put the sweetest anniversary card and note under my plate," Gabrielle said, joining the conversation. "I want to go find him and thank him."

Leander led his mother to the dance floor. "We all seem to be looking for someone," he commented. "I've also been trying to find…"

His words faded among the disquieting murmurs of several of the attendees, the flat notes of the band as their music gradually faded, and the shout of the police deputy now standing in the doorway. The sudden awareness that something was terribly wrong seemed to suck the air from the room.

Silence descended as the deputy spoke. "Uhh, m-m-may I have everybody's attention, please?" His voice trembled. He cleared his throat. "There's been a terrible, uh, happening. A terrible accident!"

At that moment, the wail of emergency vehicles pierced the air. The murmurs began anew. The rattled deputy was failing miserably in his attempts to be reassuring. "I-I'm gonna need everybody to *please* remain inside the building." His eyes reflected dismay as he frantically searched the crowd for anyone who might offer assistance.

Leander regained mobility and stepped forward just as two other uniformed officials entered, closing the bank's double doors behind them. "What's happened, sir," he asked the man who looked to be the only one in control of his emotions. "Sergeant Kennedy," Leander glanced at the name on his uniform. "Please, what is it?"

The crowd was nearing panic, pushing, albeit respectfully, each other in the direction of the doors and whatever lay beyond.

Sergeant Kennedy swallowed hard. "It's real bad. Someone—a, uh, a man—has apparently fallen from the rooftop of the bank. We've got to get him covered. You think you can keep everybody in here for a few minutes?"

Leander was about to answer when the door inched open, probably from a freshened breeze. The scene before him, illuminated garishly by the streetlights and the ever-increasing number of emergency vehicles, was paralyzing. "H-h-has the ambulance arrived yet?" he asked the sergeant as the door was immediately closed.

"No need for one, sir," came the reply. "We're waiting for the coroner."

Leander licked his lips and tried to swallow. His daddy's often-used saying of "Couldn't spit if the world was on fire," came to mind. Slowly, he turned around to the sea of faces, whose smiling expressions of only minutes ago now mirrored his own anxiety and fear.

"Lee, what's going on out there?"

"Car accident?" Somebody get hit?"

Questions were coming from all sides. He was preparing to try and address the growing concerns when a hand on his back stopped him. He turned to a gentleman unknown to him but with the unmistakable air of authority. After several moments of conversation, Leander turned his attention back to the worried faces before him.

"My friends, there has been a terrible accident. You are being directed to exit the bank building by the rear doors. These gentlemen here will escort you. Please remain in the parking lot for a brief time. You will be allowed to go to your cars shortly." He watched the crowd of people begin to move to the rear of the bank, some with arms around each other and some with eyes fixed in fear as they scanned the crowd for their partners.

Leander cleared his throat and spoke a bit louder, to be heard above the din. "It is requested that the members of the Remington and Westin families remain here." He saw her, then, and their eyes locked. Slowly, she began to sink to the floor, like an ice sculpture in August.

He stepped forward and caught her before she fell.

"Excuse me, Mr. Washington." The directive caused him to cease walking along with the family members toward the large table at the far side of the bank's lobby, where they were being escorted by Sergeant Kennedy.

Leander turned around. "Yes, sir?" It was the man who had spoken to him moments ago.

"Mr. Washington, sorry to meet you under these circumstances." The man extended his hand. "I'm Horace Beecher, County Medical Examiner. I know that you're close to these folks, but for right now, family only. You understand."

"Of course, Mr. Beecher. Can you tell us anything?"

"Not now, Mr. Washington," Beecher answered politely but firmly. "This is difficult. Please excuse me."

Leander nodded. "Folks," his voice trembled as it rose in volume, "Mama, Daddy, and I are leaving now, but please call the minute that you need me."

Vivian stepped forward. "Go to the house, Lee. Our, m-m-my house, and wait there," she stammered.

At his nod, she turned back to her loved ones. Her eyes—wide and unfocused—joined with Gabrielle's as they mutely searched the small group huddled together for the face that Leander knew they would not find.

105

As in many times throughout her life, Claire Washington took charge. The minute that she, Carl Lee, and Leander had arrived at the Remington house, she busied herself making coffee, turning on lights— anything to just keep moving. To just not think about him, to not envision his body lying in the middle of the street, covered by a sheet, the dark, wet liquid seeping from underneath. She shuddered violently, her hands covering her face in their attempt to block the image.

But she would not give in to hysteria. This family needed her. *Vivian* needed her. Claire shook off the moment of weakness, washed her face with cold water from the kitchen sink, and loaded the serving cart with coffee and cups. As she entered the dining room, Leander came forward to help her. He placed the urn, cups, and napkins on the buffet without a word.

The three of them then moved to the living room and sat down, anxiously waiting, until low voices carried in from the kitchen. Everyone moved in slow motion as hands were clasped, arms reached out, and deep, agonized sobs made words impossible.

Gabrielle sniffed, pressed a napkin to her swollen eyes, and straightened her shoulders. "Thank you, Miz Claire," she said weakly, "for making the coffee. I need something stronger, though. Anyone else?" she asked as she poured the amber liquid into a glass.

"Yes, please."

"Here, Gaby, I'll help you."

"I don't need help to pour bourbon."

"Sorry; I just…"

"No, I'm sorry. Didn't mean to snap at you."

"I-I-I'd like a brandy, please."

"Of course, Vivian. I'll get it for you.

"I'm going upstairs to lie down."

"Alone? You don't need to be alone. I'll go with you."

"I want to be alone."

And so, it continued: everyone speaking in monotones. The embraces had ended, and they now seemed afraid to look each other in the eye. All of a sudden, they avoided touching. Avoided speaking of *it*, of *him*.

Leander cleared his throat. "What did the police say?"

"They said what we all know: they said he fell off the goddamn roof. They said he's, he's…" Gabrielle walked to the buffet, refilled her glass to the brim with bourbon and turned to face the others. "Dead," she finished firmly. "They said that he is dead, Lee. *That's* what they said."

Her voice was hard. Their eyes locked as she went on: "They found a letter in his pocket. A letter written to *you*, Lee."

Some of the earlier shock was beginning to wear off, leaving an awkward silence in its wake. "A letter to me?" Leander asked with hesitation. "Whatever for? What did he write?"

"We don't exactly know that," Gabrielle replied, glaring at him, questions darting from her eyes. The bourbon, obviously fueling her emotions, sloshed out of the glass as her hand shook involuntarily. The dark stain slowly began to spread on the pale satin of her gown.

"They wouldn't let us see the letter. They did read part of it to us, though." She stopped talking only long enough to gulp the remaining liquid in her glass and wipe her mouth with the back of her hand. She turned to Leander, an expression of torment on her face that unnerved him. Her whispered words unnerved him even more. "How 'bout *you* tell *us* what that letter was about?"

"Gaby, come sit down and talk to me," Leander said. He reached out gently to take her arm. "I-I have no idea as to why he would write a letter to me."

"Don't!" she sobbed, pushing his hand away and almost falling down in the process. "Don't you fucking lie to me! I don't want to sit down, and I don't want to talk to you. I want to know what the hell he meant about an accident twenty years ago!"

No one spoke for several minutes. They moved apart from one another, a few sat down and stared at the floor while others walked aimlessly about the room, each one trying to wade through the horror that would alter the rest of their lives.

Vivian said, "Everyone will stay here tonight. That's enough, Gabrielle. Do not drink anymore. Go to bed, and I'll be up shortly." Her voice was surprisingly calm. Her words were obeyed as her daughter disappeared up the stairs.

"This *letter,* if you can call it that judging from what was read to us, seemed to be little more than incoherent ramblings. I'm sure that we will find out all the details in the next couple of days." Vivian turned and began to walk toward the stairs, her final words trailing behind her. "After the Medical Examiner has finished uh, his examination."

"I'll help you, Viv," Claire said, moving to her friend's side.

"Thank you. Thank all of you for being here."

"I'm going to go and get William. We'll be back," M'Lyn spoke woodenly.

Leander stood by the large windows, looking out but seeing nothing.

Halfway up the staircase, Vivian turned and spoke. "Lee, you will please attend to the, uh, the arrangements," she said heavily.

Without turning around, he whispered, "of course."

The grandfather clock in the entry struck two a.m. Carl Lee motioned to Claire that he was leaving. She nodded and said that she would straighten up and be home soon. Leander spoke quietly with the menfolk as they made their way outdoors. The remaining family members moved woodenly upstairs to the vacant guest rooms, leaving Claire alone.

She turned off the lights and returned the coffee service to the kitchen. Methodically, she washed, dried, and put dishes away. She gave little thought to her task. Instead, she wondered how this family—how anyone in this small town—would survive after the contents of that letter were made public.

For Claire Washington remembered. She had no need to read his words to know what had happened that fateful day twenty years ago that had robbed her precious boy of his childhood.

106

Leander sat with coffee cup in hand on the bench at the bottom of the stone steps leading from the kitchen door. He knew that she would be coming out soon. Her car was the only one remaining, indicating that everyone else in the household had already left. His mother had told him earlier that the family members were scheduled to meet with the Police Chief and the ME later on that morning. His own interview had been scheduled for tomorrow.

He hadn't been to the big house, nor had he spoken with Gaby since the night before last. The night it had happened. She needed time. But beyond that, yesterday and well into last night had been filled with the duty of managing the partnership. From the top tier of the four remaining partners to the varying levels of investors, even all the way down to the tellers in the many small banks, the dynamics of Remington Banking and Investments would change.

They had spent the day and half of the night calmly going over accounts, decreeing who should handle what, and with the blessed cloud of shock still holding emotions at bay, much had been accomplished. *His* name had not been mentioned. No one wanted to be the first one to say it out loud. No one wanted to talk about the letter. Leander knew that each of them would come to grips with the reality of his loss and with the ramifications of that letter in his own way. As yet, though, he had not a clue as to how *he* would deal with it.

The kitchen door opened. He stood up. "Can we talk? Please."

"We can, and we will," Gabrielle said calmly. "But not now. I'm on my way to Ravens to review the arrangements." She kept walking towards her car, not looking at him. "Although, I'm sure your choice of everything is fine. After that, another family meeting with more officials." She paused, her hand resting on the car door's handle. Leander remained silent, waiting.

When she seemed to be searching for words, he quietly spoke. "Gaby, I absolutely never meant to deceive you. And sparing you and your family any pain was the only thing that I thought about."

"No one will say it, Lee," she interrupted him. "No one—not even you and I—can speak of what happened twenty years ago. And I've thought all of my life that you and I could talk about anything. But we can't. We can't even say her name."

"How can I help you through this?" he asked.

She spun around, meeting his gaze head-on. "Throughout our entire lives, you have been the one person that I *could* turn to for help. With no doubt or fear, I heaped all my burdens on you, and you carried them. *My secrets!*" She paused, shaking her head sadly. "But you did not trust me to carry yours."

"That's not true, Gaby. Trust never came into the mix. I only wanted to *protect* you."

Gabrielle got in her car and started the engine. "Twenty years ago, that was our day, wasn't it? The day we made our pact. 'No secrets,' we said. You broke my heart, Lee."

* * * * *

The two men had remained silent for some time, both understanding that there was little remaining to be said. They were exhausted. Their backs ached. Their lungs craved release from air that had become stale. The staff had long since gone home for the night. It was late, and except for the harsh overhead light, the Fish Tank sat in a sea of darkness. Leander's mood appeared to mirror that darkness as he absently fingered the letter that lay on the desk in front of him.

Deshaun Freeman left him with his thoughts while he began gathering up the collection of papers that lay strewn across his desk. Some had fallen to the floor during the numerous heated exchanges between the two men. As the day had worn on, Deshaun had grown to regret his earlier attitude.

418

He hadn't apologized, though, and had no intention of doing so. At least, not in so many words. He straightened his shoulders, cleared his throat, and reached out his hand for the letter.

"You done with that?" he asked.

Leander nodded. "It's those last sentences, you know," he said. "That's, that's what hit everyone the hardest. Nothing is *ever* going to be the same for this family."

Deshaun slowly removed the letter from Leander's hand. He waited until the other man had wiped his eyes with the back of his hand, then read the words aloud one final time.

"For so long, Lee, I tried to push the memory back, tried to erase it. For a while, I succeeded. But now, I *see* her, and I *hear* her every day! I do not know when my insanity began, but I know that it will not end until I have surrendered my soul."

His eyes locked on Leander's as he placed the letter along with the stack of police reports, statements from family members, and the medical examiner's report into the waiting file box.

"There now," he said with a note of finality as he placed the lid in place, "all that remains to be done is for me to write my report of the investigation."

"And how will your report read, Chief Freeman?"

"That this town has lost a good man, one of our own, as a result of a terrible accident."

"An accident. Thank you, Chief."

"No need to thank me. I don't see any clear evidence of suicide. However, the truth about the twenty-year-old death of a child *will* be made public. Next few days, you're going to need to come back in and give a formal statement," Deshaun said. Standing up from his chair, he reached for his jacket.

"I'm dry as a powder house. Hungry, too. It's been a long day, Mr. Washington. You care to join me over at Arlene's for a beer and a burger?"

"Thank you," Leander replied as he got up from his chair, "but I need to get on back to the house. A lot to be done before the funeral."

"Gaby's the only member of the family that I know real well. Be sure and tell her how sorry I am," Deshaun said, locking the door behind them.

Leander shook his head sadly. "Gaby wants nothing to do with me right now. Guess I can't blame her. I broke a solemn promise that we made to each other. I kept a secret from her. I lied to her." Again, his voice quivered. "She told me that I broke her heart."

The two men had reached their respective cars and prepared to go their separate ways. "Gaby will come around, I'm sure. You two have been best friends since forever," Deshaun said.

"Yes, and that's what makes this so tough. No one—me included—knows what to say or what to do next. We're sinking," Leander said. He started to get into his Mercedes, then turned back to the other man. "Lately, I've often thought of one of Shakespeare's quotes."

His words drifted away. Deshaun snorted and responded. "Shakespeare, huh? Well, I can't help you there."

"The actual quote escapes me," Leander said, speaking almost as if to himself. "But the gist of it that 'hell is now a safe place, because the devil is here'."

Unnerved for a fleeting moment, Deshaun managed to shake away his sudden chill. "So, who's the devil?"

"That's hard to say, Chief Freeman. Perhaps there's a bit of him in all of us."

107

Gabrielle responded to the ping of her phone, spoke briefly, then addressed the family members. "The limos are leaving Ravens now—should be here in twenty minutes."

Everyone in the living room nodded, grunted, and checked their watches. For the better part of an hour, the family members had sat together, waiting for the appointed time of the graveside funeral service. During the past week, emotions had run the gamut, beginning with shock and anger, building to gut-wrenching sadness, and ending now in the quiet stage of *waiting*.

A minimum of conversation centered on responding to the hushed questions from Hazel or one the catering crew, who were setting up the dining room and the veranda with tables of food and drink for the mourners who would come after the funeral to pay respects. Periodically, someone would comment on the gray skies, provoking the remark of "Hope the rain holds off 'til after the service."

The grandfather clock chimed the half-hour. It would soon be time to leave. Leander leaned forward in his chair.

"We haven't spoke of it—at least not as a group—of what happened on that day twenty years ago," he began. He shook his head sadly, stood up, and walked to the fireplace. He placed a hand on the mantle to steady himself. "We haven't even said her name. I have no idea why young Tawney Simpson ventured into The Ramble that day. Nor do I know the timeline of the accident. And, yes, although he was responsible, her death *was* a tragic accident.

"But I do know why *I* was there that day." Leander smiled sadly, his eyes locking with Gaby's before she turned away. "I was walking home after the happiest day of my life. The day my best friend and I had become blood brother and sister." His voice was soothing, hypnotic. Vivian rose from her place on the sofa and came to his side, entwining her arm in his. Leander looked at her for a long time before he went on.

"I can still remember the very moment I saw the deer," he said, smiling. "Even after twenty years, I can still feel the chill bumps on my arms after seeing that beautiful buck and his doe and the little fawn on shaky legs following along behind them." He paused, swallowed hard. "That moment was the last completely happy and innocent moment of my childhood."

Vivian squeezed his arm. "You don't have to say any more, Lee," she whispered. "It's alright."

But Leander was beyond stopping now, and his words, filled with emotion, continued to flow. "I was witness to his painful, near hysterical anguish. And," his eyes closed and his voice wavered, "once I had retraced his steps and found her—Tawney—I made a decision that no nine-year-old child should *ever* have to make. I told no one. It is difficult to confess now, but I lied to those whom I held most dear. My reason was to protect Gaby and this family."

Leander looked into the faces before him. Sad little smiles and tear-filled eyes seemed to bestow forgiveness. "I also confess that, given the opportunity to go back in time," his eyes locked with Gabrielle's just as the doorbell sounded, "I would have done the same thing."

"The limos are here. We should leave."

They moved as a group down the veranda steps to the waiting cars. "I can drive Mama and Daddy in their car," Leander said.

"Absolutely not," Vivian stated firmly. "We are all family, and we'll go together. That's why we requested two limousines." She began to direct who should ride with whom.

A hand landed on Leander's shoulder.

"You should ride with us, Lee. Gaby needs you. She may not admit it right now, but I do not believe that she can get through this without her best friend."

"Thank you, Mason."

* * * * *

The rain had not materialized, although the sky remained a dismal gray. Chairs had been set up for the family members under large green tents. It seemed to Leander that the entire town of Antioch had turned out. He nodded to many acquaintances as the family processional made it way to their seats. The oak casket stood like an island amid a sea of floral arrangements.

When they were seated, the crowd of mourners quieted. Arnold Mayhew stepped forward, guitar around his neck, and accompanied by his twin daughters. Leander thought that their musical offering of *Amazing Grace* had never sounded so beautiful.

The Reverend Billy Carmichael stood from his seat, just the other side of the casket. Although hundreds of people crowded the gently sloping hill of the cemetery, the Reverend had no need of a microphone. His booming baritone voice offered comfort in the still air and, coupled with his snowy white hair and piercing blue eyes, caused Leander to picture him as a prophet.

"Dear family and friends," Reverend Billy began, "we take comfort in God's promise of eternal life as we gather today, even in sadness, to celebrate the earthly life of William Remington Westin. Our Remy—beloved son, grandson, brother, husband, father and respected friend in our town—left us all too soon."

M'Lyn had held her grief in check all week—dangerously so, Leander had thought. Her body shook now as her anguished sobs could no longer be controlled. She sat on the front row, her arms entwined tightly with William's, as the stark reality of loss overtook any sense of propriety that she might have wished to portray.

The Reverend paused in his delivery, and Leander looked at Gabrielle, sitting beside him. She sat dry-eyed and still, her expression and body language impossible to read. His thoughts turned to Vivian, who had been the soul of calm during the past week. But after losing her son, and even with Gabe's strong support, would her past melancholy rise to claim her once again? *And Will, how will you get past this? Can you get past it without losing your soul, as well?*

His mind conflicted, Leander heard no more of the sermon until the stirring of the family members roused him as they stood for the benediction. With the final blessing and "Amen," Reverend Billy announced that the family would welcome all those who wished to pay respects at the Remington home following the service. And it was over. Would the healing now begin? Could *theirs* begin? Leander rarely prayed: he did so now as they began their walk to the waiting limos.

Gabe and Vivian walked hand-in-hand behind the still sobbing M'Lyn and young William. The boy walked slightly apart from his mother and often looked back over his shoulder toward the grave site.

Gabe followed his grandson's glances. The mass of mourners had departed, leaving Will standing solitary beside the casket.

"We are going to get through this, Vivian," he said. "Together, we will survive what no parent should ever have to. But I don't know about Will. I fear we could lose him. What do you think?"

Vivian stopped in her tracks and released a sigh. "I haven't given any thought whatsoever to my father."

Gabrielle sat between Leander and Mason in the limousine. They waited on Will as the rest of the funeral processional moved slowly away from the cemetery. She had not spoken during the service, nor on their previous trip. After her initial rage at the loss of her brother, she had been rendered practically mute by her grief.

In another lifetime, her best friend's presence would have imparted strength—*their* strength. But not now. Just knowing that she had lost one of the only two souls on earth in whom she could confide, and fearing a total loss of faith in the other, had stripped her bare of any emotion.

Her hands lay still on her lap and, seemingly on impulse, Leander reached for her left hand. She allowed his touch. Gently, he fitted his left palm on that of hers, their life lines touching.

For a long moment, she searched for comfort in the gesture. Finding none, she slowly withdrew her hand.

Will nodded to the attendants and slowly, and with little noise, his beloved grandson was lowered into the ground. He closed his eyes and tried in vain to shed tears. They would not come. He longed to simply have a good cry, or an anguished release of temper such as Gaby had exhibited. It seemed to have helped her. But Will didn't know for sure; he hadn't spoken with his granddaughter. Come to think of it, he had not talked with Vivian or Gabe. Why, he wondered? Was it because he could not imagine that their grief could *possibly* equal his?

The attendants moved about nervously, repositioning the vast array of floral arrangements away from the shielded pile of dirt. Will knew that he should take his leave, as they did not want to begin shoveling dirt into the grave with a family member present.

As if reading his thoughts, Belle appeared as his side. She laid a gentle hand on his arm and said, "Will, honey, the car's waiting for us. We'd better be going."

He nodded slightly but said nothing. Words between them were unnecessary, for she and she alone knew the depth of his grief. *And his guilt.* The irony was not lost on Belle Fontenot that, while she stood just outside the realm of family, it was she who had been appointed keeper of their secrets.

"I brought this on, you know," Will said, his voice heavy. "His death. I let him carry it all on his own shoulders, let him walk that dark valley all alone. Until it got too much for him." He retrieved his handkerchief from his pocket and blew his nose.

Belle said nothing as he continued to voice his anguish.

He closed his eyes and shook his head sadly. "That day twenty years ago," he said, "I didn't know what to make of him crying like that. And Leander? I had no idea! When I figured it all out—what must've happened—I tried to talk to Remy about it. I didn't try hard enough, though. I let him down. I was a coward."

"You loved him, Will, and he loved you," Belle said. "Now, you have a responsibility to young William. He needs you."

He nodded, looking at her as if the idea had just struck him. "Yes, I have William." They prepared to leave the graveside but not before he whispered one final lament.

"Oh, my sweet boy, I simply couldn't—or wouldn't—face something that I was unable to fix. So, I pushed it to the back of my mind, pretending that it did not exist. Forgive me, Remy, for I have known *the secret* all along!"

Epilogue

Leander woke from a shallow and fitful sleep. His dreams had been vague and unremembered. He stretched his tall body, his feet bumping the footboard. His mother had not changed one thing in this, his childhood bedroom. He smiled as he looked at the kitty-cat clock that hung on the wall, its eyes and tail moving back and forth with every tick-tock.

His prized books still lined the bookshelves along the far wall. He should have them shipped home for Clarissa. How he missed her and Allure. The three weeks apart from them seemed like a lifetime. He had accomplished much business-wise, but the personal issues remained to be addressed before he could return to his wife and daughter.

He stretched once more and got out of bed. After retrieving his pants from the floor, he opened his bedroom door and made his way toward the kitchen.

"Anybody home?" he called out. "Guess not," he answered his own question. He poured a cup of coffee from the pot and found the plate of still-warm ham biscuits Claire had left. His dad had gone to work sometime earlier, and his mom would be at the cemetery. Leander shook his head, recalling the old southern tradition still practiced in his hometown of tending to the flower arrangements at recent burials. She had asked him at supper the night before if he wanted to accompany her this morning. Instead of telling her he thought the tradition to be totally morbid, he'd smiled and politely declined.

After breakfast, Leander wandered back to his bedroom. During the restless hours of last night, he'd thought of the box on the shelf of his closet and its contents. It had remained unopened for all these years, and today seemed to be a good day to expose its contents to the light of day.

The layer of dust atop the box bore witness to the fact that it had not been touched in ages. Actually, someone would have had to be searching for it to ever find it. The lid opened easily to the velvet-lined interior holding the shiny contents: his medal for spelling, his math award, perfect attendance and scouting merit badges. *More keepsakes for Clarissa.* He knew she would delight in having something from his childhood.

The remaining item awaited him, carefully wrapped in tissue and lying apart from the others. Gingerly, he lifted it from the box and put it in his pocket. He knew immediately where it belonged. He would go there one last time. It would be his final goodbye.

He left the house several minutes later and began his walk toward his destination. As he walked, the thought occurred to him that this cathartic venture of his was really no different than that of his mother's as she tended wilting flowers on a grave.

The smell of damp earth, of moss untouched by the sun and the heady scent of wild honeysuckle led him along the well-remembered path. Twenty years had passed, and he could have walked it blindfolded.

Spindly saplings still reached for sunlight, their progress slowed by the tangle of faster-growing vines. Leander had begun to sweat as he tore a path through those vines and into his destination.

"Oh, my God," he said, clutching his chest. "You just about scared me to death!" Relieved, he stepped forward and smiled. "I never expected anyone to be here."

Vivian turned to face him. She laughed lightly and said, "Did you think that I was my mother, Miz Lily, walking in her secret garden?"

"Well, that thought *did* come to mind." He stepped forward and took her hands in his. Their eyes met. Silently, he nodded toward the stone bench on which he had once sat. Surprisingly, it still appeared to rest on solid ground. "Let's sit down, Miz Vivian. What brings you here?"

"I suppose you and I have come here for the same reason, Lee, to say goodbye." She reached into the pocket of her jeans for a tissue and gently dabbed her eyes. "Not goodbye to Remy," she said as if to clarify her words, "but goodbye to a tragedy that has marked us all."

"I am so sorry." It was all he could say.

She looked at him questioningly. "Lee, I have told you before that you have *nothing* to be sorry for. Oh, how terrified and confused you must have been! I never told anyone, but I was in The Ramble that day, looking for Gabe. Had I walked in a different direction, I might have found you, you precious little boy! And I would have held you in my arms and comforted you, and we would have dealt with it together."

"And how would we have dealt with it?" he asked.

She shook her head. "I don't know. What I do know, however, is that this is probably the last time that anyone will come to The Ramble in its present state."

"Oh, and why do you say that?"

She grinned, her eyes twinkling as if she knew something wonderous. She hummed a silly little tune, so unlike her that Leander laughed out loud. "Come on, now! Don't keep me in the dark."

"The bulldozers will arrive at nine o'clock on Friday to begin demolition of The Ramble," she stated without emotion. Seeing Leander's stunned expression, she continued. "Only the large, healthy trees will remain. And the azalea and other blooming bushes and trees will be properly pruned. After the area has been cleared, the landscape designer that I've hired will begin the renovation." She grew more animated as she revealed her plans.

"We will have stone pathways, lighted, mind you, and fountains that actually work," she added, pointing to the disheveled concrete mass in front of them that had sunk into a pool of stagnant water and hardly resembled a fountain at all. "And the entire stretch of land by the road will be grass, with picnic tables and swings for anyone to enjoy."

"Sounds like you've given this a lot of thought," Leander said. "How does Will feel about the undertaking?"

"I haven't told him." She simply replied. "He'll see it when he gets back from his European tour."

"He and young William are leaving on Tuesday, right?"

"Yes, that's the plan. They will fly to New York for several days, then to London to begin their tour." Vivian grew thoughtful once again. "Remy was Daddy's heart. Everyone knew that. I suppose that he'll now try and mold William into his image as well. That's what this two-month trip is all about, you know."

"Does that worry you?"

"Not at all," she said. "In spite of Daddy's efforts—and those of my son for that matter—young William has managed to avoid their lust for *more*."

"I haven't seen M'Lyn since the service," Leander said. "How is she?"

"My daughter-in-law will be alright in time. She's staying at her parents' now. And will most likely remain there, at least until Daddy and William return from their trip."

Leander stood up and pretended interest in the activity of a squirrel that sat perched on a tree branch, twirling a large acorn. He turned back to Vivian. "Will *everyone* be alright in time, do you think?"

Vivian smiled. "Yes, Lee, in time. We all have someone we can cling to. Daddy has William. Gabe has Daddy, whom he's worshipped since he was seven years old. M'Lyn and William have each other, as do Mason and Gaby. She has you, too, Lee. Don't forget that."

"And you, Miz Vivian—whom do you have?"

"Why, Lee, I have *all* of you. I have my family." She reached out her hand. "Let's go to the house, now. After all, it's Friday night."

"I'm right behind you. Watch your step," he cautioned.

As Vivian turned and began her exit from the garden, he reached into his pocket and brought out the gold ID bracelet that had not seen the light of day in twenty years. He turned it over in his hand and studied it thoroughly. He closed his eyes and listened for the sound of a voice. He tried to conjure up an image, a connection to that fateful day.

But when he opened his eyes, he saw that it was only a bracelet. Slowly, he let it slip from his hand and disappear into the black water.

"I'm glad that we were drawn to the same place at the same time," Vivian said. They strolled, their arms entwined, from The Ramble across the wide expanse of lawn toward the Remington house. "I am at peace, Lee. And you?"

He took some time to respond. She didn't push. "I-I'm getting there," he said. "Honestly, Miz Vivian, I don't know if I can *ever* find complete peace if Gaby and I cannot get beyond this." Just voicing the possibility of losing his one true friend hit him like a blow to the gut.

She remained silent until they had reached the kitchen steps. She looked at her watch and spoke casually. "It's getting near cocktail time, and we don't want to keep Daddy waiting. I haven't seen Gaby at all today. Do you suppose you might be able to find her?"

"I'll do my best," Leander said.

She stood on tiptoe to brush a light kiss on his cheek. "Your best will be just fine."

He watched her until she reached the door. The subtleties of Vivian's life-long friendship with his mother had not escaped him during the past weeks. One woman had buried a son, and he could not ignore the fact that the actions of the *other* woman's son had added to that loss. And yet, the bond between the two women had not wavered.

"You are quite a lady, Miz Vivian," he said with emotion.

She smiled down at him. "Go get our girl, Lee."

* * * * *

Leander parted the tall bulrushes and saw her immediately. Clad in cut-off jeans and tee-shirt, she sat on the big rock in the center of Dalton's Creek. *Their* rock. He stooped down and removed his shoes. He sat down on the creek bank and put his feet in the cold water. She'd seen him, he knew, yet she ignored him.

"You want to come back to the house with me?" he asked. "It's close to time for the family cocktail hour."

Her voice held no emotion. "But all the family won't be there, will they, Lee?"

"No, Gaby, they won't. And as time goes by, there will be even fewer." He wanted to say this right, but he was sinking, and he knew it. "I'll be there, though, if humanly possible. Because, well, because you and I are more than friends: we're blood brother and sister. No matter how far away I am, I'll be there for you, Gaby. I won't ever let you down. I swear." His voice broke. She turned and looked his way.

"You left out the part about *no secrets*."

Leander removed his feet from the water and dried them on the mossy bank. After putting his shoes on, he stood up. He tried one last time to reach her.

"Maybe I made a mistake, maybe I didn't. Okay, yes, I broke a sworn oath that I made to you. So, if this is where you and I—where *we*—end, then blame me. But I'll ask one thing of you first."

After a time, she glanced in his direction. "What?" she asked.

"Close your eyes," he directed. When she kept staring at him, he repeated his words. "Go ahead, close your eyes." When she had done so, he made his plea.

"Picture that little nine-year-old boy that I was on that day. He was terrified, in shock, and all alone. All he could think about was protecting you. Now, you go right ahead and blame me, Gabrielle, but *do not* blame that little boy. He would have died for you."

He blinked the tears from his eyes. There was nothing left to be said. He turned and began to walk away when her voice brought him to a standstill.

"So," she said as she slowly began to wade from the rock back to the bank, "what do you want to do tomorrow? I know! Let's come back down here and bring our fishing poles and some bait—"

He didn't turn around and rush to wrap her in his arms like he wanted to do. It was too soon. He simply finished her sentence: "I bet we could catch our supper!"

The End